THE
ROOK

DANIEL O'MALLEY graduated from Michigan State University and earned a master's degree in Medieval History from Ohio State University. He then returned to Australia and now works for the government, managing media relations for the agency that investigates transportation accidents.

THE
ROOK

DANIEL O'MALLEY

HEAD
of ZEUS

First published in United States of America in 2012
by Mulholland Books, an imprint of Little, Brown and Company

This edition first published in the UK in 2013 by Head of Zeus Ltd

9 8 7 6 5 4 3 2 1

A CIP catalogue record for this book is available from the British Library.

ISBN (hardback): 9781908800374
ISBN (export trade paperback): 9781908800381
ISBN (eBook): 9781908800879

Printed in Germany

Head of Zeus Ltd
45-47 Clerkenwell House
Clerkenwell Green
London EC1R 0HT
www.headofzeus.com

For my father, Bill O'Malley, who read to me at bedtime,
and my mother, Jeanne O'Malley, who read to me the rest of the time.

THE
ROOK

1

Dear You,

The body you are wearing used to be mine. The scar on the inner left thigh is there because I fell out of a tree and impaled my leg at the age of nine. The filling in the far left tooth on the top is a result of my avoiding the dentist for four years. But you probably care little about this body's past. After all, I'm writing this letter for you to read in the future. Perhaps you are wondering why anyone would do such a thing. The answer is both simple and complicated. The simple answer is because I knew it would be necessary.

The complicated answer could take a little more time.

Do you know the name of the body you are in? It's Myfanwy. Myfanwy Alice Thomas. I would say that it's my name, but you've got the body now, so I suppose you'll be using it. People tend to mangle its pronunciation, but I would like it if you at least knew how to say it. I don't embrace the traditional Welsh pronunciation, so for me the w is silent and the f is hard. Thus, Miff-un-ee. Simple. In fact, now that I think about it, it rhymes with Tiffany.

Before I give you the story, there are a few things you should be aware of. First, you are deathly allergic to bee stings. If you get stung and do not take quick action, you will die. I keep those little epinephrine-injector-pen thingies around me, so find one before you need it. There should be one in my purse, one in the glove compartment of the car, and one in pretty much every jacket that you now own. If you get stung, slip the lid off the thing, jam it into your thigh, and inject. You should be fine. I mean, you'll feel like absolute shit, but you won't die.

Apart from that, you have no dietary restrictions, no allergies, and you're in pretty good shape. There is a tradition of colon cancer in the family, so you

*should get regular checkups, but nothing has appeared yet. Oh, and you
have a terrible head for alcohol. But you probably don't need to know that
yet. You've got more important things to worry about.*

*Hopefully, you will have my wallet, and along with it all the little plastic
cards that are so vital for surviving in today's electronic world. Driver's
license, credit cards, National Health Service card, library card, and all of
them belonging to Myfanwy Thomas. Except for three. And those three are,
at the moment, the most important. Tucked away in there you will find an
ATM card, a credit card, and a driver's license in the name of Anne Ryan, a
name that will not be linked to you. The personal identification number for
all of them is 230500. That's my birthday, followed by how old you are.
You're a newborn! I would suggest that you withdraw some money from
Anne Ryan's account immediately, go to a hotel, and check in as her.*

*You are probably aware of this next part already, since if you are reading
this then you have survived several immediate threats, but you are in danger.
Just because you are not me does not make you safe. Along with this body,
you have inherited certain problems and responsibilities. Go find a safe place,
and then open the second letter.*

Sincerely,

Me

She stood shivering in the rain, watching the words on the letter
dissolve under the downpour. Her hair was dripping, her lips
tasted salty, and everything ached. Under the dim light of a nearby
lamppost, she had scrabbled through the pockets of her jacket, looking for some sort of clue to who she was, where she was, what was
going on. She had found two letters in the inside pocket. The first
envelope had been addressed simply *To You.* The second envelope
just had the number 2 written on it.

She shook her head angrily and stared up at the storm, watching
the lightning fork across the sky. She fumbled in another pocket, and
her fingers closed on a bulky shape. She pulled it out and looked at a
long thin cardboard box that was getting all soggy and losing its
shape. Typed on a prescription label was some long chemical term
and the name Myfanwy Thomas. She clenched her fingers and

2

felt the firm plastic of the epi-pen, then put the box back in her pocket.

This is who I am, she thought bitterly. *I don't even get the luxury of not knowing what my name is. I don't get a chance to start a life. Whoever this Myfanwy Thomas was, she managed to get me into a whole lot of trouble.* She sniffed and wiped her nose on her sleeve. She looked around at the place she was in. Some sort of park. Willows drooped their long tendrils down around the clearing, and she was standing on what used to be a lawn but was rapidly becoming a mud hole. She came to a decision, pulled her feet out of the mire, and stepped carefully over the ring of bodies that were scattered around her. They were all motionless, and all of them were wearing latex gloves.

She was hugging herself and completely soaked by the time she made it out of the park. Recalling the letter's warning, she had been wary, scanning her surroundings for any attackers hidden among the trees. Thunder crashed above her, and she flinched away from it. The path brought her out of the park, and she stared at the scene before her. Clearly, the park was in the middle of some sort of residential area—there was a row of Victorian-style houses before her. They were no doubt pretty, she thought grimly, but she wasn't in the mood to appreciate them as they deserved. There were no lights on in any of the windows, and a cold wind had started blowing. Still, she squinted down to the end of the road and could make out the distant neon glow that promised some sort of business emporium. Sighing, she began to walk that way, shoving her hands into her armpits to stop their shaking.

An ATM visit and a phone call made from a rather battered phone box later, and she was sitting in the back of a cab being ferried to a five-star hotel. Several times, she looked back, checking to see if any cars were following, and once she asked the cabdriver to make two U-turns. Nothing suspicious happened, although the cabbie gave her some funny looks in the mirror. When they finally arrived at the hotel, she muttered something about a stalker boyfriend, and the driver nodded knowledgeably, his eyes lingering on her face. The hotel-management students who had been saddled with doorman duty on the graveyard shift lived up to their training and didn't bat an eyelid as they swung open the doors for a soaking-wet woman. She walked through the glorious foyer, leaving a dripping trail on the tiles.

The impeccably dressed and coiffed desk clerk (at three in the morning! What kind of monstrous automaton was this woman?) politely stifled a yawn and barely widened her eyes when the person who hesitantly identified herself as Anne Ryan checked in without a reservation or luggage. A bellboy did a poor job of appearing awake, but he managed to guide her to her room and work the key-card thing for her. She neglected to tip him but assumed that her shattered appearance might earn her some forgiveness on that score.

She stripped and rejected a bath on the rationale that she might fall asleep in the water and drown in some flower-scented oblivion. Instead, she showered. She saw massive bruises blossoming on her body. She gasped in pain when she crouched down to pick up the soap, then finished the shower, wrapped herself in a big fluffy robe, and staggered out into the bedroom. She caught movement out of the corner of her eye, and she stared at the stranger in the mirror.

She looked automatically at the face, which was dominated by two nasty black eyes. *Bloody hell,* she thought. *No wonder the cabdriver bought my story about an abusive boyfriend.* It looked as if she had taken two hard blows to the eyes, and the whites were bloodshot from tears. Her lips were raw red and burned roughly when she licked them. "Someone tried to kick the living shit out of you," she said to the girl in the mirror. The face that looked back was narrow, and although it was not beautiful, it was not ugly. *I am nondescript,* she thought. *Nondescript features with shoulder-length dark hair. Hmm.* She opened the robe and looked critically at her body.

Lots of adjectives beginning with the letter S *are appropriate here,* she thought grimly. *Short. Scrawny. Small breasts. Skinned knees* (although presumably those were only temporary). She remembered something from the letter and felt along the inside of her left thigh. A small hard scar. *From falling out of a tree and impaling this leg at the age of nine,* she thought. Her body was not particularly fit-looking but seemed blessedly free of cellulite. Shaved legs. A conservative and recent bikini wax. More bruises had risen to the surface, but they didn't conceal the fact that she was not possessed of an especially sexy body. *I think I could do better,* she thought. *I won't be able to hit the level of Hot, but I might be able to manage Cute. If I have a big enough budget. Or at least some makeup to work with.*

Her gaze moved from her body to the reflection of the room behind her. There it was, a huge bed with big fluffy pillows, a very soft-looking blanket, and white sheets so crisp they could be used to sculpt something. It was almost exactly what she needed. If only there was a...there was! A welcome mint on the pillow! Well, if there was a welcome mint, then the bed was probably worth staggering across that massively wide carpet to get to. The carpet was soft, and she could have collapsed on it easily, but the thought of the welcome mint was enough to impel her forward. Dragging her feet, she hobbled over and managed to fall asleep without choking to death on her mint.

She had confusing dreams, although later, when she woke up, she wondered if they were confusing simply because the people she'd dreamed about were from pre-amnesia times. But even while she was in the dreams, she was confused. She was kissing someone, but she couldn't see him. All she could do was feel him, and shiver. And when his tongue stretched down her throat, she didn't panic.

Then she was sitting down to afternoon tea in a room full of ferns with a black-and-white-tile floor. The air was hot and wet, and an elderly lady dressed in Victorian clothes sat across from her. The lady sipped thoughtfully from her teacup and stared at her with cool chocolate eyes.

"Good evening, Myfanwy. I apologize for disturbing your sleep, but I felt obliged to thank you."

"Thank me?"

"Myfanwy, don't think I don't understand what you have done for me," the lady said coldly. "I dislike being in your debt, but thanks to you, a threat to me and my family has been disposed of. If it should happen that I can ever return the favor, I suppose I am obliged to do so, tiresome as that may be. Tea?" She poured Myfanwy a cup, and drank from her own cup. Myfanwy hesitantly tried a sip, and found herself enjoying it.

"It's delicious," she said politely.

"Thank you" came the distracted reply. The woman was looking around her curiously. "Are you all right? There's something strange . . ." She trailed off and peered at Myfanwy thoughtfully. "Your mind is different. Something has happened to you; it's almost as if—" She stood up abruptly, knocking over her chair, which dissolved into vapor, and backed away from the table. The plants writhed, drawing in around her. "Who are you? I can't understand it. You are not Rook Thomas, and yet you are!"

"Myfanwy Thomas lost her memory," the younger woman said levelly with that strange detachment that comes in dreams. "I'm what woke up."

"You're in her body," said the lady slowly.

"Yes," Myfanwy said reluctantly.

"How inconvenient," said the old lady with a sigh. "A rook with no memory of who she is." There was a pause. "Bugger."

"Sorry," Myfanwy said, then felt ridiculous for apologizing.

"Yes, well. Give me a moment. I need to think." The older woman paced for a few minutes, pausing periodically to smell the flowers. "Unfortunately, young lady, I don't have time to ponder all the factors here. I have problems of my own, and I can't actively help you, here or in the waking world. Any unusual movements on my part would put us both in danger."

"Don't you owe me a debt?" asked Myfanwy. "Thomas helped you."

"You are not Thomas!" the lady snapped in irritation.

"I don't think she's going to be coming around to collect," Myfanwy said dryly. The elderly lady subsided.

"A good point. But the best I can do is keep your secret. I will not move against you nor tell anyone what has happened to you. Everything else will be up to you."

"That's it?" Myfanwy asked incredulously.

"It's more than you realize, and it could make all the difference. Now, I must go, and you had better wake up." The plants around them writhed again, and began to withdraw. Darkness flowed down from the glass ceiling above them.

"Now, wait a just second," said Myfanwy, and the lady looked startled. She raised an eyebrow, and the spreading darkness paused above their heads. "You're not going to be any more helpful?"

"No," the elderly lady said with some surprise. Once again, she was sitting at the table. "You are very definitely not Myfanwy Thomas," she remarked as she poured herself a fresh cup of tea. "Good evening."

"Good evening," said Myfanwy. The lady raised an eyebrow again, and Myfanwy felt herself blushing. Clearly she was supposed to say something else, and a vague recollection floated up—a tiny scrap of dying memory. "Good evening...my lady?" The lady nodded approvingly.

"Well, apparently you have not forgotten *everything*."

She woke up and fumbled by the side of the bed for the light switch. The clock told her that it was seven in the morning. Though she was exhausted, there was no chance she would be getting back to sleep. There were simply too many questions rushing through her head. What was the deal with the dreams? Should she be taking them seriously?

It seemed a trifle unfair to place any more importance on the conversational dream than she did on the tongue-kissing dream. However, the conversational dream had been incredibly vivid. Did she believe that the dreams were subconscious messages? She was vaguely inclined to dismiss them as her brain's sieving through the garbage of her thoughts while she slept, but she wasn't really sure.

And who was this Myfanwy Thomas person anyway? A rook?

Wasn't that some kind of bird? Clearly the dream could be discounted, since she was not a bird. The lack of feathers, she thought wryly, was just one indicator. As it was, she had no idea about anything. How old was she? Was she married? No rings on any fingers; no incriminating tan lines. Was she employed? She hadn't thought to check the balance in the accounts earlier. She'd been too occupied with not freezing to death. Did she have family? Friends? With a sigh and then a few grunts of pain, she rolled out of her comfy bed and trudged gingerly over to the table where she'd thrown her jacket. Her scabbed knees hurt when she bent down, and her chest ached if she breathed too deeply. She was about to empty the pockets when her eye fell on the phone and the menu.

"Hello, this is room five-five-three."

"Yes, good morning, Ms. Ryan," said a polished and mercifully nonperky voice. "What can I do for you?"

"Ooh, I would like to order some breakfast. Could I get a pot of coffee, some blueberry pancakes, some orange juice, some wheat toast, some marmalade, and two raw steaks?"

Astonishingly, there was no stunned pause; the voice on the other end cheerfully agreed to send it all up.

"I need the steaks for my eyes; I had an accident," she felt the need to explain.

"Of course, Ms. Ryan, we'll be up soon."

She also asked if the hotel could quickly launder her only set of clothes, and the voice on the phone promised to dispatch a person immediately to pick them up.

"Thank you," she said as she looked out the window. The storm had passed overnight, and the sky was now cloudless. After a few minutes she wandered over to the doors that led to the balcony. She was about to open them when there was a discreet knock at the door. *Remember,* she thought, *someone beat the hell out of you, and someone is still after you.* She peeked through the peephole and saw that it was a diffident young fellow in a hotel uniform with an empty laundry bag. She eyed the crumpled and damp trail of clothing leading to the bathroom and dismissed her paranoia. *I'm willing to risk it for the sake of clean clothes*. She opened the door, thanked the young man, and, flushing, hurriedly gathered up her bedraggled garments and dropped them into the waiting bag. Then, feeling guilty about the porter she hadn't tipped the previous night, she lavishly overtipped him.

She was watching the morning news and marveling at the lack of items about corpses in a park when breakfast arrived and was laid out carefully for her, prompting another disproportionate tip. She sat down, fished in the jacket pockets, and pulled out the envelope neatly labeled *2*. Just looking at it made her feel mildly irritated with the woman who'd written it, the woman who'd put her in this situation. *I'll look at it in a sec,* she decided. *Once I've had some coffee.* She set it to one side, took out her wallet, and nibbled some toast as she looked through the cards. There were two driver's licenses, one of which confirmed that she was indeed Myfanwy Alice Thomas. The address given triggered no memories at all, although she was intrigued to note that it appeared to be a house rather than a flat. It identified her hair as brown, her eyes as blue, and her age as thirty-one. She looked at her picture with disfavor. Ordinary features, pale, with independent-minded eyebrows.

The wallet also contained several credit and ATM cards and a little hand-scribbled note that said *I appreciate what you're trying to do, but you're not really the kind of person who wears your heart in your wallet.*

"Very funny," she said to herself. "It looks like I thought I was quite amusing before I lost my memory." Sifting through the rest of the pockets produced a packet of tissues, a mobile phone with a dead battery, and a pass card on a clip. She spent some minutes fruitlessly examining this last item, which was as thick as four credit cards and featured only a sulky-looking photo and a bar code. Finally she put aside her jacket and took a long drink of very good coffee. There was no time like the present for reading a letter from herself. She could only hope that this letter was more illuminating than the last. Well, at least this one was typed, rather than handwritten.

Dear You,

Have you noticed that I'm not calling you Myfanwy? This is for two reasons. First, I feel that it would be somehow rude to foist my name on you, and second, well, it's just too strange. Speaking of strange, I suppose you're wondering how I came to write these letters, how I knew they would be necessary.

You're wondering how I know the future.

Well, I have bad news for you. I'm not psychic. I can't see what's coming. I can't predict the lotto numbers for tonight, which is a real pity because it would be exceptionally useful. But over the past year, I've been approached by several people who claimed they could see my future. Random strangers. Some of them knew they occasionally had flashes of precognition, while others couldn't even explain why they'd come up to me on the street. They'd experienced dreams, visions, hunches. At first I assumed they were nothing but random crazies, but when it kept happening, it became harder to dismiss.

So I've known for some time that you would find yourself standing in the rain without any memory of who you were. I knew that you would come to surrounded by dead people wearing gloves. I knew that they would be lying on the ground having been "taken down hardcore," in the words of one particularly batty old woman who spoke to me on the street in Liverpool.

I wonder, are you made up of parts of me? Or are you a completely new person? You don't know who you are, that much I can be certain of, but what else is gone? I suppose you couldn't know that Jane Eyre *is my least favorite book in the world. Or that anything by Georgette Heyer is my favorite. I like oranges. I like pastries.*

"Do you like pancakes?" wondered the girl in the hotel room, taking a bite of blueberry-filled deliciousness. "I certainly like them. You should have said."

To tell the truth, I find this whole thing alarming. I have a tidy, comfortable life. It's a trifle unorthodox, but I have managed to make it work. And now all I can do is piece things together from what I've been told.

1. I know that I will lose my memory. I have no idea why, but I will try and be prepared and make this as easy for you as it can be.

2. I know that I or you will be attacked, will fight, and will win. I'm laying odds that the last part is you. I organize very well, but I don't fight.

The black eyes are probably mine, though. That sort of thing seems to happen to me.

3. I know that the men who attack me are all wearing latex gloves, which is very important. I know it sounds like nothing, maybe an incidental perversion. You don't understand the significance, but I do, and I will explain it to you, if you want. All you need to know immediately is that someone I should be able to trust has decided that I need to be removed. I don't know exactly who. I don't know why. It may be for something I haven't even done yet.

I can't be certain that you'll read this letter; I can't even be certain that you'll read the first letter. I've just put copies of them in every coat and jacket I own to make sure they'll be available to you when you need them. I can only hope that my limited knowledge of the future will be of use to you, and that you will gain some additional insights of your own.

And that I'll be wearing a coat when it happens.

In any case, we must face facts. There is a choice you must make, because I will not make it for you. You can walk away from my life and go create a new one. If that's what you choose, then you will need to leave the country, but this body comes with a large amount of money—more than enough to buy you a comfortable life. I have left instructions on how to build yourself a new identity, and lists of names and facts that you can use to protect yourself. It would never be a completely safe life, but it would be as safe as I, a person who knows how to prepare, can make it for you.

Or you can choose to adopt my life as your own. You can find out why you have been betrayed. I said before that mine is a good life, and that is true. The body you are in has been privileged enough to have wealth, power, and knowledge beyond the dreams of normal people. You can have those things as well, but this choice will be dangerous. For whatever reason, an injustice has been committed against both of us. An injustice against you because you did not do anything, and an injustice against me because I cannot believe that I will do anything to deserve it.

So, that's the choice you have to make. Unfair? Absolutely. But you still have to make it. There are two keys in the envelope, and both are to lockboxes at the Mansel Bank on Bassingthwaighte Street in the City;

1011-A contains all the materials you need to go away and 1011-B puts you back into my life. I would not blame you for making either choice.

I wish you nothing but the best. Whatever you do, be careful until you have opened the box. Remember, they want you dead.

Sincerely,

Myfanwy Thomas

She put the letter down on the table, picked up her coffee, and walked over to the balcony door. She hesitated, but then dismissed her fears. *No one followed me,* she thought. *There aren't going to be snipers waiting for me to come outside. Get a grip.* She opened the door and went out into the morning. It was a nice day. All around her were hotel rooms in which people were eating much the same food as she was, and balconies where they were enjoying the same late-winter sunshine and looking down on the same steam coming off the heated (and completely deserted) pool. But she imagined that she was probably the only person about to decide who she was going to be.

Well, Ms. Thomas, your story is very compelling, she mused. *You have deliberately tried to tantalize me into some sort of pursuit of justice. You give me no details of the life I would be inheriting. You want me to be curious. And although I still have no idea who I am, it seems that I do have a penchant for intrigue.*

I don't know whether I get this from you, she thought, *but I have enough sense to realize that your little mission would be a fool's errand. And I'm not even vaguely intrigued by your promise of "wealth, power, and knowledge beyond the dreams of normal people." Can you hear me somewhere in the back of this brain? If so, then hear this: Don't flatter yourself, darling. Your life holds absolutely no appeal for me.*

She stared up at the clouds, which she couldn't remember ever staring at before. She drank the coffee, and although she knew it was good, and that she liked it with milk and sugar, she couldn't remember ever drinking coffee before. She could recall the movements needed to swim the butterfly stroke, although she couldn't remember ever entering a pool. There were so many memories to build and experiences she knew she would enjoy.

If people are going to be trying to kill me, then I want to be somewhere far away, and I want to be spending as much money as you have bequeathed me. Whatever you lacked in courage, I am going to make up for in common sense. She went back in the room, picked up a pen, and firmly circled 1011-A.

She lay on the bed with a steak draped over each eye, thinking about what she would do next. There were a few issues that needed to be addressed. First, how was she to get to the bank without catching the attention (and, subsequently, the fist) of some psycho with a fetish for surgical gloves? Second, where did she want to go once she opened the door to her new life? The first problem seemed relatively simple. In her panic the previous night, she'd extracted a rather large quantity of cash. Certainly enough to hire a car and driver to take her to the bank. As to the second, well, for all her obvious faults, Miss Myfanwy Thomas as was did not strike her as a liar. She expected to find everything she would need in box 1011-A. Thomas had said there would be instructions and advice on how to build a new life. Of course, there remained the question as to why Myfanwy Thomas hadn't elected to take this wealth she claimed to possess and flee the country herself before she lost her memory. She could have precluded the amnesia and been sunning herself on some balcony in Borneo if she'd had the nerve. So what had stopped her?

Perhaps, she thought, *it was the number of predictions she received. But what kind of person believes random "psychics" off the street? And if Thomas was certain the attack would happen, she was equally certain that I could escape her life. Thomas was too timid to change her fate, but I will not be!*

Filled with a sudden certainty, she carefully peeled the steaks off her eyes and examined the results in the mirror. The swelling had gone down, but the bruising was dark and thorough. It would be days before all signs vanished, and the aching continued to be a problem. She headed to the bathroom to wash the meat juice off her face and out of her hair, pausing only to fetch a Toblerone from the minibar.

Forty-five minutes later, she stepped into a waiting car and was ferried away in comfort into the City. Her clothes were clean, her hair smelled of flowers rather than steak tartare, and her mind was intent on how she was to go about living. Clearly, she and Thomas were different people. Well, she would be grateful for what had been left to her, and the girl who used to live inside her body could rest in peace.

Taken by a sudden whim, she asked the driver to go by some of the main sights of London. As they drove through Trafalgar Square and cruised past St. Paul's Cathedral, she looked out with narrowed eyes. She knew these places, but only as if she'd read about them or seen pictures of them.

The long black car glided to a stop in front of the bank, and the driver nodded agreeably when asked to wait. *I wonder if Thomas had this same taste for luxury? If not, it's a pity, since she could afford it.* After breakfast, she'd checked the account balances for all her cards at an ATM in the hotel and had been thrilled with the number of zeros that appeared. If this was the wealth Thomas had spoken of in her letter, then she was going to live quite comfortably. If there was more, then it was going to be an excessively good life. She disembarked from the car and walked up the steps, looking subtly around her for the slightest sign that someone was watching her. Not seeing a hint of a glove or anyone staring in her direction, she relaxed and walked in.

I'll have to come up with a name, I suppose. I certainly can't go about being Myfanwy Thomas, not if I'm trying to escape the past. And I'm not particularly wild about Anne Ryan. Probably dangerous to make any decisions before I know what Thomas had planned. There may be a passport or something. Although I've always liked the name Jeanne.

At least, I think *I've always liked it.*

Still musing, she followed the signs, took the lift down to the lockbox area, pushed open the thick wooden doors, and walked over to the receptionist.

"Good morning, I'm Anne Ryan," she said, producing the driver's license.

14

The receptionist stood up, nodding. She was wearing latex gloves. And before the woman formerly known as Myfanwy Thomas could say a word, the receptionist wound up and punched her in the face.

She flew backward, the pain in her eyes flaring, and shrieked like a train whistle. Through the stars floating in her vision, she could see three men entering the room and shutting the doors behind them. They surrounded her, and one of the men leaned over her with a hypodermic needle in one hand. Filled with a sudden rage, she swung her leg up and kicked him hard between the legs. Squealing, he doubled over, and she lashed out with a fist, catching him hard on the chin. He staggered back onto one of the other men, and she swung herself up, teeth bared, panic rising as she realized that she had no idea how to fight. Still, certain things were obvious. She shoved the man she'd kicked hard, sending him and his friend against the wall. The remaining man and the woman stood back, seeming almost hesitant to touch her. She noticed that the men were also wearing latex gloves. The woman flicked a questioning look to the standing man.

Taking advantage of this, she leaped toward the woman, reasoning that she would be the easiest target. They didn't appear to have any weapons, and so far it was only the woman who'd seemed willing to hit her. Instead of slamming her target, however, she found herself quickly slung around and placed in some sort of painful armlock. She was being taken down by experts. *Sorry, Thomas. It looks as if you overestimated me.* One of the men stepped in and slapped her hard. The pain rocked her, and she reeled in the woman's grasp. The bitch shoved slightly against her arm, and it felt as if several bones were being pushed to their breaking point. Then the man punched her.

"Bastards!" she shrieked. The first man limped toward her, holding the syringe. The pain was rising within her, and when the woman jerked at her arm again, the agony exploded. She closed her eyes and screamed. There was nothing in the world but that scream, drowning out everything else, even the pain. All the air was pushed out of her lungs, and she felt and heard nothing but her voice. When she opened her eyes and took a breath, she realized that there was no one holding her. Instead, the four people were lying on the ground, twitching uncontrollably.

What the hell just happened? What did I do?

She staggered, panting, but refused to keel over. She looked around, waiting for more people to come in, but no one appeared. *Not even the bank staff?* she thought vaguely, but the doors were apparently thick enough to muffle any sounds of fighting. Her first instinct was flight, but then she was seized with a terrible resolve. Her existence up to this point had been bizarre, admittedly, but she'd made decisions based on the facts she'd collected. Now, nothing she'd thought she understood could be trusted. Any vague suppositions she had had about who Myfanwy Thomas was or what had happened to her were clearly deeply flawed. There was far more to the world than she'd supposed, and she wanted to know everything.

Carefully, she searched the receptionist's pockets, doing her best to ignore the increasingly feeble twitches. Nothing. A cursory examination of the desk revealed a drawer of numbered keys, each in its own little compartment. She found the appropriate keys to match the ones she already had, and, stepping over the people lying on the floor, she walked into the room in which the boxes were kept. With a gasp, she found an unconscious woman with an ID badge indicating that she was the receptionist. *I suppose they knocked her out,* thought Myfanwy weakly. *How could they have found me? And gotten in place so fast?*

She stepped over the bank employee, scanned the rows of enormous drawers until she found the right ones, and matched the keys to the two locks. For a moment, she was tempted to change her mind, but a glance over her shoulder at the bodies on the floor decided her. She set her jaw and opened box 1011-B.

Inside were two suitcases. She opened the first and saw a number of objects wrapped in bubble wrap. She turned to the second suitcase, opened it, and took a step back in surprise. The case was filled with stacks of envelopes, all numbered in the unmistakable handwriting of Myfanwy Thomas.

2

Her initial disappointment at finding a suitcase full of paperwork rather than high-tech gadgets or gold coins gave way to intrigue. She hadn't been certain what she would find, and she supposed that letters made about as much sense as anything else. Hopefully, Myfanwy Thomas had left instructions for a situation such as this. But was there time to peruse them? She risked a look over her shoulder and saw that the four figures had not roused themselves and were not headed toward her but in fact had ceased their twitching and were lying still. The receptionist did not seem to be in any danger of waking up. She sucked her teeth for a moment, weighing possibilities in her mind, and then reason won out over curiosity. *Fuck it, I'll read in the car.*

She tucked the first envelope, labeled *3,* in her back pocket, then hefted the two suitcases, which were much heavier than she had anticipated, out of the drawer and onto the floor, and then precariously wheeled them out of the vault. She maneuvered carefully around the bodies and found the lift, which whisked her up to the lobby.

Be calm, she said to herself. *Be calm. Not everyone in the bank is going to be wearing latex gloves.* In fact, nobody was wearing gloves, and nobody appeared to pay her a blind bit of attention. *Well, that will last right until someone goes to check his lockbox,* she thought, and hurried outside. The stairs down from the bank presented some problems, but the driver noticed her struggling and obligingly toted her luggage to the car. Myfanwy thanked him and slid into the backseat.

"Just drive," she said. "Just go, please." She leaned back weakly and focused on controlling her breathing and not having a heart attack.

Okay, you're safe, she told herself. *Well, what's next?* She took the envelope from her pocket and tore it open.

Dear You,

    The odds of your reading this are slim to none. Who would choose uncertainty and vaguely worded warnings over a new life of wealth and luxury? I can only assume that you were put under a massive amount of stress, touched someone's skin, and they were paralyzed. Or blinded. Or lost the ability to speak. Or befouled themselves. Or one of several other effects that I won't outline right now. In any case, I know what it's like the first time it happens. It's like a door opening up inside of you, isn't it? Like you've been hit by a truck. It can't be ignored. So even if you would have preferred to open up the other box (which, by the way, would have had you living out the rest of your life as Jeanne Citeaux), I'm glad you made this choice.

    Take both suitcases with you and go to the address below. The key in this envelope will get you in, and you should be safe there. It has no connection to me, officially. Open the next envelope when you are established. Try not to be followed.

This note was unsigned, and the key she fished out of the envelope bore no identifying marks. The address given was not the one on either of her driver's licenses and appeared to be some sort of flat. The letter and key were put into a pocket, and she gave the next destination to the driver with the message that he should try not to be followed. The driver nodded and began to follow a course with so many doublings-back and abrupt changes in direction that she was certain nobody could pursue them without being noticed. When she commented on this, he smiled slightly.

"I'm used to it, miss. Many of our clients have the paparazzi after them." Nodding her head thoughtfully, Myfanwy took out the key and turned it over and over in her hands as she looked out the windows. They had by now moved out of the City. At points, they drove along the Thames, which was very pretty, with tour boats cruising along. Then they would curve away, switching lanes and twisting through residential districts. As the car meandered east, to the Docklands, she began to digest the events in the bank.

Eventually the car stopped in front of an apartment building. The driver carried her suitcases into the lobby for her. She gave him a generous bonus for his excellent driving, then dragged the suitcases into the lift. On the ninth floor, she found the appropriate apartment and opened the door.

It was clear that the apartment had been empty for weeks, if not months. A little light trickled in, but the curtains were drawn. She flicked on the light. The entire place smelled of abandonment. It was eerily quiet. She hesitantly took a few steps, feeling as if she were intruding or had broken into someone's house.

Before her, the living room opened up, with some pieces of furniture sitting solidly under dust sheets. There were no pictures on the walls. To her right was a kitchen. She opened the refrigerator and found some six-packs of bottled water and cans of soft drinks. The freezer held a variety of Lean Cuisines and some plastic-covered trays of frozen meat. There was cutlery in one of the drawers, and crockery in a cupboard. She moved into the living room and dragged the sheets off the furniture, revealing some big, squashy-looking couches and chairs of a dark burgundy color. There was a large TV hanging on the wall.

"How minimalist," she remarked to herself. The bedroom was similarly devoid of character, with a large bed under yet another dust sheet. She peeled back the sheet and saw that the bed was already made up with some soft-looking blankets. A surprising waft of scent rose up when she uncovered the bed, and under the blankets she found a few sachets of lavender. There were soap, shampoo, and towels in the bathroom. A few fresh toothbrushes in their boxes, with toothpaste and mouthwash in the cupboard above the sink. No makeup, but there was a hairbrush and, surprisingly, a few bottles of hair dye.

Don't tell me I'm going gray at thirty-one! she thought in horror, but she noticed that none of the colors were her own. *Probably in case I need to disguise myself,* she concluded. There was also a large first aid kit on a shelf.

The other bedroom had been made into a sort of office, with a large computer and a complicated-looking printer under more plastic. There was a low bookshelf with some folders on it, and she pulled one out and opened it at random. It appeared to hold the details of the rental of the flat she was standing in. Struck by a sudden thought, she went back into the main bedroom and opened the wardrobe.

There were a few exceptionally bland garments, mostly black and gray. Some white blouses, a couple of suits, a skirt, and two pairs of jeans. All had been carefully hung up and all appeared designed to encourage people not to look at the person wearing them.

Well, apparently I had absolutely no taste, she thought, bemused by the plainness of the range offered. She shuddered, because there was something unsettling about the thought of those clothes on her body without her mind being present. However, as she fingered the clothes, she found that all of them still bore price tags. She carefully closed the doors and went out into the living room, where she pulled back the curtain and let in all the sunlight.

The windows were huge and looked out on the river, with all its traffic. The furniture seemed much more cozy suddenly, and she could see that everything had been carefully positioned in the very best spots. *Thomas put some thought into this place,* she reflected. *This wasn't just a bolt-hole but somewhere to be comfortable.* She felt a little pang of fondness for the woman who'd lived in her body. You couldn't help liking someone who put all this effort into making you feel welcome.

Besides, she's the only person I know, she thought, a little ridiculously. She dragged the suitcases into the living room and opened the one that had no letters but was instead filled with objects packaged in bubble wrap. She plucked one out and weighed it in her hands. It was heavy, and a label reading JUST IN CASE had been stuck on. She carefully unwound the tape and wrappings, and then sucked in a breath of surprise. In her hand she held a small but evil-looking submachine gun. She eyed the suitcase warily, lest it suddenly eject more weapons, and then gingerly rewrapped the gun before putting it back in the case and shutting the lid.

She turned her attention to the other suitcase and plucked out the next letter. It was much thicker than all the others had been, and written in a cheerful violet ink. She kicked off her shoes and sat on the couch, which was extremely comfortable, just perfect for napping.

Dear You,

I am just going to have to assume that you are where you're supposed to be and stop making all sorts of vague conjectures as to where you might be. That said, you'd better be in the apartment I set up for you because it's taken me ages to prepare it. There were all sorts of things I wanted there waiting for you, and it's been exceedingly difficult to get all this done without being noticed. I (and now you, I suppose) exist under a certain amount of surveillance. And so the establishment of this secret hideaway, where I sit on the right-hand side of the couch writing to you, was quite an accomplishment.

She looked over at the other side of the couch, where her old self had sat. It was kind of companionable, despite the lack of a companion.

There are all sorts of things I must explain to you, but I will have to prioritize carefully. Before I can tell you all about who I am, what I do, and so on, there are a few more immediate things you should know. I assumed in my last letter that you touched someone and disrupted their control of their own body. I'll keep on assuming that, since it's the only reason I can think of why you would have picked the box you did. As an aside, I'll tell you that I feel really bad for you — it takes quite a large amount of pain to trigger your gift unconsciously. Hopefully, nothing has been broken or ruptured inside of you, since that would be really inconvenient. But no, I resolved I wouldn't go down all the avenues of "what might be." You're in the apartment, and safe.

The first time it happened to me, I was nine years old and had climbed a tree. Somehow, I managed to fall and get a sharp branch jammed into my leg. Shrieking with pain, I was bundled into the car by my parents and driven to the hospital. I was wearing a tracksuit at the time, and so I must assume that's how my parents managed not to touch my skin during this whole thing. Anyway, the ride was dreadful for everyone concerned, for me because I was bleeding and am a terrible coward when it comes to pain, and for my parents because I didn't stop wailing.

Finally, we arrived at the hospital, and either there weren't many people waiting or my shrieking prompted some sort of queue-jumping privileges, because I was quickly taken in to the doctor, who gently cut off my track bottoms (they'd glued themselves to my leg). When he brushed his hand against my skin, he immediately fell over and started screaming. It turned out that he'd lost control of his legs. Some other hospital person rushed in and tried to tend to both me and the doctor. When she touched my bare skin, she lost her sight.

So now we had three people shrieking and flailing about, although I was so thrown by the whole thing that I was getting much quieter by this time and gave out only the occasional whimper when I remembered to. The third medical person had the good sense (or perhaps it was just good luck) to tend to the others first. And the next person to touch me had the even better sense to be wearing gloves, and so my leg was stitched up and bandaged, and when I woke up, it was safe for people to touch me again.

But I knew that I had caused the chaos, and I knew I could do it again if I wanted to. Search your mind, think back, and you'll see that you know how to do it too. If you haven't done it yet (I can't avoid this conjecture, because it's too important), then you're going to have to jump-start your powers. There's a red folder in one of the cases that you can consult for suggestions.

She's got to be kidding, the woman on the couch thought incredulously, but she put the letter aside for a moment and sifted through the case until she found the red folder. Inside, there were detailed descriptions on how best to push her own arm or leg to the near breaking point (without actually breaking it) and how to induce a number of other ghastly sounding but nonpermanent types of damage. "Unbelievable," she murmured. The incident at the bank hadn't been pretty, but at least she hadn't had to do anything like this.

At first it seemed that the bizarre afternoon had passed without consequence. There were no lawsuits, and my parents never spoke to me about it. But somebody somewhere must have mentioned it, and the talk must have eventually made its way to an exceedingly interested party. I found out later that three months after my visit to hospital, my father received a letter from an obscure branch of the government. I like to think that he and my mother talked it over, but the end result was that my father and I were driven to an old stone building in the City, and I was introduced to Lady Linda Farrier and Sir Henry Wattleman of the Checquy Group.

My father and I were led into a sort of drawing room lined with books and prints. We sat down carefully in armchairs and were brought tea and biscuits, and then Sir Henry and Lady Farrier proceeded to explain to my father why it was both necessary and legal that I be taken away from my family and placed in the care of the Checquy Group. I was not really paying attention to all of this because I was only nine and a half and because I could not stop staring at Lady Farrier, who was strangely familiar.

She was not young, but she was very thin, with hair that had been drawn back and up. Her eyes were a dark, dark brown and she spoke in a very calm manner. Nothing seemed to shake or surprise her, even when I managed to drop my teacup onto the floor, where it shattered into a million pieces and splashed tea everywhere. She didn't even blink, although Sir Henry's head whipped around in alarm and I half thought he was going to punch someone.

I do remember my father objecting to my being taken, but in a sort of halfhearted manner, as if he already knew he would lose. Lady Farrier very patiently repeated some lines of the law she'd quoted earlier, and there was not the slightest bit of mercy in her voice, but Sir Henry seemed to have a bit more pity in him. This is ironic, since I later learned he was one of the most dangerous men in the country and had been responsible for a great many assassinations—most of which he had carried out himself. Nevertheless, at that time he was by far the more human of the two and was doing his best to console my father. He even patted him on the shoulder.

I was finding it increasingly difficult to pay attention to this conversation because of my fascination with Lady Farrier, who ignored me completely. Just as my father finally bowed his head and agreed that he would be leaving *without me, I recalled where I knew her from. My mind was whirling as I submitted to a final kiss and hug from my father, and I honestly cannot recall what our parting words were. He left with Sir Henry, and I stood, absentmindedly wiping my father's tears off my cheek, staring at the woman whom, impossibly, I recognized.*

Do I sound like a terrible child for ignoring my father as he walked out of my life? Looking back, I cringe and am amazed. I was not normally self-centered. I adored my family and had a little sister and an older brother who were my favorite people in the world. In the days to come, I would dissolve in tears at the thought of them. But at that moment, there was nothing but her.

Every night for the previous two months I had dreamed of her. I'd sat with this woman in a room with black-and-white tiles and told her everything. She was stiff and formal, but I had found myself adoring her. Food would appear on the tables, and she would patiently extract every detail of my life from me. She was especially interested in my day at the hospital but endured my descriptions of all my possessions and the minutiae of my day. I think it was her patience that endeared her to me. How often does a nine-year-old child have such a fascinated audience? In any case, she had listened, and now I found myself face-to-face with her.

In the apartment, she put down the letter for a moment and stared thoughtfully at the ceiling. This woman, Farrier, sounded eerily like the woman from her own dream. And the room Thomas described was exactly the same. Even the name the Checquy Group stirred the hairs at the back of her neck and along her arms. Was her memory returning? Even a little? She turned back to the letter.

"Well, Miss Myfanwy," Lady Farrier said thoughtfully. "Here we are again." Numbly, I nodded in agreement, too filled with amazement to say anything. "And now it seems you are going to come and live with us," she added, staring at me meaningfully. It was then that the realization hit me, and I began to sniffle. Perhaps I expected that, like a kindly aunt, she would hasten to comfort me, but all she did was take another sip from her teacup. As I broke down into sobs, she simply nibbled her crumpets and waited for

me to finish. When Sir Henry came in and sat down in his own chair, he didn't do anything either. Though he had been moved by the distress of a grown man, he did not react to the weeping of a little girl. Eventually I managed to get hold of myself, and, wiping my nose on my sleeve, I began thoughtfully eyeing the tray of biscuits. Lady Farrier nodded slightly, and I made a grab for something intriguing and chocolate.

And that was the beginning of my association with the Checquy Group, which has continued since that day. They wanted me because of what I could do — what you can do. Hopefully some of my training has remained with you, because it took me years to attain this level of mastery. Now, with a touch, I can seize control of someone's physical system. I can take away any or all of their senses, paralyze them, make them feel anything I want.

The Checquy Group thought I could be some sort of ultra spy, traveling the world and, I don't know, making people throw themselves in front of cars or something. Unfortunately, at least for the Checquy Group, I am not the spy type. I'm not an aggressive person, I get violently ill in planes, and I'm really quite shy. The Court was disappointed, but I was too valuable an asset for them to simply drop. Instead, I have become an in-house operative. It turns out that I am an extremely capable administrator and have a very good head for numbers. I use my powers only rarely. Thus, while other members of the organization attain high positions through their remarkable accomplishments in the field, I became a member of the Court simply through my work in the bureaucracy.

Does that sound lame? I'm very, very good. There's not a formal timeline for ascending to the Court. In fact, most people never get in. I am the youngest person in the current Court. I got there after ten years of working in administration. The next-youngest got in after sixteen years of highly dangerous fieldwork. That's how good an administrator I am.

"What a geek," she sighed. Shaking her head, she put down the letter and went into the kitchen, where she pulled a bottle of water from the fridge. She gulped it all down and reached for another. A thousand questions were whirling through her head. What was this power over others that she had inherited? Thomas claimed that it required skin-to-skin contact, but back in the bank, she had managed to take out four people, all of whom were wearing gloves and three of whom hadn't even been touching her. And what was this Checquy Group? They sought out people with powers. They were led by a woman who could enter dreams. They were empowered by the law to take a child away from her family. And Thomas was a part of it. Slowly, she walked back to the couch.

So, I suppose you're wondering all about the Checquy Group. Oh, and please note that it is pronounced Sheck-Eh. *French influences, I think. Or possibly just warped by generations of employees mispronouncing it. Don't worry if the name means nothing to you. Most people never hear of it at all, but it has been in existence for centuries. It worked closely with the House of York, tended to ignore the Tudors, and endured the House of Stuart. However, it does not really matter who is ruling—from the earliest days, the organization's loyalty has been to Britain rather than to a particular ruler. When Oliver Cromwell became Lord Protector, the four leaders of the Checquy Brotherhood (a pompous and inaccurate early name for the organization) were waiting to offer their services to him. You might think that Cromwell, a dedicated Puritan (indeed, the dedicated Puritan), would not have suffered such a group to live, let alone employed them. The records I saw describe the exhibition the leaders gave the Lord Protector, and as a result of that demonstration, the Brotherhood continued its existence. We weather the vagaries of history, welcoming new rulers and bending knees to those in power, whoever they may be. We are a tool of the nation, an asset of the British Isles. Those who work within the Checquy can accomplish what no one else can, and so they are the secret arm of the kingdom.*

If I sound like I'm proud to be one of them, that's because I am. Threats arise every day, threats normal people cannot be made aware of. It is the Checquy Group that protects them, though it goes largely unrecognized. Although I don't go out into the field, I know that I play an integral part in defending normal people. I love my job, and that's why those random psychics' predictions have hurt me so badly. I don't know which member of the Court will turn against me, but if one does, it means there is something rotten at its core, which means that everyone is in danger.

The Checquy Group is composed of hundreds of individuals. Some are like me—they possess powers beyond the normal population. The non-powered members are simply the cream of their respective occupational crops. This shouldn't be taken as meaning that I don't admire them. Unlike most other members of the Court, I do not regard the non-powered as being lesser. Perhaps it is because I lack the courage to go out and face what they do, but in any case I know they are just as good as me. Still, by long-standing tradition and policy, non-powered individuals cannot become members of the Court—the ruling circle. The Court answers to the highest individuals in the land only, and not always to them.

Those of us with powers are sought out by the Checquy through a variety of means, and the group was long ago granted the authority to claim any citizens it wanted. Parents are coerced or duped into releasing their children, sometimes with massive payoffs. Adults are lured in with promises of power, wealth, and the opportunity to serve their nation. The initiation is a mixture of ancient oaths and modern contracts under both the official and unofficial secrecy acts of the government. By the time an individual has become a full member, he is bound by a million different ties. Do you realize now what your leaving would have meant?

I've only ever heard of three people who tried to leave the Checquy, and I know the history inside and out. Of those three, the first was a powered individual called Brennan the Intransigent who made a break for it in 1679. He was about to step across the English Channel to France, where he had been lured by the promises of the French government, when he was taken into custody. He was crucified on the cliffs of Dover.

The second was a soldier in 1802 who was driven insane by something he saw in a burrow at John o'Groats and who fled to his parents' home. He was carefully brought back to the Checquy stronghold and then buried alive in his village's graveyard.

The third was a woman who could grow tentacles out of her back and exuded some sort of alarming toxin through her fingertips. In 1875, she fled to Buenos Aires and managed to live there for three months before the hand of the Checquy caught up with her. Her stuffed body is currently displayed above the mantelpiece in one of the London offices. The little bronze plaque indicates that she lived for six months after they caught her.

See how the Checquy Group deals with those who try to leave? They like to make examples of them, and they tend to be creative about how they do it. And did I mention that none of those who tried to escape were members of the Court? Can you imagine how much more creative they would be if you had fled and they caught you? Don't worry, you would have escaped safely. As soon as I accepted what was going to happen to me, I began to consolidate all my resources and knowledge into designing a means of protecting you.

You don't need to know all the details, but suffice it to say that I created a series of contingencies that if activated would have simultaneously crippled the Checquy's ability to pursue you and disrupted the daily functioning of the organization in such a way that they could not have spared the staff or the resources to pursue a Myfanwy Thomas—especially a Myfanwy Thomas who had had plastic surgery and drastically corrupted the records that contained her personal details.

How? *I can almost hear you ask. Well, it involved a few things.*

1. Lots and lots of research, which started as an attempt to figure out who would have a reason to attack me and ended up giving me a far better understanding of the organization and how to evade it. It also allowed me to build up some rather detailed dossiers on the various Court members. Some of those dossiers describe—well, let's call them indiscretions. They're not crimes on the level of a bring-down-the-government scandal, but they're grave enough that if certain highly placed officials found out about them, it would prompt some inconvenient investigations that would take up an enormous amount of the Court's time.

2. The systematic alteration of most of the files that describe me, including fingerprints and DNA details. The hard copies, anyway. I've used my rank and a few little computing skills to write a program that will corrupt the electronic copies.

3. The insertion of a virus into the computer systems that will, if put into motion, hamper even the most mundane work. The Checquy would still be able to carry out its day-to-day activities, but with far less efficiency than usual. The resulting confusion would give you ample time to get out of the country, get a new face, and attend to a few other things.

If you had elected to leave, I would have had you stop by an unmanned Checquy outpost office in Waterloo Station, log onto the terminal, and e-mail keywords to some accounts in the Checquy mainframe. Once you'd activated these contingency plans, you would technically have been guilty of committing treason against the nation by (temporarily) weakening its defenses. So in some ways, staying and assuming my life is safer. It's a very complicated business, I'll admit.

If it's any consolation, I'm really glad you made this decision.

So, while I don't know exactly who is currently trying to kill you, there are seven candidates — the other members of the Court. One of the psychics confirmed that.

Oh, but before I give you any more details, check your watch and see what day of the week it is. If it's a weekday, well, I suppose it's fairly obvious that you've missed work. Is it too late to call in sick?

Automatically, she checked her watch and saw it was Saturday. Then she did a double take.

Yes, you're going in to work. Yes, you're going in to an office where someone is trying to kill you. You chose not to leave, and this is the only way you can stay. There's a purple binder in the suitcase with the letters. It's thick. That's because it describes the Checquy and what you do for them. You'll probably need to consult it a lot. If it's a workday today, then you should call in sick. Instructions on how to do so are at the top of page 1. Otherwise, you'll want to pick out a businesslike outfit for your first day at work. If it's a weekend, read on.

When last we left our heroine (us), she was nine years old and about to stuff her gob with a chocolate digestive. As I recall, we had all finished our tea, but neither Lady Farrier nor Sir Henry spoke directly to me. I remember feeling somewhat irritated by this but not so irritated that I didn't start wolfing down everything on the pastry tray. And then Lady Farrier sent me away to the Estate.

The letter continued, but she was too tired to read further. The pages fell back into her lap, and soon she was asleep on the couch, a couch that had been chosen for its extreme coziness.

If she had any dreams, she did not remember them.

3

My name is Myfanwy," she said, concerned by how unsure her voice sounded. The face she saw in the mirror might belong to someone named Myfanwy, but it was taking her a little while to think of herself as such. She was, however, beginning to think of the person who had previously occupied her body as Thomas.

"I'm Myfanwy," she said again, a bit more convincingly this time.

"Were you a morning person, Thomas?" she wondered aloud as she struggled up out of bed. She'd spent most of the previous day sleeping and reading through the dossiers that Thomas had left her. She'd fallen asleep around midnight, her face covered by a report on the Checquy's diplomatic relationship with the Great Barrier Reef. Now it was five o'clock on Monday morning, and she'd woken with a start, petrified that she was late.

For a moment she'd toyed with calling in sick, but a number of factors had dissuaded her. To begin with, the letter writer had seemed reluctant to suggest that missing work was even an option. In addition, the prospect of staying alone in the contrived apartment another day was, well, kinda creepy. Nope, it was definitely time to go in to work and figure out what the hell was going on. She stumbled to the shower and ran through a variety of possible wardrobe combinations in her mind before settling for a suit. It was Myfanwy Thomas who had picked out the clothes, so at least she didn't need to worry about turning up and not looking like Myfanwy Thomas.

She'd noticed the previous morning that the cupboard was surprisingly bare of breakfast foods. *Slipping a little, aren't we, Thomas? What kind of "extremely capable administrator" doesn't take care to leave breakfast for the woman inhabiting her future amnesiac body? Not even a Pop-Tart? A frozen croissant? Honestly.* Still, there were coffee beans and a grinder, and she was able to sit down with a cup of coffee and that big-ass purple binder.

Thomas seems like a decent sort, but she's a glorified paper pusher, she thought ruefully. *Even if she does work for a paranormal version of the MI5, she's probably dealing with the boring bits. "Heavens! Some kind of werewolf is eating the Queen! Fetch some forms and ask her to fill them out in triplicate, and then perhaps we can attend to her needs at some point during the next quarter."* Snorting to herself, Myfanwy opened the binder and read the instructions Thomas had left for getting ready for the office.

Half an hour later, she was wearing one of the ugly suits from the wardrobe, holding a briefcase, and anxiously explaining to the man on the phone that she'd like a cab as soon as was humanly possible and admitting that yes, she was in a hurry, and so, yes, she should have planned ahead. The next fifteen minutes were spent in the lobby of the apartment building looking out for the cab. When it finally appeared, she gave the address to the extremely scruffy driver and was then forced to concede that she didn't know where it was.

As the driver perused his map, she thumbed through the purple binder. She'd only managed to read the summary, which had been mind-bogglingly intricate. She'd found some sticky notes in the flat's office and was marking various important-seeming passages. As a result, every page was marked, some of them three times. Apparently Thomas had not felt an index would be necessary, although there was a vague table of contents.

"So, you have no idea where this house is?" the driver asked. He was elderly and wearing one of those dubious flat caps.

"No," she admitted as she turned a page and found an entirely new alarming topic.

"Whose house is it, then?"

"Oh, it's mine," she said distractedly and was sufficiently absorbed in her reading not to notice the look he gave her. In fact, she kept her head down for the entire trip and so had no idea where the house was located even when they arrived. She thanked the driver as she stared in utter bemusement at the building in front of her. *Goddamn! I must be loaded!*

"You live in a big house," the taxi driver remarked.

"Yes, it seems I do," she replied.

"Tasteful too," he added. "I'd say it's mid-nineteenth century."

"Oh?"

"Yes. The features around the windows and the gables are a dead giveaway," he said.

"Those and the engraved *1841* above the door."

"There's a Rolls-Royce pulling in the other end of the driveway, and the driver is dressed in purple," he pointed out.

"Yes, that's my ride, I think," she said; she closed the purple binder, paid the man, and got out of the cab.

"If you ever feel the need for a taxi and a driver you can tip heavily, ask the dispatcher for Hourigan," he called after her. "I'll even put on a purple shirt if you like."

"Thank you," she called back over her shoulder. The driver of the Rolls stepped out, and she eyed him carefully. There had been a note about this in the binder:

The Retainers

Rank is complicated in the Checquy Group, the result of centuries of tradition and leaders who look upon a lack of change as evidence of cultural stamina.

But to put it very, very simply: If you have powers and you're not in the Court, then you're a Pawn. If you don't have powers, you'll never be in the Court, and you're a Retainer.

Of course, there are a lot of different levels within that framework. Pawns aren't automatically higher ranked than Retainers—at least, not anymore. A Pawn and a Retainer can possess the same level of authority; they can both be supervisors or section heads. A Retainer can be in charge of Pawns, and vice versa. Admittedly, prejudices endure. For the most part, if it comes down to a choice between a Pawn and a Retainer, a Pawn will get the job. But there are more Retainers than Pawns.

Retainers are drawn from a variety of places. Of course, we gather from the government, the military, and the clergy. We have drafting agents in the universities keeping eyes out for those who have skills and can manage to be discreet. There's always competition for the best and the brightest, but we have an outstanding budget, and our people have a talent for spotting the exceptional at an early age. And we also draw them from the private sector.

Retainers are crucial to the Checquy Group. They work in administration, intelligence, security, medical—everything. There are only a few sections of the Checquy where a Retainer cannot be employed, and those are positions where having powers is vital.

One subset of Retainer that you should know about is the personal staff of the members of the Court. That includes secretaries, drivers, bodyguards, etc. Bodyguards attend members of the Court only during ceremonial occasions or at times of high alert. So, yes, you'll have several people who periodically guard your body, but presumably, they weren't around when I lost my memory. In any case, you can distinguish the personal staff from regular Retainers because they dress in purple—it's a livery thing, dating back centuries. I've included a list of your personal staff, with photos, in the back of this binder.

The Retainers are bound to the Checquy through a variety of means. Legal contracts. Religious oaths. Oaths of fealty. Penalties under the Official Secrets Act. Penalties under various unofficial secrets acts. Vaguely worded threats of nebulously horrible vengeance. People don't learn the real secrets of the Checquy until they're a part of the group, and then they can't get out. Of course, there's no real reason why they would want to. They're doing good and earning well, and we provide an excellent and understanding staff of therapists.

"Good morning, Rook Thomas," said the man in purple, opening the car door for her.

"Good morning," she said awkwardly.

"To the Rookery then?"

"Uh, sure. I mean, if it's Monday, then I have to go to the Rookery, right?" she said, trying to pass her befuddlement off as a joke.

"Monday through Friday," said the driver ruefully.

"It's the price of having a job, I guess." He smiled but looked a little surprised. *Great, I'm already breaking character,* she thought dismally. "Well, we'd better be off."

She'd skimmed some material about the Rookery earlier but now decided she should better acquaint herself with it. She scanned anxiously through the binder's table of contents and then turned to

The Rookery

Of all the Checquy strongholds, the Rookery is simultaneously the most obvious and the most well concealed. Located in the City, the Hammerstrom Building was acquired some years ago under the auspices of then-Rook Conrad Grantchester. It serves as the headquarters for in-country operations and the barracks for the Barghests, and it features a temporary holding and interrogation facility. It also contains one of the key arsenals for the Checquy as well as alternative residences for the Rooks to use in times of emergency or on occasions when we stay at work too late to go home. Both situations arise with depressing regularity. As far as the outside world knows, the building is used only by several law and accounting firms, none of which have any non-Checquy clients on the books. In the areas open to the public, there is a bank, a restaurant, and a pub. The restaurant is terrible; avoid it.

It took years for the building to be refurbished to Grantchester's specifications, which involved a multitude of secret passages, special wiring, and concealed security fortifications. He was also responsible for the astonishingly tasteless decor in your secure residence. How tasteless? *you ask. Well, since you'll be seeing it, I probably shouldn't ruin the surprise. But what the hell— I'm facing betrayal, personal attack, and the prospect of my entire identity being wiped away, so I think I should be allowed to take what pleasures I can. Besides, it's absolutely hideous. We're talking about the ultimate bachelor pad, with lots of attention devoted to the sound system, and a carpet so thick and deep and verdant that you need a machete to get to the bathroom. It was designed specifically to get women to go to bed with its occupant.*

In many ways, the residence is the worst part of your new life. Compared to the decor, the fact that someone is trying to kill you is almost tolerable. There are two such apartments; it's just my luck that I got the one whose previous owner didn't die but instead rose to become the second most powerful man in the group, and my immediate superior. He insists on asking about the residence every time we meet, which is at least three times a week. So I've never been able to redecorate it.

In any case, as a Rook, you are one of the bosses of the Rookery. Thus, you have access to all areas and know all the secret passages, and everybody has to do what you say. All the secret passages are marked down on an electronic organizer in your office desk drawer and in the schematics in the binder, and the locks are keyed to open to your fingerprints, your palmprints, or the access code I gave you in the first letter. Officially, the secret passages were put in for the sake of the Rooks' privacy and security, but I'm convinced that really they're there because Grantchester's years as an agent in the field made him utterly paranoid—and also because he liked to sneak chicks in.

That's the Rookery. It is hidden from the eyes of the populace, a secret fortress that protects the normal people even as they remain ignorant of it. It is a testament to the willingness of humanity to ignore the obvious.

"Front door or garage, Rook Thomas?" asked the driver.

"Oh, it's a nice day," she replied. "I'll go in the front door."

The car slowed and she looked up in anticipation, eager to view this bastion of concealed power. Her eyes widened when she saw that there seemed to be an encampment in front of the building. Various small tents had been set up on the sidewalk, and badly dressed people were picketing the doorway, wielding placards that screamed with red exclamation points.

NO MORE CONSPIRACIES! blared a sign held by a man with a lot of beard. THE TRUTH IS IN HERE!

WE KNOW THE TRUTH! proclaimed several placards clutched by small children. The protesters were chanting some sort of rhyme that failed to scan but did manage to establish that the Hammerstrom Building was the secret headquarters of the government's department of the supernatural.

"I don't believe it," she muttered to herself, watching bemusedly as the denizens of the business district walked past the protesters with averted eyes. Looking up at the building, she had to sympathize with both parties. It was the last building in the world one would expect to contain anything interesting. About nine stories tall and constructed of an unprepossessing gray stone, the Hammerstrom Building looked like the kind of place in which the most tedious of businesses conducted their most tedious endeavors. There were no sculptures or decorations, no clue as to what might be inside. You would never just wander in to see what was in there. You'd have better things to do.

The driver had the door open, and she realized with a jolt that she should probably get out of the car. Thanking him, she accepted his hand and took a few hesitant steps toward the front door. The protesters, seeing a short woman looking around uncertainly with wide eyes, thought she was a possible convert and converged upon her.

"Miss! Miss!" There was a cacophony of voices, but finally the man with the beard established himself as their ambassador.

"Miss, it might shock you to know that this building is home to one of the greatest conspiracies in history!" he declared.

"Oh?" she said weakly.

"In this building the government keeps its secrets about the truth!" he explained.

"The truth?"

"Yes!" he said, and he paused impressively.

"About what?" she finally asked.

"Excuse me?"

"The truth about what?" she prompted him patiently.

"Everything they've been concealing! Are you aware that the British government has been hiding evidence of alien landings for the past twenty years?"

"They have?" *We have?* She resolved to look up aliens in the files Thomas had left for her.

"Yes! And that's not all! They have teams engaged in secret operations all over the countryside. We're not sure what it is they're doing, but we demand to know! Would you like to sign our petition and be put on our mailing list?" With one hand he thrust a clipboard under her nose, and with the other he fanned several pamphlets.

In the end, she signed the petition. She declined the mailing-list offer but did accept some of their home-cranked pamphlets, slipping them into her briefcase before, to the horror of the protesters, walking straight into the building through its rather shabby-looking revolving doors.

Inside there was a small, bland lobby with a large, bland security guard behind a desk. There were three lifts, and a building directory listed an assortment of businesses that she knew were fictitious. She looked around and saw that the guard was hurriedly standing and straightening his tie.

"Good morning, Rook Thomas," he said, dragging his gaze away from her bruises and black eyes and looking her square in the shoes. "How was your weekend?"

"It was nice," she said, caught slightly off guard. "Yes, very, very...nice," she added, failing to provide any details. There was an awkward pause, but to her secret delight, the large security officer seemed much more ill at ease than she was.

"Yes, well, if you'd just like to step on through then," he said as he reached under his desk and pressed a button, which buzzed her through a discreet frosted-glass door. She stepped forward, thanking him, and found herself in a painfully bright corridor that took her (unless she was mistaken) around behind the lifts, through a metal-detector archway, and into a lobby that was slightly larger and more nicely appointed than the one she'd just come from. A slightly larger and more nicely appointed security guard was getting up from *his* desk.

"Morning, Rook Thomas," he began

"Morning. I had a shit weekend, longest I can remember," she said with perfect honesty.

"Uh, yes, they look nasty," he said awkwardly, presumably referring to her bruises. "Well, if you'd like to swipe your pass and go on through," he said, gesturing toward the four revolving doors set into the wall. The partitions were made of heavy steel bars and intricately pierced metal plates. She carefully ran her pass over a small black panel and heard a series of beeps and heavy clunks. The metal doors began to rotate, and she stepped through smartly.

Here was the real lobby, obviously. A high ceiling arched

gracefully. Elevator doors lined the walls, and she recalled from her reading that some led to the underground garage and some to the upper levels—a deliberate move to ensure that everyone entering the building had to go through multiple layers of security and pass the exceptionally large and prominently armed guards who sat at the ring of desks in the center. It was a beautiful room, and it was filled with people bustling about.

Her heels clicked on the marble floor, and she caught her breath as all the people stopped talking and parted in front of her, opening the way to a specific lift. All eyes were fixed on her and she was very aware of her mud-spattered shoes and her black eyes. She straightened her spine and walked carefully to the doors. Was it her imagination, or had that woman started to curtsy? She nodded carefully and kept walking. One man gave a small bow, and an older gentleman in tweeds gave a brief, flickering salute. What was she supposed to do? Seized by a sudden impulse, she paused before the man who'd saluted and smiled. His eyes were fixed firmly ahead.

"Yes, Rook Thomas?" She was surprised by the deference that this man, who was at least twenty years her senior, showed her.

"Oh, um. Are you busy?" she asked awkwardly, without any idea of what to say.

"Not if you need me, ma'am," he said, keeping his eyes ahead.

"Please, come with me to my office. I would like to hear your thoughts on the project you are working on." And with that, she began walking to the lift. The only way to do this thing, she decided, was to be brazen about it. Until this man had answered her with fear and respect, she hadn't appreciated the power that came with being Myfanwy Thomas. It wasn't just the fear of what she could do to him should she touch him; it was also the authority of her position.

As the doors snapped shut, she could sense how uncomfortable her escort was. She'd made certain to stand at the back so that he was obliged to push the button for the floor, since she'd forgotten which one her office was on. He stood ramrod straight and very carefully avoided eye contact with her.

"So—" she began, but he cut her off immediately.

"Yes, Rook Thomas?"

"Ye-es," she said slowly. "What is it you are working on right now?"

"My section is concerned with tidying up after that outbreak of plague in the Elephant and Castle. All the bodies are being dissected more thoroughly, and the witnesses coached."

"Oh, good," she said weakly. "And everything is proceeding well?"

"Yes, indeed."

"Excellent; that is very... satisfying." And then there was a long pause. "Do you have any... observations? Or... suggestions?" What had started as a brief test of her authority was now turning into a humiliating interview in which neither person knew what to say.

"No, no, we are following standard procedure," he said hurriedly.

"Hmm," she said, as an ingenious way of not having to say anything. Another nightmarish pause ensued.

"However—" he began.

"Yes?" She pounced on the opening like it was a welcome mint.

"I must confess, and please don't take this as a criticism of the group, that the process is not as effective as it might be."

"Really?" she said, as breathless as if he had just come down from Mount Sinai with a few footnotes. "Let's make an appointment so you can expand on your ideas. We'll go to my office, and you can set a time with my assistant." At that, the lift doors opened on her floor, and she very carefully let him go first, since she had no idea where her office was.

Her executive assistant, whom the binder had identified as Ingrid Woodhouse, looked exactly like her photo. A distinguished woman in purple, Ingrid rose and greeted her politely.

"Good morning, Rook Thomas," her secretary said. "How are you?"

"Great, thanks. Now, this gentleman has a few ideas that I'm quite keen to hear about, so if you could find a mutual opening in our schedules, that would be grand." She looked around curiously while Ingrid and the man, whose name she hadn't managed to pick up, made an appointment for him to tell her all about something to do with a plague. *Eh, it was probably worth it,* she thought. *I was never going to find my office otherwise. Plus, the poor man actually seemed to think he had some interesting ideas.* She smiled an absent good-bye at the perspiring man (whom Ingrid addressed as Colonel). He left, visibly relieved, and Myfanwy turned her attention to her executive assistant.

"How was *your* weekend?" she asked, purposely heading off any questions about her own experiences.

"Oh, it was nice," said Ingrid. "You remember I told you my daughter Amy was coming home from York for the weekend?"

"Oh, right. And you had a good time?"

"Yes, very pleasant," said Ingrid. "Here's the current situation précis," she said, handing Myfanwy a leather folder. "Now, can I fetch you some coffee?"

"Yes, coffee would be wonderful. Please," Myfanwy said as she walked hesitantly into her office. For a moment, she paused there and looked around, trying to drink in the lingering traces of her predecessor. It was a large room, and beautifully furnished. Two of the walls were massive sheets of glass looking out on the city. A collection of portraits hung on the other two walls. In one corner of the room, a vase holding an arrangement of roses stood on a heavy table. There was a large antique desk before her, and off to the side was a sitting area with couches and a coffee table. She gingerly sat down behind the desk and eyed the many piles of paper stacked on it with a certain amount of trepidation. They all looked official and important. She carefully cleared a space on the desk and cracked open the folder Ingrid had given her.

There was mention of the plague in the Elephant and Castle and the wrap-up details related to that. There had been three incidents over the weekend, none of which had required the presence of Barghest commandos (whatever they were), and there was a scheduled assault on an antler cult that morning, with E. Gestalt attending. Seven people were under surveillance in the greater London area, and thirty-four overall in the British Isles. Preliminary preparations had begun for the annual review.

Well, that's all very nice, she thought. *If I knew what it meant, I'm sure*

I'd be thrilled. Anyway, it seems to be under control, so back to my scheduled programming.

Myfanwy was looking through the desk drawers curiously when Ingrid came in with a cup of coffee and an appointment book so thick it could be used to bludgeon a cow. Myfanwy took a long contemplative sip as her secretary began to describe her schedule.

"Ingrid?" she said.

"Yes, Rook Thomas?"

"Um, I'm sorry to interrupt, but can I get some cream and sugar in this coffee, please?" Her secretary looked at her blankly. "I've decided to change the way I take it." Myfanwy felt the need to explain the abrupt change in a habit that (for all she knew) had been established for years. "I'm doing that because..." *Why? Because I want to put on weight? Because I've been told I need more sugar in my diet?* "...because I've been sleeping badly. And so I wish to dilute the caffeine. But not to cut it out entirely. Because of the headaches." Ingrid looked at her a little strangely, for which Myfanwy couldn't blame her at all, but took the coffee and went to modify it. *God, who knew it would be so horrendously complicated impersonating oneself?* she thought, and opened up Myfanwy's folder.

Assassination of Court Members

One of the reasons this whole plot has been so difficult for me to suss out is that there has been relatively little internal assassination of Court members in the history of the Checquy. Given that it's a centuries-old militant organization that operates under a shroud of secrecy with a plethora of baroque (and sometimes rococo) traditions and bureaucracy, and that most members are trained to kill and equipped with supernatural capabilities, and that members of the Court wield authority with a terrifyingly free hand, you might expect there'd be more internal violence.

But no.

Oh, there's been some assassination by outside organizations (supernatural and otherwise — Lord Palmerston had a Bishop shot), and plenty of deaths in the field, but as far as I can tell, there have been only four illegal deaths of Court members that were the work of other Court members. There have been a few legal executions, of course, including a monumental slaughter in 1788 that was only later declared legal, but the big four illegal ones are notorious:

1. *In 1678 Lord Charles Huxley was thrown down a well on the orders of his wife, Lady Adelia Huxley.*
2. *In 1679, Lady Adelia Huxley was beaten to death with a kettle by her husband's lover, Bishop Roger Torville.*
3. *In 1845, Rook Angelina Corfax was run over by a barouche. It was eventually discovered that this was done at the command of her counterpart, Rook Cassandra Bartlett.*
4. *In 1951, Bishop Donald Montgomery was strangled with his own tie by Rook Juniper Constable.*

Naturally, it is illegal for one member of the Checquy to kill another—not just because it's murder, but because it strips the British Isles of part of their defense. In the cases above, all but one of the murderers were briskly tracked down, briskly tried, and then executed with a conspicuous lack of briskness. The exception was Rook Cassandra Bartlett, who successfully concealed her part in Corfax's death; it was discovered in her journals years after she'd died. She must have been a fucking genius to avoid the tracking abilities of the Checquy.

My point is, it isn't done.

And it certainly isn't done to me.

Whoever tries to have me killed, whoever succeeds in destroying my memory, well, they're placing themselves in an awful lot of danger to do so. I can't imagine their risking doing it in the Rookery.

Now, one of my initial thoughts was that you could request a full-time bodyguard, but you'd have to explain why, and that would lead to all sorts of speculation about you. You'd then have someone with you all the time, and, frankly, we don't want to draw that much attention to you. The reason I didn't get a bodyguard was I knew it wouldn't do any good.

"Rook Thomas, I just got a call from your counterpart's assistant— all of the bodies were out of town on different assignments over the weekend, and none of them will be back for a few hours, so your

Monday-morning meeting is going to be pushed back," said Ingrid, coming in with the renovated coffee.

"My counterpart? Yes..." replied Myfanwy, beginning with a question but frantically shifting it into a musing declarative sentence. She now scrabbled for some sort of comment to make and settled for stating the obvious. "So, the meeting is being pushed back."

"Yes," said Ingrid. "All of Rook Gestalt should be back after your meeting with the headmistress from the Estate, except possibly Eliza, depending on how the antler-cult assault goes."

"Oh, okay," said Myfanwy, trying to work out what had just been said.

I think I get it, she thought. *One of the two Rooks. There are two Rooks. Like chess. I am one, and the other is my counterpart. Rook Gestalt.* It was making a modicum of sense. She had a vague idea about what to do, but now something else was bothering her. *What does she mean by* all *of Rook Gestalt?*

"At nine thirty, you will be meeting with the accountants from Apex House to go over the budget for the Elephant and Castle operation," continued Ingrid, apparently having decided to overlook her boss's problems understanding the English language.

"The plague one?" Myfanwy asked brightly, pleased that she'd remembered.

"Yes. At ten fifteen you have a half-hour meeting with the head of the Estate, and then at eleven, you have your meeting with Rook Gestalt. I will cancel your appointment with the Minister of Defense."

"And that's okay?" she asked, thrown by the ease with which her secretary dismissed the Minister of Defense.

"Of course."

"Well, okay," said Myfanwy dubiously. "Now, I was hoping to have some time today to review some figures." *And acquaint myself with the organization that I appear to be running.*

"If there is any spare time, I shall endeavor not to fill it," Ingrid said.

"I'd appreciate it."

"Yes," her secretary agreed. "Now, you have nothing booked for lunch—shall I order something in so you can eat in the office?"

"No, I want to go somewhere nice for lunch," Myfanwy said. "See if you can't book me a reservation at a place with very good food."

"All right," said Ingrid, looking a little surprised. "Christifaro's?" Myfanwy nodded. "I'll arrange for your car to be ready. And after lunch, Security Chief Clovis is coming over from Apex House, and then you're having dinner with Lady Farrier."

"Okay. So, what are these meetings about?" she asked, getting out a pen and preparing to take some notes.

"The head of the Estate wishes to go over a list of potential acquisitions, and you made the appointment with the head of security. I'm afraid I don't know why."

"Oh, well, I'm sure it will come back to me," Myfanwy said.

"For dinner you are booked in at Simpson's," said Ingrid. "I'll let you know when your car is ready." Myfanwy agreed and Ingrid sailed out of the office like a clipper under full, tailored sails.

I suppose I should do some more homework on how this organization actually works.

How This Organization Actually Works

There is a constant stream of information coming from the civil service to us. Unnatural occurrences aren't limited to graveyards, morgues, and funky cult headquarters. Don't get me wrong, a lot of them happen in those sorts of places, but many more turn up in entirely mundane situations, which actually makes them far more upsetting. People are more likely to cope with the appearance of an animated corpse in a graveyard than one in an ice cream parlor or the changing room of a boutique. They won't be happy with the appearance of the animated corpse in the graveyard, but they tend to be less outraged.

In order to detect all the things that concern us, we receive a torrent of information, most of it completely unimportant. Stacks of reports, pages of figures, and tons of files. We have teams of analysts who sift through the information and intelligence that is forwarded to us and, out of all the details and minutiae, find the trends that reveal when the wheat market is being manipulated by a vampire.

We're also connected to the bureaucracy through the Panic Lines. Various high-placed officials from all branches of government, both national and local, are given discreet briefings that are designed to be simultaneously specific and vague. We don't tell them to be on the lookout for gremlins or storms of bile, but a few judicious slide shows and the generous use of the adjective unnatural ensure that they get the drift. As a result, we receive panicked calls from police chiefs, government ministers, members of the aristocracy, military officers, councillors, intelligence agents, churchmen, surgeons, diplomats, hospital administrators, etc. We also have people placed in key organizations who keep us abreast of significant developments.

Still, despite all these connections, we maintain our secrecy. Our name does not appear on any piece of paper outside of our organization. In fact, very few on the outside know that we exist. People are given a phone number to call, and information comes to us through twisty channels. Our computer network is not connected to any external system. If you try to track us down, you will not find us, but we will find you.

The meeting with the people from accounting proved spectacularly uninteresting as Myfanwy learned how cheaply one could surreptitiously remove plague-infected bodies and dissect them. The credit for the cost-effectiveness went to the very polite gentleman whom she had coerced into taking a lift ride with her (his name was Colonel Hall). She made a mental note to pass on some sort of praise to him. Despite her boredom, Myfanwy took care to be pleasant to the accountants, who squirmed uncomfortably in their seats and seemed terrified of her. *I guess Thomas wielded some authority,* mused Myfanwy. *Pity she controlled the nerds.*

"Rook Thomas?" Ingrid asked. She'd come in silently behind the poor little accountants, and her voice scared them half to death.

"Yes, Ingrid?" she replied, looking up from rows of figures that made a surprisingly large amount of sense. Thomas had said she was an able administrator, and apparently some of that talent had been passed along.

"The headmistress from the Estate is here." Judging from the accountants' reactions, Myfanwy assumed this person was similarly impressive and terrifying to them, so she politely ushered the accountants out and welcomed in the headmistress. Or at least she tried to, but Ingrid insisted on standing in the doorway and loudly announcing the woman.

"Frau Blümen, Chief Instructrix of the Estate!" the secretary bellowed into the office.

"Yes, thank you, Ingrid," Myfanwy said and stood up to welcome the rotund woman who waddled in. Frau Blümen was almost perfectly round and could get through the door only by turning sideways and sucking in her chest. Her blond hair was piled up high in intricate coils and braids, and she descended on Myfanwy with arms outstretched.

"Little Miffy! My *Liebchen!* Whatever has happened to your eyes?" she bellowed in a thick German accent. She was the first person who had dared to comment on the black eyes that still adorned Myfanwy's face. Before a response could be given, she had enfolded the hapless Rook in her fleshy arms and was embracing her tightly.

"It's lovely to see you, Frau Blümen," Myfanwy said, gasping; the arms tightened and then released her.

"Frau Blümen?" she said. "Why are you so formal, Myfanwy? No, we agreed when you rose to the Court that you would call me Steffi. You have not been fighting, have you? Of course not! From when you were a little girl you hated to fight, and now do you see what has happened? Yes, I see you do." The woman's obvious affection was nice, although her habit of asking questions and then answering them herself was a little disconcerting.

"I was, um, some people tried to mug me."

"Those poor idiots!" The fleshy woman chuckled.

Myfanwy hesitated. Clearly this person had a great deal of affection for her, but until Myfanwy knew exactly who she was, she was wary of revealing too much, so she shrugged.

"You are very calm! I would have anticipated that you would be shaking and weeping. Come, let me look at you." Myfanwy was gripped gently by the shoulders, and her face brought up close to the eyes of Frau Blümen. "Hmm, you were hit...what, two days ago? Maybe a little more? Oh, my poor little Miffy! Of course, they were common assailants? Nothing supernatural? After all, your powers are certainly no secret. No one in the community would be that stupid. Now I would like some hot chocolate. Be so good as to have your secretary bring some...ah! Wonderful. Thank you very much. Come, Miffy, fetch your coffee and we will sit on your very comfortable couches and have a nice long talk." She ushered Myfanwy to the couches and settled her ponderous bulk upon the cushions.

"Steffi...," Myfanwy began hesitantly. "What did you mean about my powers not being a secret? I mean, obviously as a member of the Court—"

She was cut off briskly. "*Liebchen,* even if you had not ascended to the Court, everyone would have known about your powers. My God, you were the most exciting find in decades! All of us knew about your potential. The tutors at the Estate were babbling about you to everyone!" She took a long contemplative drink of hot chocolate and rubbed her jowls. "And of course, I was always aware of your intellectual gifts. You would have risen to the Court even if you hadn't had such powers." Myfanwy's interest was piqued. The letter had spoken a little of her predecessor's shyness, but here was an opportunity to get another person's opinion about her.

"I've been thinking a lot about these matters lately, Steffi. I'd like to hear your take on my potential."

Frau Blümen raised an eyebrow. "Well, I'm glad to hear that you're taking a stronger interest in your career these days." Myfanwy lowered her eyes, trying to project the image of a shy yet able administrator. One who hadn't lost her memory and wasn't trying to glean any and all information she could. "Very well. When you were brought to me at the Estate, you were clutching the driver's hand, chocolate smeared all over your face, and your eyes brimming with tears. My poor little *Liebchen.* You were attached to that man like he was an inflatable bath pillow and you were floating in the Black Sea. Farrier was all you had left at that point, and when you realized that she had no loyalty to you, I could see the last little light of confidence die in your eyes. That stupid woman! You adored her, and she was too self-important to see it.

"In any case, before you came to us, we'd heard about your powers, and we were very careful. I read through all the files and the records, and at the end of my research I could safely conclude that yours was an entirely new ability, unlike anything that had ever appeared in the British Isles.

"Now, naturally we were eager to learn the full extent of your capabilities, but we were leery of pushing you. Most of the children who come to us are extracted with a great deal more finesse than you were. This is what comes of allowing the leaders to do something they are unqualified for. She can walk through your dreams and he killed all those Nazis while he was naked, so we kowtow to them, but let me tell you, they do not have the best people skills."

Steffi shook her head at the stupidity of those set above her and then inquired as to whether there might be any biscuits forthcoming. Myfanwy allowed as how there might be, and orders were relayed to Ingrid, who came in with unruffled calm and a plate of little confections.

"Excellent! Thank you, Ingrid. Anyway, as soon as we heard about your powers, we told Farrier and Wattleman. It's routine to keep the Court abreast of any promising talent. After all, that's why I came this morning! But they got wind of just how excited we were, and they wanted to see you for themselves first so they could make a connection with you—make you loyal to them. But the power and authority that befuddled your father was enough to completely overwhelm a child like you. So you came to us traumatized, and, much to my regret, you never really healed."

Myfanwy was sitting with her coffee clutched in her hands. She could see it clearly, although she was certain it was not a memory resurfacing. It was simply that it all made sense. The letters she had read had given her the impression that Myfanwy Thomas had been damaged in some way.

"Go on," she said quietly.

"Now, Miffy, you mustn't think that I am not proud of you, but your potential power was obviously much greater than you've ever lived up to. You must know this. After all, you never seemed to enjoy using your gifts. You obtained exactly as much control as you had to—never more—and it was clear you were never going to be an effective field agent. Heavens! You would drop your keys if someone yelled at you. Can you imagine what would happen if we gave you a gun?" Steffi smiled and gave a little rueful laugh.

"No, it was clear that you could not be sent out to whatever sewer or forest or semidetached house some monster had decided to live in. You had a good memory, a quick mind, and you were so thoroughly immersed in the Checquy that there was no question of releasing you back into the real world. So we let you slide into admin. But not without some regret."

"Hmm," hmmed Myfanwy. She was about to ask how powerful Thomas had had the potential to be when the secretary came back in.

"I'm sorry to bother you, Rook Thomas, but Rook Gestalt will be here in fifteen minutes for your appointment."

"Coming here?" Steffi asked in surprise. "Tell me, Ingrid, which body is Gestalt wearing today?"

Which body? thought Myfanwy in bemusement.

"The twins will be visiting today, Frau Blümen," said Ingrid.

"Ugh, well, in that case I shall leave now," said the portly woman with a shudder. "If ever you worry that you did not flourish in your powers, Miffy, look at that one. An astounding warrior, a master of supernatural gifts, and, in my opinion, a complete failure as a person." She shook her head.

"In any case, we will make another appointment soon. We got so caught up in reminiscing that we didn't even have a chance to go over the candidates for the Estate." Blümen laid a folder of profiles on the coffee table, patted her old pupil on the cheek, and went out. After she left the room, Myfanwy went to the desk and added a few notes to the list of terms and names she needed to look up. The Court. The Estate. Steffi Blümen. Wattleman (killing Nazis while *naked?*). Farrier. But to deal with the immediate future, she returned to the couch and paged hurriedly to the section on Gestalt.

Rook Gestalt

Nine years before I was born, some poor woman had to give birth to four children in one sitting. Three boys and one girl. Two of the boys were identical. That's not the weirdest thing, however. The weirdest thing was that when all four pairs of eyes opened, only one mind was looking out from behind them. This was Gestalt.

Gestalt is kind of disconcerting, because it/he/she/they is/are spread over four bodies. People try to avoid calling Gestalt anything but Gestalt because they get confused about the grammar. However, it's very tiresome to constantly write Gestalt instead of using a pronoun. So, when I need a pronoun in this description, I'll refer to Gestalt as it. I don't do it in general conversation — that would be rude.

Its parents were, understandably, terribly distressed by their peculiar offspring. I suppose that when you have four children and all of them do exactly the same thing at the same time or one of them does something while the other three lie comatose on the floor, you're going to be freaked out. Plus, there's the stress of recuperating from having four babies at once. So, when the Checquy turned up on the babies' first birthday and offered to take them off their parents' hands, the couple was relieved beyond words. Sadly, this is often the case with the children that the Checquy acquires. They're weird children and they have weird needs.

Gestalt took to the Checquy like four strange, hive-minded ducks to water. Or maybe that should be one strange mind inhabiting four ducks. Damn it.

This is why Gestalt is so irritating to work with.

In any case, the Checquy took Gestalt to the Estate. They taught it, trained it, and brought it up in as loving an environment as that sort of place will allow. It was with other children, children who were also strange. Little boys with tusks. Teenage girls who could talk with clouds and get intelligible answers. Some poor youth who possessed a psychic control over flamingos. Speaking as someone who lived at the Estate, I can tell you that it's not a bad place to grow up, especially if you are different and have abilities beyond the ken of mortal men. But Gestalt did not make it work.

To begin with, it made very few friends. You may be thinking, Hey, there were three brothers and a sister, they didn't need anyone else, *but you'd be wrong. You must always remember that Gestalt is one person with eight eyes. It's a common mistake to think of the four as different people. Gestalt takes advantage of that. The bodies have different voices, and somehow it has developed different mannerisms for each body. The bodies don't move in unison or just sit still in some rigid way unless it decides it wants them to do that. It's a brilliant actor to the extent that it can make its bodies have an argument or a conversation. So much so that you will forget that there is one mind controlling the puppets.*

The other children at the Estate forgot that Gestalt was one mind. They just thought that the Gestalt siblings were snobs. I know, because I was there. There was only one year when we were both at the Estate, and then Gestalt turned nineteen and graduated. Now, keep in mind that I was a painfully shy nine-year-old, and Gestalt was four stunningly beautiful blonds slated to be the next big thing in the Checquy. And I had a massive crush on one of the brothers — the one who wasn't a twin. So I watched them, and it was brought home to me that Gestalt was very definitely not a normal person. Not even four slightly peculiar persons. But it was a spectacularly powerful person, and everybody knew it.

I've read Gestalt's files, and as a student, Gestalt excelled. It had an excellent memory, could think quickly (four brains to draw on, remember), and absorbed the instruction rapidly and easily. The normal education was sucked up by those four heads immediately, and under careful tutelage, it gained a brilliant control of its powers.

By the time it was nine, Gestalt could control varying combinations of the bodies, could hold multiple conversations at once, and was coordinating bizarre tournaments in which its bodies would fight one another.

By the time it was twelve, it was demonstrated that Gestalt could be continuously awake by letting one of its bodies sleep whenever the others stayed up. It did this for five months.

By the time it was fifteen, the bodies had been carefully moved about the globe to investigate the distance that could safely exist among them. It was demonstrated that they could be placed on opposite sides of the planet without ill effect.

Gestalt graduated from the Estate and immediately went into the field. It earned its Rook status through outstanding operations work. With four bodies, it constituted its own team. During its sixteen years in the field, it achieved a series of seemingly impossible tasks, culminating with the destruction of a 488-year-old vampire who had been secretly controlling the wheat industry for 252 of those years.

Keep in mind that in an episode that occurred in 1980, it took forty-five soldiers to kill a sixty-four-year-old vampire.

Gestalt is tough.

It rose to the rank of Rook five years ago, and I've been obliged to work with it on many, many operations. I see it every day, and meet with it every Monday, Wednesday, and Friday at nine in the morning. Generally, because of the whole multiple-bodies thing, Gestalt has at least two faces in the field overseeing operations. Normally, a Rook isn't called out unless there is a particularly large problem, but Gestalt likes to kick arse, and I have to admit that it does a very good job of coordinating things on-site. On the downside, there's generally at least one of Gestalt's bodies hanging around in the office. Still, it's better than having four of them, especially since none of them seems to know how to deal with the filing system.

If it turns out to be Gestalt who wants you dead, you will need to be very careful.

"Rook Thomas?" Ingrid asked quietly. Myfanwy looked up with a start. "Rook Gestalt is here to see you."

4

Oh? Yeah? Rook Gestalt? That's...cool," Myfanwy fumbled. "Just give me a moment to get my flesh to stop crawling." Was it her imagination or was her secretary regarding her with a hint of sympathy? "Yeah, all right, Ingrid. Show Rook Gestalt in." She got up to scurry around her desk and compose her face into an appropriate mask of authority.

For a moment, Myfanwy wondered if she had time to put her hair up in some sort of professional style; right now it was just pulled back in a clip. But it was too late. *And besides,* she reasoned, *the two black eyes are bound to detract from any air of professionalism. Plus, who knows how Thomas carries herself?* As Ingrid came in and announced the entrance of Rook Gestalt in ringing tones, Myfanwy gave a mental shrug and threw caution to the wind. *Nobody really knows anyone anyway.*

"The Rooks Gestalt, as I live and breathe!" she exclaimed in apparent rapture. Two identical blond men looked at her with startled eyes. "Gentlemen, please, have a seat," she invited, gesturing to the chairs in front of her desk. "Well, you're both looking very nice," she said.

"Thank you," said one of them.

It was true, she had to admit. Whatever the other bodies looked like, these two were gorgeous. Thick blond hair, blue eyes, and golden brown tans. *In this country? How in God's name do they manage that? Do their weird genetic powers include the ability to bronze without sunlight?* They were clearly twins, but some care had been taken to make them look different from each other. The twin on the right had shorter hair, artfully tousled with gel, while the twin on the left had a more standard haircut, carefully brushed. They wore different suits. One twin sprawled in his chair, and the other sat attentively, although neither of them seemed particularly comfortable. And one was staring at her thoughtfully while the other directed his attention to straightening his pants. She mentally christened them Cool Twin and Tidy Twin.

It was downright eerie when Myfanwy remembered that there was one mind in those two heads. It was even eerier when she remembered that there were two other bodies wandering around somewhere, controlled by the same mind. *Stay calm,* she thought, *and try not to be freaked out by the fact that you're talking to a hive mind that freaks out the freaks in the Checquy. And don't automatically assume that this is the one behind the attack on Thomas. And even if it is, it probably won't make a move in your office.*

"We only just got back from that operation in Essex," Cool Twin was saying. "You're looking, ah, a little different, Myfanwy."

"It's the black eyes," suggested the other twin.

"No," disagreed his brother. "It's something else." Myfanwy tried to look enigmatic and probably failed. She watched them shift in the chairs.

"So, what happened to your eyes?" asked Tidy Twin.

"Oh, uh, someone tried to mug me," she said.

"But you're all right?" he said.

"I'm fine," said Myfanwy. "A bit achy, but fine."

"Interesting...," mused Cool Twin.

Crap, this isn't in keeping with the traditional meek and mild Myfanwy Thomas, Myfanwy realized. She thought about trying to appear more traumatized but instead opted for misdirection.

"So, where are your siblings hanging out nowadays?" she asked. Thomas's notes hadn't included photos, and she was keen to see the brother her predecessor had had a crush on.

"Eliza is leading a team in Aberdeen, chasing down that antler cult," one of them said dismissively. "Robert is back in our office."

"Well, I hope they're keeping well," she said pleasantly. *This*

Gestalt is good, she thought. *It's like they really are three brothers and a sister.* Myfanwy realized that one of the twins had been speaking and she hadn't been paying attention. "I'm sorry, what did you just say?"

"Alex was just explaining that we know they're fine," explained Tidy Twin.

"Ah, of course, of course," Myfanwy agreed sharply, suddenly irritated with his patronizing tone. "They're fine. You're fine. I'm fine. We're all fine. Can I get you a beverage?" she offered. One ordered coffee and the other ordered orange juice. "Certainly. Ingrid?" The secretary, who must have been listening through the open door, appeared miraculously with a tray. "Thank you."

"I understand you came in a little late this morning," said Cool Twin.

"Huh?" replied Myfanwy with startling presence of mind.

"Well, normally you're the second person in the Rookery, after that assistant of yours," said Tidy Twin.

"Yes?" said Myfanwy. *What, do these guys keep tabs on my comings and goings?* "Well, I...had an appointment." They regarded her with expectant eyes, and she was suddenly filled with a desire to shake up those proprietary stares. "A gynecologist appointment." She smiled triumphantly at the twins. "To have my vagina checked," she added. They nodded in unison and, to her private satisfaction, seemed somewhat disconcerted. *Of course, they do have a female body,* she remembered, slightly crestfallen. *They probably aren't going to be freaked out at the mention of female matters.* "And...it's still...there. And okay."

"That's...good," said Tidy Twin.

"Yes, anyway, let's get down to business." Fortunately, Thomas had left an agenda for her meeting with Gestalt, and Myfanwy was able to run down the list—or would have been if she hadn't moved the meticulous piles around. "Okay, let's see..." She shuffled through papers.

"I be*lieve* you have some documents for me to sign," said Cool Twin.

"Yuh," she said shortly, finding the stack exactly where she'd left it. "So, um, you need to sign these...things...which I have already signed, I think." She flipped through them hurriedly and saw the signature of Myfanwy Thomas. "Yes, I *have* signed them, and now you need to. So, here is a letter to the...Prime Minister...of Great Britain that states that we are aware of nothing he needs to know about." She passed the documents over to the twins, who began signing them. She watched with fascination as they produced identical signatures simultaneously, one with the left hand, one with the right.

"You missed this one," said Tidy Twin, handing her a contract.

She took it and had a dreadful moment of realization. *Crap. Signature. What did Thomas's signature look like?* She'd seen it a minute ago, and Thomas had signed at least one of the letters to her, but she hadn't really spent much time contemplating its form or shape. In retrospect, that had been a mistake. *Oh God.* She took a breath and was aware that Tidy Twin was staring at her. She smiled tightly at him, and then signed it. *Is that it? It looks familiar.* Still, neither twin seemed overly interested in her signature. Nor did either compare the new one with the old ones. "All righty, thanks. I'll take those and make sure they get to...where they need to go.

"Now," Myfanwy continued, "this week's schedule. Okay, it looks as if I've got rather a lot of meetings with accountants about—are you all right?" she asked. Both the twins Gestalt were staring blankly into space. *That's creepy.*

"I'm about to go into the headquarters of the cult," said the twins in unison. "Do you want commentary?"

"Uh, sure," said Myfanwy. "Should I take notes?"

"Not necessary," said Gestalt through two mouths. "The teams are equipped with recording material. We're gathering at the door, and Pawn Kirkman is looking through it. He's signaling that there are three people on the other side—armed. *Cooper, once Meaney brings the door down, launch stun grenades.*" Myfanwy looked up in surprise—the twins' voices had shifted, becoming higher, intent. She realized that she was hearing the voice of their sister giving orders. "I'm giving the countdown: Three! Two! One!" The twins' left arms jerked slightly, presumably mirroring the motions of their sibling more than two hundred miles away.

"Meaney has punched down the door, and we've drawn back to avoid the concussion. Now we're in, with five men in front of me. They've covered the foyer and—*take him! Take him!* Okay, a man with antlers is down. *Team one, hold the foyer. Teams two and three move in. Keep in mind, people, that we want as few deaths as possible. Immobilize them.* Kirkman is scanning surrounding rooms. *You four—secure that room. Move forward.*"

For the next forty-five minutes, Myfanwy listened intently as Gestalt led the assault. Soldiers were directed, orders given, cultists restrained or dispatched (depending on the extent of their dedication to the cause). She was treated to a blow-by-blow account as the female Gestalt was surprised by an attack, and her guards were impaled on the prongs of a high priest's antlers. She watched as the twins' muscles tensed while their sister kicked and spun and punched, with only sharp, shrill exclamations shooting out of their lips. Finally, after a high-pitched *kiYAA!,* they settled back, breathing heavily, and explained that Eliza had just broken the neck of the leader of the antler cult, and that the complex was secured.

"Wow. Great," said Myfanwy. "Nicely done."

"Hmm," said Tidy Twin absently. "Eliza has blood on her boots."

"That's lovely, Gestalt," Myfanwy said, trying to keep her cool. "More coffee? Or more orange juice? No? Perhaps I could have Ingrid fetch you a couple of moist towelettes."

Once the twins had left (still somewhat unsteady on their feet), Myfanwy sat for a long time turning things over in her mind. After their commentary on the strike, the twins had had trouble focusing on the rest of the agenda, and they'd agreed to attend to the remaining administrative details later. Watching the satisfaction with which the twins narrated the attack and hearing the play-by-play of their sister's skill, she'd felt her own muscles tensing. The bruises on her body ached, and she could easily imagine the twins beating her, their eyes coming alive with violence.

I cannot meet every member of the Court and automatically assume that he or she is the traitor, she decided. *It's entirely possible that Gestalt didn't order the attack on Thomas and that I spent the entire meeting sweating through my clothes for nothing. But who* did *give the order?* Myfanwy leaned back in her chair and laced her fingers behind her head.

Too many questions. And I don't even know everything that Thomas knew. Not yet. But I will.

She reached for the purple binder.

The Rooks

For the first few centuries, the Rooks were the martial leaders of the Checquy. That is to say, they headed all military actions. Traditionally filled by members of the noble class, the position called for an encyclopedic knowledge of tactics and strategy, but little else. If the Pawns were the blade the Checquy swung, then the Rooks were its hilt.

The old leaders of the Checquy looked upon the Rooks as weapons and nothing more. They were the hounds to be released, and even if they were the heads of the pack, they were still only hounds. In 1702, it was the Rooks who led the four-pronged assault on Brigadoon and burned every structure in the place. Some of its citizens were put to death, and the rest were shipped down to Wales, where they were set to mining lead. The properties of the mines prevented any of those extraordinary people from escaping, and they all perished in captivity. (In the late 1960s, however, an individual claiming to be "the last son of Brigadoon" surfaced and wreaked havoc for years before being subdued and dissected.)

One notorious Rook, Rupert Chamberlain, was kept chained up in the vaults beneath the White Tower until he was needed, at which point he was transported in a cage to the appropriate location and unleashed upon whatever hapless target the leaders had selected. During his tenure, he devoured the Duke of Northumberland, the ambassadors of France and Italy, an archdeacon, and one of his fellow Rooks.

Then, in 1788, the situation changed drastically. A massive redistribution of power led to the new status of the Rooks. Rather than being the generals of the Checquy, the Rooks were placed in charge of all domestic affairs. They became the administrative guardians of the United Kingdom. Now if something strange comes up within the British Isles, the Rooks are the ones who deal with it. We are executives, and though we still periodically mete out violence, it is by delegation. We don't have to get our hands dirty unless we want to. I, for one, prefer to remain in the office, but Rook Gestalt seems to enjoy fieldwork.

Your main concern will be to master the running and politics of the domestic Checquy forces. You'll be meeting with and coordinating the teams of Pawns who work in the country and assigning them to various tasks. You will also oversee the management of the Rookery, working closely with Gestalt.

Oh, that's going to be fun, Myfanwy thought.

And you meet regularly with the other members of the Court to coordinate the Checquy's movements.

It's all fairly self-explanatory, really.

Oh, well, thanks an awful lot, Thomas, Myfanwy thought bitterly. *It sounds like I'm the Defense Minister of Ghosts and Goblins, but as long as the job is "all fairly self-explanatory," I've no doubt it will be fine. The country might get overrun by brownies and talking trees, but what the hell— there's always Australia!* Seething, Myfanwy threw down the purple binder and realized that she had been chewing her nails. *Great, that's probably a new habit. I can't see Rook Thomas, administrator extraordinaire, biting her nails. This must mean that I'm finally developing my own identity.* Myfanwy was staring sourly at the portraits of the Rooks and wondering which of the subjects had been chained up in the Tower of London when Ingrid came bustling in.

"Rook Thomas, I've canceled your lunch at Christifaro's," she said.

"Why?" Myfanwy asked in dismay. "That's the only thing I've had to look forward to!"

"An emergency has emerged, and both you and Rook Gestalt have been summoned to an interrogation," the secretary replied in an unruffled manner.

"Oh. Okay." Myfanwy looked down at her desk, thought for a moment, and then looked up. "Are we getting interrogated, or are we doing the interrogating?" she asked. Ingrid looked a little startled but explained that some poor twerp the Checquy had captured would be interrogated. Apparently, a specific member of the staff would be doing the questioning, and Myfanwy and Gestalt would be there serving in an audience capacity.

"So I don't have to do anything?"

"No, ma'am."

"Should I bring anything, do you think?"

"What, like snacks?" her secretary asked.

"I'll bring my notepad," Myfanwy decided. "And a pen."

"They have stenographers there, you realize. And video cameras," Ingrid pointed out.

"Yes, I know," Myfanwy replied tartly. "But I like to take my own notes."

"Very good, ma'am."

"Yes. Now, would you accompany me to the interrogatory...the interrararium...the interrogation...place? I would value your observations." After all, she could hardly ask for directions, could she?

"Certainly, ma'am. After you." Ingrid swept aside to allow Myfanwy to walk ahead.

"No, no," Myfanwy said hurriedly. "After *you*."

"That's highly irregular, Rook Thomas," Ingrid observed.

"Humor me," Myfanwy answered.

"As you please."

The two women walked briskly down the hallways, and the people ahead of them pressed themselves against the walls so the Rook and her secretary could get by easily. Heavy wooden doors dotted the corridors. Whenever she passed an open doorway, Myfanwy slowed down and snuck a peek. In one room, three men were poring over a map and shouting at one another in hushed voices, like angry librarians. In another, an elderly Pakistani gentleman with a monocle

brandished a walking stick under the nose of a short fat man in a caftan. Through another door, there was a room filled with bookshelves. Seated at a massive wooden desk, a man with curly hair was reading intently from a ledger and absentmindedly stroking the head of a large condor that perched proudly on his wrist. He looked up as they passed, and his eyes widened in surprise.

Finally, they came to a pair of massive iron doors with a metal plate set into them. Ingrid stepped aside and looked at Myfanwy expectantly. Fortunately, Myfanwy vaguely recalled reading something about this. She moved forward and placed both her hands flat against the plate. The metal warmed underneath her palms, and the doors opened slowly, with a sound of grinding gears. Behind those doors was, in a stunning anticlimax, another set of doors, which slid open. A lift.

They descended for many floors, until it was clear that they were several stories beneath the ground. Neither of them said anything, but Myfanwy took the opportunity to eye her secretary in the mirrored walls. Ingrid was tall, in her late forties, and her auburn hair was immaculately coiffed. She was slim and fit-looking, as if she spent every afternoon playing tennis. She wore a few pieces of discreet gold jewelry, including a wedding ring. Myfanwy breathed in gently through her nose and smelled Ingrid's good perfume. The business suit she wore was of a light purple, and exquisitely cut.

Myfanwy looked herself over in the mirror. The hair she had swept back into a clip was coming loose, and her suit (although far more expensive than Ingrid's) was rumpled. She'd neglected makeup entirely, and those damn black eyes lent her the appearance of a raccoon. A raccoon that had gotten hit in the face. After a lifetime of poor nutrition.

The silence was broken only by the humming of the lift, and it felt conspicuous.

"So, Ingrid," Myfanwy said conversationally. "Do you ever get tired of purple?" The secretary turned surprised eyes on her boss, but before she could answer, the doors opened.

5

Dear You,

I'm not bipolar, I've just had a bipolar life foisted upon me.

My personal life consists of my coming home, sitting on my couch with a bowl of popcorn, and combing through long and tedious files.

My professional life consists of long hours of general executive responsibilities broken up by . . . well, as an example, this evening at work I had to deal with a visiting Argentine government official who spontaneously manifested the ability to create animals out of ectoplasm. The only problem was that she couldn't control these animals, and it happened in the middle of the city of Liverpool.

The first I knew about it was the flashing of my office lights. I'm not entirely certain who arranged to have the lighting in the Rooks' offices and quarters hooked up to the Panic Lines, but it has taught me to flinch violently when a lightbulb ceases to work. It's not even necessary, strictly speaking, because if there's something big happening, my desk phone flashes a red light and rings with a particularly shrill tone, my mobile phone rings with a different shrill tone, and a message pops up on both my computer screens.

All of which happened tonight.

I then had details flung at me. Four civilian deaths. Thousands of pounds' worth of property damage. The Argentine woman seemed to be having a nervous breakdown, and no one could get near her because there was a herd of ghostly green tarucas, jaguars, and llamas surrounding her.

At that point, my palms became soaking wet, but my mind was absolutely dry. I'm good in a crisis, but it's not because I'm not afraid. I'm always afraid. I'm so stressed I want to throw up. But I am good in a crisis because I am very, very good at making preparations. I try to cover every angle, to plan for every eventuality.

As you've probably figured out.

But back to the newly spawned luminous fauna of Liverpool. The man on the other end of the phone was the shift commander for the Crisis Office, which was located in London.

"Our troops have been mobilized?" I asked.

"Liverpool teams are either out there or on their way, but this is looking to be major," he said, and I could hear concern in his voice, which was very worrying. Crisis officers tend to be the calmest people in the entire organization. Possibly the calmest people on earth. If this one sounded worried, then I could almost believe there wasn't going to be a city of Liverpool the next morning. "I'm not certain that they will be able to handle this," he continued.

I opened a spreadsheet and scanned down until I found what I wanted.

"There's a team of final-years from the Estate doing covert maneuvers half an hour away from the city limits," I offered. "We'll dispatch them for initial assistance."

"Is that legal?"

"Yes. According to the charter of the school. One sec." I held the phone away and called for Ingrid to inform Frau Blümen. Then I returned to the call. "What's the situation with the press?" I asked.

"None so far" came the tense answer over the phone. I could hear people in the background being frantically busy. "There's been some chatter, but we got this very quickly."

I weighed the situation and took a deep breath.

"Cut the city's communications," I said.

"Excuse me?" came the startled response.

"Do it, and call me back when it's done—wait, Lewis! Are you there?"

"Yes, Rook Thomas."

"How dark is it there now?" I asked.

"What?"

"How dark is it there? It's ten past six in the evening here, and it's dark. Liverpool is farther to the west than us, so the sun will have set later there. How dark is it?" There was an indistinct voice behind Lewis. "What did he say?"

"He said it's dark there. As dark as here."

"Okay then . . . we'll have to cut the entire power supply. We need a blackout," I said, wincing at the problems this was going to cause. "Now."

"We can do that?" he asked.

"Rookery techs have placed backdoor computer entry into the power facilities of the sixteen biggest cities in the UK," I said, revealing the existence of a project I'd initiated nine months ago.

"I never heard about that," he said.

"It's . . . restricted." In fact, knowledge of it was restricted to the Court and the techs who had accomplished it. "I'll put the order through, and we'll turn it off."

"The whole city?" he said weakly.

"Relevant area if possible, whole place if necessary. But communications need to be down. I want it difficult for the press to find out the details, and I want it very difficult, if not impossible, for them to record anything."

"Okay, well, I'll let the teams know." And we simultaneously hung up. Then I made a call down to the IT section and plunged the city of Liverpool into darkness.

"Ingrid, the subject's from Argentina?" I called through the doors.

"Yes."

"I'll need to speak to one of the Chevs then. Get me a line to whoever's there. And why hasn't Gestalt called me?"

"Eckhart's in Paris, Gubbins is on line one, and Gestalt is on line two" came the composed answer. I snatched up the phone and stabbed at line one.

"Harry?"

"One sec, Myfanwy." I heard him putting the phone down and speaking to someone else. "Yes, Minister, it turns out that there was a mysterious force that caused that plane crash. Yes. Yes. What was it? We call it gravity." He sighed as he picked up the phone connected to me. "You know, Rook Thomas, this is why we keep ourselves secret. People look for the most ridiculous excuses. No wonder the age of reason was so welcome. It finally allowed the supernatural to take a break."

"Mm-hm, that's fascinating," I said, scanning the details that had been e-mailed to me. "Look, an Argentine government official has spontaneously gone critical in Liverpool. We may have to take her out — read the e-mail

I'm forwarding to you, figure out the implications if we kill her, and be ready."

"Jesus Christ!" he exclaimed, and hung up. I hit the button for line two.

"Gestalt? Where are your bodies?"

"One in is Wolverhampton, one in Nottingham, both are on their way to Liverpool. I'm also in the Rookery in my office."

"All right. We've cut the power in the city. You'll be able to handle crowd control as well as tactics?"

"Yeah."

"We need to end this ASAP," I said, and hung up.

"Lewis is on line one," Ingrid called.

"Lewis? Is the power off?" I asked him.

"Yes, but—" He broke off.

"But what?"

"But there's a TV crew out there, and we can't find them."

"Oh. Shit." I ended the connection and dialed the extension for Media Cover. "It's Rook Thomas here. I hear there's a TV crew wandering around in downtown Liverpool—why is that?"

"They have a television station in downtown Liverpool" came the dry voice of Caspar Dragoslevic, the head of Media Cover.

"We permitted that?"

"Remarkably, I do not have the supernatural ability to influence the placement of media outlets' facilities. We have someone in the station who will let us know what kind of footage they have once they have it, and we may be able to do something to it."

"Good luck." I snorted. "If it's the kind of footage I think it is, they'll guard it with their lives. What do your Liars have?"

"I wish you wouldn't call them that." Dragoslevic sighed. "They're the Tactical Deception Communications Section."

"Caspar, we will need something to tell people, and an Argentine woman who coughs up ectoplasm that turns into animals that chase people—well, that falls into the category of things that we are very specifically supposed to prevent people from finding out about."

"You know, Rook Thomas, with language skills like that, it's amazing you weren't placed in my department."

"Give me something, please," I said, and hung up. Almost immediately the phone rang again. "Yes?"

"Lewis here—we've had three more deaths, and there are two more news crews out there."

"What's the situation with the troops? Do I need to send the Barghests?"

"I don't think so; they're closing in on the target. Hold on—she's down," said Lewis.

"Dead?" I asked intently.

"Yes, it's confirmed."

"And the animal constructs?"

"They're evaporating," he said, the relief in his voice mirroring my own emotions.

"Okay, remove the woman and try to sweep up any incriminating stuff. We're turning the lights on and giving the phones back in ten minutes."

"Yes, ma'am."

I gave the orders for the services to be returned to the city, looked at the clock, and saw with bemusement that only thirty-one minutes had passed. I smiled. We really are very good. But then Ingrid buzzed through and told me that we were getting frantic calls from people high up in the Home Office; the Department for Environment, Food, and Rural Affairs; the Liverpool City Council; the Liverpool Police Department; the power company; and the Royal Society for the Prevention of Cruelty to Animals.

"Okay, put them through one at a time." I then had to endure a series of irate ministers (Prime and otherwise) and members of my own organization. Though the whole incident had taken only half an hour and the lights had been cut off for just fifteen minutes, cleaning up the aftermath took more than an hour and a half. Even as I mouthed platitudes, I was watching three television sets, waiting anxiously for footage.

"Ingrid," I said, after putting the phone down on Bishop Grantchester, one of my immediate superiors, "call Caspar Dragoslevic and find out what the hell we're going to tell the public." I opened a drawer in my desk and took out some aspirin. The phone buzzed, and I flinched away from the sound.

"Rook Thomas here."

"It's Caspar."

"And where are we?" I asked wearily.

"I have exceptionally good news, Rook Thomas," said Dragoslevic. "Thanks to the lack of electricity and the number of people trying to get out of the city, the media crews weren't able to get to the epicenter of the event. They were only on the outskirts, and it turns out that cameras couldn't record the constructs—the ectoplasm didn't register on film or digital."

"Thank God." I sighed. "Have you come up with a plausible story?"

"We have some very nice things that aren't particularly specific having to do with escaped animals from a cargo ship and the power outage and resultant looting," he said.

"Sounds convoluted. How much do I need to worry about people reporting herds of ghost animals?" I asked.

"It's the business district at six in the evening in the middle of the week, so nowhere near as bad as it could have been. But there were still quite a few. They'll accept the news stories' explanation, especially once we release a few animals out there and have them caught on television," said Caspar. He'd worked in television for twenty-three years before I'd headhunted him, and I had confidence in his ability to gauge what humanity would accept. I wanted to ask what kind of animals and where he was going to get them, but I decided my life would be easier without that knowledge.

"Great, well . . . just try not to go overboard," I said. "It's not going to look good to my bosses if we kill more members of the public by releasing water buffalo among them," I told him, and I hung up on the evening.

Now I am exhausted, but the necessity of being prepared for you combined with the work habits instilled in me at school mean that I am still in the office at eleven at night. The Liars' explanation went out hours ago and has been broadcast, and though there will inevitably be questions and a difficult cleanup, disaster has largely been averted yet again. But still I sit at my desk, doing research into the past to prepare for your future.

I am combing through old files, looking for something—the merest hint of impropriety—to help me figure out who is trying to destroy me, but so far, I haven't had much luck. The one good thing is that when people are brought up within the Checquy, pretty much everything they've ever done is written down in their files. This is going to call for old-fashioned detective

work, *for which I have neither the time nor the inclination. It's not like
I can just drop everything and tail these people around, and I worry that I'm
running out of time.*

*I keep having these embarrassing little episodes where I break down crying.
Being a Rook is an exhausting job as it is, and this threat has not made my
life any easier. Fortunately, these crying jags usually happen in the office,
and I can just go up to the residence and have a little bawl. Then I wash my
face and go back to the desk. My secretary comes in with another appointment
or a stack of files, and I wonder if she's noticed.*

*I'm glad I have these letters to write. At least I can confess my fears to
somebody, even if we will never meet and you won't find out what I've been
through until after the fact.*

Exhaustedly yours,
Me

6

The room before Myfanwy and Ingrid was large and surprisingly luxurious. There was a thick carpet on the floor, and pictures hung on the walls. A sideboard along the left held a selection of cheeses and fruit, and on the right an ornate bar was stocked with an array of decanters and bottles. A chandelier hung from the ceiling, and curlicues traced their way along the plaster. At the far end of the room, facing a wall covered in heavy red drapes, were a number of chairs. A few men in suits were milling about by the buffet.

"Rook Thomas?" A man dressed as a butler was at Myfanwy's elbow. She turned to him, startled.

"Yes?" she asked.

"Can I fetch you a beverage?" He gestured toward the bar.

"Oh, that would be lovely. Could you please get me a coffee? Ingrid, what would you like?" Both her secretary and the butler looked nonplussed, but eventually an arrangement was entered into whereby Ingrid also would receive a cup of coffee. Judging from the frozen expressions, Myfanwy realized that in the Checquy the people in purple were there to do the waiting, not to be waited on. Shrugging, she went to the sideboard and loaded up a plate with strawberries and cheese.

"Ah, Rook Thomas!" exclaimed one of the men there. He was heavyset and loud and had very large teeth and a red face, and he bore down upon her like a truck. Myfanwy stared at him, smiling politely, and stood her ground, popping a strawberry into her mouth. He paused and looked a little puzzled, as if he had expected her to step back or cringe, but then he gamely continued on until he was standing uncomfortably close and she was obliged to tip her head back to look at him.

"Good afternoon," she said coolly. *Who is this guy, and am I supposed to curtsy or is he supposed to bow?* It seemed as if he anticipated some hesitance or deferral on her part, but when he didn't receive it, he did not give the impression of being insulted, only surprised. *Perhaps he's accustomed to the painfully shy Thomas,* she thought. *The Rook who doesn't dare to speak loudly.*

"Quite inconvenient, having to clear our schedule for this procedure, eh?" he said, although there was less gusto in his voice now than there had been. Under her fixed stare, he actually seemed to be wilting. Still, he tried to make up for it with volume and, apparently, flow.

"You're spitting on me," Myfanwy said coldly. He stammered something as she wiped her face with a napkin. She continued to look him in the eyes and saw his gaze dart nervously behind her. He stepped back and gave a polite nod to whoever had just arrived.

"Rook Gestalt," he said in a respectful voice. "Good afternoon." *Ah, so that's the way it is,* Myfanwy thought. *Gestalt gets the deference, and Thomas does the bookkeeping.* She swung around and then stepped back in confusion. It was not the twins who were emerging from the lift but a much taller and more powerfully built man. She realized this must be the third of Gestalt's bodies, and she looked at it with interest. *Oh, Thomas. You had good taste,* she thought. Robert Gestalt was handsome and strong. Dressed casually in khakis and a short-sleeved shirt, he moved forward with a palpable air of confidence.

"Good afternoon, Perry," Gestalt said smoothly, and then he turned his attention to her. "Myfanwy, you are looking well," he said with an extra dose of charm. Only the eyes gave him away. *Don't forget,* she reminded herself, *you just finished a meeting with this man and heard him kill a bunch of people. He may have been wearing different skin, but it was still him.* "I'm dreadfully sorry this has come up," he said to her. "I know how these questionings upset you. We shall simply have to endeavor to endure it." He offered Myfanwy his arm to escort her over to the chairs, and she hesitantly took it.

As their skin made contact, she felt a shock.

It was as if she had been plunged into a pool of water whose currents were winding their way around her. Each stream was distinct, separate from the others. She felt as if she could reach out and disrupt the course of that movement—re-channel it, warp it, or stop it entirely. The ribbons were complex, horrendously complex, but she could tell that the system encompassed the physical being of Gestalt.

Oh my God! Myfanwy thought. Suddenly, she had control over this man—not through violence but with all the force and power of her own mind. She was no longer defenseless; she was dangerous. *Thomas, I can see why you were hesitant, but you never needed to be afraid of it!*

Bemused, she allowed herself to be ushered into one of the chairs in the center, and she received her cup of coffee. She looked at Gestalt in wonder and saw smug satisfaction on his handsome face. *You think I'm in a daze because you're handsome? I'm in a daze because I could crush you.* She looked around and saw other people settling themselves in the chairs. Two rows of comfortable chairs, in a horseshoe pattern, the inner row sunken slightly so as not to obstruct the view of those behind them. It was like being in a very expensive private box at a very small, underground soccer game. A distinguished-looking gentleman in a suit stood before the curtains. He cleared his throat awkwardly.

"My Rooks, lady, and gentlemen," he began, "we have had this individual under surveillance since he entered the country three days ago. His passport is for a Peter Van Syoc of Holland, and his cover was a business trip for his employer, the Zeekoning Fishing Company. Upon his arrival at Heathrow from Amsterdam, certain factors caught the attention of our agents, and in accordance with the procedures codified by Rook Thomas, he was placed under discreet observation. His room in a bed-and-breakfast was entered, and subtle listening devices and cameras were placed there by our people.

"The Checquy agents observing Mr. Van Syoc noted that in the course of his movements about the city, he passed by the Rookery several times and devoted some attention to the building. Yesterday evening he engaged the services of a prostitute and paid her to remain in his accommodations for the entire night. This morning, the subject activated inhuman abilities and began the murder and, we believe, consumption of the prostitute.

"At this, the Pawns moved. When they appeared, the subject demonstrated further abilities, demolishing part of the architecture of the bed-and-breakfast before he could be restrained." The man's voice was carefully dry, giving away no emotion. His subdued tone made the entire recitation ridiculous. "He was then transported immediately to the Rookery."

Bloody hell, thought Myfanwy. *That's pretty hardcore.* She twisted around to find Ingrid and saw that her secretary was sitting behind her. She was obviously ill at ease but carried herself well. Myfanwy smiled at her, and caught by surprise, Ingrid smiled too. As Myfanwy turned back to the curtains, there was a crumpling beneath her, as if she were sitting on a sheet of paper. She felt about and pulled out a carefully folded wax-paper bag.

"Gestalt?" she said, turning to the body seated next to her. "What's this?"

"But Myfanwy!" he exclaimed. "You always have a paper bag. You know how often these interrogations make you ill," he said with a tone he might have intended to be comforting but that she found patronizing.

"Oh, of course. I simply did not expect to sit on it," Myfanwy replied, placing the bag on her lap. *Thomas got sick at these things?* She could just picture the timid person in this little body throwing up in front of these men. Aside from Ingrid, whom Myfanwy had invited on the spur of the moment, she was the only woman in the room. *Poor Thomas,* she thought. *How humiliated she must have been.* And then, eyeing the curtains in front of her dubiously, she wondered: *What exactly is going to happen?*

The curtains trembled and then parted. As the red cloth flowed to the sides, the lights in the room dimmed. *It's exactly like a theater, and we are in our private box,* she thought uneasily. In front of them was a thick pane of glass, and beyond that a room tiled in a pale blue. Soft lights glowed from the ceiling. Myfanwy's imagination had summoned up a slab of stone with some poor soul bound to it by chains and straps, but instead she saw something more like a thickly cushioned dentist's chair. Seated upon it was a man with his eyes closed. The sleeves of his shirt had been carefully cut off, and the pants legs had been rolled up. He was still. There were soft cloth straps binding him to the chair at his wrists, waist, and ankles. Something about the clinical matter-of-factness of it all was more alarming than the medieval images she'd conjured up.

"Oh God," Myfanwy murmured to herself, and drew a pitying glance from Gestalt. She tensed as a man entered the room. He had glasses, was dressed in scrubs, and wore a surgical mask. She looked about for his tools, some tray or trolley with gleaming metal instruments on it, but she saw nothing. Tension was building within her. If there was no equipment, then how did the Checquy members gather their information? Would there be some surreal torture, the man's flesh and bones rending themselves? Would a psychic tear the thoughts out of his brain? What had horrified Thomas so much that she'd vomited regularly during these sessions? Myfanwy's fingers gripped the arm of her chair, dimpling the soft cloth. She squirmed back against the cushions as the interrogator lifted his latex-gloved hands and reached for the man. Beside her, Gestalt leaned forward intently, and a hush descended upon the room.

The interrogator rested his hands on the man's hair and then began probing with his fingers, tracing the contours of the scalp. He leaned back slightly and spoke rapidly into a microphone that hung from the ceiling.

"His ancestors hail almost exclusively from Western Europe, except for a great-grandfather from Poland," he said. The loud man who had tried to intimidate Myfanwy gave a snort, and the interrogator froze. He drummed his fingers angrily on the subject's head, and then continued. "He is predisposed to be talented at music and mathematics but is also prone to self-doubt. He has extraordinary physical courage and little to no sense of humor. He has no compunctions about killing."

The interrogator ran his fingers carefully down one of the man's arms and paused at the wrist. Squinting, Myfanwy could see that he was pressing lightly and had closed his eyes.

"He is thirty-two years old, the second-oldest child. He was born in June. He has undergone several major surgeries and received various implants. Among other organs, his kidneys and lungs have been replaced." There was a long pause, and the interrogator cocked his head as if listening for something. "That surgery took place four years ago. He is right-handed. He is allergic to dairy." The interrogator turned the man's palms upward. He got down on one knee and leaned closer to the armrests of the chair, peering carefully at the lines crisscrossing the man's palms.

"He was born in Brussels, and his father died when he was four. In university he met a tall dark stranger. Female. It did not work out. He learned how to type. For several years, his employment was sporadic. Mainly manual labor. And he did a great deal of traveling. Then, when he was twenty-five, he joined the military. He learned martial arts. He did a great deal more traveling. There was violence. And he was committing most of it." The interrogator stood up and walked over to the sink in the corner. He moistened a paper towel and carefully wiped the man's hand with it. Then he fetched a magnifying glass and polished it. He peered at the hand again.

"After two years in the military, his life took a major turn."

"Dr. Crisp, what was this turn?" called out the loud man, interrupting. The interrogator looked up in irritation.

"I'm not sure," he said testily. "Some sort of professional shift, but a drastic one."

"How can you tell?" asked the loud man. The man sitting next to him tried to shush him. "Perry, please don't start," Myfanwy heard him whisper to the big man.

"Because his fingerprints have been removed," the interrogator replied.

Myfanwy jotted down a note on her pad; Gestalt subtly tried to sneak a peek, but she covered it.

"What else do you see, Dr. Crisp?" she asked. He removed his glasses and squinted more closely at the hand.

"A great deal more travel, and then he encountered a short, fair person whom he already knew very well. He appears to have found true love. And had three children. One of whom died. Twice."

"Twice?" exclaimed Perry. "How do you figure that?" The interrogator threw down his magnifying glass in exasperation.

"All right, who is that?" Crisp asked.

"What, can't you tell by my voice?" Perry sneered.

"The voices are electronically disguised, you colossal fool! But let me hazard a guess...is it someone whose eldest daughter hasn't gotten married yet and never will?"

"Well, of course she won't *now*, you fraud! What kind of person tells an eighteen-year-old girl she'll never get married?" Perry stood up and pounded his fist on the glass.

"An accurate one!" yelled Crisp, striding over to the glass. He yanked his mask down to reveal a mustache and a goatee.

"How dare you? You are a hack! A filthy liar!"

"My talents are indisputable!" shrieked Crisp, spitting all over the glass in his rage. Unfortunately, he was unable to see through it, and he had chosen to stand right in front of Myfanwy, his eyes fixed on some imaginary point.

"I dispute them!" Perry yelled back. "You scarred my daughter with your slanderous stories. What kind of swine drools all over a young girl's hand at a Christmas party and then lies to her about her future?"

"To begin with, *you* told her to consult me. And I said nothing that wouldn't have been perfectly obvious to every hapless fool she spoke to! She has all the personality of a drink coaster!" They were both pounding on the glass now, and their shouts devolved into an incomprehensible roar of insults. *This is unbelievable,* thought Myfanwy. Everyone else was watching in rapt fascination, and so it apparently fell to her to do something. *I'm the Rook, after all. And Gestalt doesn't appear to be stepping in.* She snuck a glance at her counterpart, who was looking on in amusement.

"Gentlemen," Myfanwy said calmly but to no avail because all the other men in the room had risen and were adding to the clamor. "Gentlemen," she repeated, raising her voice a little. Still no response. *Right, that does it,* she thought in exasperation. Her patience had run out.

"Gentlemen!" she finally shouted, and her voice cut through the noise like a scythe through a poodle. There was dead silence, and everyone stared at her, stunned. "You all need to shut up and stay focused on the task at hand. Dr. Crisp, if you will turn your eyes back toward the interrogation, I wonder if you could revive the subject and question him." All eyes swiveled back to the man in the chair, and there was some embarrassed clearing of throats. Everybody sat down abruptly, except Dr. Crisp, who pulled his surgical mask up again and strode back to the chair.

A nurse had entered, carrying a polished steel tray on which lay a syringe filled with indigo fluid. Crisp took the syringe carefully, nodded his thanks to the nurse, and injected it into the subject's arm. The man's eyelids flickered, and Crisp took the opportunity to change his gloves. Finally, the prisoner came awake, looking around him with confusion.

"Good morning," said Dr. Crisp, attempting to sound calm and collected.

"It's afternoon," corrected Perry dryly.

"Shut up!" exclaimed Crisp, flashing the glass a dirty look. "Now," he said, turning back to the subject. "I am going to ask you some questions, and you will answer truthfully. If you lie, I will know, and it will not be good for you." The man stared at him, unblinking. "I'm sure you understand." He gently laid his hand on the man's wrist, placing his fingers on the pulse point. "Let us begin."

Myfanwy felt uneasy as she stared through the glass. She had relaxed a little earlier, when Crisp had read the lines on the subject's hands. The physical examination had been passive, noninvasive. But now she could tell there would be pain and violence. She sat still, aware of Gestalt's eyes on her. Her heart began to pound.

"What is your name?" Crisp asked.

"Peter Van Syoc," the subject replied. His Dutch accent was thick, and although he spoke calmly, his eyes were wide open, staring at the glass. Myfanwy knew he could not see through, but she shifted uncomfortably in her seat.

"True," said Crisp. "Now, for whom do you work?"

"Zeekoning Fishing Company," Van Syoc answered. There was a pause.

"That is, at best, a partial truth," said Crisp finally. "Now that you can see I know a lie from the truth, I will ask you, for whom do you work?"

"I told you, Zeekoning Fishing Company!" Van Syoc exclaimed. There was a little sound as Crisp sucked his teeth regretfully behind his mask. He kept one hand on Van Syoc's wrist and placed his other hand on the subject's fingertips. He carefully positioned each finger in a specific place, and Myfanwy saw his arms tense for a moment. Van Syoc flinched and drew a sharp breath tinged with shock.

"For whom do you work?" All he received in answer was a terrified stare. Crisp sighed and pressed again. Van Syoc cried out, and this time it was words. Myfanwy listened closely; to her it seemed simply a collection of random syllables, but all the men in the room gasped. She twisted around, startled. The various section leaders looked pale, and Gestalt looked absolutely stricken. It was as if they had just received confirmation that Satan had arrived and was in the process of eating Glasgow.

"Hmm," she said, as if she understood the significance of Van Syoc's words. She'd ask Ingrid later. Meanwhile, Crisp was gearing up for another question, and judging by the intent stares of the rest of the audience, Myfanwy thought this would be the truly important one.

"Why are you here?" Crisp asked with a terrible focus. His fingers had tensed on the delicate pressure points of Van Syoc's hand, and it was evident that the pain was increasing. "What are they doing?" he demanded. The muscles of the subject's face were straining. His jaw was clenched shut, and his eyes bulged. Nevertheless, he did not speak. Gestalt made a sound in his throat, and the doctor released his grasp on the prisoner's hand. Crisp moved closer to the glass and looked straight ahead, his hands by his sides.

"Yes, sir?" he asked. Gestalt steepled his fingers, seemingly lost in thought, and stared at the man slumped in the chair. Eventually Perry summoned up the nerve to break the silence.

"Rook Gestalt, we really must know what is going on here."

Gestalt assented dully. "Extract the information, Dr. Crisp. You are authorized by the Rooks," Gestalt said.

"Excuse me?" Myfanwy spoke without thinking, surprised at not being consulted, earning herself a startled glance from her counterpart.

"That is, if you have no objections, Rook Thomas?" said Gestalt, a little bemused. The entire room was again staring at her in surprise.

"Um, no. I suppose I have no objections," she said. "Please proceed, Dr. Crisp." The interrogator gave a short bow and turned back to the man in the chair. He placed himself carefully behind Van Syoc and spread his fingers wide, then cupped them around his victim's skull. He began to press and stroke the skin.

"Why are you here?"

Van Syoc *writhed* in his chair, his limbs fighting themselves. Beneath his shirt, there were strange shudderings, as if his organs were attempting to rip themselves from his torso. A peculiar popping sound chattered through the room, echoing eerily through the microphones. For a moment, Myfanwy could not see the source of this sound, but then she realized it was Van Syoc's teeth, rattling in their sockets. A thrill of horror went through her, and her flesh crawled.

"What do they want?"

The agony of the man was palpable. Indeed, she almost fancied that she could *see* the man's sensations. They throbbed in front of her, like burning ribbons that flared and ebbed as impressions flowed through the channels of his body.

"Why are you here?"

Myfanwy shook her head, trying to focus on Van Syoc rather than the torment that washed out of him. In desperation, she turned to look at those around her and blinked in surprise. Around each person shivered an aura of sensations, concentric rings that over-lapped one another. She felt that with a brush of her mind, she could leave every person there lying comatose on the floor. Her attention was dragged back to Van Syoc and the pain he was enduring. His senses flickered against hers, and she reeled internally. Her stomach heaved. She swallowed back her bile. *This is why Thomas was always ill,* she realized. She stared at the subject and felt pity.

Myfanwy reached out to the man with her mind. Hesitantly, without really understanding what she was about to do, she touched the current that blazed most brightly, and turned off his pain.

"Why are you here?"

Van Syoc's body continued to rack itself under Crisp's touch, but Myfanwy could tell that his mind no longer felt it. Though the cords in his neck still stood out, his eyes darted around, looking for an explanation.

Sitting on the other side of the glass, the explanation maintained her contact with Van Syoc's system. *Amazing,* she thought, tracing the paths of his nerves. *So this controls pain.* She turned her attention to another portion. *And this web is linked to the eyes. But what is* this? *This can't be right.* As she examined the anomaly, she frowned. Much of his system seemed obvious to her, almost self-explanatory, but there were sections that made no sense at all. Then a pulse rippled through his system, the work of Dr. Crisp. With an effort, she dragged her attention back to the rest of the world, where all was not well. The interrogator had clearly sensed that something was wrong, and he was sweating profusely.

"What do they want?"

Crisp dug in deeper and felt for the most sensitive junctures of nerves and energy, disrupting and agitating. Behind the glass, Myfanwy noticed his efforts, felt them crashing up against the barriers she had placed. There was only so much she could do against Crisp's abilities, she admitted to herself. His influence was flowing over the walls she had created, and eventually it crashed down on the subject with unimaginable force.

"Why are you here?"

Van Syoc shrieked, a long shuddering wail. His mouth opened and closed, his lips flapping obscenely, and he struggled against himself. *Are those words?* Myfanwy thought. *Is that an answer?*

There was an angry buzzing coming from somewhere, building in volume. They all looked around, except for Crisp, who was intent on his project. Then there was a wet pop, and the doctor snatched his hands away from his patient and stepped back with a startled yelp. Perry gave a short laugh when he saw the doctor shaking his fingers and swearing.

"Don't be a fool, Perry," Myfanwy said sharply. "Look at the body!"

"The body," echoed Gestalt. They all stared at Van Syoc, limp in the chair. He remained firmly bound, but there was an alarming stillness.

Faint trails of smoke drifted around the earthly remains of Peter Van Syoc.

What the hell was that, Crisp?" yelled Gestalt. The doctor had been brought into the observation room and was standing in front of a group of accusatory executives and an irate Rook. Myfanwy and Ingrid were still seated, but all the men had risen to their feet, presenting a united front. "You said that you could break anyone, that you could get us all the information we wanted!"

"Rook Gestalt, you know my record is perfect," Dr. Crisp said, staring down at the floor. His hands were clenched by his sides, but if Myfanwy was any judge, the man's tension was the result of fear rather than anger. Of course, with Gestalt raging in front of him, his fear could be forgiven, but she could sense his puzzlement as well.

"If your record is so goddamn perfect, then why is that thing in there dead?" Gestalt demanded. The lift doors swished open, and the twins were there, similarly enraged. They strode in, and everybody in the room stepped back.

"I'm not certain myself," said Crisp nervously. "The man had incredible tolerance, but I would have expected nothing less from someone with his training. I pushed him well beyond normal boundaries, but frankly, he should have broken much sooner."

"And died?" snarled Tidy Twin.

"Was *that* supposed to happen much sooner, Crisp?" asked Cool Twin, curling his fingers into claws.

"We need answers, Crisp!" yelled the handsome Gestalt. "*I* need answers, and thanks to you, they will not be forthcoming!"

"Sir, I'm sorry, I honestly can't understand it," Crisp replied, sweat beading on his brow.

"No?" asked all three of the Gestalt brothers together. "Perhaps I can help you understand." And their hands shot out and linked around Crisp's neck. Working together, the brothers lifted the doctor off the ground. "Can you understand *this?*"

"Gestalt," said Myfanwy tensely. *Is Gestalt actually going to kill this person in front of us all?* she thought. *Is this normal? What the hell kind of organization* is *this?* "Stop." All attention snapped to her. She could feel three pairs of beautiful blue eyes staring, frantic and enraged. "While I have no doubt of Dr. Crisp's talents, I think it is quite beyond him to make a body burn itself. Isn't that right, Dr. Crisp?" The man nodded frantically even as he squirmed in the grip around his throat. "There is something at work here that we do not see. So let us be sensible and put the good doctor down." *You psycho.* She saw reason return to all three faces. Crisp was lowered to the ground.

"Does anybody have any ingenious suggestions?" the Robert body asked, suddenly calm. The twins had turned and were walking away to the lift. Dr. Crisp was gasping on the floor, and all the men were looking at Myfanwy expectantly. Presumably they thought Gestalt was less likely to throttle her. "Well, Rook Thomas, what would *you* suggest?"

"There are a couple of things," she said slowly, stalling for more thinking time. She opened her notebook and flipped through the pages, her brow furrowed as though she were looking for some obscure piece of information. Then she remembered something. "I'm curious about what Van Syoc shrieked at the end. Dr. Crisp, would you agree that our subject was compelled to answer you?" The doctor was still on the floor, gasping for breath, but he managed to nod his head.

"Yes, Rook Thomas," he said hoarsely. "Whatever he was trying to say, he was not lying. I would have known."

"In that case—" she began, but she was cut off by Perry, who was looking entirely too skeptical for her liking.

"Ahem. While I am certain that we all appreciate Myfanwy's little suggestions, it is dangerous to place too much emphasis on this idea. After all, it is clear to *anyone* who has experience in operations that this man"—he gestured toward the window and the slumped body of Van Syoc—"was simply reacting to the crude pain he was feeling. I understand why it would frighten you," he said to Myfanwy, patting her on the shoulder, "but you can rest assured, it's all very normal in these circumstances." Perry's patronizing tone set Myfanwy's teeth on edge.

"Indeed," Myfanwy answered, staring at Perry fixedly. "Thank heavens we have you here to tell us when your superiors should be listened to and when they should be ignored." She could see the lines of his mind traced out around his body and resisted the urge to cut his legs out from under him. Instead, she watched his cheeks flush and his eyes bulge. "I must confess, Perry, I don't recall that particular responsibility listed as part of your office, but perhaps it is just a service you provide to the community for free." The room's focus was him now, and he was so red he would have stopped traffic.

"In any case"—she waved a hand absently—"have someone figure out what this man Van Syoc was attempting to say." Out of the corner of her eye, she saw the butler turn to a Pawn and send him hustling away, presumably in search of some sort of expert. *How satisfying,* she thought to herself, and took a long sip of coffee.

"Also, I should like to know why there is smoke coming out of his body. Dr. Crisp, why did you snatch your fingers away?" she asked, doing her best to ignore the open mouths of the men around her. By this time, Crisp had managed to lever himself up and was edging himself away from Gestalt.

"Well, ma'am, it felt as if I'd been bitten, as if something had snapped at my fingers," he said apologetically.

"Let me see your hands, please," Myfanwy said, and he held them out. Crisp was still wearing the latex gloves, and she turned his hands over to examine them closely. His fingers were unusually long, with massive knuckles and joints. "Dr. Crisp, there are small burn marks on the fingertips of your gloves. Take them off, please." He peeled them off and presented his fingers for inspection. They looked like pink bamboo. Myfanwy reached out, and he flinched away.

"Don't be foolish, I'm not going to hurt you," she assured him, gently taking his hands in hers. His hands were soft and were lightly dusted with powder from the gloves. Nevertheless, she could see tiny pinpoints of soot on his fingers. "Fascinating. We'll want to have both the gloves and your hands analyzed. And of course, the late Mr. Van Syoc will also need to be examined. Thoroughly." She looked around and saw that nobody was doing anything. All of them were too busy watching her incredulously. She snapped her fingers several times, and they all startled. "All right, people, now! Start thinking some thoughts, and let the Rooks know when you've come up with anything. Ingrid, shall we adjourn?" Her secretary stood up beside her, and they walked to the lift.

Well!" Myfanwy burst out in frustration as soon as the lift doors had shut. "What the hell was that about?"

"Perhaps—" began Ingrid, but she was cut off by Myfanwy's rant.

"I mean, that prat Perry comes barreling toward me as if I'm walking in a no-crossing zone and then sprays his spit in my face!" she said, wiping again at her cheek, this time with her sleeve. "And that bloody patronizing Gestalt! 'Oh, here's your little girlie paper bag to have a nice little girlie vomit if you feel the need,' while the entire time he's looking at me hoping I'll lose it."

"Although to be—" Ingrid attempted to interject, but Myfanwy was going full throttle now, and barring a chop to her throat, there was little to no chance of stopping her.

"Perhaps I should have let them do nothing because they proved so capable of *that* when Gestalt was strangling the staff." Myfanwy waved her hands in the air, shaking her head so violently that her hair tumbled out of its clip. Ingrid reached out and removed the dangling clip from her hair.

"Those obnoxious twits! Thanks, Ingrid. Who do they think they are?" Myfanwy ended.

"Well, they *thought* they were the Rookery section leaders, the elite, the most trusted and powerful of the executives," said Ingrid dryly. "But you've probably disabused them of *that* notion."

"Whatever," said Myfanwy. Her spleen now completely vented, she put a hand out against the wall and leaned forward, panting, her head bowed. There was a reflective pause.

"Of course, it's not entirely unexpected," Ingrid said quietly. Myfanwy looked up from her leaning position.

"I beg your pardon?" she asked. The older woman was looking straight ahead, deliberately not making eye contact.

"Rook Thomas, you know I have never commented on the way you conduct yourself," Ingrid began.

"Oh...um, yes. I've always appreciated that," said Myfanwy, trying to conceal the fact that she had no idea if it was true.

"And of course you know that I hold your professional abilities in the highest regard. So please don't be offended..." Ingrid paused, and Myfanwy waited. "Please don't be offended when I say that you have never taken a dominant role in commanding the Checquy."

"Oh, that's it? Gosh, I'm totally not offended by *that*," Myfanwy said dismissively as the lift doors opened.

"Are you certain?" Ingrid asked. *What does she think I'm going to do, go fetal on the floor?* Myfanwy wondered.

"Yeah, no problem. Now, what's the rest of the day look like?" Suddenly she was ready and raring to go. She felt as if she'd drunk six cups of coffee. Ingrid was looking at her strangely. "What? Come on! Meetings, et cetera. Didn't I have some sort of meeting with the security...boss...guy?"

"Not until three," said Ingrid. "Did you still want to go out to lunch? I had to cancel your reservation, but I could see if they have an opening."

"No, I loaded up on cheese and strawberries at the interrogation. What are you doing right now?"

"Me?" Ingrid asked, looking startled.

"Yes, I want to hear your thoughts on what we just saw," Myfanwy said enthusiastically. "Did you think I brought you along for kicks? That was a classic date, with snacks and a show, and now I expect you to deliver the goods. We'll order some afternoon tea, and you'll give me your critique." *And hopefully I'll find out what in God's name that poor guy choked out, the thing that made everybody else gasp as if he'd revealed he was the heir to the throne in disguise.*

"Well, that would be very pleasant," said Ingrid. "Give me a few minutes to get it all arranged."

"Fine," said Myfanwy as they entered the office. "I have a couple of things I need to take care of as well." There were a number of readings she wanted to look over, and unless she was mistaken, her brief look in the desk cupboard had revealed a mini-refrigerator. *I hope Thomas had the good sense to keep the minibar stocked.*

Twenty minutes later, Myfanwy had taken a break from reading and was cheerfully contemplating a Toblerone when Ingrid entered, looking apologetic.

"Rook Gestalt is here to see you, ma'am," said Ingrid.

"Oh. Goody. Well, wait one second," Myfanwy said, somewhat dispirited. She composed herself, flipped her hair back out of her face, and straightened her coat. "Do I look all right? Professional?" Ingrid nodded dubiously and turned to welcome Gestalt. Myfanwy fixed a look of calm on her face and then quickly snatched the chocolate off the desk. The twins filed in and took their seats on what, judging from the way they kept shifting awkwardly, Myfanwy could only conclude were her deliberately uncomfortable chairs.

"Gestalt. Hello." There was another one of those long expectant pauses. "Toblerone?" she offered finally.

7

Dear You,

So, I told you how Farrier and Wattleman acquired me from my parents. They had just ushered a very shaken Mr. Thomas out of the building and were now faced with the prospect of a little girl who was smeared liberally with both tears and chocolate. Morning tea was finished, and Farrier and Wattleman had a talk with me about how important they were, why I should do my very best to make them proud and happy, and how I would be going off to a sort of boarding school. Thrown as I was by the events of the previous hour, I just nodded in a stunned manner and consented to be led out of the building and put into the back of the car, in which I was driven for many miles, far away from London.

It seemed like the journey was endless. I remember looking around help-lessly. Everything I knew was gone, and I was being driven away into the wilderness. I was alone in the back of a limousine. I sniveled and then did a bit more weeping before the driver took pity on me and brought me up front with him. I ended up falling asleep stretched awkwardly across the gear stick, my head on the driver's knee, my face welded to his uniform trousers by an unholy combination of chocolate, drool, and the products of a runny nose.

When the car finally arrived at the Estate, I was prodded awake and greeted by a large woman with a strange accent who was horrified by my traveling circumstances. Eventually, when she had finished denouncing the carelessness of her superiors, she introduced herself to me as Frau Blümen, the headmistress of my new school.

Frau Blümen was jolly and gentle, good with children, and looked tremendously comfortable to fall asleep on. But I was horribly wary of everybody now. As soon as I was out of the car, the driver on whom I had napped drove away without so much as a good-bye. It seemed as if no one could be relied on, no one could be trusted.

That belief would remain with me for a very long time.

Frau Blümen sent me straight off to bed, where I passed out immediately, exhausted by the day's events.

The next morning, I woke up in a new life, a different person than I'd been the previous day. It's a little odd to think that you're experiencing the same sort of thing—how many people do that ever, let alone in the same body? I wonder, will you remember every moment of your first new day? I know I certainly do.

It was the most disorienting, exhausting day of my life.

I had been awakened by the sound of a rooster crowing. It was dark out, but people were stirring in the room, and the lights were slowly turning themselves on. It was clear that I had no option but to get out of bed, especially when I felt someone poking me hesitantly in the shin. When I finally managed to crack my eyes open, I saw a Chinese girl my own age looking at me expectantly.

"Good morning!" she chirped. "I'm Mary, and I'm supposed to show you around! It's time to get up!" Everything she said came out in a cheerful exclamation, and she proved to be one of those people who are always in a good mood.

Still, it seemed unnatural to me, even at that age, that anyone could just spring out of bed and be alert. What I didn't know was that all the students at the Estate received extensive training and indoctrination that was designed to make them as efficient as humanly possible. This included becoming "a morning person." To make matters worse, all the students in my year had been at the Estate since they were infants. There's no set time when people's powers manifest, it can happen at any point in their lives, but it usually happens before adolescence, which is convenient for the Checquy, because people are much easier to indoctrinate then. I was the only person of my age group whose powers hadn't been detected in the womb. Everyone else had spent practically every minute of the past eight years together, so that in addition to already being fitter than most professional athletes and possessing more self-discipline than the samurai, the children had formed themselves into a tight, cohesive group of friends.

Into this was plunged little Myfanwy Thomas, who was still absorbing the knowledge that she'd never go home again and was laboring under the vague but pressing injunction to make Lady Farrier and Sir Henry proud. And there was something else nagging at me, something that made this whole scenario all the more distressing. It was the first night in months that I hadn't been visited in my dreams by Farrier. No discussions, no explanations—she'd simply abandoned me.

When I got up, I was dressed in a navy blue uniform, my hands were slathered in moisturizer and covered in latex gloves, and then I was made to go out to the quadrangle, where we warmed up before embarking on a series of high-impact aerobics classes and then a type of yoga that was designed to improve contortion skills.

The five minutes at the end of our session during which we were allowed to lie on our backs and pretend to be dead was the sweetest period of that day. The two-mile jog we had to run afterward was the worst.

Throughout the entire ordeal, I was encouraged by Mary, but I could tell that she was keen to rejoin the rest of the group, who had finished the run almost as soon as they began. In the time it took me to complete this little expedition (which took us up a steep hill, over a stretch of sand, and through a creek), we were passed by five higher age groups that had been released at appropriately staggered intervals. This was followed by a long warm-down period, which involved having your limbs pulled on by enthusiastic peers and then putting on a swimsuit and marching in a queue under a long line of showers whose temperatures were calculated to change in exactly the right way to ensure that your muscles didn't explode.

After that was chapel, for a mercifully brisk sermon on duty and patriotism, and then we adjourned for breakfast, or at least, breakfast for everyone else. Mary apologetically (but cheerfully) explained that the doctors were going to do some tests on me. As a result, I wasn't allowed to eat anything yet. Thus, I got to watch as a dining hall full of people wolfed down food that had been specially designed to supply maximum energy, promote healthy growth, provide all the valuable nutrients, produce glossy hair, and ensure good digestion. To make things worse, it looked and smelled delicious. I sat in the middle of a group of girls and boys who chatted nonstop, making references to things I had never heard of and laughing at jokes I didn't understand (which was unsurprising, considering they were reading at a level *five years higher than me and were expected to be fluent in two foreign languages). They tried to draw me into the conversation, but I was exhausted, bewildered, and starving.*

At the end of breakfast, the sun was just beginning to rise. I found out later that the rooster crowing that woke us was a recording, presumably of some rooster whose crow had been identified as the most archetypal and whose voice would strike a primitive part of our brains and kick-start them just as it would have our ancestors'.

That's the way it was at the Estate. Every aspect of our lives had been carefully designed and coordinated to be as efficient as it could possibly be. And so had we.

From breakfast we moved to the classroom, where the subjects included the classics, chemistry, and field-stripping three different kinds of assault rifle. Lunch was delicious-looking, but instead of that I was given some pills that I was told would help "flush me out" in preparation for my tests. I had no idea what this involved until the middle of the next class, when I was obliged to leave the room abruptly in the middle of a lecture on observation techniques. I also had to leave the room during my introductory French class (which I was quite relieved to do, since I was surrounded by three-year-olds). And during judo class. And computer skills class. By the end of choir, I was feeling drained—emotionally and intestinally.

Finally, when everyone else went out to the ranges to work on his or her powers, I was directed to the sanatorium, where a battery of medical staff wearing unthreatening yellow lab coats and latex gloves embarked on a series of tests and examinations that left no part of me unscanned, unscraped, unprobed, or unanalyzed. I was photographed, x-rayed, and interviewed. They took a sample of every fluid in my body, as well as some of its solids. I was fingerprinted, toeprinted, palmprinted, eye-scanned, and voice-scanned, and the content of my exhalations was recorded. I received a new haircut (hair down to shoulders was not acceptable for our "adventures"), had a cavity filled, was given glasses, was scheduled for laser eye surgery and braces as soon as I was old enough, and was assigned a special weightlifting regimen designed to bring me up to the standards of my age group as soon as possible.

They checked for allergies, and found one for bees. They checked for phobias, and found some for enclosed spaces, the dark, open spaces, snakes, spiders, and speaking in public. I was assigned a psychiatrist and a course of therapy. When I came out of the san, they had enough details on my physical, mental, and spiritual condition to fill a filing cabinet. And that was only the beginning.

From there I was sent across the lawn to the solidly built building that housed the department concerned with the students' special features, those advantages that had led to their coming to the Estate in the first place. I walked past practice rooms where children sang little animals to death, lifted refrigerators above their heads, and had in-depth conversations with pine trees. I finally arrived at the office of the head of the department, who interviewed me for a good two hours on exactly what had happened when I fell out of the tree.

This interview stands out in my memory as one of the most excruciating experiences of that entire excruciating day, and that includes the hurried visits to the bathroom. But we came out of it with the understanding that I thought I could repeat my little trick with touching people. It didn't occur to me at the time to wonder what would have happened if I had decided I couldn't do the trick again. Years later, I learned that the Estate's approach to such situations is something along the lines of "birds that can sing and won't sing must be made to sing."

I settled into the classes, the routine, and if I ached like hell for the first couple of weeks, well, that was the price of getting fit. These people knew exactly how far they could push their charges. This wasn't some fanatical ballet school's attempt to ensure the pupils never entered puberty or a cram school whose pupils were going to commit suicide if they didn't get into the appropriate university. The Estate took a great deal of care not to push us too hard. After all, it was in the administrators' best interests to produce excellent adult human beings, and putting undue pressure on our fragile bones and psyches wasn't going to do that.

That said, it turns out that children can handle a lot more pressure than is traditionally put on them.

The battery of medical tests was a monthly thing, and standard for every pupil. The Estate was mad for unraveling the sources of the students' unnatural abilities and was not discouraged by the almost complete failure to do so. One boy was linked to atmospheric phenomena in Iceland, but on such a deep and complex level that no one really understood how they were related. Another boy could only try to explain how he was tapping into the emotional state of every left-hander on the planet. It was a situation that led to widespread hair loss among the medical technicians as they tore at their scalps and suffered from stress-related shedding. Still, the staff took their readings, did their analyses, and stockpiled the information, vaguely hoping that future Checquy workers would have the technology or the insight to understand the data.

I didn't make friends. The first few weeks consisted of my frantically trying to adapt to the routine, the expectations. By the time I relaxed enough to notice those around me, I found it difficult to talk to them, and because they were constantly talking to one another, no one really noticed I wasn't saying anything. I could never keep pace with them in the runs, not because I wasn't fit (I became extremely fit) but because with their years of training, they were preternaturally athletic. In terms of academic achievement, I was in the top ten, but in the bottom half of the top ten. I was never really one of them.

The work the instructors did with my abilities progressed, although not, I think, to their satisfaction. Training an individual with supernatural powers is a difficult gig to begin with. There is enormous variety in the types of abilities that manifest, and it is very hard to train someone to do something when you can't actually do it yourself. At the very least, though, students at the Estate are taught from a very early age to be enthusiastic about their powers. They are encouraged to explore the boundaries of their abilities, and they want to learn.

I, however, did not.

I associated my powers with blood, pain, and doctors screaming and flailing about. I also understood that it was these powers that had led to my abruptly being taken away from my family. Combine that with a new wariness of other people, and you have a child who is extremely disinclined to touch people at all, let alone try to connect with their nervous systems.

It was lucky, however, that although it had taken a great deal of pain and stress to activate my powers the first time, from then on I was able to engage them easily. But although I was able to do it, I didn't want to. I didn't want to reach out across the table and place my finger on the bared arm of the lab assistant. I didn't want to see if I could make her clench her fist. I didn't want to extend my senses through that connection and explore her body. I didn't want to be near people and I certainly didn't want to put my mind inside them.

Of course, I did it in the end. Progress was achingly slow, but over the months and years, I gained the power to touch people and possess instant control of their bodies. I could make them move however I pleased. I could read their physical condition, detect pregnancy, cancer, a full bladder. Over time, I developed much more subtle control, introducing new sensations into their perceptions or, in some cases, activating their special abilities without their consent.

It was horrible; I hated it.

In addition, everyone at the Estate knew about my abilities and my limitations. People went out of their way to avoid physical contact with me. I won't say I was shunned — they were nice enough, and no one was cruel or bullied me, but they would step aside in corridors as I was passing. I was given more personal space than the twins who could render you color-blind with a touch or the girl whose right hand raised boils. Pretty much the only skin-to-skin contact I had was in a clinical setting. And I was fine with that.

When I graduated from the Estate, I had an ability that was unique in recorded history, and a deep aversion to using it. I also had the impression that my powers had not advanced nearly as far as the Checquy had hoped.

8

"No, neither of us would like a Toblerone," said Tidy Twin. For a moment, Myfanwy toyed with eating the chocolate right there and then, but Cool Twin was busily opening a folder, and Tidy Twin had begun to speak.

"Myfanwy, it seems that your suspicions were correct. The interrogation department began a full examination of the tapes and transcripts, as you suggested. It appears you have put quite the fear of Rook Thomas in them." Tidy Twin sat back while Cool Twin finished consulting his documents and jumped in.

"Dr. Crisp ordered them to pay particular attention to the last few moments, the death shrieks. Almost immediately, the technicians realized that those *were* coherent words. And as soon as the translators figured out what was being said, they dispatched a runner to your office." The twin paused. "The runner tripped over me in the hallway, and I said that I would share the dispatches with you." Myfanwy did her best to look calm, but inside she was seething. *How dare he read my mail?* she thought. When Gestalt offered her the note, she practically snatched it out of his hand. Ignoring the surprised scowls on both twins' faces, she hurriedly skimmed the message. She was not surprised to see that Dr. Crisp had dreadful handwriting. Nevertheless, she was able to make out what the last, gasped words of Van Syoc had been.

I scout for the invasion . . . we will kill you all.

"Invasion," she breathed. She looked up at the twins and realized that the grimaces on their faces were not from displeasure, but fear. "Gestalt, we need to know more."

"I agree," said Tidy Twin. "But the Court must be informed as soon as possible, and this information is too sensitive to entrust to any more messengers. Do you concur?"

"I do," Myfanwy said seriously.

"Ingrid," called Cool Twin. The woman in purple came in immediately. "How long until sundown?"

"Approximately three and a half hours, Rook Gestalt," Ingrid replied without batting an eye.

"The days had to start getting longer," said Tidy Twin, seething. "Contact Apex House and tell them that the Court needs to convene as soon as possible—the meeting will need to be moved up to tonight, as soon as the sun has set." Ingrid nodded and stepped out of the room quickly. "Well, Rook Thomas, it appears that we shall be up late. I would advise you to take a nap and get a very early dinner." Myfanwy stared at him, incredulous that he was ordering her around like this. Also, she wasn't thrilled with the tone he'd taken with Ingrid. Under her gaze, the twins cleared their throats uncomfortably.

"Rook Thomas, I also wish to apologize for losing my temper so violently during the questioning when the subject mentioned the Grafters. You know the stories they told us at the Estate."

"Yes," agreed Myfanwy solemnly, without any idea what Gestalt was talking about.

"I, um, spoke to Crisp, and he's agreed that nothing more needs to be said about the incident," continued Tidy Twin, staring at her meaningfully. After a pause, Myfanwy agreed. *Who are these Grafters that can freak out Gestalt so much it* strangles *someone?* The twins were looking relieved as they stood up. "Thank you very much, Rook Thomas—the, uh, the shock, you know. I must say, you're taking this very well. Much better than I would have expected," said Tidy Twin. And with that, the twins left the room.

Myfanwy noted down *Grafters,* and Ingrid came in.

Lady Linda Farrier shifted uneasily in her sleep, her face twisting briefly in anxiety. Her eyelids moved faintly, and she bit her lower lip in concentration. The tall thin woman was lying on a Roman-style couch, facedown, one arm under her head, and the other thrust out and down so that her fingertips grazed the floor. Periodically, a lady-like snore would issue forth.

The room was circular and dimly lit. There were no windows, and the walls reached up to a viewing gallery that stretched all the way around the room. On this gallery stood several men, all of them heavily armed. They were still, like gargoyles dressed in purple.

Then she opened her eyes and rolled over, blinking. A massive yawn split her features, and she sat up. A small man in purple who had been sitting by the door stood up and walked over.

"Harrison, please inform the Foreign and Colonial Office that the ambassador to China will have to be replaced immediately. He craves money too strongly to resist temptation. Also, there is a young gentleman in the town of Milton Keynes who is rapidly becoming murderously insane. I couldn't get his name, but he lives in a white house, number fifty-seven, on some lane. It has a blue mailbox, and a willow on the front lawn. He has red hair and is uncircumcised." Her secretary nodded obediently and took notes on an electronic organizer.

"My Lady, the Rooks have called an emergency meeting of the Court. They've requested that the executive meeting be brought forward from Friday."

"*Both* of them?" she asked in surprise.

"Yes, ma'am."

"Interesting. So when is this emergency meeting?" she asked, straightening her coat.

"Fifteen minutes after sundown tonight" was the diffident answer.

"Oh, of course. We have to take that into account, don't we?" She sighed in exasperation.

"Indeed, ma'am."

"All right. Let Rook Thomas's office know that I would still like to dine with her, and move our reservation up."

"Yes, ma'am," Harrison replied.

"I'm going back to sleep," she said, lying back down. "I shall see if there's anyone interesting asleep in America."

"That seems rather like a contradiction in terms, ma'am."

"God, you're such a snob."

Chevalier Heretic Gubbins (Harry to his friends) was staring in vexation at his computer. The damn thing had frozen with twelve unsaved pages of directives on the screen, and he was trying to figure out how the hell he was supposed to reboot the computer without losing everything he had written. He licked his teeth thoughtfully, evaluating the possibilities. Finally, he gave the thing a good slap.

Nothing.

"You piece of crap!" he exclaimed. He took a deep breath, trying to calm himself. Deep breath in. Slowly breathe out. Then he gave the thing another good slap.

Nothing.

"Unbelievable!" His secretary came in. "Fetch somebody from technical support or that woman who claims she can negotiate with computers and have this fixed." He turned his attention back to the computer, and then looked up again. "What?"

"You're balancing on one hand again, sir," the secretary replied. "And you're getting footmarks on the ceiling. The cleaning staff has been complaining."

"Oh. Fine." Gubbins flipped himself up the right way, and his secretary rolled her eyes.

"In any case, sir, the Court meeting has been moved up. It's now today right after sunset — emergency."

"Okay," Gubbins sighed, and he took one leg off the ground. Then he lifted himself up onto one toe. "Piece-of-shit computer!"

And *that,* Minister, is why you may not go to Australia!" snapped Conrad Grantchester. "You will die, and it will be in a very public, messy, media-filled environment." He clicked a button, and the next slide came up on the large projection screen. An awful lot of it was red, but it was really the green bits that got the minister's attention.

"You have made enemies of some very powerful people. And they keep *these* things as pets. You see these pointy bits? You do? *Those* are designed to go into *these* soft bits, causing the soft bits to come out, and those soft bits, Minister, were not meant to leave your stomach." Grantchester ignored the weeping and continued. "The government, the people, and the Checquy want those soft things to stay in your stomach. Therefore, you will not go to Australia." And with that, he stood up and walked briskly out of the darkened conference room, trailing wisps of inky fog behind him.

"He'll need a few minutes," Grantchester said to the ministerial aides who were standing about awkwardly in the hallway. "Joan!" he called to his secretary, who was right behind him. "Send someone in to clean up all that vomit, please. What's next?"

Joshua Eckhart was walking down a long dim tunnel. Water dripped on the tiles, where a thick layer of mold was growing. Eckhart's rubber galoshes splashed in the ankle-deep water, which swirled murkily. Overhead the fluorescent lights (what were left of them) flickered. Behind Eckhart slogged a petite woman in purple waders and a purple raincoat. She was grimly holding on to a plastic-wrapped folder. Behind *her* were two men in purple holding plastic-wrapped guns.

Finally, they came to a massive door bound in strips of brass, lead, and copper. Eckhart pressed his hands against a plate in the center and felt it heat against his palm. Little bubbles rose up in the metal around his fingers. There was the sound of hydraulic machinery. The door split open and each half was drawn back into the wall. He was about to step inside when his secretary tapped him on the shoulder.

"The Rooks have called an emergency meeting of the Court, sir," she said, holding up a waterproof mobile phone. "Fifteen minutes after sundown."

"Fine," he sighed. Then he stepped through the doors, and his entourage followed. There was an unholy shrieking, a clashing of a multitude of chains, and the sound of huge rubbery limbs smacking against each other in impotent rage. Then Eckhart's voice.

"Good afternoon, Your Highness. You look unchanged. Now, perhaps we shall talk about your country. Your subjects are very vulnerable without the unique protection you can bring them. And that is why you will do as we say."

There was a frenzied wailing in response.

"No? Well, we shall see. Gentlemen, please shoot His Highness. In the left head this time, I think."

It was an old room in an old building and was decorated in a very specific style that showed the decorators were lacking both imagination and a second X chromosome. The paint, which had not been vibrant to begin with, was now faded to a distressing beige. The carpet didn't shag and very likely never had. Even the light filtering through the windows was tired and respectable.

Leather-covered armchairs were occupied by the elderly, the plump, the male. This is not to imply that the occupants possessed only one of the above characteristics. They were all, without exception, male. Plumpness or age or both were preferred, but not mandatory.

Cigars were chewed, pipes sucked, and snuff snuffled. One clump of chairs was occupied by a group of men whose names you wouldn't have recognized unless you were a particularly eager scholar of tedious politics and obscure government offices. Still, they had power.

Sir Henry Wattleman was seated among these men and was wondering if he could fake some sort of seizure. After engaging in several hours of conversation, even tedious old men can get tired of being surrounded by old tedious men. He nodded thoughtfully as some person in charge of an obscure mineral pontificated on how important it (and, by extension, he) was. A waiter came up bearing a cordless telephone on a tray. The bylaws of the club forbade members to carry mobile phones on the premises, which was not that great a sacrifice since very few of them knew how to use them.

"Sir Henry, there is a call for you."

"Thank you," he said, inwardly giving three cheers. "Hello?"

"Sir Henry, this is Marilyn," said his secretary from the lobby of the club, which was the farthest she was allowed into the building, having failed to fulfill any of the criteria of membership. She had mentioned that she could easily go back to the office and carry out her duties from there, but it was a sign of status at the club to have one's aides waiting about, ready to dance attendance upon one. "The Rooks have called an emergency meeting of the Court. You'll be gathering at Apex House right after sundown."

"I understand. I shall be right there," he said with thick tones of false regret.

"No, no, sir. You have several hours yet."

"Yes, absolutely. Have the car ready," Wattleman replied. "Gentlemen, I'm terribly sorry, but it appears that I am needed. Duty calls. Right now."

The Toblerone proved to have been well worth the wait, and Ingrid had shyly accepted a few of the little mountains. Now they both sat on the couch, one with impeccable purple-clad posture and one slumped back on the cushions with her stocking feet up on the coffee table.

"So, Ingrid, what did you think of the interrogation?" Myfanwy asked.

"Very interesting," said Ingrid.

"Oh, yeah? You know, Ingrid, I don't think *interesting* is a suitable response from an intelligent person. It means 'I have no idea, but I think I'd better say something.'" She looked at her secretary, whose cheeks were flushed. "Let's be a little bit more specific: What did you think of poor Mr. Van Syoc's responses?"

Ingrid took a deep breath and looked down at her hands. "Well, Rook Thomas, I suppose that the most startling thing is the fact that the Grafters are sending operatives back into the British Isles. The second most startling thing is that the Grafters still exist. I was under the impression that their organization was dissolved and their leaders executed several hundred years ago."

"Yes, the Grafters," said Myfanwy thoughtfully. "I was struck by that too." She surreptitiously underlined the *Grafters* notation in her notepad.

"Although…" Ingrid hesitated.

"Yes?" Myfanwy said quickly, eager to seize the informational opening.

"I'm not entirely certain the rest of the audience was so shocked." Ingrid paused, and Myfanwy gestured for her to continue. "I mean, they were appalled, but only Rook Gestalt gave the kind of reaction I would have expected."

"You would have expected him to strangle Dr. Crisp?" asked Myfanwy.

"Well, no," said Ingrid with a shudder. "Although it didn't really surprise me. I mean, you know how short a temper Gestalt can have, and remember, the female Gestalt was in combat just this morning. Gestalt's assistant told me that all the siblings were still fairly energized." Myfanwy nodded, thinking of the twins' unsteady walk as they'd left her office after recounting the antler-cult raid. "Plus, the Grafters are something of a bogeyman for graduates of the Estate, as you know yourself."

"Hmm," said Myfanwy, at a complete loss. "I agree." It was almost a relief when the phone rang and Ingrid got up to answer it.

"Rook Thomas's office, Ingrid speaking. Yes? Certainly. I'll inform the Rook immediately. Good-bye." Ingrid jotted something down, and looked over at Myfanwy. "Lady Farrier has requested that you still join her for dinner before the meeting at Apex House. You may wish to change your clothes."

"Why?" asked Myfanwy. "This is a designer suit."

"Oh, it's quite respectable," said Ingrid awkwardly, "but, well, you know how Lady Farrier likes women to dress at dinner."

"Yes, of course. Lady Farrier and her dress requirements," said Myfanwy. "I guess you should arrange for a car to take me back to the house."

"You're not going to use the residence?" Ingrid asked in surprise, gesturing toward the massive portraits on the wall.

"Oh, um, yeah, good point," fumbled Myfanwy. "I didn't think there was anything that I could wear to dinner, but now that you mention it, there may be. I'll go and check. Maybe I'll take a nap too. Thanks, Ingrid."

"Don't forget, you have an appointment with the head of building security at three. Shall I page you when he arrives?"

"Please." Myfanwy watched as Ingrid left the room, then picked up her notepad and the purple binder and walked to the wall of portraits. She tried to peer behind the first one. Nothing. In the process, she nearly knocked the picture off the wall and was obliged to scrabble frantically to make sure it didn't crush her. She almost had to call for help but eventually managed to manhandle the large picture back up. She approached the other portraits much more carefully and finally found one that had hinges on one side. She stepped back and contemplated it for a moment.

It was of a tall, handsome man with dark hair. His eyes gleamed black. The background was highly stylized, with the dark paint sloshed on boldly in curves and waves. A small copper plate read CONRAD GRANTCHESTER, ROOK. Under her touch, the portrait swung aside to reveal a heavy metal door with the by-now-familiar metal plate that warmed under her palms. The door slid open, and carpeted steps led up.

Dramatic, she thought. *I wonder whose portrait conceals the door to the bathroom?* She rearranged the heavy binder in her arms and walked hesitantly up the stairs. The staircase switchbacked twice before suddenly opening onto a huge room filled with light. Large windows that looked out on the city of London also illuminated the decor that had been personally selected by Conrad Grantchester, Rook.

"Oh," she said out loud. "Okay, I see what Thomas meant." *He must have thought he was the most pimpariffic man in the entire world.* The flat had clearly been designed two decades ago for the express purpose of seducing young women. They would have been brought here, discreetly, would have gasped over the black leather and the dark wood paneling, and would have had sex on the luxurious purple carpets in front of the fire. Their reflections would have appeared on the many brass fittings, and the massive amplifiers would have blared out the latest music track. Myfanwy resisted the urge to giggle and then burst out laughing instead. She had to sit down to get a grip on herself, which spilled the binder onto the floor.

Eventually she got up and wandered through the residence, her left eyebrow aching from all the raising it was being forced to do. There was a very large gold bathtub shaped like a shell, and an orange billiard table. Track lighting cast spotlights on the abstract paintings and sculptures. *Oh, I have to see the bedroom. I wonder if there's . . .* There was. A round bed, with mirrors on the ceiling. *How in God's name did Thomas ever manage to look this guy in the face?* The study, mercifully, was fairly businesslike and modern, with shelves full of reference works, a large number of which were anatomy textbooks. Myfanwy guessed that they were Thomas's and resolved to cast an eye over them later in order to acquaint herself more fully with how human beings were actually put together.

Okay, study time.

9

The Grafters

The Grafters, or the Wetenschappelijk Broederschap van Natuurkundi-gen, date back to the fifteenth century. Now, as far as I can determine, there were a number of alchemists wandering around Belgium. Or at least, the territories that would eventually grow up to become Belgium. Anyway, I'm sure you can imagine the sort of people these alchemists were. Most of them were squirrelly little men hanging around in cellars doing rather unfortunate things with mer-cury and dung for the cause of greater human knowledge. There were, how-ever, a few of their brotherhood who were nobles — men of exceeding wealth who had gotten involved to achieve greater financial returns.

Personally, I find it difficult to believe that anyone seriously thought these little mole men were going to make gold out of lead, or tuna, or whatever the hell they were working with. But the Duke of One Thing and the Count of Something Else decided that this was a worthwhile investment and poured an obscene amount of money into financing the brotherhood. This is something that would normally really irritate me, the thought of all that wealth being lavished on some totally useless endeavor, except for one funny little fact.

They succeeded.

Of course, they didn't actually turn lead into gold, but those grimy, deluded scientists came up with a discovery of equal value. Somehow or other, they mastered the art of fleshcrafting, of radically altering the properties of the human body. This brotherhood of medieval geeks could mold and re-form the raw materials of people. They could liquefy the flesh and bones of a person, resculpt them. They could attach new limbs. They could create new creatures.

Now, I like to think that these grubby alchemists had only the best of intentions. Hopefully, they had in mind the repairing of mangled peasants or the augmentation of...whatever. The noble investors, however, had some different ideas. With the sort of power these new processes granted them, the members of the brotherhood were in the perfect position to seize power. In any other country, a massive, bloody war would have ensued. Horrors would have stalked the land, unholy amalgamations of flesh would have fought on the fields, and the nights would have held new, unspeakable terrors.

Fortunately, this is Belgium we're talking about.

Rather than creating an army of monstrosities striding across the green, green fields and stomping on soldiers, the wealthy sponsors met with the current ruler and had a very polite and civilized conversation. Possibly over some sort of soup made out of cream. Thanks to that conversation, the brotherhood became officially affiliated with the government, such as it was. I mean, not to cast aspersions on Belgium or her predecessors, but this was the fifteenth century. Nobody was really very organized.

For the next couple of centuries, the Grafters did not do a great deal to influence the affairs of Belgium or, indeed, anywhere. They had been given a large sum of money and a mandate to pursue their studies, which they did with a level of focus that is quite remarkable given that the lands they were living in changed rulers and were divided up several times. Fortunately, the new rulers were apparently not informed of the Grafters' activities, and the Grafters took no interest in political developments, or we would have had Hapsburg Grafters, Spanish Grafters, and possibly even Imperial Abbey of Stavelot-Malmedy Grafters running around the place.

Instead, the Grafters used the funds that had been allocated to them to improve and refine their techniques. The Checquy were vaguely aware of them but did not consider them to be terribly important. Let's face it, they were Belgian geeks chilling in a big-ass basement and doing atrocious things to swine. No one cared. But by the beginning of the seventeenth century, the Grafters were able to produce killing machines of such breathtaking efficiency that a Checquy operative who happened to observe them in action wrote a panic-stricken thirty-page report heavily streaked with tears and vomit. He also became a much more religious man.

As a result of this report, the Checquy began paying a great deal more attention to the Grafters. The Alabaster Lady of the time, Margaret Jones, dispatched seven Checquy operatives to Belgium for the express purpose of observing the Grafters. This was made difficult by the fact that the Grafters worked out of several different estates that were rigorously guarded and patrolled by large chitinous creatures with the scent capabilities of bloodhounds and the hospitality instincts of sharks. Still, the Checquy improvised and were able to gather some important intelligence. One agent, who made his observations while in the form of a seagull, confirmed that there was an entire regiment of augmented soldiers, all of them mounted on huge creatures that were described as "the bastard offspring of spiders and Clydesdales." The Grafters were now of major international concern.

Lamentably, at the same time that the Checquy realized that the Grafters were a big deal, the Grafters did too. They suddenly became aware of their glorious, monstrous muscles and were rather excited about the prospect of flexing them. They tentatively reached out to the head of the government of the time, who was quite impressed and saw great opportunities for his own personal advancement. Accordingly, he did not feel compelled to inform his boss, the King of Spain, about the Grafters and instead urged them to explore their potential. The only problem was that they lived in a fairly religious time, and there was some concern about the public reaction if they unleashed a force of creatures that looked as if they had been shat out of the anus of hell. You see, for all their brilliance in creating strength and resilience, the Grafters had absolutely no aesthetics. I've seen charcoal sketches and oil paintings of the products of that estate, and they were terrifying in their appearance.

Thus, the use of these things would have to be discreet. The Grafters needed a relatively small, contained arena in which to try out their assets. I have no idea which genius thought of the location, but I hope he suffered from excruciating piles because he proposed, and it was agreed, that the Isle of Wight would make an ideal preliminary target.

In 1677, monstrosities walked out of the ocean and supernatural war began on British soil. In response, the Checquy unleashed the Pawns under the direct command of the Rooks. For three weeks, battles raged and hundreds of civilians died. We slowly sliced away at the invaders, each Grafter creation brought down at the cost of dozens of Checquy soldiers.

Twelve of our troops — the last anthropophagi in the British Isles — banded together and slaughtered seventeen monsters. During that battle, an entire village was leveled and the surrounding fields rendered toxic. Pawn Hamish

McNeil, a leper, released a virulent and abnormal disease upon the Grafter troops, causing their bodies simply to fall apart under their own shuddering exertions.

Finally, all that remained of the invaders was their general, a massive warrior who proved invulnerable to all forms of attack the Checquy could muster. Eventually, one of my—our—predecessors was driven to extremes. Crimson Rook John Perry, the only surviving Rook, linked his mind to that of the Grafter general and then shot himself in the head, killing them both.

And that was the end of the Grafter incursion into England. From what I gather, the English ruler of the time, Charles II, would have liked nothing better than to invade Belgium (I know it was called something else then, but it's all in Belgium now, and it's less confusing if I just call it Belgium), the Checquy forces having (it seemed) proven their superiority. The Lords and Ladies of the Checquy, however, pointed out tactfully that not only were our forces decimated but our most competent generals were dead. Remarkably, the King saw reason, and negotiations with the Belgian ruler were entered into. All efforts were made to prevent the Grafters from learning of our precarious status, and a treaty was brokered in our favor.

Under the terms of the treaty, the Belgian ruler agreed to dissolve the Grafters. All funds were withdrawn, all experiments put to death, and all estates and chattels confiscated. If these seem like massive concessions, they were. But for all the Belgians knew, the might of the Checquy forces was poised to descend upon them and wreak unknowable horrors. So they agreed.

As far as the Checquy (or anyone) could tell, the Grafters were no longer a threat. Under the rigorous supervision of the Checquy Chevaliers, the entire project was dismantled. There are detailed records of how the leaders were executed before dozens of highly placed witnesses, and their remains obliterated. The scientists were killed discreetly by Checquy soldiers, their remains were fed to pigs, and then the pigs were killed and burned. The facilities and barracks were burned and the estates redistributed to the church. All entities that had been altered, even the humans, were put to death—a process that took months, not because of the number (although there were many of them), but because of the tenacity of the creatures. All servants and bureaucrats involved were strongly encouraged to forget everything they knew and find new occupations.

There were no mysterious disappearances (besides those the Checquy engineered), no member unaccounted for. There was no reason to suspect the Grafters were not finished. They were an interesting chapter in the history of the supernatural, and some regretted the loss of their revolutionary knowledge, but most agreed that it was better that they were gone.

Most of the Checquy believe that that's where the story of the Grafters ends. They were obliterated, at a horrendous cost, and the entire incident stands as an example of how important the Checquy is and what it can accomplish. World without end.

Amen.

Except.

Except that the elite know better. During the Great War, our agents routinely collected bodies from the no-man's-land between the trenches. It was a dark time, the country was desperate, and secret endeavors were undertaken by both sides. Among the darker echelons of the Checquy, a project was under way; cadavers were needed, and fewer questions were asked if the corpses were acquired from the battlefields rather than from England. The project was a dismal failure in the end, and it was ordered forgotten. Only through the most diligent research did I learn about it.

However, in the process of their work with the corpses, the scientists found some disquieting phenomena. They knew that these anomalies could only be the work of the Grafters. Not only did the Grafters still exist, but their skills were now far greater than they had been when the Belgians were at the height of their power.

Naturally, the organization had to be informed. The Grafters—one of the most dire threats that the Checquy, indeed the nation, had ever known—were active. Still, the heads of this project were wary of coming to the Court with nothing but assertions based on corpses that were, admittedly, in advanced stages of decay. After all, they were men of science. They decided to gather more information.

Two Pawns were quietly dispatched to the front to investigate. One, Thomas Ryan, was a proficient soldier who possessed telescopic vision and could see through human skin. The other, Charlotte Taylor, could cook a human being from the inside. They traveled discreetly and made their way to Ypres, where those suspicious bodies had been gathered.

Ryan sent back regular dispatches, keeping the project leaders abreast of all developments. He reported on the stories the soldiers in the trenches recounted. The boys told of things that were out there in the wasteland, that lollopped among the craters and breathed in the mud and the blood. They spoke about the unnatural men they'd glimpsed in the night, walking silently among the bodies and slipping over the barbed wire with inhuman grace. A face might be seen for a moment laughingly gulping in poisonous gas before it moved back into the roiling fog. Bullets might be fired, but no body would be found.

Ryan and Taylor had great respect for the soldiers around them—young men who would almost certainly die. Fear was always present in the trenches, and they did not want to add to it. Nevertheless, the Checquy operatives coaxed out as many details as they could, and they resolved that they would have to "go over the top."

On a night of storms, the Pawns carefully climbed out of the trench and made their way into no-man's-land. The rain pelted down, drowning the soil and turning the terrain into a devastated expanse of mud. Lightning forked across the skies, augmented by explosions and flares. Thunder roared and machine guns screamed. I can't imagine how they negotiated the territory, but I know that they had to step over the bodies of their countrymen and slog through thigh-deep mire. The files do not record how far they walked, but somewhere in that territory, they found what they were looking for.

They found nightmares.

Taylor's only dispatch was brief and to the point:

Have lost my boots to the mud, Ryan to an explosion, and an eye to the claws of something unnatural. The evidence you desired has been collected and is en route.

The samples Taylor brought back were enough to provide firm evidence that the Grafters were continuing their work. The Court panicked, convinced that the Grafters were poised to sweep down on them, and more Pawns were dispatched to the front. But though they ventured out into the most dismal and dubious areas, after months of observations, they found nothing.

The war ended, and there were still no developments regarding the Grafters. There was no hint of them during the Second World War, and the Checquy allowed themselves to relax a little. Although they knew their enemies were out there, no hostile moves had been made. Perhaps, the Court members told *themselves, the Grafters have no interest in settling old scores. Perhaps they are devoting themselves exclusively to their obscure, if disturbing, studies. Perhaps we can afford not to think about them.*

Perhaps.

For decades, there has been no reason to be concerned. Through conflict and peace, the Grafters have not surfaced. A lingering doubt remains, but with so much to divert its attention, the Checquy strives to remain focused on its responsibilities. The Court agreed that the memory of the Grafter invasion still holds too much terror among the Checquy rank and file for the evidence of their existence to be widely shared. The students at the Estate tell stories about the Grafters to scare one another.

For the Checquy, the Grafters remain one of the most frightening foes we've ever faced. Should they surface in force, it will be a disaster.

A mazing, thought Myfanwy, shaking her head in disbelief. Thomas had included some photocopies of old sketches, and though they were rough and blurry, those details that could be made out were enough to turn her stomach. Glittering carapaces, jagged barbs. *How big were these things supposed to be?* She looked at the description. *In 1677 they were breeding horses the size of Humvees? Well, animals like horses—horses with scales and fangs. I'll be goddamned.* Then she thought back to the revelations of the interrogation.

These *are the people invading us?* She flipped through some more recent pictures. She bit her lips as she perused the details and notes.

Oh, well, we're totally fucked.

And I'm supposed to be going out to dinner with Lady Linda Farrier.

We're being invaded by evil Belgian fleshcrafters, and I have nothing to wear.

Myfanwy grimly contemplated the contents of the residence's wardrobes. *Did Thomas wear nothing but black and gray?* she asked herself. *I mean, there are thirty good-quality suits here, and not a single one with any personality. No skirts cut above the knee, no blouse that isn't white.* She trailed her fingertips along the coats and then, struck by a sudden thought, slid her hand into the inside pocket of one of them. She pulled out two envelopes, carefully marked *To You* and *2*. The rest of the coats yielded identical envelopes, and she put them in a little precarious stack on the floor. *I'll have to go through every coat I possess and shred all these envelopes,* she thought.

She grimly opened another closet and found a number of dresses in the same vein as the suits. *More offerings from the House of Puritan Blah,* she thought. Still, she made the best of a bad lot and managed to put together an outfit that said both *elegant* and *I control a secret government organization.*

The meeting with the head of building security turned out to be easier than she'd anticipated. She'd actually been dreading it, since it was her predecessor who had called it, but fortunately the head of security opened the discussion, and Myfanwy learned why there was a small group of fanatics camped outside the building. Apparently, they were convinced that the Rookery was the government base for covert supernatural agents.

"I realize that this may sound a trifle naive, but isn't it?" she asked, somewhat confused. "I mean, that's what we do here, right?"

"Oh, yes," agreed the head of security, a tall man of Sudanese descent named Clovis. She realized that he'd been one of the men at the interrogation, standing quietly at the back and observing everything. "They're completely right." He smiled cheerfully.

"And you're not concerned that our elaborate smoke screen, the safeguards designed to deceive the public and conceal our existence, has been penetrated by a group of computer nerds and conspiracy theorists?" she asked. "I mean, our best minds have gone to a great deal of effort so that we can operate in secrecy."

"This is true," he said and nodded.

"And they have failed."

"Yes. In fact, the group is doing its best to educate the passersby about the nature of our operations."

"Are we trying to do anything about this?" she asked.

"No," he replied calmly. Myfanwy sighed. She'd taken an instant liking to Clovis and had decided not to make him sit in the deliberately uncomfortable chairs. She ran her fingers through her hair in agitation.

"Okay, Clovis—may I call you Clovis?" she asked.

"Certainly, Rook Thomas," he said.

"And in private, you can call me Myfanwy," she invited, on the spur of the moment.

"Thank you."

"Now, explain to me why we are not bothering to drive off these people."

"Myfanwy—"

"These people who have built what amounts to a tent village outside our service entrance," she said, rapping her fingers sharply on the coffee table.

"Yes, but—"

"These people," she continued, "who are trumpeting the truth about us to every Kev or Nigel who wanders past." She took a breath and stared at him with her two black eyes. "Explain that to me, please, Clovis."

"Nobody pays any attention to computer nerds and conspiracy theorists," he replied blandly.

"Excuse me?" she asked, taken aback.

"Myfanwy," he said smoothly. "Nobody pays any attention to protesters. Even environmentalists are routinely ignored, and *their* arguments make sense. Think about what these people are claiming, and you will realize that no sane person walking through the financial district is going to listen to them. They're not even going to give them pity money."

"Are you certain?" she asked. "It seems like a distressing breach of security."

"Please," Clovis said. "These *X-Files* fans are shooting themselves in the foot. Have you seen the way they dress?"

"Well, if you're certain, then," said Myfanwy.

"Quite certain," said Clovis. "Now, there was just one more thing."

"Oh?"

"Yes, and I believe it may be a matter of deepest concern to our national security," he said in ominous tones.

Bloody hell, she thought. *This is all getting a bit much for my first day of work.*

"Someone has been Googling you."

"I—what?"

"Someone has typed your name into Google," said Clovis, leaning forward as intently as if he'd just announced that the Prime Minister had exploded.

"Gosh," said Myfanwy. "That's, um, yeah. Are we sure it was me?"

"What?"

"Well, I mean, Myfanwy is a Welsh name—they didn't just make it up for me. And Thomas is a pretty common name too. There's got to be a few Myfanwy Thomases running around the place."

"There are twelve that we know about," said Clovis seriously. "Nine of them are in the United Kingdom, one in Australia, one in the United States, and one in New Zealand."

They keep a list of Myfanwy Thomases? thought Myfanwy. *Well, that's your tax dollars at work.*

"However," continued Clovis, "you are the only Myfanwy Alice Thomas. Plus, they typed in your birth date."

"Oh," said Myfanwy.

"Yes."

"Wait, how do we know that someone's Googling me?" asked Myfanwy. *We don't own Google, do we?*

"We've placed the names of all the members of the Court on a watch list," said Clovis. "The various organizations with which we have agreements and relationships inform us if any of those names pops up."

"Okay," said Myfanwy. *I don't suppose it's the Grafters. I mean, they already know where the Rookery is; Van Syoc was observing it. And I like to think that they'd have greater resources at their disposal than Google.* "Well, do we know where this Googler was?"

"This morning they were in London," said Clovis. "In an Internet café. They paid with cash."

Who would be looking for information on me? Myfanwy wondered. *Other than me, that is.*

"They wouldn't have found anything, would they?" she asked.

"No, you have no presence on the Internet," said Clovis. "We're very careful to keep all Checquy personnel off the Web, of course. But can you think of anyone who would be looking for you? Someone outside the Checquy? Who else knows you exist?"

Are you kidding? thought Myfanwy. I *didn't even know I existed until a couple of days ago.*

"I have no idea," she said.

"Well, it's very strange," said Clovis. "But we'll keep watch for any more hits on you."

Myfanwy was asking if there was any other way someone might be able to track her down when Ingrid sailed in.

"I'm sorry, Rook Thomas, but your car is here," she said.

"My car?" Myfanwy said.

"It's time for your dinner with Lady Farrier."

"Oh, crap," she sighed, then noticed Clovis's shocked expression. "I mean, oh, good, this should be delightful."

10

Lady Linda Farrier

Is regarded nervously by everyone in the Checquy. It's not just that she's the boss. Or that she is an actual aristocrat from an old family and is close personal friends with the monarch of our nation. It's not even the fact that she can actually enter your sleeping mind.

It's that she exudes authority. And she looks at you as if she knows everything you're thinking and everything you've ever done wrong. Her gaze makes you want to straighten up and pee yourself at the same time.

The extent of her power and influence is uncertain. Although everyone in the Checquy knows that Lady Farrier can enter and control your dreams, there are also whispered rumors about other powers. That she can place hypnotic suggestions in your mind (some say she has gone all Manchurian Candidate on several key members of Parliament). That she can lock you into a dream permanently. That she can drive you mad.

I wonder—if she can enter one's mind and do as she pleases, then is she perhaps the traitor? Is it she who will sneak into my head while I sleep and obliterate my memories?

If it is, you're screwed.

11

Why was Thomas so afraid of using her powers? Myfanwy mused as the car whisked her away from the Rookery and toward a much more gastronomically inclined district. She herself was terrifically aware of her abilities. Even as she looked through the tinted glass behind the purple-clad driver's head, she knew that she could cut the light out of his eyes. Of course, that would probably have led to his veering the car directly into a crash barrier. But the point was that she could if she chose to. She didn't need to touch him, as Thomas had implied in her letter. It seemed that her predecessor had misjudged the extent of her powers.

However, it was evident that the years of training Thomas had undergone at the Estate had given her a much finer control than Myfanwy currently enjoyed. Thomas's letters had mentioned feats that Myfanwy had no idea how to accomplish. At the moment, she felt she could affect only the most basic bodily functions. But unlike her predecessor, she was eager to explore her abilities. *If I could sit down with somebody for a few hours and just read his system, I'd have a much better understanding.* Unfortunately, she couldn't think of any way to do that beyond engaging the services of a prostitute. *Which would definitely be out of character.*

Myfanwy was still musing when she was delivered to the front door of Simpson's. All of the hippest young things were dressed as formally as their budgets would allow, while the powerful old things dressed as they normally would. A charming maître d' led her through the crowds, her black eyes drawing a few stares, to the table where sat, in all her importance, Lady Linda Farrier.

"Good evening, my Lady," Myfanwy said, debating whether to curtsy. It was the woman from her dream, of that there was no question. Those eyes, that intense concentration, and the unflappable poise that came with power. The last time they had spoken, both had been asleep, and Myfanwy had been only a few hours old.

There was a pause in which Farrier looked at her steadily, and then she gestured for her to sit. Under that gaze, Myfanwy busied herself with tidying her skirt and examining the cutlery.

"Do you know who I am?" the lady finally asked.

"You are Lady Linda Farrier, the female head of the Checquy," Myfanwy replied smoothly.

"Do you know who you are?"

"To a certain degree."

"Indeed?" Farrier said. "When last we spoke, you had no idea who either of us was. At least one problem has been solved."

"Yes, ma'am."

"And you have managed to turn up on Monday at the Rookery and start conducting business. Very impressive. It was never an option that you leave. After all, *I* knew you had lost your memory, but I doubt that any of the others would have believed it. And, of course, no one leaves the Checquy. Myfanwy Thomas was privy to state secrets at the highest level. Even if you have not retained those memories, simply by showing up to work today you have learned things that no one outside our organization can know. You are a horrendous security risk. Still, I had vaguely hoped to make some sort of arrangement for you. Perhaps some sort of sequestered retirement."

"That's it?" Myfanwy asked. "Didn't you owe Myfanwy Thomas a debt?" *Which reminds me, I need to find out what that debt was,* she thought to herself.

"Young lady, I don't know what kind of relationship you think I had with Myfanwy Thomas, but we were not friends. She fought me, in her own way, on many issues. We were civil, and that itself was not easy. My keeping your secret—a secret of massive implications, by the way—and permitting you to assume this life served to pay back that debt."

"But what if I had been killed? I have enemies, clearly. You can't just leave somebody wandering around without any memory of who she is!" She didn't know what she thought Farrier should have done, but leaving her to sink on her own didn't seem like much of a favor.

"Of course you can. And I'm very sorry, but if you'd been killed, that would simply have served to tidy up an inconvenience," Farrier said calmly, taking a sip of wine.

"An inconvenience," repeated Myfanwy.

"What do you call a Rook who has no memory of who she is? At best, you were a liability, at worst a danger. Fortunately, you have proven far more resilient than I anticipated," Farrier said with some satisfaction.

"Oh?"

"Of course. You knew nothing, and now, only two days later, I learn that you have been firmly ensconced in the Rookery, meeting successfully with some of the most powerful people in the land, and ruling on matters that are both secret and terrifying! Do you not find that a trifle peculiar?"

"Lady Farrier, that's not the most peculiar thing I have heard today. It doesn't even make the top ten," Myfanwy said levelly.

"No, I suppose it would not," Farrier said, with a small smile. "That's the problem with our profession. Hardly anything manages to strike us as unlikely." The waiter arrived and, sensing the tension between the two women, was very nervous in taking their orders. "However, we can still be surprised. And you, you are the most surprising thing I have seen in a long time. I wonder, how did you learn about who and what you are?"

Myfanwy stared at her, and, for a moment, she was tempted. Could she explain that Thomas had known what was coming—had known and had made preparations? Farrier wielded power and would make a valuable ally. *And besides,* she thought to herself, *it's hard going through this alone. It's only been a day at work, and already I know so many terrible things. A monstrous army is about to descend upon the country. Somebody in the Court wants me dead, and I still don't know why. I am responsible for fixing these things, and I can't even remember my middle name! I want to tell somebody!*

It was tantalizing, and yet Myfanwy knew that she could not. If she had inherited Thomas's powers, she had inherited her enemies too. Whether Farrier was a true enemy or not, she was not a friend.

"It appears that I am a quick study," Myfanwy said and took a long sip from her water glass.

"Do you mind if I ask you a personal question?" Farrier asked.

"Please," said Myfanwy.

"This may sound strange, but who do you think you are? Do you think of yourself as Myfanwy Thomas, Rook of the Checquy? Or are you just the person wearing her body? Do you have any memories of being her?"

"Good question," Myfanwy said with a small smile. "I'm still coming to a decision on that one."

"But..."

"But I'm not her. She blinked, and when these eyes opened, a new person looked out."

Alrich woke up.

"May I ask you a question?" Myfanwy asked Lady Farrier.

"I suppose so" was the dubious reply.

"What was Thomas like?" she asked, and she was rewarded with a startled look.

"Oh, er, my goodness," fumbled Farrier, who was somewhat taken aback. "She was...nice."

"Nice? She was *nice?*"

"You must understand, it's a little disconcerting to be telling *you* what I thought of Myfanwy Thomas," Farrier pointed out, not unreasonably.

"Certainly, but I'm not asking you whether you would have trusted her with your Bentley. I just want to know what she was like."

"Ah, well, give me a moment," said Farrier. Her eyes got the same faraway look they had had three nights ago when she had been surprised in Myfanwy's dream. "Thomas was simultaneously a tremendous disappointment and a surprisingly valuable asset.

"When we acquired that child, it was a coup. An entirely new talent with no alarming weaknesses or deformities. Do you know how rare that is? On an island this small? The organization screened her life intensely. If you like, you could probably find in the Estate's records what kind of dinner she had every night for the three months between the manifestation of her powers and our acquisition of her. I watched that little girl's dreams for weeks and recorded every minute detail, looking for any sort of mental instability. I interviewed her, taking care that every dream was set in a place that would test her..." Farrier trailed off.

"And?" Myfanwy prompted.

"And it was fine. She was healthy, she was happy, she was sane. She was *ours*."

An attractive young man was led into Alrich's room, and Alrich's eyes brightened.

"So, how was she a disappointment?" asked Myfanwy, already knowing part of the answer but wanting to hear Farrier's perspective on the events.

"It was one of those things that can't be anticipated. A bright little girl, seemingly resilient, but she just didn't respond well to the transfer. Many children have problems when they're taken from their families, but the Estate is designed to minimize the impact. Its purpose is to welcome students in rapidly, make them feel comfortable and loved, and train them in the effective use of their powers. But Myfanwy Thomas withdrew into herself. She seemed almost pathologically shy. In some instances, I suppose, that's acceptable. But with a talent that turned out to be linked exclusively to physical contact, it was disastrous. And we'd pinned such high hopes on you...I mean her." Farrier stopped and looked thoughtfully at the woman sitting across from her.

I know what you're wondering, Lady Farrier. You're wondering if Thomas's powers came with the body. You're thinking, Hmm, *when all those brain cells gave up the ghost and Thomas vacated the premises, did* that clump of lobes that let her control other people's bodies get broken too? *That's why you didn't make a move to shake hands with me.*

"So, there we were with this little girl who, in addition to being able to control other people, seemed to have the ability to grow an impermeable emotional and social shell around herself. And there was no question of letting her go, because no one leaves the Checquy."

"Not even children?" asked Myfanwy quietly.

"Not even they," said Farrier. "We were stuck with her, this constant reminder of unfulfilled potential. And don't think that we simply gave up on you as a bad deal! The staff and teachers at the Estate spent years working with you. So disappointing." Farrier shook her head.

You forgot, for a moment, that I'm not the same person, Myfanwy thought as Lady Farrier scanned the room. *Is there a little residual guilt there?*

There should be.

Alrich sat at his desk, reading reports carefully and wiping his lips, while behind him, on a couch, the man snored.

"When it became clear that Myfanwy Thomas's powers would be hopelessly limited, the Court did not pay as much attention to the rest of her education," Farrier continued. "She quietly beetled away through the training, receiving, by the way, a top-notch education, and then came into the Checquy organization."

She continued unremarkably, and you shunted her off into some tedious little position in a relatively unimportant department, went Myfanwy's mental subtitling.

"And then, thank God, she was redeemed. She proved quite capable. More than capable, really...she was brilliant. Under her hands, the Checquy's administration was revolutionized, and she rose to the rank of Rook."

Oh, and I'll bet you were just thrilled with that. The failure that you'd hoped to sweep away into a corner was now sitting in the middle of the room.

"She was one of the most capable executives in the history of the Checquy, an organization that has endured for centuries and has had its pick of the nation's top minds. Make no mistake, Myfanwy Thomas earned her position as Rook," said Farrier.

Myfanwy and Farrier took separate cars to the meeting in Apex House. Thomas's notes had said that the Checquy had facilities all over the country, but the big three were the Rookery, the Annexe, where foreign operations were based, and this place — Apex House — their ultimate headquarters. As they approached the building, she regarded the large crescent-shaped structure with curiosity. It was distinguished-looking, with columns and restrained decorations around the windows. Myfanwy skimmed through the background on the building. The base of the Lord and Lady and the Bishops, it contained much of the legal and financial apparatus for the organization. It was also the place where the Court of the Checquy met every Friday to coordinate the activities of the department.

Where did my day go? Myfanwy thought desperately, paging through the binder. *I don't know whom I'm meeting or what they do. Oh, crap crap crap. Some administrator you were, Thomas. You couldn't have put in a cheat-notes section?* Myfanwy was freaking out when she finally flipped to a section entitled

The Court

The Court of the Checquy is the executive council charged with overseeing the entire organization. And for as long as the game of chess has been recognizable in the British Isles, the hierarchy of the Checquy has been based around chess pieces.

It's a terrible system.

Problems:

The Checquy is a government organization in a country that has a monarchy. You can't have people running around calling themselves King and Queen when they're not the King and Queen. Especially when they wield supernatural powers and command a private army. Inevitably, word gets back

to the actual King or Queen, who is unimpressed. Accordingly, after a few pointed conversations, the titles of the leaders of the Checquy were changed to Lord and Lady, which departs from the chess motif and is still pretty obnoxious but could be worse.

The Lord and Lady titles are gender specific, which makes it awkward when a vacancy appears and the most qualified person has the wrong kind of genitals. As a result, during the 1920s, the organization was inflicted with the uncomfortable tenure of Lady Richard Constable, a large bearded man who once bit the head off a possessed Irish wolfhound. He succeeded Lady Claire Goldsworthy and out of sheer bloody-mindedness declined to change his title. Even when the then-Lord died, Constable refused to switch positions.

Although, as we've seen, the Checquy has occasionally departed from the chess theme, there is still adherence to the idea that there should be two of each rank. (Well, technically, there should be four of each rank, but that's a whole other story.) We share responsibility for our bailiwicks with our counterparts, and the boundaries are not at all clearly defined. It's a nightmare for logistics and responsibilities. It is implied that the Rooks, for instance, will consult and cooperate on all domestic affairs. In some cases, this works out all right. Rook Gestalt and I complement each other, insofar as I do all the paperwork and Gestalt does all the fieldwork. However, there have been less successful partnerships. On one memorable occasion in 1967, the Rooks accidentally led simultaneous but completely separate strikes on the same nest of gorgons, simply because they had refused to talk to each other.

The Bishops are not actually members of the clergy. Not anymore.

The Chevaliers have not necessarily been knighted.

Our titles cannot be used in front of civilians, which periodically makes for awkward situations.

Some people feel that the title Pawn has unpleasant connotations. We are brought up knowing that we may be sacrificed at any time for the greater good, but the implication that we may be sacrificed easily and without any thought is sometimes disheartening.

Not everyone in the organization gets a chess title. If you have no unusual powers, then you're not a Pawn, you're a Retainer. Setting a large portion of our staff apart from everyone else doesn't do a great deal for corporate morale.

Occasionally, someone will point out these flaws and attempt to institute a change, but that person is slapped down. The reasons for this down-slappage are:

> *If you're in the Court, you have an impressive title, and you don't want to change it for something generic.*
> *Tradition.*
> *It's supposed to remind us of the importance of strategy and of rank.*
> *It's cool.*

Still, here are the members of the Court, reduced to the barest bones— their names and offices. There are also flash cards in the top drawer of your office desk.

Rooks (responsible for domestic operations; based at the Rookery)

> *1. The Gestalt siblings (Alex, Teddy, Robert, and Eliza)*
> *2. Myfanwy Thomas (that's you)*

Yes, thanks for that, she thought in irritation.

Chevaliers (responsible for foreign operations; based at the Annexe)

> *1. Major Joshua Eckhart*
> *2. Heretic Gubbins*

Bishops (supervisors of the Checquy, aides to the heads; based at Apex House)

> *1. Alrich*
> *2. Conrad Grantchester*

Lord and Lady (heads of the Checquy; based at Apex House)

> *1. The Right Honorable Linda Viscountess Farrier*
> *2. Sir Henry Wattleman*

Unfortunately, there were no photographs or even sketches. *I suppose I'll just have to wing it,* Myfanwy thought. *I'm getting pretty good at that.* She looked up when the car stopped. Up close, the building reeked of old money and discreet authority. The fattest man she'd ever seen, dressed all in purple like a pampered plum, opened the car door.

"Good evening, Rook Thomas. May I carry that to the board-room for you?" he asked, gesturing toward her purple binder and briefcase.

"No, thank you," she said absently, staring at the grand pillars that marked the entrance of the Apex.

"Actually!" she exclaimed, reconsidering. *Seeing as how I have no idea where I'm supposed to be going...* "If you could, that would be wonderful."

She followed the man as he waddled to the lift and then through vast hallways. She took the opportunity to read his system. Com-pared to the radically altered Van Syoc, the biology of a normal human being was harmonious, elegant. She concentrated, tracing the impulses and connections of every movement. It was fascinating, the play of muscles and neurons, the complexity that went into tak-ing a step, turning one's head. She reached out a tentative thought, and his hand opened, dropping her briefcase to the floor.

"Terribly sorry, Rook Thomas," said the Retainer, looking sur-prised as he bent down. "Butterfingers."

"Not to fret," she said easily, smiling at him. They proceeded along, and she became absorbed in the frantic energy of his spine, the messages humming back and forth between his brain and the rest of him. It was the most beautiful thing she had ever seen.

"Rook Thomas?" said a distant voice.

"Hm?"

"Uh, we're here," said the fat Retainer, warily proffering her pos-sessions. She pulled her thoughts back into herself and took the case and binder.

"Sorry about that," she said. *I'll have to be more careful,* she thought. *I'm getting better, though.* Every time she used her powers on someone, she gained a greater understanding of how things worked, intuitively sensing connections.

The Retainer opened the door, and she stepped through into the boardroom, where she was a little taken aback. With all the talk of the Court, and the impressiveness of her own office, she'd been expecting something pretty amazing. She'd wondered if it would be traditional, with lots of polished wood, or high-tech, with glass and metal. She hadn't been anticipating a rather stark room that needed a fresh coat of paint. A battered-looking table sat in the center, and two men were on each side of it. Two of the four were Gestalt. The twins.

"Rook Thomas," said one of the men who was not Gestalt, rising to greet her. He was tall and slim, in his fifties, and extremely handsome. His wavy black hair was making a slight retreat at the temples, but his blue-gray eyes were mesmerizing. Was it her imagination, or were there faint tendrils of black smoke coiling off his shoulders? He looked vaguely familiar, but she couldn't quite place him.

"Good evening," she said, flashing him a faint smile. Despite the difference in ages, Myfanwy found herself warming under his ardent gaze, and she blushed slightly when he took her hand. "I don't suppose you'd care to tell us why the meeting has been brought forward?"

"Um, well, I think we should wait until everyone is here," Myfanwy said.

"Fair enough," he said, smiling. "And how is the residence? Does the decor continue to delight?" he asked. *Oh! Ho ho ho! This is Conrad Grantchester, the man from the portrait, the man behind the circular bed,* Myfanwy realized and then again flushed at the image this had conjured up. *I bet that round mattress got quite a bit of use,* she thought, and she resolved not to sleep on it if she could possibly help it.

"Well, Bishop Grantchester, the decor continues to continue," Myfanwy said politely, restraining an unladylike snort. She turned her attention to the other stranger in the room, who had also risen and was waiting to greet her. He had a full head of thick, curly brown hair, no eyebrows, and a large walrus-style mustache. He was not a particularly attractive man, but his eyes were kind.

"Rook Thomas, it's good to see you," he said, his smile apparently genuine. She liked him immediately. "What on earth happened to your eyes?"

"Muggers, of all things," she replied, trying desperately to figure out who he was. "Two men jumped me and tried to take my purse."

"Good God!" he exclaimed with concern. "Are you all right?"

"Oh, yeah," said Myfanwy. "You know, whoever takes one of us on is going to regret it."

"Well, of course," said the man. "I know several people who absolutely pray for the chance to smite some evildoers. One of my accountants actually hangs around in rough areas, hoping to get attacked. He's always disappointed, poor chap. I suppose no one is going to try and mug a man who's built like the Colossus of Rhodes," he mused, absently lifting one leg off the floor, and curling it up into the small of his back.

"Yes, anyway, you look like you're...well," she commented, trying not to let her eyes bug out of her head. He had rocked back on his other leg and ended up balancing on his heel. "Anything, uh, new happening in your office?" Fortunately, further conversation was precluded by the arrival of Farrier. She was hanging on the arm of a tall, gruff-looking old gentleman, and everybody bowed his or her head respectfully. *Sir Henry Wattleman,* Myfanwy surmised. The Lord and Lady greeted everyone by name, which helped Myfanwy figure out that the curly-headed contortionist was Heretic Gubbins, one of the two Chevaliers.

When the Lord and Lady greeted Myfanwy, she gave her most charming smile and a tiny curtsy, which earned her an approving look from Wattleman and a flat stare from Farrier, who could detect Myfanwy's amusement.

They had only just gotten seated when another man walked in hurriedly, smoking a cigarette and talking speedily on a mobile phone. He nodded to each of them and continued to give directions into his phone.

"No, no, no. You let her get off the plane, you let her walk to Customs. Then you claim there is a problem with her visa, and you have her escorted to the interview room we have set up." There was a pause. "She receives no food, she may go to the ladies' room as long as she is accompanied, and you ensure that anything that comes out of her is collected. Keep her *away* from any pipes connected to the greater system. She may be given water. Don't answer her questions." He clicked off the phone and made his greetings. "Good evening, all. My apologies for being late. Am I the last? Of course not, we're still waiting for Alrich, aren't we?" *So he must be Eckhart,* she thought.

He sat down across from Myfanwy and quickly lit a new cigarette off the old one. Myfanwy looked at him with interest. Joshua Eckhart had thinning blond hair and a hardened look about him. He was tanned in a way that suggested he'd spent a good deal of time in the sun doing actual work. His posture was military issue, and his eyes were alert. As he brought his cigarette up to his lips, Myfanwy noticed the many scars on his hands.

Then Bishop Alrich entered, and Myfanwy caught her breath.

Alrich was tall and had ivory skin dusted with light freckles. His features were angular, androgynous, and perfect. His blood-red hair flowed down straight to the small of his back, and he was dressed in an exquisitely cut navy blue suit.

"I am sorry you had to wait for me. Working the night shift means this is my busiest time." Alrich spoke with a husky, growling voice, which was a little jarring coming out of someone so smooth and polished. "Rook Thomas, you look different somehow."

"Well, I recently got the shit kicked out of me," she said.

"Ah, that would be it then," Alrich replied, and he settled down into the chair next to her with a sinuous grace. "Now, what is the emergency that has necessitated this early meeting?"

"The Grafters," said Myfanwy calmly. *Gestalt is going to have to run this show, so I'd better get my licks in while I can.* She looked around at the various Court members as they took in the information. Reactions varied from a narrowing of the eyes on the part of Eckhart and Grantchester to Heretic Gubbins looking like he was going to throw up. She noted with passing interest that there was utterly no change in Alrich's position or demeanor. "This morning, a Grafter operative named Peter Van Syoc was apprehended in a darling little bed-and-breakfast in Harrow. During the subsequent interrogation, we learned that he was sent here by the Belgians. Gestalt?" Tidy Twin looked up in surprise and then fumbled for his notes.

"Uh, thank you, Rook Thomas. To begin with, we have just received the footage of the acquisition. Although neither I nor Rook Thomas have viewed it, I understand it serves as an effective demonstration."

The lights dimmed, and behind Myfanwy and Alrich a screen descended from the ceiling and then flickered on. Everyone turned to watch.

It was a *very* nice bed-and-breakfast. Evidently, the Grafters had a good travel agent, because the bed looked comfortable, and the room was tastefully decorated. Certainly, Van Syoc seemed at ease there as he puttered about the room. It was a bit eerie to see the man moving about casually when earlier that day she had seen him bound to a chair and tortured. His body had been smoking then, but now she watched him check out the minibar and eat some peanuts.

Myfanwy felt vaguely ridiculous as the secret powers in the land watched a video of a man sitting on his bed, slowly eating snacks before putting on his socks and shoes. The time seemed to drag on interminably as Van Syoc tied his tie and checked his hair in the mirror. Through it all, Joshua Eckhart smoked his endless cigarettes, and Heretic Gubbins contorted his body into upsettingly intricate shapes. They all shifted in their executive chairs, except for Alrich, who sat as still and perfect as a Donatello sculpture. Myfanwy was beginning to wish she had some popcorn or a novel when on the screen a woman wandered in from the bathroom, doing up the front of her dress.

"Was she there the whole time?" asked Sir Henry. "Is she also a Grafter?" Clearly, he hadn't read the report.

"That's the whore," said Lady Farrier icily, and everyone flinched.

"Well," said the woman on the video. "If you ever need anything else, you have my number."

"One thing," said Van Syoc, and the woman looked surprised. He reached out a hand toward her.

Ooh, don't take his hand, thought Myfanwy, cringing. But the woman did, with a little smile. Van Syoc was wearing the same little smile, which tightened as he pulled her to him smoothly. Myfanwy watched, transfixed, as the woman twirled into his arms like a dancer. For a moment, they looked like golden-age Hollywood stars, his hand cupping her chin and her eyes turned up to his, and then he tensed and tore her face off.

Myfanwy's hands had been knotting themselves uneasily in her lap, but they were suddenly pressed against her mouth in horror, clutching back a scream. She was breathing rapidly, and it felt as if her heart were about to punch itself out of her chest.

Oh, my holy fuck, what kind of job have I gotten myself into? As Van Syoc casually broke the woman's neck, Myfanwy looked at those around her and was slightly relieved to see that all of them were aghast. Even Alrich, who had struck her as a pretty cool customer, had his eyes wide open with surprise.

On-screen, Van Syoc was pursing his lips as if for a kiss when there was a thundering knock at the door, which made everyone watching jump. Van Syoc also jumped and dropped the body and the face on the floor; the squelching thud made the audience wince.

"Just a moment," Van Syoc said, staring at the door while he stealthily reached into his suitcase, pulling out a pistol.

"Mr. Van Syoc?" came a woman's voice, hesitant and polite.

"Yes?" he asked, doing whatever intricate mechanical things were needed to get a gun ready to shoot.

"This is Louisa, from the front desk. I'm sorry to bother you, but there's been a problem with your paperwork." Van Syoc didn't put down the gun. Instead, he backed across the room, away from the door. "So," continued Louisa, "if you could step out, then perhaps we could resolve this."

"Yeah, I'm sorry, I was just getting in the shower," Van Syoc lied as he brought the gun up and pointed it at the door. "Perhaps I could come down to the desk when I am through?"

"Oh, yes, absolutely. I'm sorry to have bothered you."

And the door exploded inward.

Myfanwy jumped in her chair and gave out a little squeak. Fortunately, so did Gubbins, so she didn't feel too ridiculous. They exchanged a look of embarrassment across the table. All the others kept their gazes fixed on the screen.

Smoke was roiling in through the doorway, and the top of the frame hung crazily, as if it had been punched off the ceiling. Van Syoc hadn't jumped or squeaked but was standing absolutely still, his gun trained carefully on the door. Nothing could be seen through the clouds of smoke billowing in. Tension built, even among the members of the Court. Then, three men burst out of the smoke, toting large guns. They were dressed in black armor, clunky helmets, and goggles with ominous green lights. They looked, Myfanwy thought, like samurai beetles.

"Freeze, motherfucker!" yelled one of the soldiers. "Drop that g—" He was cut off as Van Syoc shot him through the goggles. There was a deafening roar, hastily muted on the video, as torrents of lead poured out of two extremely large guns and slammed into Van Syoc's torso. His body shuddered and dropped to the ground.

Wow, thought Myfanwy. *That was amazingly brief. I wonder if*—her thought was cut off as Van Syoc sat up and, with two casual shots, killed the heavily armored Checquy soldiers.

Myfanwy was proud of herself for not squeaking again, and Gestalt said something in the background about armor-piercing bullets. Her jaw dropped, however, as Van Syoc flipped himself to his feet and bullets began to force themselves out of his flesh. Now a young woman came out of the smoke, and Myfanwy noticed in bemusement that she wasn't wearing body armor or carrying a gun but was dressed in a tracksuit and had a bandolier of pouches slung across her chest. On her hands, she wore bulky padded gauntlets made of a dull black material.

Van Syoc also appeared slightly taken aback, but Myfanwy had to give him credit—he didn't hesitate before firing at the woman. Her hands blurred as she reached up and snatched the bullets out of the air. Myfanwy could hear the dull thwaps as the bullets thudded into the gauntlets. Van Syoc looked shocked, but he was a professional and stood up straighter. His body shook for a moment, and then the muscles in his arms began to grow and swell. Like bunches of grapes, nodules of strength popped up along his limbs. Was it Myfanwy's imagination or did she actually *hear* Van Syoc's flesh manipulating itself?

Then his face began to change shape. His forehead swelled, and his brows plumped themselves; the skin around his eyes grew out to protect them. His neck expanded until it was as wide as his head, then wider. It was as if his body simply tapered off at the top. Van Syoc's nose hinged itself up and shrank back, leaving two small teardrop slits in his face.

Myfanwy was appalled by the transformation; she stared as Van Syoc's hair retracted back into his scalp. She bit her lower lip hard and looked over at Alrich, whose eyes were fixed on the screen.

"You don't have a paper bag, do you?" she asked quietly. He looked at her and then gave his head a minute, apologetic shake. Fortunately, by that time the transformation appeared complete. Another Pawn came into the room, a middle-aged man dressed like a history professor, leather-patched elbows and all, and carrying a backpack. Van Syoc launched himself at the woman, who flung off her gauntlets and reached forward with that same dizzying speed. She slapped him around the neck and shoulders, striking at specific pressure points. Her hands bounced off the neck, which seemed to be composed of a springy, spongy material. Van Syoc grabbed her by the shoulders and shoved her forcefully against the wall. Her hands blurred about his face, but he continued on stolidly, literally pushing her through the plaster into the hallway.

The professor Pawn was staring, horrified, and obviously wondering what he should do. It was clear that he lacked the strength to take Van Syoc out. He reached into the backpack and, with a brisk movement of his hands, drew out a long, delicate whip. The Pawn snapped it up around Van Syoc's torso and hauled with all his weight, tugging Van Syoc off balance. The behemoth in the recently created doorway turned awkwardly, and in the deep recesses of his skull, his eyes narrowed. He absently flung the woman down the hall and took a step back into the room, putting his hand firmly on the whip. The Pawn, recognizing that this was a tug-of-war he was unlikely to win, dropped the whip, reached back into the pack with both hands, and drew out two more.

"How many of those things does he feel compelled to carry about?" asked Eckhart around his cigarette. They all watched as the Pawn deftly entangled Van Syoc's legs and yanked them out from under him. Another brisk snap of his wrists and the whips were stretched up and around the enemy's neck. The woman Pawn reappeared behind Van Syoc, looking rather the worse for wear after her trip through the wall, and reached down with her quick hands, hog-tying the Grafter so that his head was pulled down between his ankles. Still, his massive arms flailed around, bashing at everything within reach. Two more whips were produced, and the Pawns pinned and immobilized his arms, wrapping him in lengths of thick, braided cable. Then the woman produced an enormous hypodermic from her bandolier and injected him carefully behind the ear. For a little while, Van Syoc continued to struggle, but his thrashings slowed to twitching, and eventually he lay still. His muscles shrank, and the man and woman tightened the knots. Van Syoc's body slumped into unconsciousness.

"I need a drink," said the woman tiredly, checking for pulses on the dead soldiers.

"I need a Band-Aid," said the man, examining his hand. Suddenly, Van Syoc began to writhe against his bonds. "Jesus Christ! I thought that stuff was supposed to be able to knock out an elephant."

"It *is* used to knock out elephants. It's elephant tranquilizer," snapped the woman, putting a hand to her ear. "We've got him secured for now, but send in Pawn Depuy." She looked down, saw that Van Syoc was straining against the whips, and sighed. "Is he going to break those?" The professor (as Myfanwy had mentally christened him) eyed the writhing killer on the floor and nodded in resignation. He pulled out several more cords from the backpack and began to add more to the web around Van Syoc. "Jesus, he's going to break those too. Get Depuy up here *now!*"

An elderly man with a walking stick appeared in the doorway, accompanied by a woman in a nurse's outfit. He hobbled painfully to the squirming mass of ropes on the floor, leaned over his face, and breathed out a single quick breath. Van Syoc immediately went limp, and Depuy turned around and hobbled out.

"All right," sighed the female Pawn. "We'd better move him. Drape some sheets over him, get the dollies, and let's start cleaning up."

Van Syoc was transported to the Rookery," said Gestalt, "where he was placed in a system of restraints that could ensure he would not activate his implants. Dr. Crisp then woke him from his sedation and began an interrogation, with the Rooks and some of the section leaders present. We learned that he was an agent of the Grafters and that they have a specific agenda." He paused, and Myfanwy seized the opportunity to continue the story.

"Van Syoc died during the questioning, under circumstances that are being investigated. It has been put forward that some sort of self-destruct mechanism was activated. But certain details were extracted. It appears that Van Syoc was a scout and that he was there as a precursor to an invasion by the Grafters." Gestalt was nodding seriously, but all the others looked incredulous. *I guess it must be difficult for them. It's like saying that the Normans are staging a comeback.* Finally, Wattleman came out of his trance and addressed the Chevaliers, Eckhart and Gubbins.

"Gentlemen, you are responsible for foreign operations. Have you had even the vaguest idea that this might be on the horizon?" Myfanwy suddenly felt bad for the Chevaliers, one with his cigarettes and the other who appeared to be braiding his arms.

"Well, Sir Henry, you must remember that we do not actually oversee the entire world," pointed out Eckhart mildly. "If that were so, then we would require a much larger budget."

"If this country is about to be invaded, then it does not seem unreasonable to expect that you might know about it," said Lady Farrier.

"I suppose not," Eckhart replied, "but we are really not an in-depth espionage operation. We are weapons. We are pointed and unleashed. There are other branches of the government that deal with international intelligence gathering. They tell us what poses a threat, and we take care of it."

"Well, your domestic siblings appear to have identified the problem, and now it falls to you to *take care of it,*" Wattleman said coldly.

"Forgive me," said Conrad Grantchester, "but could someone refresh my memory about these Grafters?" Everyone turned expectantly to Myfanwy, and she froze. *Ah, looks like I'm the nerd here. Thank heavens I did my homework.*

"The Grafters are the Wetenschappelijk Broederschap van Natuurkundigen, which translates roughly as 'the Scientific Brotherhood of Scientists,' " she began.

"Catchy," said Eckhart.

She gave them a quick rundown, and Farrier gave her an approving (and somewhat surprised) nod.

"Well," said Grantchester, "whom do we inform?"

"The Palace," said Farrier.

"The Prime Minister," said Wattleman.

"The Minister of Defense," said Eckhart.

"The chiefs of the intelligence agencies?" suggested Gubbins.

"Oh God, must we?" asked Grantchester tiredly. "They're always so obnoxious if we turn up something they don't know about, and anything even vaguely unusual makes them nervous. Can you imagine what they'd do if they saw this tape? It's so embarrassing when spies start crying."

"How much are we obliged to tell them?" asked Gubbins, who was cracking his neck, having twisted his head to the right substantially more than was normal for a human being.

"You'll all recall that when the major-incident-response system was installed after the London bombings, special capabilities were put in for the Checquy," said Eckhart. "We can have the airports and ferries up their security, focusing on new arrivals from the Continent. They needn't even check luggage."

"Why bother?" wondered Grantchester. "Apparently they can store all the important stuff inside their bodies anyway. And I'm assuming their enhancements don't show up on metal detectors."

"That's true," conceded Myfanwy. "But sniffer dogs seem to notice them. They were quite wary of Van Syoc—that was one of the things that drew our attention to him. His possessions were searched at the airport, along with his internal cavities. When airport security couldn't figure out what was driving the dogs crazy, they notified the Checquy."

"Did Van Syoc offer any explanations for the dogs' interest in him?" asked Alrich.

"He said that he'd come from Amsterdam, where he'd enjoyed doing things that were legal there even if they weren't here," replied Myfanwy.

"Clever," said Sir Henry. "And plausible."

"Except that the dog handler was one of our agents," said Myfanwy. An idea was forming even as she spoke. "She had enhanced olfactory abilities, and she couldn't smell any drugs on him. Couldn't smell anything out of the ordinary, in fact. So, I'm thinking that we keep an eye on anyone the dogs take an unusual interest in and have them searched. If no drugs turn up, tag the suspects for Checquy attention. That way we can target the Grafters without alerting the rest of the government that we're facing a serious problem."

"Very clever, Rook Thomas," said Wattleman benevolently.

"I know," she agreed, earning herself a few startled glances.

"But how best to implement all this under the radar?" mused Farrier. "No formal announcements—they'd raise too many questions we don't want asked."

"And you realize that not all individuals coming in from the Continent are automatically checked?" asked Alrich.

"Damn that entire EU business!" said Wattleman. "It's all very well to have nice cheap cheeses, but did no one stop to think that the

European continent is connected to ones that aren't necessarily so . . . so . . ."

"Friendly?" offered Myfanwy.

"Secure?" suggested Eckhart.

"Full of nice cheap cheese?" said Gubbins.

Farrier shot Gubbins a dirty look.

"Perhaps if the new procedure was gently put forward to the appropriate people?" suggested Grantchester.

"Yes, capital idea! I could bring it up to the Home Secretary at the club," agreed Sir Henry enthusiastically. "He'll know how best to arrange it. That's settled. Now, what's our next immediate move?"

"But how do we know they're not invading tonight?" asked Gubbins. "I mean, there could be some cobbled-together monstrosities parachuting out of the sky somewhere. Some poor prats in some little village could be getting eaten alive right now."

"I doubt it," said Eckhart. "You don't send your preliminary scouts the morning before you invade a country."

"Yes, good point," said Grantchester. "That's only common sense."

"Can we be certain he was only a preliminary scout?" asked Farrier.

"Absolutely," said Eckhart firmly. "If three Pawns can subdue him, then he does not represent the height of the Grafters' powers."

"Plus," noted Tidy Twin, "he said so during his interrogation."

"We don't have enough information to plan our next move yet," said Myfanwy. *Some of us don't even know who our enemies are.* "We need to learn more."

"Excellent! Good thinking, Rook Thomas!" said Wattleman happily. "The Rooks and the Chevs will work together and present their conclusions to the Bishops tomorrow evening. Unless, of course, we're invaded tonight. In which case, you may have us woken up. Ah-ha-ha." No one else laughed as Wattleman and Farrier rose from their chairs and made their way toward the door. Grantchester nodded and smiled faintly at them all, the smile of someone who has not been obliged to take any responsibility for the problem at hand. Then he left the room also, smoke trailing behind him.

The Rooks and the Chevaliers were left with Alrich, who simply sat there. *God, he's gorgeous,* thought Myfanwy. *If only he'd blink once in a while. Or move. It's kind of creepy.* In fact, Bishop Alrich seemed to be freaking the others out as well. Gubbins appeared to be dislocating his fingers out of nervousness, and Eckhart was paying his cigarette far more attention than it warranted.

"I do not envy you," Alrich said, suddenly rising from his chair with eerie smoothness. "Still, I am quite certain you will come up with some good solutions." And he was gone.

The four remaining members of the Court (well, five if you wanted to include Gestalt as two, which Myfanwy didn't) stared at one another.

"Bring it up at the club?" said Gubbins. "What is he going to say? Ah, nicely played bit of backgammon there, Chumsey. Fancy another brandy? Oh, by the way, damnedest thing. Some arcane group of Belgian mutants that tried to conquer us a couple of centuries ago are coming back to finish the job. Foreigners, eh? Now, where's the sporting section of the *Times*? Unbelievable." He had stood up, kicked his feet into the air, and was now balancing on the table on the points of his elbows.

"Could you please stop that?" asked Myfanwy. "It's just not pleasant to look at."

"Sorry," said Gubbins, easing himself down to his feet.

"Now," said Eckhart. "What do we need to do?"

"Secure the country," said Cool Twin, as if it were obvious.

"Of course! It's only twelve thousand four hundred and twenty-nine kilometers of coastline," said Eckhart with withering sarcasm. "Maybe we could mobilize the lighthouse keepers and the fishermen."

"We could put the nation on heightened alert," said Gubbins slowly.

"We'd have to tell them why," pointed out Myfanwy.

"And then we'd need to enlighten the Americans," said Eckhart. Nobody looked pleased at the prospect.

"Stop a moment and think," said Myfanwy. "We are as well

informed as anybody. Have any of you noticed anything that would prompt you to believe that some sort of invasion is imminent?" They all shook their heads. "So, presumably, we have at least a bit of time. Invading Britain is no small endeavor," she went on thoughtfully. "We need to gather information on the Grafters. Their activities abroad, and their activities here.

"We'll need to assign teams. So far, our one lead is Van Syoc. I know we have a team back at the Rookery cutting him open, so we'll be able to gather some idea of the Grafters' current abilities. Sound reasonable?" No one responded, but Gubbins managed to rouse himself to nod before Myfanwy continued.

"We'll have to assign another team to trace his movements back and find out exactly where he came from. The Rookery staff will get all the details we have on him and distribute them among us. You two gentlemen," she said, pointing at Gubbins and Eckhart, "you must have operatives on the Continent whom you can order about. You'll need to set them chasing down the Grafters. We'll meet tomorrow morning and coordinate."

Myfanwy stood up. "Now, I have had a very long day, I have a splitting headache, and I am going home." Everyone followed her as she walked out, and hers was the first car to pull up.

It whisked her away to Myfanwy Thomas's house.

12

Dear You,

I've realized that I never entirely explained to you how I came to know that I would lose my memory. I mean, I've mentioned that there were psychics — but that's about all I've told you. Sorry about that.

Psychics are not generally held in the highest esteem in the Checquy. I know, it seems like it would be the most common and the most useful sort of power around. After all, everyone's granny is supposed to be able to read tea leaves. And what could be of greater use in the Checquy than knowing what someone else is thinking or what is going to happen in the future? Plus, it would be supremely useful for funding purposes. But in fact, genuine psychics are rarer than rare, and extra difficult to detect.

"I'm getting an impression . . . that you're thinking of . . . this! Am I right? No? Well, does that mean anything to you? It does? See, I'm psychic!" Even worse are the vague predictions and prophecies that seem to maybe have come true. If you look at them with your eyes sort of squinted.

Actually, the most effective psychics are the ones who never realize they're psychic and instead manage to live excellent lives by consistently making the right decisions. Their powers effectively guide them through the shoals of life without their knowing. And one major shoal tends to be the Checquy. The best psychics pop up on our radar only after they've died, when their powers no longer keep them out of our sight.

There are so many impressive fakes around, and it's such a vague sort of power anyway, that the Checquy maintains a very skeptical stance. (This is partly the result of a frantic two weeks under a previous Lord during which the members of the entire organization had orders to imprison any tall dark stranger they met.) We're far more likely to accept that a subject might have the power to turn people into footstools than that he can read minds or see the future. The closest we're likely to get are the palm-reading efforts of Dr. Crisp, and he deals only with a person's past. So when I started receiving warnings from random people, I was dubious.

The first prediction came during a lunch break—one of those rare occasions when I didn't have a meeting and wasn't obliged to eat at my desk. It's a little eerie to look back at that. It was the last day that all I had to worry about was running a major government agency and coordinating covert operations that deal with the supernatural. It was the last day that I woke from an untroubled night's sleep.

I'd decided, since it was such a nice afternoon, to go out into the city and get myself some lunch at a little pub I knew. Every so often, it's pleasant to walk around with the normal people. Of course, one can't help scanning the passersby looking for any little tells that give them away as special. The training we receive is so rigorous that even Checquy desk jockeys are always on the lookout for an ultra-perfect manicure that suggests self-sharpening retractable claws or a cleverly tailored suit that conceals skin made of cheese graters. Checquy statistics indicate that 15 percent of all men in hats are concealing horns. But going out for lunch is still an enjoyable thing to do.

So I was strolling down the street, savoring the sun on my face and with no more thoughts in my head than what kind of sandwich I wanted. The footpath was full of people, and while I was careful not to bump into the normals around me, I rather liked the sense of being lost in the crowd. I was just coming up to the Ivy and Crown when I heard something that caught my attention.

"Ruck."

I looked around and spotted a homeless gentleman squatting against a wall. He had a hat in front of him with some coins in it, and he was staring at me intently.

"Are you talking to me?" I asked. He brought up a hand and pointed a dirty fingernail at me.

"You," he said. "Your memories will be taken. They'll be licked out of you, everything that makes you who you are. Gone forever. You'll flee to a park, and there, in the rain, someone new will open the eyes that used to be yours." He spoke in a voice that cracked, and I stared at him in horror.

"They'll open your eyes, your black eyes, and see corpses all around them. Corpses wearing gloves."

"I—I beg your pardon?" I asked.

"You heard me," he said, lowering his hand.

"I'm not giving you any money," I said faintly.

"Fine," he said. At this point, I realized that, unlike most painfully awkward interviews I take part in, I was able to walk away from this one. So I turned aside from the homeless crazy person, though I didn't fully turn my back on him, and walked into the pub.

Now, London is a big city with the requisite number of homeless crazy people. And I'll freely concede that I am not an expert on their behavior. But a few things struck me as kind of... off about this guy. Like the fact that he didn't ask for money (not that I would have given him any). And that he singled me out of the crowd. But since his body didn't explode into ravens, and he didn't call down a hailstorm, I put it down as an upsetting encounter with someone outside of the Checquy and resolved not to go out to lunch again for a while.

Then I had a roast lamb sandwich, which quieted my mind significantly. But the incident still nagged at me.

The next day, Gestalt and I had to go to the Estate in our capacity as governors of the school. We don't give speeches on graduation days, that's strictly the role of the Lord and Lady of the Checquy, but we are obliged to go up four times a year to make sure the students are being taught and that the entire campus hasn't been reduced to a big smoking crater. It's tedious and a waste of a day, and being forced to spend several hours in a car with one of Gestalt's bodies has always been kind of a drag. Generally it'll put the body to sleep and then go on conducting business elsewhere with the other three.

This time, I got the female body, Eliza, as company. She's everything I'm not: tall, blond, exquisite, with large breasts. I realized abruptly that I hadn't actually seen Eliza for months and was secretly pleased to see that she'd put on a bit of weight. I was even more pleased when she stretched her long legs up on the seat with a sigh, closed her eyes, and left me to read through my reports.

I was reviewing enrollment records for the Estate but found my attention wandering. I kept thinking about the homeless guy. He'd obviously had some *problems, of which being homeless was only one, and I couldn't be certain that he'd actually said* Rook. *It sounded more like* Ruck *or possibly even* Rewck. *It could very well have been that he'd wanted to tell some guy named Rick about the memory-licking thing. In any case, it soon became abundantly clear that I was not going to make much progress with my files, and so I contented myself by looking out the window and watching the landscape glide by.*

The Estate is lovely. It's located on an island off the northeast coast of England. Up until the 1950s, young inductees into the Checquy were trained under a rotating master-apprentice scheme. Wattleman was instructed under this old system. Every year he was placed with a new mentor, who would train him in a variety of disciplines. The teacher would take him into his home and instruct him in everything from diplomacy to a pointed lack thereof. Of course, the Checquy also tried to categorize and study different powers, but our powers somewhat baffle scientists even now, so you can imagine how unsuccessful their studies were in previous decades.

After World War II, however, one of the Bishops did a little evaluating. The bombing of Hiroshima and Nagasaki had brought home like nothing else just how far science had come. For the first time, a man-made device had surpassed the highest-known power level of any operative in the history of the Checquy. Everyone was nervous about that, but people were also curious about what else science could do. Could it provide answers about the Checquy operatives and their powers? Perhaps a more rigorous testing regimen was needed.

Also, it had become evident that not every Checquy mentor was equipped to be a teacher. Agents were being produced who exhibited deficiencies in certain areas. So, Bishop Bastin set about designing a curriculum in the finest tradition of the public service (preternatural or otherwise): he put together a committee.

Unlike most committees, however, this one was designed to get things done. It was composed of dons and professors from universities, generals and sergeants from the armed forces, and a variety of scientists (even a few folks with German accents and some very original ideas who had abruptly found themselves without homes). As a result, we got the Estate.

So, back to this trip. Eliza and I soon stopped at a tiny little village and got on the Checquy boat that ferries us across to Kirrin Island, where the school is. We disembarked at the dock and were met by Steffi Blümen, who shook both our hands but gave me a kiss and observed that Eliza had put on weight (yes!) and looked tired (double yes! If this makes me a bitch, so be it).

We walked up to the school, which is a collection of handsome brick buildings with red roofs, gardens, shooting ranges, gymnasiums, and all sorts of carefully sculpted terrain suitable for specialized training. It has cliffs, a specially designed bog, and large glasshouses with mini-jungles and rain forests. I saw the dormitory I'd lived in and the heavily buttressed medical center in which I'd undergone a deluge of tests every month.

We walked around the classrooms and quietly sat in on some classes, and the students looked at us out of the corners of their eyes. I thanked my lucky stars that this wasn't one of the visits where we had to meet with any students, and from Eliza's weary step, I gathered she was thanking hers too.

"You look a little stressed, Rook Gestalt," said Steffi. "Perhaps we should go somewhere a bit more calm." She opened a door and ushered us into a softly lit room.

I looked around with interest because the room contained the most precious resources of the Checquy: nine babies, drawn from all parts of the United Kingdom. I'd reviewed their files the previous evening and could name each of them. Two little boys of Indian descent. An African girl. Three tiny Anglo-Saxons. Two Arab-Britons. And a perfect little Japanese girl who had delicate silver antlers spiraling out from her temples.

"Shuri Tsukahara," I murmured. "That must have been a nightmarish birth."

"She was a cesarean, of course," said Steffi. "Performed by Checquy surgeons in Checquy facilities as soon as was safe for both mother and daughter. We'd been making preparations and tracking her progress since the very first ultrasound."

"She's beautiful," I said. "What was the cover story?"

"Complications," said Steffi. "It's a word that encompasses a lot, and thanks to the surgery we provided, the mother survived and will be able to have more children." We stood in the nursery looking at the future and breathing in the soft smell of babies. It had been a particularly fecund year,

and the nine infants represented a strong continuation for the Checquy. And in time, they'd be joined by others, those whose powers hadn't been revealed in the womb.

Back in the 1800s, when the theory of evolution was being bandied about, there were some concerns raised that the gifted of the Checquy might be an endangered species. It is rare for a supernatural individual to produce a supernatural child, and while the members of the Checquy were only distantly aware of Mendel and regarded Darwin's work with a certain amount of skepticism, the principles of breeding were well known to them. A bit of digging in the archives and an ongoing count have shown, however, that the Checquy population remains relatively stable in relation to the British population and, even more interesting, remains relatively stable in relation to the number and level of threats that arise. Mostly. Read into that what you will.

In any case, it was very pleasant looking at the babies, right up until one of them stirred and began squalling. A nurse came in, gently scooped the little Arab girl up, and carried her over to a rocking chair. She briskly undid her shirt and put the child to her breast. Cheeks flaming, I jerked my head away and was surprised to see Eliza doing the same thing. She had so many bodies, I wouldn't have thought she'd be prudish. At that moment, her phone rang. She answered, and listened intently.

"Right," she said. "I understand. Stay on the line." Eliza put the phone against her chest, and turned to us. "Steffi, something has come up—is there a room where I can take this call?"

"Of course," said Steffi, ushering her out of the nursery and into an empty classroom.

"Anything I can help with?" I asked her as she left.

"No, it's something that really only I can handle," said Eliza. "Go on with the tour, and I'll catch up."

"We're heading to the san next," said Steffi. "If we finish there before you finish here, just give Miffy a call." We left Eliza and walked down the hallway. "Well, that's extremely convenient," she remarked. "You and I can have a nice wander without her." And we entered the san.

They say that smell is the sense most closely linked to memory. I can't confirm that, but if you ever happen to be at the Estate, stop by the san, open the door, take a big breath in through your nostrils, and see what happens. I tell you this because, although I had never before been to the nursery, I was intimately acquainted with the sanatorium. In the course of my time at the Estate, I had been taken there with multiple bouts of flu, night terrors, crying hysterics, skinned knees, nervous diarrhea, stress-induced vomiting, anxiety-based nosebleeds, sprained ankles, and exposure to the elements after getting lost on a camping trip; in one memorable incident, I was decanted there after being dredged from the bottom of the pool half drowned. So I felt a trifle uncomfortable as I walked in.

One of the medical staff immediately grabbed Steffi to discuss the recovery of a child who'd injured his spinnerets on the obstacle course, leaving me to stand awkwardly by myself. The sick children and I regarded each other with a certain amount of wariness. They were there for a variety of things, ranging from sports injuries to having multiple appendices removed to tonsillitis to a bad case of laminitis.

They knew who I was, of course, and although they had been educated about the awesome authority of a Rook, and although the potential of my supernatural gifts was legend, I was sure that humiliating anecdotes of my youth had been handed down in the dormitory from student to student. I was slightly heartened, however, to see them quail a little under my gaze. Finally, having stood silently for a few minutes, I felt compelled to go over to the child who was regarding me with the widest eyes.

He was Martin Heyer, a nine-year-old whose touch could literally curdle one's blood. He was a darling little thing with dirty blond hair and was wearing the child-size latex gloves the Checquy gives to youngsters who haven't quite gained control of their touch-based powers. I had been forced to wear them for a few weeks at the beginning of my time at the Estate. I mentally reviewed Martin's files and recalled that he enjoyed soccer and science and was being fast-tracked toward research. And apparently he had pneumonia.

"Hullo," I said hesitantly. "My name is—"

"I know, you're Rook Myfanwy," he wheezed. "I had a dream about you last night."

"Oh, yeah?" I asked. "What did you dream?"

"I dreamed that a member of the Court gave the order," he whispered, "and then a man took your memories." He stared at me in terror, and I stared back at him, completely stunned.

"What?" I whispered.

"You won't know who you are," he said, beginning to draw in deep shuddering breaths. His pupils were enormous, and his eyes were glassy as hell. I noticed with alarm that he was starting to turn faintly blue. My mobile rang, and I looked around. The other children, far from being concerned at their compatriot's apparent impending respiratory failure, had turned their attention to their books, electronic music thingies, and handheld computer games. "I tried to tell you," he whispered, "but you didn't know who you were. You just stood there, with black eyes."

A nurse approached. "Ooh, my darling, are we having some trouble?" she asked the gasping child. She easily unlooped a clear plastic mask from a stand by the bed and held it to his mouth. "All right, sweetie, big deep breaths." His eyes were huge over the mask.

My phone was still ringing in my bag.

"This is Rook Thomas," I said. My mind was whirling, and I was racking my memory, trying to recall if young Martin's files had mentioned anything about propensities for future-telling.

The call was from the chief lawyer at the Rookery, and I received a briefing on a minor procedural issue. I replied to every statement by nodding absently, which must have unsettled him somewhat, since it was a telephone conversation.

But I was having a quiet freak-out. You see, I was beginning to entertain the possibility that young Martin and the homeless guy were onto something. In fact, I'd become quite convinced of it. Both of them seemed so intensely certain, and their predictions matched. Not to mention there was little chance that they'd collaborated.

I stumbled through the rest of the tour without really absorbing anything. While thunder crashed overhead, I was shown the new indoor target ranges and inspected the boundary guards. I was introduced to the new surgeons, and I picked up Eliza Gestalt. All these events were a distant blur. We got on the boat, and the trip back to the mainland was stormy and rough. Lightning forked overhead as night fell. It rained most of the way back to London, and we passed the time in complete silence.

"Everything that makes you who you are." That's what the homeless man had said to me, and that's what kept repeating in my head. "Gone forever."

Everything that makes me who I am. My memories. My personality. My soul. Gone forever. Obliterated. That's worse than dying.

I asked the driver to stop and let me out before we got to the Rookery—we were in the East End. I got out, and the car drove away. That was when I lost it. Standing there on the dark street, I began to cry. For half an hour I stood there, weeping, weeping, weeping.

When I finally ran out of tears, I started walking. Something about the darkness and the streets appealed to me. My denial and sorrow were giving way to numbness. I wandered into the most disreputable pub I could find and then realized that I couldn't think of the name of any cocktails. Finally, I asked the man to make me something that would kill the pain and not taste like arse. He eyed me thoughtfully and then produced a drink with an alarming number of layers. I accepted it dully, took a long sip through a bendy straw, and swung around to face the room, my legs dangling from the stool.

It was kind of interesting to watch normal people interacting. They sat and had conversations, speaking much more loudly than Checquy people did. They didn't automatically scan the room for threats, and hardly any of them had taken seats that allowed good visuals of the entrances. They hadn't all situated themselves in positions that would permit them to control important lines of fire. And I was willing to bet that none of them had ordered their alcoholic beverages in an effort to cope with the knowledge of impending obliteration.

I took a few more gulps and became aware that there were two blond Cockney girls down the bar from me, commenting freely on society in general and the patrons of the pub in particular. One was tall and thin, and one was built like a normal person. They were both leaning against the bar and surveying the room.

At the Estate, they teach us high-level observation and evaluation skills, but the intense analytical breakdown that these two girls were working up on the customers of the Eight Bells was astounding.

"The lad in blue is gay."

"Gay and doesn't know it."

"The girl in the hat is from Eastern Europe."

"And has only had access to good clothing stores for two days."

"*Okay, that short girl in the suit down the bar from us . . .*"

"*Is going to lose her memory, I* know!" *I shouted at them.* "*I'm* aware. God!" *I removed the bendy straw, threw back my head and drained my ridiculous drink, then stalked out of the place.*

That's how I found out that I was going to lose my memory and eventually acknowledged it was true. When I finally got home, as I was unlocking the door, I remembered something else the homeless man had said.

"*Someone new will open the eyes that used to be yours.*"

There would be someone new in my body. And little Martin had said that person wouldn't know who she was. I hadn't come to terms with any of it—that took a lot longer—but it was the thought of that person, of you, of someone even more alone than I was, that got me through that night and led me to write these letters to you.

The next morning I found out that little Martin had died in the night, from complications.

13

Myfanwy woke up in Thomas's very comfortable bed. She glanced at the clock and saw that it was still early. Apparently, she was a morning person. At least she had a few minutes to snuggle back among the cushions and scheme before she needed to face the day.

The big problem is that I've got no idea how to impersonate Myfanwy Thomas. Nobody seems able to agree on what she was like. Painfully shy, yet bold in policy. Quiet and withdrawn, but she rises to the Court. And my taking the lead last night certainly seemed to throw the Court off balance. Am I in danger of blowing my cover? They can't say that I'm not Myfanwy Thomas, because I am Myfanwy Thomas. They can do all the physical tests they like, and I'll pass them. And if Rook Thomas starts behaving differently, well, she has the power to do as she likes, as long as she gets the job done.

So all I have to do is get the job done.

Myfanwy got out of bed and set out to explore. The previous night, after she'd left the meeting, the car had taken her to Thomas's house. She'd entered it, deactivated the beeping alarm (good old 230500), and wandered blearily upstairs until she found a room with a bed. For all she knew, she might be in the guest room. Still, judging by the bedside table with its little dish filled with coins and receipts, this was probably Thomas's room. Which meant that these were Thomas's closets. She opened one and then the other, disappointed to find that the clothing kept at home was just as boring as the clothing in the flat and in her chambers at the main office.

In stark contrast to her wardrobe, Thomas's house was lovely, beautifully designed and decorated and packed full of interesting things. Along the walls were tall bookcases crammed with books.

In the kitchen, she found a note on the counter.

Ms. Thomas,

I got the call from your secretary, so I won't stay. I know you're going out to dinner, but I've left a cold meal for you in the fridge, just in case, and changed Wolfgang's litter tray. Unless I hear different, I'll see you tomorrow afternoon.

Val

Okay, so I have a housekeeper, thought Myfanwy. She investigated the fridge and found a delicious-looking assortment of meats, cheeses, and vegetables. *And she cooks! And I've got a cat! Named Wolfgang.* After snagging a fistful of baby carrots, Myfanwy wandered through the house.

"Wolfgang?" There was no mewing or pitter-patter of little feet. She checked the doors for a cat flap and found none. *Oh God, it better be a cat. If she has some sort of bizarre hairy thing wandering around . . .* "Wolfgang?" There was a flicker of movement through a doorway, and Myfanwy found herself staring at a rabbit with extremely long droopy ears.

"Oh! I have a bunny!" Myfanwy knelt down and reached out a hand. Wolfgang continued to look at her but submitted to a tentative stroking and accepted a carrot. "How are you, Wolfgang?" Receiving no answer, she settled her mind that he was not a supernatural rabbit and turned her thoughts to what needed to be done.

Obviously, the issue of the Grafters had to be addressed—especially if they sent over any more operatives. Wattleman had seemed irate at just one Grafter's stepping on British soil. Any more, and he'd be spitting bullets. But the normal day-to-day operation of the Rookery could not go on hold, and Myfanwy had to learn all she could about her job. She still had no idea who in the Court had ordered the attack on Thomas.

Myfanwy returned to the bedroom to get dressed. The Rooks

and the Chevaliers would be meeting, and she wanted to know who she'd be dealing with. They'd seemed all right the previous evening, although no one is really at his best when he learns of an impending invasion. She'd quite liked Heretic Gubbins, although she suffered from an almost overwhelming urge to get out an eyebrow pencil and make some corrections on his eyebrowless face, and she was impressed by the massive number of cigarettes Eckhart had managed to consume. Grantchester, she was willing to admit, was pretty damn attractive, even if he was a couple of decades older than her, and the image of the pimped-out residence seemed to hover behind him. Gestalt was disconcerting. And what was the deal with that Alrich? He was gorgeous to look at, but his presence gave her a funny feeling in her stomach — and not in a good way. It was time to get back to the purple binder.

Major Joshua Eckhart, Chevalier

Was born to a nothing family in York. Now, keep in mind that I'm not in any real position to judge, since as far as I can recall, my family was in no way special. But my parents were decent people, and we ate dinner together, and I loved them. I feel relatively safe in asserting that there is no way little Joshie Eckhart loved his parents. They seem to have been two of the nastiest people ever born in Great Britain, and I regard it as a miracle that after meeting, they elected to marry and have a child rather than kill each other. Of course, their killing each other would have done the rest of the world a favor, so I suppose it's in keeping with the typical conduct of Mr. and Mrs. Eckhart that in this regard they screwed humanity over.

You know, I learn a lot of depressing facts in this job, but very little gets me as down as knowing that Chevalier Eckhart's parents are not dead but are in fact still living together in York and receiving a discreet Checquy stipend. Their one redeeming feature is that they had only one child, and he was taken away from them.

Eckhart Senior, Joshua's father, engaged in any number of stereotypical criminal activities. Let's not, however, ascribe any talent or glamour to Mr. Eckhart. We are not talking about some lithe cat burglar, or even a deft little pickpocket. His career was limited to the least sophisticated crimes. If it didn't require any skill or morals, he was willing to do it. In fact, it was pretty much the only thing he was willing to do. He was a stupid, violent man who enjoyed breaking things such as windows, bottles, and his six-year-old son's jaw.

Mrs. Eckhart was little better. The only reason she didn't set about delivering vicious beatings for money was that she lacked the appropriate strength; that, and the fact that she rarely emerged from the bottle long enough to do anything except acquire the next bottle.

The reports from the social worker who went to the Eckhart household read like Stephen King writing for House & Garden. The woman who was inspecting the place used many more exclamation points than is normal in a government report and sustained bites from both a bulldog and Joshua himself. As a result of his negligent upbringing, the boy was filthy, malnourished, and feral. He slept under his bed and stole food from those around him, and his knowledge of the English language was based in great part on the conversations he heard between his parents. To this day, he retains a massive vocabulary of obscenities, although he doesn't generally use any of them.

Joshua was taken into the government system, and he flourished. The poor kid never actually left the orphanage but was fortunate enough to be placed in the care of good people. For the first time in his life, Joshua was loved and valued. He proved to be both intelligent and personable—at least, once they got him to stop biting people.

Thanks to the glowing endorsements Joshua received from his teachers and guardians, he secured a full scholarship to university and graduated with a degree in military history. From there, he proceeded into the army, where he soon distinguished himself as an excellent soldier. He was entrusted with many responsibilities, and by the time he was thirty-five, he was being sent all over the world on highly sensitive assignments. Thus, even before he entered the Checquy, Joshua Eckhart was well acquainted with the more subtle aspects of national security.

Unlike those of most members of the Checquy, Eckhart's powers did not manifest until adulthood. During an assignment in Jakarta, he incurred the wrath of the city's pickpocket population with his habit of grabbing a thief's hands while they were in his pocket. He would then loudly point out the situation to those around him, causing much embarrassment for the hapless would-be pocket-picker. Apparently, he thought this was terribly funny. Eventually, they came after him with knives. In a normal world, he would have died from seven stab wounds.

I mean, he would have died from stab wounds if the knives had stabbed him. But they didn't. Instead, those seven knives splashed off Joshua Eckhart's body, the metal trickling down his shirt.

It is unknown who was more surprised, the thieves or Eckhart.

Rumors travel fast, and it was whispered on the streets of Jakarta that Joshua Eckhart was a witch. Three days later, an attempt was made to behead him with a pair of hedge clippers. The attackers failed miserably, and when they attempted to escape, they found their car folded up into a cube around them. The Checquy immediately approached Eckhart, offering to help him explore his new abilities. They also hinted at the rewards and satisfaction that could be found working in the more unorthodox sections of the government.

Eckhart was flown immediately to England and transported to the Estate. There, among the bizarre children of the United Kingdom, he tested the scope of his powers. He left two years before I arrived, but I hear the students adored him. There were few adult students at the Estate, and Eckhart was very kind to the children. The instructors are always careful to provide a nurturing environment, but they deliberately do not take the place of parents. Eckhart did not need to be so careful, and as a result, he was—and is—highly popular among the Pawns.

When he entered the Estate, Eckhart was already married and had his own children. In this, he was unusual. Ever since the Checquy began a systematic acquisition of gifted children, there have been few powered operatives with families. We are trained so rigorously, and our dedication is focused so deliberately on our mission, that the children who come out of the Estate are not really equipped for personal lives.

I'll admit, though I could confide this only to you, that I represent the extreme consequence of this. I'm just not comfortable with the idea of . . . intimacy. But even the most gregarious and outgoing of the Pawns have trouble with it. Dating is difficult even within the organization, especially since we are all brought up together. And that's just as well, I suppose.

Myfanwy caught a hint of wistful regret as she read this.

This is why the Checquy is a force that is focused and dedicated, without any inconvenient attachments.

Still, Eckhart has his family and they are close. I was curious to see how he managed the whole training thing, but it turns out that he went home every weekend. As far as his wife and children were aware, he was working on some special government assignment. Which was largely true. Still, I can imagine it. In the mornings, Eckhart sat between a little girl made of steam and a set of siblings named Gestalt and learned about the secrets of the world he lived in. In the afternoon, with a team of scientists, teachers, and fighters, he carefully tested the boundaries of his abilities.

Eckhart can manipulate metal. Under his touch, it becomes fluid, malleable; it assumes any shape he desires. It isn't magnetism. He can't attract or repel it. He sculpts it, gathering it up in great glistening handfuls and molding it into new shapes. With his tutors, Eckhart developed entirely new techniques of fighting. The weapons he carries change their form to suit the situation, and bullets are no longer an issue. If it turns out that Eckhart is the traitor, you'll want to bludgeon him with a cricket bat, assuming he doesn't kill you first. There's a heavy marble paperweight on your desk if it's ever necessary.

After graduating from the Estate, Eckhart was placed in charge of seven other Pawns, and they operated all around the globe, troubleshooting. If a situation arose that a normal team could not deal with, Eckhart and his team were called in.

In Greece, they rescued three British citizens who had been possessed by Spartan ghosts.

In the Northern Territory of Australia, they suppressed a seam of sentient opal that had entombed an entire district.

In Germany, they led a battalion of Pawns in a five-month campaign against the Foot Soldiers of the Nacht.

In Tuscany, they acted as bodyguards to a defecting sorcerer. Aside from the inadvertent trampling of the sorcerer's familiar, a rare and expensive type of iguana, the operation was a success.

This sort of marvelous career went on for several years and culminated in Eckhart's rising to the Court the same year that I graduated from the Estate. He was made a Chevalier, overseeing the international works of the organization.

He's been a member of the Court for seven years and remains the go-to guy for military expertise. Eckhart is not only a brilliant fighter but also probably the most skilled tactician in the Court. His experiences in the army and his studies at university have left him with an encyclopedic knowledge of military applications. Eckhart has masterminded operations on every scale.

He inspires loyalty and affection and seems like a genuinely good man. I can't help wishing that he'd been at the Estate when I was there. It might have made all the difference.

Myfanwy was startled by a knock on the door and looked up. She glanced at her watch and put down her binder.

"Rook Thomas? It's your driver," the man called diffidently.

"Right, just one second," she replied. She gathered up her things and said good-bye to Wolfgang.

Morning, Ingrid. Has anything frightfully bizarre happened?"

"No more so than usual, Rook Thomas," replied her secretary. "Dr. Crisp is waiting in your office, and then your morning will probably be entirely taken up with this meeting of the Rooks and the Chevs. I've rescheduled the other appointments. Your afternoon is going to consist primarily of seeing those people who expected to see you in the morning." She handed Myfanwy a cup of coffee and a large folder. "And here are the latest reports from around the Isles."

"Thanks. How long until the meeting? Oh, and are we holding it here?" Myfanwy asked, absentmindedly paging through the reports.

"Yes, it's here. You have half an hour."

Myfanwy nodded and wandered into her office, where Dr. Crisp was sitting awkwardly on one of the deliberately uncomfortable chairs.

"Good morning, Dr. Crisp," she said brightly.

"Rook Thomas, I'm going to have to retract my apology," he said firmly.

"Huh?" she replied. She sounded like a complete twit, but Crisp was so focused on what he had to say that she could have had a seizure and he probably wouldn't have noticed.

"Yes, I'm sorry."

"You're sorry for retracting your apology?" she asked bemusedly.

"I didn't kill Van Syoc," said Crisp.

"Okay," said Myfanwy. She'd felt a little guilty interfering with the interrogation, but there was no way she was going to let someone be tortured in front of her. She suddenly wondered, with a twist in her stomach, whether she'd caused Van Syoc's death by shoving her abilities into the mix.

"Rook Thomas, I appreciate the confidence you have in me. Your intervention with Rook Gestalt after the interrogation meant the world to me, but I myself was doubtful. I thought I had made a mistake, inadvertently done something I hadn't intended, but..." And here he paused, before saying the sweetest words Myfanwy had yet heard in her short life. "But that man's death came from within himself. No external force could have killed him like that."

"What?" she asked in a shaky voice.

"Rook Thomas, I'm not sure if you're familiar with the details of what I do," said Crisp carefully.

"Dr. Crisp, I am sorry to admit I know practically nothing of what you do," said Myfanwy. "But I can honestly say that right now I would really like you to explain it to me."

"Oh!" he said, looking a little flustered. "Well, to begin with, I don't inflict pain."

"Yes, you do," she contradicted.

"No, I don't."

"Yes, you do," she insisted. "I saw it."

"Oh, you mean the reactions?" he asked. "The teeth rattling, and those eruptions on his torso? No, no, that wasn't me. No. I would never do something like that." He shuddered. "No, those were his Grafter implants."

"But Dr. Crisp, I *saw* the pain. I saw it washing through him," she said. "With my powers."

"Good Lord, really?" he asked, fascinated. "How remarkable.

But, if you'll forgive me, Rook Thomas, what you saw was not pain. It was compulsion."

"What?"

"I compel. Under my fingers, they *want* to talk. They want to answer. That's what I do. Their bodies and their minds are not harmed."

"Then what happened?"

"To begin with, the Grafters chose a remarkable man as their agent. I have never encountered anyone who resisted the compulsion so effectively."

"And this compulsion doesn't hurt them?" asked Myfanwy. This was a point on which she wanted to be very certain.

"They just desire it. There is no physical pain, none at all. They just want to answer, to tell the truth. Van Syoc must have been a model of self-discipline not to speak sooner. He wanted to. He looked forward to telling."

"But then what happened? Why did he die?"

"The Grafters have come very far, Rook Thomas," said Crisp. "Their skills are amazing. Van Syoc's body was laced through with fibers, with devices. What I and my team have found, however, is that he was not in total control of his augmentations." Myfanwy was silent, thinking of herself. Was she in total control of her powers? But Dr. Crisp was still speaking, and she brought her attention back to him.

"I am afraid that it was not only Van Syoc looking out through those eyes in that interrogation room."

"The Grafters," she breathed in horror.

"Yes. When it looked as if Van Syoc might speak, his implants were set to work against him. And when he finally did speak, Van Syoc's masters ordered his body to destroy him. His brain was forced to crash. Several of his organs contracted and ruptured themselves, and controlled electricity coursed through his system."

"That was why your fingers were burned," Myfanwy realized.

"Yes."

157

"Dr. Crisp, I have to apologize to you. And I must confess something. I interfered with your interrogation."

His brow wrinkled for a moment and then he listened, fascinated, as she explained the details.

Gentlemen, Van Syoc's enhancements are high-tech with an old-world charm," Myfanwy announced, looking around at the three men in the room. This morning, Gestalt was just the Tidy Twin, whom Myfanwy could now identify as Teddy. Gubbins was bending his fingers back to touch his wrist, and Eckhart was smoking intensely. For a moment, her eyes lingered thoughtfully on Eckhart. Out of curiosity, she'd pulled his file up on her computer and seen the pictures of him as a little boy. A pathetic, malnourished child when he'd been taken into custody, Eckhart had a photographic history that showed his recovery and growth into a healthy young man. Now, in middle age, he appeared to have settled into a hardy combination of soldier and executive. She couldn't help smiling at him, and he smiled back around his cigarette.

She turned to her notes again. "The implants proved to be far more extensive than we originally believed. To begin with, his spine had been thoroughly coated with a sort of silica."

"To what end?" asked Gubbins.

"Armor?" suggested Eckhart.

"Dr. Crisp and his team are still investigating," said Myfanwy carefully, watching Gestalt for some reaction. His eyes had narrowed speculatively when she began the presentation; he was obviously aware that she'd received information he hadn't. Myfanwy was fairly sure that she would need to attend to this little intradepartmental problem. "However, it's a little delicate for armor. The MRI actually showed the brush marks from when the Grafters applied the material to the bone. They suspect it may be some sort of antenna. It has some interesting piezoelectric properties and is tied into Van Syoc's brain."

"So the man was a walking mobile phone," said Gubbins, twirling his mustache. "Fascinating."

"And a digital camera," added Myfanwy. "Van Syoc would have been capable of transmitting pretty much anything he wanted."

"So why the computer?" asked Eckhart.

"Huh?" said Myfanwy intelligently.

"There was a laptop in his room," Eckhart reminded her. "Hooked up to the Internet. Why bother if you've got a mobile phone that goes wherever you go?"

"There could be any number of reasons. Maybe it's a dedicated line," suggested Gubbins. "Or it's a one-time-use thing."

"We didn't find anything particularly revealing," said Myfanwy. "The lads in the computer department are crawling all over his laptop, but as far as they can determine, he was just e-mailing his family." She took a breath and went back to her summary. "That appears to have been the only modification to his skeleton. Now, as to his musculature, that's quite a different story. You probably noticed that he's had some work done."

"Well, the massive inflation of his head and shoulders kind of gave it away," said Gubbins.

"My guess is that was designed to shield his eyes and nose," she said. "And to boost his strength so he could punch through walls. Always useful."

"This is all very interesting, but we are all well aware of the Grafters' capabilities," said Gestalt icily. His fingers were drumming frantically on the table.

"Yes, Rook Gestalt, but the details are important because they represent a drastic shift in the Grafters' methods," Myfanwy replied just as icily. "Traditionally, they have gone for complicated alterations. Van Syoc is sadly lacking in any number of potential augmentations. There are no weapons concealed in his frame. No truly impressive modifications. The last time a Grafter set foot on British soil, it was the size of a draft horse and looked like its mother was some sort of sea urchin. They have never been known for their subtlety, and the restraint they've shown with this man's modifications is rather disturbing."

"I agree," said Eckhart. "Although, Rook Thomas, I put it to you

159

that they may simply be trying a different tack. It makes much more sense to send discreet spies to scout out the land."

"Do you think there are more of them out there, then?" Gubbins asked. "Other Belgians with bulging heads who will be taking snapshots with their eyes, and mailing them back to Brussels through their vertebrae?"

"I don't know," Myfanwy replied. "Van Syoc was immediately marked at the airport by our people in Customs. It seems unlikely that any other spies could have slipped through."

"I have trouble believing that they will really try and invade us," Eckhart continued. "Last time they had the resources of an entire country behind them, and all they tried to take was one island. Now they have nothing, and we're worried that they're trying to take over the entire country? It makes no sense!" Eckhart stopped short when Gubbins cracked his knuckles. Then his wrists. Then his elbows. Then his shoulders.

"Sorry," Gubbins said, under their collective gaze.

"We are making too many assumptions," said Myfanwy. "We don't know anything for certain." She risked a glance at Gestalt. Teddy had slumped back in his chair but was looking a little calmer. "Heretic, have you and Joshua heard of any recent developments that might be linked to this?" They shook their heads. "Nothing? No unusual deaths or disappearances?"

"None that are any more unusual than usual," said Gubbins wryly. "If we'd had even the slightest inkling about the Grafters, we would have informed the entire Court."

"Then what?" Myfanwy asked in frustration. "I'll accept the possibility that there's a secret supernatural group that wields power in the affairs of men without revealing its work. I have to, because we're in one. But there are limits to how big a secret can be successfully concealed. Just think how large and strong they would need to be to conquer us. Joshua, do you think there could be an army preparing to invade? A force that could subdue this entire country?" Eckhart was playing with a coin. As Myfanwy watched, he flipped it over his knuckles and the metal melted and trickled between his fingers. He opened his hand to reveal a solid coin.

"No," Eckhart said finally. "We would know. There is no army. There can't be."

"Then it's something else," said Gubbins. "Something we do not see."

The rest of the meeting produced little of value except resolutions on the part of all to send out all the feelers they could and to meet regularly. Eckhart and Gubbins would direct specific teams of their operatives overseas. Gestalt unenthusiastically offered to spearhead the domestic investigation. "If, Rook Thomas, you would be willing to oversee normal domestic operations."

Myfanwy may have had a choice, but if she did, she didn't know it. As far as she could tell, this was standard operating procedure.

"Yes, that would be fine, Gestalt."

"I realize that you don't normally take such a direct role in field-work and aren't generally keen on being called out to situations," said Teddy, "but I'm sure you'll muster up some sort of enthusiasm."

Or perhaps I'll take away your bladder control, she thought about saying. *I could probably figure out how to do that.* But she restrained herself and gave him a smile that showed many more teeth than normal.

"Someone will need to present to the Bishops," pointed out Gubbins. "And I can't do it, because there's a situation in China."

"Yes, a situation that requires the attention of both Chevaliers," said Eckhart hurriedly. *Subtle, boys. Real subtle,* thought Myfanwy. Before Gestalt could come up with some sort of lame excuse, she stepped forward.

"I'll do it, but I expect all sorts of guilty concessions from all of you." *I can't believe these are the people entrusted with the security of the nation.* She watched them file out and thought glumly about another evening spent under the disconcerting gaze of the Bishops.

"…and those are our findings, gentlemen," she concluded. She couldn't help but be a little distracted by the two Bishops, who were seated across from her. Although both were attractive, they couldn't have been more different. It wasn't just that Alrich looked as if he was five years younger than her while Grantchester was in his fifties. Everything about them represented two different extremes.

There was something alien and hypnotic about Bishop Alrich's beauty. His features seemed almost delicate. His lips were very red and glistened in the lamplight. His eyes met and held hers. In that deep, glorious gaze Myfanwy caught a glimpse of something that was both mesmerizing and frightening.

With an effort she dragged her eyes away from his and looked at Conrad Grantchester, who was taking rapid notes on his electronic organizer. Whereas Alrich was asexual, this man was definitely masculine. He gave the impression of sophistication blended equally with lust, and there was something intriguing about his sardonic manner.

It was like speaking to a sculpture and a sculptor.

The silence dragged on for at least a minute, and Alrich didn't blink once. She tried looking down at her notepad and then sneaking a glance at him, only to find that he was still staring at her. Distracted by the two handsome Bishops, she kept losing her place in her notes and thinking of inappropriate scenarios.

"I propose, then, that we put select members of the Apex assessment staff onto the task of running up a high-priority strategic risk analysis," said Grantchester, looking up from his stylus and PDA. "Such an analysis would help us identify potential targets and allow the proper security measures to be put into place.

"Rook Thomas, all new information that arises regarding the Grafters, whether it comes from the examination of this Van Syoc person or the investigations of the Chevs and Rook Gestalt, will need to go through to the Bishops so that the analysis can be as well informed as possible," continued Grantchester. Myfanwy nodded and made a note.

"Then, for the time being," said the Bishop calmly, "we shall simply allow things to unfold. All visitors entering the country will pass through stringent examination. We have both Chevs and Rook

Gestalt's bodies seeking out additional intelligence. I am confident that we have nothing to be concerned about. Not yet, anyway." It sounded as if he were rehearsing for his presentation to the Lord and Lady. "Thank you, Rook Thomas."

Grantchester stood up and left. Myfanwy turned to look at Alrich and saw with a start that he was gone. Spooky. And apparently she was dismissed. She looked at her watch; it was a bit past eight. Well, this had taken less time than she had expected. Maybe she would be able to watch some reality television that night.

14

Bishop Conrad Grantchester

If Gestalt rose to the Court on the strength of its abilities as a soldier and Eckhart because of his genius as a tactician, then Grantchester rose to power based on his skills as a financier and diplomat. After all, the Checquy Group is not just an army, a school, a prison, or a research facility—it is all of these things, and more. Someone has to keep track of everything, make sure it's all working right and that the bills are paid.

That's where people like Grantchester and me come in.

Conrad Grantchester did not join the Checquy until he was well into his thirties. He was born to an upper-middle-class family in London and attended Eton before going on to the University of Geneva. He was popular, although he did not take part in any extracurricular activities other than cutting a rather broad swath through his female peers. At university, he distinguished himself in his studies of law and finance.

After he graduated, various intelligence agencies (including the Checquy) tried to recruit him into their service, but Grantchester was not interested. All reports agreed that he was quite ambitious but did not hold any political ideologies to which anyone could appeal. Instead, Grantchester entered the world of money and profit.

His work with an investment firm proved that when he wasn't shagging girls with long hair and short skirts, Grantchester had picked up a very good education. His employers sent him all over the world, where he made large amounts of money and lots of useful contacts. He was focused and driven, and worth several million by the time he was thirty. Though he was still popular with the ladies, at age thirty-two he married Caroline Marsh, who came from a very good family and moved in all the right circles.

At the age of thirty-three, Grantchester began experiencing stinging sensations at specific points on his skin. Naturally, he went to the best doctors in the country, whose thorough examination of him yielded some very interesting findings, which were passed along to us.

Conrad is able to manufacture a variety of chemical compounds inside his body and then vent them through his pores in the form of a fine mist. The properties of these compounds range from a deadly toxin to a nonlethal lachrymatory (tear gas) to a spray that has no effect at all. All of these gases, however, emerge as a dark cloud that blacks out the area it covers.

But in spite of his obvious suitability for the Checquy, Grantchester still proved to be extremely difficult to recruit. As I mentioned, he had been courted after he finished university, and he had developed a sort of immunity to government recruiters. He was already making a tremendous amount of money. It was going to be tough to buy him.

Eventually, however, the opportunity for adventure, intellectual stimulation, and genuine power persuaded him, and he joined us.

He also received a massive pay package.

Grantchester went through a few courses at the Estate, receiving some acclimatization to the world as it actually was, and then he was moved into our foreign affairs section. He traveled everywhere, demonstrating that not every supernatural problem needs to be solved with a cross, stake, or shotgun. Many of them can be solved with some discreet diplomatic maneuvering and a few minor concessions. Also some judicious wining and dining—it wasn't just Grantchester's language skills and business acumen that made him valuable. As it turned out, his handsome face and excellent manners proved useful as well.

He brokered a treaty with the Sirens of the Mediterranean Sea (some of the diplomacy even took place standing up), oversaw the tactful deposition of a dictator in Antarctica, and facilitated the installation of a tyrant in a small African nation. It was automatically assumed that he would rise to the Court, but everyone was fairly surprised when he was given the position of Rook rather than Chevalier.

As Rook, he did a great deal of consolidating and streamlining of the Checquy's domestic finances. I've had the opportunity to review what the situation was like before he took it in hand, and it was a veritable Gordian knot *of trusts, accounts, inheritances, discretionary funds, and properties. We weren't exactly hemorrhaging money, but there was some gradual seepage. Grantchester tidied that up.*

Grantchester has also proven very, very good at assigning people to the tasks they're best suited for—he has an excellent understanding of others' strengths and weaknesses. I suppose it's a corporate thing. Anyway, he's made several unorthodox promotions that many people questioned and that later turned out to be genius. His experiences in business also taught him how to be an effective headhunter. He brings in exceptionally skilled people from outside the Checquy.

He oversaw the design and reconstruction of the Rookery, which gives extra insight into the kind of mind he has: respectable on the outside and sneaky on the inside. Grantchester likes to be prepared, with all contingencies covered and everything organized into nice, methodical systems. He's not much of a combat person, although he has no problem with ordering assassinations—but he does that only when all other negotiations have failed.

After eight years as a Rook, Grantchester made the jump to Bishop, giving him oversight of the entire organization. He examined the greater financial structure, which proved to be even more convoluted and leaky than the domestic ops. Grantchester rolled up his sleeves and made us profitable.

Personally, I respect the hell out of him. His administrative innovations revolutionized the organization, and he's brilliantly businesslike about everything. I inherited his position and his bachelor pad (he wasn't a bachelor when he built and decorated it, by the way). He is a shoo-in to lead the Checquy when Wattleman or Farrier shuffles off this coil (if they ever do), so I imagine I'll be working under him for quite a while.

And did I mention how handsome he is?

In addition, it's worth noting that he doesn't limit his amorous activities to outside stakeholders and has slept with quite a few female Checquy employees. Not me, I hasten to add, which I have rather mixed feelings about. His conquests have always been very discreet, but I've uncovered a few liaisons in the course of my research that form the basis of my blackmail material. There have been no illegitimate children, but one girl, a very popular member of the Checquy, killed herself when he broke it off. Her suicide rocked the organization, but only I and Grantchester know that he was the reason.

15

R ook Thomas?" Ingrid carefully made her way into the office. Myfanwy looked up, startled, from the reports she was reading. *Amazing,* she thought, *I don't think I've ever seen her really freaked out before.* The secretary was actually perspiring.

"Ingrid, are you all right? You look quite flushed. It's not..." She trailed off in embarrassment. After all, Ingrid *was* of a certain age.

"No, it's not that!" snapped Ingrid. "I just received notification that the Americans are coming!"

"All of them?" asked Myfanwy.

"You know, it's not wise to be sarcastic with your executive assistant," remarked Ingrid tightly. "And it isn't the American people, it's the American Bishops."

There are American Bishops? wondered Myfanwy. *There's an American Checquy?* This was probably explained somewhere in the purple binder, but over the past two days, she'd gotten so caught up in the work at hand that she hadn't had much time to consult it. Overseeing all the details and making sure everything tied together well was absorbing. And whatever talent had resided in Thomas's brain appeared to have stayed. Once or twice she'd forgotten that she wasn't the same Myfanwy Thomas everyone assumed she was. She was no longer worried that each thing she said or did would clash with everyone's mental image of what Rook Thomas would say or do. And she'd learned that betraying a bit of ignorance wouldn't automatically reveal her secret. She was finally coming to appreciate the power that came with being a member of the Court.

"Okay, so the American Bishops are coming," Myfanwy said.

"I'm guessing they're here to bother Conrad and Alrich. All the old diplomats getting together for snifters of brandy, sitting 'round the fireplace, wheeling and dealing and deciding the fate of nations over nibbles, eh?" She cocked an eyebrow at Ingrid.

"No, Rook Thomas," said Ingrid. "They're here to see you."

"Me?" she asked incredulously.

"You," said Ingrid with finality. They stared at each other.

"Is this because I was sarcastic about the Americans coming over?" Myfanwy asked at last.

"No," said Ingrid. "Although it certainly makes up for it."

"Well, when are they coming?" asked Myfanwy.

"Forty-five minutes."

"Forty-five minutes! Forty-fucking-five minutes!" Myfanwy stood up behind the desk and started frantically tidying. The dish of biscuits went into the drawer, and papers were hastily stacked. Then the stacks were knocked over. "You know, I could order a pizza and have more time to get ready for it." She looked at her clothes critically. It wasn't quite a casual-Friday outfit, but she'd dressed for a day with no meetings. "Why do they want to talk to *me?*" she asked desperately.

"You wrote the report, Rook Thomas."

"What report?"

"The report on the Grafters, the one you wrote after the Rooks and the Chevs met."

"That was classified!" Myfanwy exclaimed. "That was for the eyes of the Checquy only!" She stacked the papers again.

"The Grafters are on the List, those subjects that initiate automatic alerts," explained Ingrid. "Certain matters are automatically communicated throughout the community."

"Well, okay, but if I had known that other people would be reading it, I would have . . ."

"Yes?"

"I don't know! I'd have used the spell-checker more!" Was it Myfanwy's imagination or was Ingrid amused by all this? "Okay, so they'll be here in forty-five minutes. Is there some sort of reception ceremony or anything?"

"The heads of the Checquy will be hosting a formal gathering to welcome our guests tomorrow evening. It's supposed to give them time to get over their jet lag. But for today, according to long-standing tradition, I perform the sacred cancellation of your other appointments and make reservations at the hallowed temple of Italian food." Myfanwy looked suspiciously at her secretary. Ingrid had been getting more and more smart-assed lately. Then she spoke in her mum voice. "Rook Thomas, you don't need to panic. Go up to the residence, get yourself changed and ready, and I'll let you know when they're here." Myfanwy nodded obediently, opened the door behind the portrait, and went up to the bachelor pad.

The Americans

The moment the English arrived in the New World, the Checquy was there too. The second person off the boat at Jamestown was a Checquy operative who spent most of his time cringing at the appalling things the other colonists were doing and quietly applauding as they succumbed to the subtle magical warfare tactics of the natives. He returned to England with a newfound penchant for corn and a fervent desire not to go back to the colonies. He convinced the Court that a more effective (and better funded) effort was going to be necessary to evaluate the supernatural potential of the continent. They took notice and dispatched several agents to the New World.

The most important of these was Richard Swansea, who faced the rather daunting task of being a secret paranormal agent for the government in the colony of Plymouth. His letters back to England make for fascinating reading, especially since the poor man did not subscribe to the religion of his neighbors.

Surrounded by sour-faced fanatics, Swansea was obliged to put on a brilliant performance; if his neighbors had discovered any of the records concealed in his house, he would have undoubtedly been hanged. Because of his public good works and seemingly burning piety, however, he was a local hero, regarded with a greater reverence than even the community elders. No man dressed more soberly or was quicker to condemn laxness on the part of others. The poor man must have been in hell.

Back in London, Richard Swansea had enjoyed a life of remarkable decadence. The child of a successful madam, Swansea grew up wandering freely between two worlds. Half his time was spent running wild on the streets and the other half becoming acquainted with the many upper-class customers of his mother's . . . stable. One of these customers was a high-ranking member of the Checquy, so as soon as Swansea's powers of chameleonic skin, body-part regeneration, and hypercontortionism manifested, at the age of twelve, he was snatched up.

During his training, Swansea amazed his teachers and earned the adoration of his fellow pupils. Upon his graduation, he became the most prominent operative in the organization. Swansea's extensive contacts in polite society and his in-depth knowledge of the underworld allowed him to pull off some of the most remarkable operations of the time. Accordingly, when the opportunity arose to create the first major American Checquy outpost, the best Pawn was sent.

I can only imagine his frustration as he wandered about in his hat with a buckle and glumly toted his blunderbuss. A man who used to be a dandy, a favorite of the London whores, a gentleman who'd slithered through the dining rooms of society and the sewers beneath it with equal ease, condemned to a tedious backwater populated entirely by religious fanatics whose idea of fun was not having any.

If it had not been for his overwhelming loyalty to the Checquy, Swansea would have stood aside and welcomed any roving monsters into the town of Plymouth. Hell, he probably would have provided them with detailed maps and then cheered as they devoured the Pilgrims.

I gather that his only release was the extended expeditions he took into the wilderness, where he became good friends with the natives. He did his best to warn them of the dangers that his countrymen posed and urged the tribes to move away. The natives nodded kindly, showed him the secrets of their land, and ignored his warnings completely. He watched the outcome with sadness but without any real surprise.

For the next hundred and seven years, Swansea set about creating a resilient operation, one that maintained its close ties to the parent organization. This American Checquy, which became known as the Croatoan, spread out over the colonies. In many ways, the members faced an unimaginable challenge. Technically, they were charged with recording all supernatural entities and goings-on in the New World. If there was a threat, they were encouraged to suppress it and, if possible, ship it back alive to England for examination. They tried to follow this mandate, but resources and necessity often dictated that they simply terminate any menaces. Each colony was a tiny outpost; the entire enterprise was a thin archipelago spread out before an ocean of wilderness.

Every colony had its Croatoan office, but don't think of the organization as more than it was. It lacked the massive population resources that the Checquy could draw on, so the Croatoan's forces consisted of a mishmash of troops, any powered individual its members could get their hands on. Swansea approached the tribes for recruits and explained the situation; he had noticed that the natives had a far higher incidence of powered births. They politely declined. Apparently, they felt that thousands of years of experience had left them well equipped to deal with any danger their homeland could muster up. But they wished him the very best of luck.

Swansea faced major problems. The religious and independent nature of the colonies meant that the Croatoan could not rely on governmental authority to acquire children. If the colonists resented paying taxes on tea, they were going to be even less excited at the prospect of handing over their progeny. And no one knew better than Swansea the danger of bringing up the supernatural around Puritans. It set them to thinking about nooses. Thus, he was pushed to adopt extraordinary measures to build a force that could protect the populace.

Children were acquired. Those children whose families were willing to apprentice them to prominent local "tradesmen" became operatives with relatively little fuss. Children with less flexible parents were, well, seized. Swansea and his operatives snatched those likely children off the streets or silently grabbed them from their beds and sent them off to another colony. There, they were given new identities and taught the importance of the Checquy mission as embodied by the Croatoan. They received an education, learned a trade, and protected their community.

Adults were lured. Periodically, the Checquy would send out reinforcements, who were welcomed ecstatically. Otherwise, Swansea did what he could. In an ironic twist, sailors were press-ganged off their ships. Any adult manifesting powers had a better than average chance of being executed by the community (although it is worth noting that Swansea never found any

manifestations, adult or child, in the village of Salem). In any case, the Cro-
atoan rescued a number of these "witches" and reeducated them. Swansea's
charisma and dedication helped a great deal in converting these late bloomers.
Slaves were rigorously screened and purchased. Upon their integration into the
Croatoan, they were granted their freedom. Some operatives spoke out indig-
nantly at the prospect of freeing slaves and letting them operate as equals.
These protests died down quickly when the general level of ability among the
Africans outstripped that of most of the other operatives.

There were many threats to the colonies—in fact they rose with a terrifying
regularity—and the Croatoan tried to meet them. When possible, colonies
dispatched reinforcements to their stricken siblings. It was this unity that enabled
the group to weather the revolution. Maybe it was also the fact that none of the
members were obliged to pay taxes (a privilege that has never been extended to
the Checquy in Britain, I might add. You wouldn't believe how much I pay in
taxes) and that visiting Checquy representatives treated them with profound
respect. Still, they were realists, recognizing that their mission was as much
about protecting the people as it was about being loyal to the throne.

During the Revolutionary War, the Croatoan operatives did not fight on
either side. The massive carnage and chaos of the various battles excited some
of the more exotic local wildlife, and teams were occupied with quelling the
gigantic mollusks that liked to descend upon isolated farmsteads and feast on
the families. By the time the war was over, the Croatoan had been decreased
by half, with heavy casualties inflicted by the desperate operations and by
incidental violence from the war.

At this point, the remaining Croatoan forces found themselves in an awk-
ward situation. They were agents of a government that had been firmly invited
to leave the country. If they revealed themselves to George, Ben, Thomas,
and the rest of the gang, they might be told to bugger off. Or there was always
the good old hanging. Jefferson and Franklin were supposed to be fairly open-
minded, but some of the older Croatoan members were still wary of revealing
themselves to anyone. However, the country was as much theirs as it was
anyone else's. And it was clear that no one in the new, still somewhat confused
government was close to even comprehending the supernatural horrors that
strutted across the nighttime landscape, let alone doing battle with them.
Bewildered and exhausted, the remnants of the Croatoan continued to protect

their neighbors and sent out politely desperate letters to the Checquy asking for instructions.

Meanwhile, the members of the Checquy Court back in England had been having its own problems. Something unpleasant had been born in Cornwall, and putting it down had occupied the attention of the entire Court. On September 3, 1783, when the Treaty of Paris was signed and ratified, the Checquy were recuperating, burying their dead, and just starting to turn their attention back to the parts of the world that weren't Cornwall. The arrival of letters from the Croatoan prompted the Crimson Lord to scream "For fuck's sake!" while in church.

Although the Croatoan was performing vital services for the good of humanity, the Checquy decided that they couldn't really ask King George for the funding to keep their American counterparts in business. The new country's government would need to be approached, subtly. The Croatoan would send one person to the new government to explain their mission and offer their services. Someone with abilities garish enough to impress the authorities. Someone who could easily escape if the newly elected president hastily reached for a musket. Until they could be certain that the government had accepted them, the Croatoan was urged to keep their heads down and behave.

The chosen representative was a Bishop, a former slave named Shadrach. His appearance in George Washington's home was suitably inexplicable and would have made a great impression on the president had he been there. Unfortunately, Washington had elected to spend the day inspecting some troops. Fortunately, Shadrach's entrance out of a cloud of moths and his impeccable manners bemused Martha Washington enough that she agreed to let him stay until her husband came home. For several hours, the first First Lady and the ex-slave sat in the parlor and Shadrach explained all about the Croatoan and their mission. Martha was a remarkably open-minded person and was sensible enough to appreciate that having the Croatoan would be a good thing for the fledgling nation.

Over a cup of untaxed tea, Martha and Shadrach hammered out the details of the Croatoan's absorption into the government. The negotiations were terrifying in their complexity, and the supernatural community still disputes who was the shrewder negotiator. Regardless, when George Washington arrived home, he found himself in possession of a covert supernatural agency.

Historians have noted that George Washington was quite the spymaster and spent a large portion of his budget on intelligence. Well, I can tell you that a sizable cut of that was spent on the activities of the Croatoan. In many ways, the Croatoan's organization mirrored that of the Checquy. It, too, received a ridiculously oversize budget and retained a hierarchical structure, despite protestations by Martha that it was not in keeping with the new ideals of the nation to have a ruling Court. Shadrach, however, had been very firm. But unlike the Checquy, the Croatoan was denied the right to forcibly extract powered children from their families. Martha, in fact, had been all for it, but the president was adamant on that point. Instead, the Croatoan members were obliged to lure their operatives with exuberant references to duty and responsibility, which worked almost as well as force and had the advantage of not being a flagrant mockery of the Constitution.

Finally, and crucially, it was agreed that the Croatoan, like the Checquy, would not interfere in nonsupernatural affairs. Its remit was strictly confined to the realm of the unnatural.

As the nation grew, so too did the Croatoan. However, they did not grow proportionally. For some reason, far fewer powered children were born in the continental United States than in the United Kingdom. This would have been cause for concern had it not been for the fact that there were also far fewer supernatural threats. This is not to say that there were no problems. It was in America that the mathematically created Irregularities arose, warping the very material of time and space while secretly manipulating the silent-film industry. The Cult of the Estrangement. The Horseman of Famine. The Rattling God. All of them were dire, but in terms of sheer number, supernatural threats did not seem to be too much of a problem in the United States.

Richard Swansea, before he died of repeated decapitation by a spurned (and increasingly bewildered) civilian lover, had noticed this trend, and a possible explanation was found in his diaries. Swansea's close friendship with the Native Americans had allowed him to observe their rites and practices. He postulated that a series of protections had been laid in place, woven into the very fabric of the land. Even as the tribes diminished, their work endured, and the continent remained relatively free of paranormal manifestations.

Despite the state-mandated separation of the two organizations, the Croatoan and the Checquy continued to maintain excellent relations. Formal *arrangements were avoided initially, but they communicated regularly. Scarcely a decade went by without a member of one Court visiting the Court across the ocean. In 1850, a formal agreement—the Sororitas Pact—was entered into, codifying the many bonds of friendship between the two groups. Among the features of this agreement were the establishment of the List, the commitment to the extradition of transgressors, and the solemn and binding promise that neither organization would consent to be part of a war against the other's country. The List was a catalog of threats each group regarded as most dire. Any developments that involved a threat on the List were to be shared immediately.*

There were even a few collaborative efforts. During the American Civil War, the Croatoan called in reinforcements when the gigantic mollusks, excited by the violence, rose again and stalked the land. In 1903, the Checquy appealed to their American siblings when a portal opened in Hong Kong and demons began infiltrating the community. In 1989, the two groups coordinated the suppression of the animated dead on Hawaii—a state that did not enjoy the mystic immunity of its continental brethren. The success of these campaigns served to strengthen the bonds of friendship.

Today, the Croatoan members are our staunchest allies. They know secrets that not even our countrymen know. They are fewer than we are, yet they police a territory many times larger than ours. Personally, I have nothing but the greatest respect for them.

Well, that's all very nice, thought Myfanwy. *But did you ever actually meet any of them? Am I going to need to acknowledge any private jokes? Do I need to be asking after their kids?* Myfanwy flipped helplessly through the binder, but nothing caught her eye. She looked at her watch and realized how little time she had to get changed. Fortunately, the one thing she was not lacking was a whole bunch of appropriately businesslike suits. By the time Ingrid came to announce the Americans, she had pillaged the wardrobe, scurried back down to the office, and was looking sufficiently formal.

16

Rook Myfanwy Thomas of the Checquy, I present Bishop Shantay Petoskey of the Croatoan," announced Ingrid in ringing tones. *What did she do, take elocution lessons?* thought Myfanwy, blushing furiously. The echoes were still bouncing noisily around the room when Bishop Petoskey walked in and Myfanwy opened the eyes she'd closed tight in embarrassment. She looked at Petoskey and felt her eyes widen. Whatever she'd expected, Shantay Petoskey was not it.

The woman was maybe five years older than her, and lovely. She was black, slim, and tall tall tall. She was dressed in something that might have been either horrendously expensive or distressingly cheap, and it looked absolutely glorious on her.

Please let her have slept her way to the top, thought Myfanwy. *No one deserves to be this beautiful and clever too.*

Petoskey had an expression on her face that implied she was trying not to burst into laughter.

"Yes, thank you for that lovely introduction, Ingrid," said Myfanwy.

"It's tradition," said Ingrid calmly.

"Yes, of course it is," said Myfanwy. "Bishop Petoskey," she said, nodding her head in a bizarre gesture that was intended to be formal and gracious but probably looked ridiculous.

"Rook Thomas, it's lovely to meet you," said Petoskey. "And please, call me Shantay."

"And I'm Myfanwy," she replied. *Oh, thank God, we've never met!* she thought. She looked carefully beyond Shantay, but all she saw was Ingrid going back to her desk. "I'm sorry, I thought Ingrid said both Bishops were coming."

"Bishop Morales wasn't feeling well, so she stayed at the hotel."

"Oh, I hope it's nothing serious," said Myfanwy.

"It's the traveling. It exhausts her," explained Shantay. "We knew she wouldn't be coming to this meeting."

"Never mind. Three-quarters of an hour ago I didn't know that there was going to be a meeting, so really it's no big deal."

I can't believe I just said that.

"I can't believe you just said that," said Shantay. There was a brief moment of terrible tension, during which Myfanwy braced herself for a declaration of war. Then Shantay smiled broadly. "You're much funnier than they led me to believe." She winked, and Myfanwy smiled back, liking this woman very much.

It dawned on her that they were both still standing. "I'm terribly sorry," she said. "Let's sit down. Not there!" She stopped Shantay from sitting in the deliberately uncomfortable chair. "Let's sit on the couches. Would you like a steaming beverage of some sort?" Soon, they were ensconced in the depths of the couch and Ingrid had furnished them both with cups of coffee.

"So, Shantay!" said Myfanwy, settling back comfortably and letting the cushions absorb her.

"Yes, Myfanwy?" asked Shantay with equal comfort and amusement.

"What brings you so abruptly to England? Not that we're not ecstatic to see you."

"Oh, naturally. To begin with, our entire Court was very impressed with the report you penned," said the Bishop, carefully arranging her dress around her. "And it proved remarkably timely."

"Oh?"

"Yes. Four hours ago, a team of our Pawns acquired an individual who entered the country through LAX. She was examined thoroughly and proved to have some very specific implants." Shantay paused meaningfully. "They weren't silicone."

"Let me guess," said Myfanwy dryly. "Grafter enhancements?" Shantay nodded grimly. "Crap," she sighed. "Was it the dogs that brought her to your attention?"

"No," said Shantay. "We hadn't set up the dog thing yet."

"Oh, really?"

"Yeah, we followed her because she was from Belgium," said Shantay bluntly.

"Interesting," said Myfanwy weakly. "I don't know if that's going to work here. And she just went nuts in the airport?"

"Well, she *might* have been freaked out by the three albinos who were following her" came the answer. "But they were pretty discreet. Seriously, she just popped without any provocation."

"That's alarming."

"Extremely. As soon as we were informed, Bishop Morales and I made arrangements to come here." *And all this happened two hours ago,* marveled Myfanwy. *It's probably best I don't ask.* "The Grafters represent a credible danger to both our countries," continued Shantay. "The appearance of one was cause enough for concern, but two in such a short period of time... well, that's a bit more disturbing."

"Is the subject still alive?" Myfanwy asked.

"Yeah, although it wasn't easy subduing her," said Shantay darkly. "She managed to kill thirteen people in the airport."

"Not civilians?"

"Four civilians, nine Pawns."

"Oh God. I'm so sorry," Myfanwy said. "Is the public aware?"

"It's impossible to conceal something like this when it happens in an airport. The only things we managed to hide were some of the more bizarre aspects. Fortunately, none of our Pawns activated their powers in view of the public."

"Then how—" wondered Myfanwy.

"Sharpshooters" came the terse answer.

"Really? Our guy turned out to be bulletproof."

"We didn't use bullets."

"Ah. Please accept my deepest sympathies, and those of the entire Checquy, for this tragedy."

Shantay nodded her acceptance. "Your Chevaliers will be officially informed within the hour, but we wanted to be here for the inevitable conference."

"Right. Forgive me, but you said that the subject is still alive. Have you begun to interrogate?"

"We've had no luck. We've secured her in our place in Nevada, but she's put herself into some sort of coma state, and so far none of our folks can rouse her."

"One of our Pawns had some success waking Van Syoc," said Myfanwy, thinking back to the careful ministrations of Dr. Crisp. "I'm sure we could work out some sort of arrangement. Dr. Crisp is our chief information extractor. He's a palm reader and haruspex, so he can read a person inside and out. He's currently up to his elbows in Grafter, but he must be able to get more information out of a living person than a dead one."

"If he can't, we have a woman who's pretty good with the dead," said Shantay. "And I don't mean to be rude, but didn't Dr. Crisp kill the last person he interrogated?"

Myfanwy paused. "No, Dr. Crisp didn't kill Van Syoc. The Grafters did." She explained everything Dr. Crisp had told her.

"Christ!" said Shantay. "So the woman we have in custody... they could order her to self-destruct?"

"No one has to order anything," said Myfanwy. "They can do it themselves."

"Even worse," said Shantay. "I'll get on the phone and see if they can put her somewhere that's signal-proof."

"Good idea. But don't be disappointed if it doesn't work out. We had Van Syoc stored five stories beneath street level. I'll ask Dr. Crisp to talk to them; he may have some ideas." For a few moments the two women ignored each other as Shantay spoke urgently into her cell phone and Myfanwy explained the situation to Ingrid. When they had both given instructions, they turned back to each other.

"Lunch?" asked Myfanwy.

"I'd love to," said Shantay.

Dear You,

I find research, even research to find out who wants to kill me, rather soothing. After all, dealing with vast amounts of information is what I do anyway. Most of the information is available through our in-house computer system. It's a closed network, so no computer that contains any reference to Checquy material is connected to the World Wide Web. E-mails from one Checquy office to another go through one of our satellites, so there's no chance some obnoxious American teen with too much time on his hands can hack into our system. There are no crossovers, and if you think setting up that sort of thing is expensive, you have no idea.

Anyway, I can pull up most of the stuff on my computer, and my position as Rook gives me access privileges to practically everything. So I scan through files and files and files. Every once in a while, I need something that hasn't been put into the computers. If the material is available in the Rookery, I walk down to the archives, which are a very handsome part of the building. Dark green carpets, large oaken bookcases, quiet scholars—I like it there. I like following a trail of information, moving from shelf to shelf, passing by glass cases that hold dignified dead things, and then moving through the metal door to the vaults.

In the vaults, there are aisles and aisles of secrets. Tall cabinets with shining wood drawers. Folders sealed with wax. Boxes of orderly papers. And then I go past those rooms, put on a coat, and walk into the cold-storage area, where heavy steel cabinets guard the details.

It's always there in the details.

Some things, however, aren't available online or in the Rookery, and if they're in one of our other London facilities, I go over on the weekend and prowl through the stacks of the Annexe or Apex House. If the records are somewhere else, I have them shipped over, and battered folders that Ingrid has to sign for show up on my desk, shrink-wrapped in plastic, with various seals stuck all over them. I always like looking at the names of the places they've come from. Bath, Stirling, the Orkneys, the Isle of Man, Manchester, Portsmouth, Edinburgh, Whitby, Exeter. We're all over the place.

And now I am trawling through the financial figures, which are not hundreds but thousands of pages long. The old Checquy financial methods and systems were nightmarishly convoluted, and even the new arrangements are as complex as you would expect of any gigantic quasi-independent government agency that operates all over the world in secret. Numbers writhe in front of my eyes—account numbers, transaction numbers, staff ID numbers, authorization numbers, destination numbers. I have gotten my feet wet in slush funds, been dubious about trust funds, and asked discerning questions about discretionary funds.

Why am I trawling through the financial records? Well, it's because I have found in the course of my career that even in this secret world of power and mysticism and hidden wonders, it still usually comes down to the money. And I wonder if my abilities with figures and finances combined with my access to the records of the Checquy are the reason that someone in the Court will destroy me. Perhaps they fear that I will catch them out in some financial wrongdoing.

Which, as it turns out, I may have done. It's not huge, but it looks as if Sir Henry's and Gestalt's finances are both a little . . . unorthodox. Now, it may simply be the result of both of them having very peculiar lives. Sir Henry enjoys an extended life span and has operated under a couple of different names and identities, so there are issues there. Money has gotten lost. Meanwhile, Gestalt receives the salary of four people, but it's not clear how many people's worth of tax he pays.

The thing is, this is not concrete. I don't know for certain that any fraud has been committed by either of them. To confirm any wrongdoing—to go through their finances—would take more time than I have. What I have found would be enough, however, to warrant a massive investigation. Which is why it forms part of my blackmail contingency plan.

But I don't think either one's financial impropriety is enough to warrant my destruction. It's got to be something else that leads to my betrayal. Thus, every evening, every morning, every car ride, and every lunch hour (on the rare occasions that I get one), when I'm not scrutinizing the details of the Court's personnel records, I'm going through financial records. Of course, the Checquy's assets are vast and varied, and I can't account for everything. But in my role as Rook, I've ordered double audits of the major vaults and had them done by rival sections in an effort to ensure that there's no collaboration. In the meantime, I'm personally reviewing the finances of the bigger projects in the Checquy portfolio. These are quite complex, which makes it easy for financial jiggery-pokery to take place.

It also makes them a complete bitch to review.

At the moment, I am mired hip-deep in the funding that is allocated to the Estate every year, and make no mistake—it's a lot of money. It would have to be. Every person who comes out of there at the age of nineteen has the equivalent of a thorough education through university, rigorous military training, and as complete a mastery of his or her powers as possible. The budget has to include the facilities of the best public school in the country, the equipment for diagnosing and testing a wide variety of superhuman abilities, the accommodations for a student population of genetically unstable people, the wages for the best-qualified and most open-minded teachers in the world, and security to keep all this a secret. Not to mention therapy for everyone concerned.

I'm telling you all this because, as a result of my weeks and weeks of after-hours studying and reviewing and anal-retentive tracings of moneys, I have found another irregularity, one that may be big enough to justify destroying me.

And as soon as I've taken an aspirin, I am going to chase it down.

Yours with a headache,

Me

Well, this is going to be much nicer than the homemade sandwich I brought to work," said Myfanwy after they'd been ferried to the most exclusive restaurant in the city and seated in a pool of sunshine. "Shantay's an interesting name. Is it short for something?"

"Not so far as I know," said Shantay. "Why, is yours short for something?"

"Myfanwy? What could it be short for?"

"God alone knows, but people's names are weird. Especially those made-up names."

"Is your name made up?" Myfanwy asked curiously.

"No," said Shantay.

"So what kind of name is it?"

"Uh, Shantay comes from French," said Shantay, accepting a glass of wine from an obsequious waiter.

"And what's the Petoskey part? You don't look Polish."

"It's Chippewa, means 'the Rising Sun.' Don't feel bad, it always confuses people."

"At least you can be relatively certain that you're pronouncing yours correctly."

"Yeah, where *does* Myfanwy come from? Is it Scottish?"

"Welsh."

"Really? I know nothing about the Welsh," said Shantay conversationally.

"No, me either."

"Didn't your parents tell you about your heritage?" asked the American Bishop distractedly as she beckoned the waiter back over. "My folks are always telling me about my various cultural and ethnic backgrounds. Actually, we'll take the whole bottle." This last part was said to the waiter, who was clearly going to be earning his tip today.

"I don't actually know my parents," said Myfanwy, carefully adjusting her sunglasses. The terrace of this restaurant was *the* place to be eating in London of a sunny afternoon. The air was cool, but elegant heaters had been set up. Normally, one needed to be extremely famous to get a table on the terrace, but somehow, Ingrid had managed to cultivate very good relationships with every restaurateur in the city. When Myfanwy and Shantay turned up, one carrying a credit card that appeared to be made out of actual gold and the other looking like a Nubian goddess, they had quickly been placed in the favored spot, seated ahead of a group of shrill movie stars who had apparently been waiting for ten minutes.

"You don't know your parents?" Shantay repeated.

"No, I was taken from them at the age of nine," said Myfanwy, hazarding a taste of the wine.

"Oh my God, I forgot. That's what you do here, isn't it?" said Shantay in horror.

"Mm-hm," confirmed Myfanwy.

"You know, not to be rude," said Shantay. "But I really can't believe that you take children from their parents."

"It's tradition," Myfanwy replied, deciding on a food item that had a long and detailed menu description. If she was going to be charging massive amounts to the Checquy expense account, she wanted something that would involve a lot of work for the chef. "People like us are sort of considered to be the property of the nation."

"Well, we had a similar tradition over in the States—people as property. And then we had a little war that sort of established that tradition would end."

"Of course," said Myfanwy. At that moment, a waiter appeared and took their orders—a procedure that took longer than usual because both women insisted on reading out the descriptions of the food in their entirety.

"So do you remember your parents?" said Shantay once the waiter had tottered away, weighed down with culinary adjectives.

"Not at all," said Myfanwy, with complete honesty.

"And that doesn't bother you?" asked Shantay.

"Not really," said Myfanwy, shrugging. She wondered vaguely how Thomas had felt. "So how did *you* end up in the Croatoan?"

"I tested early. We have this whole program—very thorough. We've got so few manifestations that we can't afford to miss any possibilities. Anyway, there my parents were, in Flint, Michigan. Ever been there?" she asked suddenly.

"I think I've heard of it," said Myfanwy. "Wasn't there a unicorn running around there last year?"

"Nah, that was East Lansing," said Shantay dismissively. "Anyway, back when I was little, my parents were having a pretty hard time of it, especially with three kids."

"I think I was one of three as well," said Myfanwy.

"Oh, yeah? Which one were you?"

"I'm fairly certain that I was the middle child," she replied, trying to remember.

"I was the oldest," said Shantay. "And though we weren't starving, we weren't far away from it. Then they get a very official-looking letter."

"From the government?"

"No, from some extremely expensive boarding school out in New Hampshire, offering free room and board and tuition."

"Well, then," said Myfanwy. "Thank heavens for the scrupulous honesty of the American government's supernatural department." She paused in her good-natured use of sarcasm as a blunt instrument. "But how does this constitute a more ethical system than ours?"

"My parents had a choice in the matter. Yours, I am led to believe, did not."

"Yes, although there are certain advantages to our approach. Were there any other perks?"

"I got to go home during vacations," said Shantay.

"Well, you've certainly got me beat there," said Myfanwy.

The food proved to be delicious. After dessert, they discussed the intricacies of their nations' security arrangements as they were whisked back to the Rookery.

"Rook Thomas," said the driver, "it looks as if those protesters have decided to set up a barricade in front of the parking entrance. Security is working at moving them on, but it may take a while."

"You can just drop us out in front then," said Myfanwy, pulling on her gloves. "Thank you, Martin." As the two women got out of the car, they eyed the protesters with distaste.

"Have you thought about siccing the police on them?" asked Shantay.

"I think it would just bring the press here," said Myfanwy, whose eye had been caught by a familiar-looking woman across the street.

"Maybe you could blame it on some sort of gang turf war?"

"This is London, not LA," Myfanwy said. "And besides, this is the financial district." The conversation broke off as the familiar-looking woman crossed the street and approached them.

"Excuse me," said the young woman. "I'm sorry to bother you."

"Yes?" asked Myfanwy. *She really looks familiar—is she in the Checquy?*

"Is...are you Muvvahnwee Thomas?"

"I guess," said Myfanwy. "I'm sorry, have we met?"

"My name is Bronwyn." The girl looked at her hesitantly, waiting for some reaction. "Bronwyn Thomas. I'm your sister."

17

They stared at each other, the woman claiming to be a sister named Bronwyn with a look of expectancy in her eyes, and Myfanwy completely stunned. Even watching Gestalt strangle Dr. Crisp hadn't struck her as forcibly as this revelation. She looked at the woman, recognizing her own features, albeit much prettier (gorgeous, really, let's admit it), along with a taller body and long, fashionably highlighted blond hair.

That's why she looked familiar, Myfanwy thought numbly. She could see Shantay gaping, but all the sounds in the world appeared to have been muted. Instead, there was only Bronwyn, and she felt a connection, a feeling almost of familiarity. As if this girl fit into her life, filling a sister-shaped hole.

What is this? Is it even possible? she thought, looking at eyes that were exactly like hers. *Is this really my sister?*

I should say something, it's been a minute.

"My God," she said, and then couldn't think of anything else to say. "Hi." She hesitated, and then put out her hand. The woman calling herself Bronwyn looked a little startled, but then took it with a smile, and they squeezed tentatively.

"This must be a tremendous shock," said Bronwyn. "Me just coming out of nowhere."

"It's the most astounding thing that's ever happened to me," said Myfanwy. "The most astounding thing..." She trailed off, still staring, and still holding Bronwyn's hand.

"I'm Shantay. I work with Myfanwy," said Shantay flatly, stepping forward. "It looks like she's in a little bit of shock."

"Hi," said Bronwyn.

"You know, I am *so* sorry to do this to you," said Shantay, "but there is a really important thing we have to get to. And it just can't wait."

There's a thing we have to get to? thought Myfanwy weakly.

"Bronwyn, you must give me all your contact details. Your address and so on," Myfanwy said. "And I'll give you mine, and we'll make a plan to meet." She let go of Bronwyn's hand reluctantly and looked down. *She has the same hands as me,* she thought giddily. *Christ, and I didn't even take off my gloves when I held her hand!* She winced. "You can come to my house, and we'll learn about each other," she said in a rush. Even as she spoke, though, she was already aware of the hundreds of complications spooling out from this development.

They traded details and made arrangements for that evening. Myfanwy said that she would call later to set a time. There was an awkward good-bye, and she let Shantay lead her into the Rookery.

"Well," said Shantay, once they were in the elevator, "that kind of came out of left field."

"Yeah." Myfanwy sniffed. Shantay handed her a tissue. "I didn't take off my gloves when I took her hand," fretted Myfanwy. "I was so gob-smacked, I didn't even *think* of it."

"Thank God!" exclaimed Shantay. "Girl, if that woman had tried to swoop in for a kiss, or *any* skin-to-skin contact, I would've beat her skull in right there on the sidewalk."

"What?"

"Are you serious? Some girl comes up to you on the street, you don't know *what* she is! Hell, she could be a Grafter agent!"

"I know that I have a sister, and this woman looks exactly like me—well, bits of her do," amended Myfanwy, thinking of those long legs.

"Oh, please, you know what the Grafters can do," said Shantay. "Sure, she looks a lot like you, but we're tussling with people who are pretty much the gods of plastic surgery and weird biological weapons. Shit, forget touching you—if she'd looked like she was gonna even *breathe* on you, I'd have moved in."

"Shantay," said Myfanwy, "if this woman was going to kill me, she didn't need to use some Grafter weapon. That guy in the B and B had a gun." She felt a sinking feeling at the thought.

"True!" realized Shantay. "That girl is lucky she isn't a headless corpse on the street right now."

"Well, that might have caused a few problems," said Myfanwy. "But you're right about this chick. I don't know anything about her. I'll need to have her vetted before I let her in my house. I'll need dossiers on Bronwyn Thomas, including photos, personal history, travel history, where she's living. The real Bronwyn Thomas could be in Australia now..."

"You okay?" asked Shantay. "I'll help you with the background check. We can tear through it."

"Yeah, I just...I hope it really is her, and that there are no problems. It would be nice to have a sister."

"Maybe she really is your sister," said Shantay. "We'll check everything, and if it all works out, then you'll be having drinks with her tonight. In which case, you've got a whole bunch of other problems."

"Like what?"

"Like where you're gonna tell her you've been all her life."

Myfanwy sat on one end of her couch at home, her bare feet propped up on a footstool, her head leaning back. Despite a brimming glass of brandy in her hand and the placid presence of Wolfgang on her lap, she was still feeling nauseated about the prospect of Bronwyn's arrival.

She and Shantay had spent the afternoon in a frenzy of security vetting. Myfanwy hadn't liked the idea of anyone—not even Ingrid—knowing that she was researching her birth sister. Questions would have been asked, and the Checquy might have said there was no way

Myfanwy would be permitted to see her. If this Bronwyn really *was* her sister, then Myfanwy was determined to know her.

And if she wasn't, well, then something would have to be done.

So Myfanwy had had Ingrid scrub all afternoon appointments from her schedule, and she and Shantay had gone into her office and shut the door behind them. Then they'd set about learning everything they could about Bronwyn Laura Thomas. Being Rook meant that she had practically unlimited access to government information about its citizens, and her predecessor's focus on research and preparation meant that she could do most of it from her office.

Bronwyn Laura Thomas did not live in Australia. She was living in London, in a flat near Marble Arch. She was enrolled at the University of the Arts London. No criminal record. She'd never left the country to go anywhere, let alone Belgium. Her Internet use was orthodox—almost painfully so. No e-mails to anyone in Belgium, or anyone dubious. There wasn't time for them to check every person she'd e-mailed in the past six months, but a random selection had shown nothing suspicious. The number for her mobile phone was the one Myfanwy had been given that afternoon.

The person in the photos they accessed was identical to the one they had spoken to.

"Well, it all looks okay," Shantay had said. "It could actually be her."

"I think it's her," said Myfanwy. "I really do."

"So, what are you going to do?"

Myfanwy sat and bit her lip. Since she'd entered into this life, there had been very little that filled her with genuine pleasure. The balance in her bank account. The meal she'd eaten while dining with Lady Farrier. Her spontaneous friendship with Shantay. The prospect of meeting—of *having*—a sister was delightful. She was tired of being an orphan. She wanted a family. Or at least more than one friend.

"I'm going to call her," decided Myfanwy, and she reached for the phone.

"Wait," said Shantay. "Don't call the mobile number—call her home number."

"She didn't give me her home number," objected Myfanwy. The penny dropped. "Okay, fine."

She'd dialed the home number, and gotten a Bronwyn Thomas who had been expecting her call. They'd chatted a little and agreed that Myfanwy would send a car to pick up Bronwyn. Which would be happening in five minutes. Val, the housekeeper, whom she'd finally met, had been very excited about the prospect of Myfanwy's sister coming.

"You know that I've always worried about you, Ms. Thomas," she'd said in her thick northern accent. "You keep too much to yourself. It's not healthy for you young women to work all day, and then come in and fall asleep on the couch. I'm so glad your sister is visiting. Maybe she'll be able to talk some sense to you." And she'd insisted on preparing a huge tray of food. "It's been how long since you saw each other?"

"Years," said Myfanwy, with perfect accuracy.

"Years! That's absolutely dreadful! That's typical with you career girls. You get the job, and just forget entirely about everything else. Do you know that this is the first time I've heard you talk about your family?" Myfanwy had realized when she'd met Val that Thomas had employed her for two reasons. First, it was kind of comforting having someone boss you about your life, and second, she was a marvelous cook and housekeeper. Fearful of offending her, she'd just meekly agreed with everything Val suggested, including the brandy.

"Normally, I don't encourage drinking," she'd said. "But I've never seen you this nervous." Val poured Myfanwy a drink and told her to sit back and relax. "I'll let your sister in, and then I'll head home."

So now Myfanwy was stroking Wolfgang's fur, although she hadn't yet drunk any of the brandy. Instead, she was trying to simultaneously remain alert and relax her aching muscles. Those damn shoes, the ones she felt obliged to wear when playing the role of Rook, were murder on her ankles. She was so focused on staring at the ceiling that she didn't hear the doorbell ring, didn't hear Val open the front door, and then didn't realize that Bronwyn had entered the room.

"Myfanwy?" said Bronwyn shyly. Myfanwy startled, and looked around anxiously.

"Hey! Come in. I'd get up, but I have Wolfgang here, and he doesn't like to be jostled," she explained, gesturing helplessly toward the rabbit, who seemed quite comfortable. Bronwyn's face lit up, and she came over to stroke the bunny.

"He's darling!" said Bronwyn. "How long have you had him?"

"Oh, gosh, I don't know," said Myfanwy truthfully. "Do you want to take him?" Bronwyn sat down beside her on the couch, and Myfanwy carefully transferred Wolfgang. "So," she said nervously.

"So."

"I don't know about you," said Myfanwy, "but when I woke up this morning, this wasn't at all what I expected to happen. How on earth did you manage to find me?"

"It wasn't easy," said Bronwyn. "I was in a café in the city, looking at stuff on the Web, and you know how you look yourself up? I did that, and then, out of curiosity, I typed your name in to see what would happen."

Ah, the mystery Googler, thought Myfanwy. *Well, I guess we can close that case file.*

"I got absolutely no results, other than some chick in New Zealand who knits and felts woolen pears and sells them on the Internet. But it made me curious about you, so I looked around. I looked for a death certificate—they're public-domain documents, you know—but I couldn't find one anywhere."

"I did not know that," said Myfanwy. *I would have thought the Checquy would have tidied that sort of thing up.*

"Oh, yes. So I knew you were alive, and I have a friend who works in the tax office. He didn't want to, but he tracked down a Myfanwy Alice Thomas who lives here. You're the only Myfanwy Alice Thomas in the UK."

Of course, thought Myfanwy. *Death and taxes. They get you every time.*

"That's really impressive," said Myfanwy.

"I've always been a pretty good researcher," said Bronwyn modestly.

Oh, so that *we share,* thought Myfanwy, *but you didn't inherit the power to make people shit themselves. You've got to love the randomness of genetics.*

"I still wasn't sure that it was you. I came to this address, and I was trying to get the nerve up to go and buzz at the gate. But then I saw you and you looked so much like my mum. So I followed you to that building in the city. I went in the front, but your name wasn't in the building directory.

"I know it was kind of stalkerish," continued Bronwyn, "but I hung around the building. I thought that if you didn't come out the front, then I could just come back here and try buzzing at the gate. And then you were there, right across the street." She shook her head in amazement, and it was clear to Myfanwy that Bronwyn was trying to figure out how to ask all sorts of questions. So she beat her to it.

"Bronwyn, you're twenty-five, right?"

"Yeah, I was only three, when you . . . went away. So I really didn't remember you at all," she added guiltily.

That makes two of us! thought Myfanwy, as she tried to think of what else to say. There was an awkward pause, and then Bronwyn settled for the easiest opening gambit. "I like your house a lot. How long have you lived here?"

"Oh . . . a couple of years," said Myfanwy vaguely. Since she'd spent most of the afternoon vetting Bronwyn, she hadn't had a great deal of time to prepare any convincing stories. "I got a big promotion and bought this place. And then spent ages decorating it."

"It's lovely. So, what is it you do?"

"I work for the government," explained Myfanwy. "I'm a specialist on domestic affairs." She watched the light of interest die in Bronwyn's eyes, just as it was meant to. "I do a lot of supervisory stuff.

Long hours, not much social life, but I like it." And that was true, she realized. It wasn't just the administration she enjoyed, although she was good at it. She liked the whole thing.

"Okay, so I have to ask," said Bronwyn. "What happened? Jonathan told me that we had a sister, and there were some photos of you, but Mum and Dad never talked about you. For ages, I thought you'd died or something."

"Jonathan's our brother, right?" asked Myfanwy hesitantly. She had to be careful here, but she was also intensely curious.

"Don't you remember?" Bronwyn was incredulous.

"Not really," said Myfanwy. "I was young when I left, and then a lot of stuff happened."

"What kinds of stuff?"

"Well, it's complicated. What did your...*our*...father tell you? Or our mother?" asked Myfanwy, wary of contradicting any established stories.

"They never said. When Jonathan and I tried to talk to them about you, they just refused. Dad especially, he said that he didn't want us ever to ask him about it. That you were gone, and we should try to forget about you, and just get on with our lives." She kept her eyes firmly on Wolfgang as she talked, and Myfanwy got the impression that there had been bitter arguments over this matter. Shouting and silence and shame. People had been sent to bed without supper. She felt obscurely guilty.

"I had a medical problem," said Myfanwy. "And it was a very big deal—the odds of my living were really slim." Bronwyn looked at her with concerned eyes. "I'm pretty much okay now," she assured her, "but for a while, it was touch and go. Most of the time I was on a lot of drugs, completely out of it, in the closed wards," she invented on the spur of the moment.

"And that's why you couldn't visit," continued Myfanwy. "Our parents knew I was going to die and that they couldn't see me. So it must have been easier for them just not to think about it."

"What was wrong?" asked Bronwyn hesitantly.

"Complicated stuff, really rare," said Myfanwy vaguely. "You don't need to worry, it's not a genetic problem. But I really don't like talking about it."

"But you got better?"

"About four years ago, they figured out a drug regimen that let me function. Still, it was a huge deal getting me cleaned up. I'd been on some of the medication for years, and had a few pretty serious addictions going on," said Myfanwy, mildly impressed with how easily the lies were coming.

"That's dreadful!" exclaimed Bronwyn. "But you never thought of trying to contact us?" It was clear she didn't want to offend Myfanwy but also felt hurt. It was incomprehensible to her that her sister wouldn't immediately try to find her family.

"There was so much coming at me so fast," said Myfanwy. "I'd been living in this drug-induced fog. I was given help finding a flat, a job. I was so used to focusing exclusively on just one thing, there didn't seem room for anything other than work, and detox. I still hardly go out in the real world. I get nervous." She looked intently at Bronwyn, willing her not to be upset. "And my memories of you all were so vague. It was like a dream, when I thought about it at all."

Bronwyn nodded, looking dazed. It turned out her sister was a recovering drug addict and an agoraphobic.

"I don't know what to say," said Bronwyn. "This is a lot to process. It must have been so hard for you."

"Yeah, well," said Myfanwy, shrugging easily. "Them's the breaks, and I'm really grateful for how everything turned out."

"Yeah," said Bronwyn softly. She looked down at her hands, stroking Wolfgang.

"You okay?" asked Myfanwy uncertainly.

"Yeah, it's just that it would be intense if it were just a friend telling me this, and you're my sister," said Bronwyn, still staring down. She took a deep breath. "I feel like I'm already supposed to know all of it, like this is supposed to be part of *our* past, and the family just let you go. You must feel that way too, like we didn't even care." She looked up, and Myfanwy saw tears in her eyes. "There's no reason for you to feel anything for me, but I want you to know that even though I don't remember you, and maybe you don't remember me, I'm glad I found you. I really do want you to be my sister."

And Myfanwy felt those words within her heart.

"I do too," she said.

Then she was moving forward, and she and Bronwyn were holding each other and weeping, but laughing at the same time. As she embraced the woman, Myfanwy felt a flaring in her powers, as if gasoline had been poured onto a fire. She could sense the genetic ties she held with this girl, her own patterns mirrored, to a certain extent, within her sister. Myfanwy pushed gently away, examined Bronwyn at arm's length, and then drew her back in, laughing again.

Everything else seemed like a part of Thomas's life, she thought. *Something inherited. But this, this is mine as much as it could have been hers. This girl is the sister of this body, and this is just as much my body as Thomas's.* And with that, she felt herself finally relax into her own self.

Now," said Myfanwy after they'd calmed down and wiped their faces. "Tell me all about you. And the family."

"Oh God. Well, I hate having to tell you this, but our parents are dead," Bronwyn said sadly. This didn't come as a surprise; Myfanwy had read it in the files. But now, when her sister said it, she felt a shock go through her. Somehow, it was more real, more relevant. They weren't just the parents of a body she'd inherited, they were *her* parents. She felt a piercing regret, and she knew it showed on her face.

"They died eight years ago in a car accident," her sister continued. "It was a drunk driver. I moved up to London to live with Jonathan. He's a banker; he's thirty-three. When Mum and Dad died, he became my legal guardian. It wasn't easy, being in a new school and everything. I finished, but just barely. And then I bummed around for a couple of years, worked a bunch of crap jobs. Then Jonathan said I'd had enough time to get over it, so now I'm studying. We Thomases do better when we have a mission. You probably figured that out for yourself." They smiled at each other, and Myfanwy felt very strange. Seeing her own features stamped on someone else's face was somehow comforting.

"We believed you were still alive," said Bronwyn quietly. "Jonathan and I went through all their papers and found some documents."

Christ, have I just given a brilliantly detailed lie, only to get totally busted? Myfanwy thought in horror. *What did these documents say?*

"They were financial records. Mum and Dad had been receiving regular payments. Jonathan traced them through his work and found out that they were from the government. Some obscure department. We tried to track you down, but it was miles of red tape. And we had no idea where you were, what was happening. It just turned out easier not to think about it either. But the payments kept coming. They're paying for my university," said Bronwyn shyly.

Compensation from the Checquy, thought Myfanwy. *I wonder how much I'm worth.*

"What are you studying?" she asked.

"Fashion," said Bronwyn.

"Oh, fantastic! Maybe you can educate me," said Myfanwy. "I'm completely ignorant about all aspects of fashion."

"What? Look at the suit you're wearing!"

Myfanwy looked at herself. "Yeah?" It wasn't a suit that screamed *Look at me!* In fact, it looked like it would prefer if you didn't look at it at all.

"Well, it's really good quality," said Bronwyn, fingering the cloth appreciatively. "And it costs more than I make in three months of work as a waitress."

"Yeah, well, my general approach is that if I pay a horrendous amount of money for a garment, people will overlook the fact that it looks terrible on me," said Myfanwy.

They stayed up late, and Myfanwy found out a great many details of her sister's life. She still lived with Jonathan. The only reason she hadn't brought their brother to Myfanwy's was that he was in Japan for a few weeks on business. Bronwyn wanted to be a designer but doubted both her talent and the possibility of finding employment.

She'd made only a few friends since moving to London and had no boyfriend.

"I know how that goes," said Myfanwy. "I've *never* had a boyfriend." *And no time even to think of having one,* she thought dispiritedly. Thomas's written explanation of her lack of a social life had been short, mildly regretful, and awkward. Much like Myfanwy imagined Thomas herself had been. That whole aspect of her life was going to require some thought. She'd found a battery-powered item in the drawer of the bedside table but was somewhat wary of using it. *Admittedly, it is mine. And it's only ever been used on my body. But not by me. This is an aspect of amnesia that people don't normally talk about.*

After she'd shown Bronwyn to the guest bedroom, Myfanwy went back down to the living room and finished the last of the brandy. She scooped up Wolfgang and put him in his night hutch. Then she lifted up the pillow on her end of the couch, took a gun from where it had been hidden, and locked it away in her office desk.

18

Dear You,

Well, I have hit an extraordinary amount of pay dirt. You know, there's a reason the FBI employs accountants and computer geeks. It's always about the money. And the whole electronics revolution has caused a tremendous amount of trouble for the illegally minded. Used to be, you could just take a handful of doubloons and spend them. The authorities couldn't really trace a doubloon. Now, however, there's always a trail. Especially if you're dealing with big bucks. That irregularity I mentioned earlier? Yeah, well, it turned out to be a lot of money. And I've figured out where it was redirected.

Tracking the missing money was actually kind of fun, especially compared to all those records of corporate credit card transactions that I had to wade through. That shit was just tedious. There's a reason that there's no TV show called CSI: Forensic Accounting. Although I will say that I now really, really know the Checquy, inside and out. And I know where the missing money went.

Compared to the total budget for the Checquy, the amount that was missing over the years wasn't that much, but it was enough to buy up a lot of land in the south part of Wales, throw up some buildings, and set about building a small army of superkids.

That's right: there's a second Estate.

Maybe that doesn't strike you as terribly astonishing, but I couldn't have been more surprised if there'd turned out to be a second royal family stashed away in the back valley where this second estate is. That's how big a deal it is. The first Estate represents the real core of the Checquy's power. Paranormal ability isn't what makes our operatives the best in the world, although their supernatural skills certainly give them an edge. They're the best because they're brought in at an early age and trained rigorously. This is how the Checquy remains so powerful and the reason the nightmares stay under the bed rather than climbing into it with the rest of us. And now there's another one, so whoever controls it holds an awfully big weapon, illegally.

I couldn't believe it, so I made myself go down there. I had a weekend off, and it was either go on a mini-break to Wales or stay in my house and go over administrative records. So, Friday afternoon after work, I loaded the car up, packed Wolfgang in his carrier, got behind the wheel, and began to drive.

I actually like to drive. One of the many perks of my position is not having to worry about speeding tickets, and I have enough money to afford a nice frivolous car with a good stereo. So, tearing down the road I managed to sing loud enough to justify the speed but not so loud that Wolfgang wouldn't be able to stand up without falling over.

Ah, Wales! Land of my forefathers! Our forefathers! You're part Welsh, did you know that? I mean, our family moved out of Wales a few generations ago, and though we probably have relatives scattered around somewhere, I don't recall ever meeting them.

Ever since I learned that in the near future, one of my compatriots will try to have me killed, I've become kind of paranoid. Frankly, I think that's justifiable. So I elected not to check into a B and B and slept outside in a sleeping bag.

I haven't slept outside in years, not since the wilderness training at the Estate. God, I hated wilderness training. I hated everybody in my group, and it didn't help that I was made to share a tent with Emmie, the girl who shot insects out of her mouth. But this time, I actually found it very soothing to sleep out in the open air. All snuggled up in my new sleeping bag, looking up at the stars, listening to Wolfgang fidget around in his carrier. There was no moon that night, and I was out in the dire wilderness of Wales, so there was no light pollution. Just five hundred million stars glittering down at me.

The next day, I drove farther into Wales, to some little nothing village where I made some very discreet inquiries. I felt uncomfortable at first, starting conversations with people I'd never met. I was worried that they would correct the way I pronounced my name. I mean, I look at that w in the middle, and I always worry that I don't say it right. Whoever heard of a silent w? Plus, I really thought that they were going to yell at me for sticking my nose into other people's business, but it was actually fairly easy. It turns out that ordinary people like to tell you about their lives, and the old ladies in the hair salon were gold mines of information.

As far as the residents of the village are concerned, the secret estate is some military installation that deals with very hush-hush materials. At least, I think that's what they said. Everybody I talked to had pretty thick accents. On the upside, I did get a nice haircut.

Nobody from the estate ever comes into the village. Trucks full of supplies drive down the main street early in the morning, but the drivers never so much as stop to pick up cigarettes. The estate itself is back in its own little steep-walled valley. There's one road in and out, and it goes through these woods that must date back to before the Romans. I found some underagers hanging hopefully around the pub and pumped them for information. It's funny; the bad kids of my childhood rebelled by trying to sneak off a secret military installation, and these kids do their best to sneak onto one.

According to Darren, Lucy, Ricky, and Maysie: "There's a place where the fence kind of skips over a gully, and you can slide underneath. You can sit under the trees with a six-pack and a pair of binoculars, and just watch the show. It's totally amazing."

This estate's very hush-hush reputation is likely the result of the weird things seen in the sky above it. Shapes coursing through the night, brilliant light bouncing off the clouds, and people ghosting along the lawns doing bizarre gymnastics routines. To the bored teens of the village, it's like having the Cirque du Soleil and a jet stunt team living next door. To me, it sounds like home.

Now, let me make this clear for you. There is only one Estate. It's not a case of putting all your eggs in one basket; it's a matter of keeping your valuables in a safe. All the genetic potential of the British Isles is there, a vast resource of wealth and power. And by putting them all in the same place, we ensure that they mesh. The Pawns of the Checquy work together so well because they all receive the same education in the same place.

One time I watched a documentary about guns. The thing that really struck me was how big a deal it was when gun parts started being interchangeable. You could take the hammer out of one gun and put it in another, and it would work. It meant that no gun was unique, and that they all could be repaired easily. It's the same with the Pawns. Most of them, despite their gigantic variety in terms of supernatural ability, can be slotted easily into a new team.

Ironically, it's generally the misfits who rise to the Court. None of us is standard Checquy. Even among the unusual, we're strange.

Anyway, the secret estate needed further investigation, and I wasn't about to trust anyone else, so I was going to have to check it out. The kids assured me that guards would periodically come along on these "mega-cool four-wheeler things with lights," but you could easily see them coming and hide. I wasn't terribly impressed with the security arrangements of this school. On the real Estate, hiding in the woods wouldn't protect you from the guards. For that matter, there wouldn't be a quaint little village nearby either. Still, this place was on a budget (I should know), and its main protection was its secrecy.

So that night, I put on the infiltration clothes I'd brought with me. Black everything, and a ski mask to boot, under which I was sweating like a goldfish in a wok. Most important were the gloves. I'd cut holes just big enough to reveal the very tips of my fingers.

Stepping into those woods, I was petrified. I'd felt so calm camping the night before. Now, every little sound was enough to freak me out. There was hardly any light and I could easily imagine some great beast from the dawn of time burbling out of the forest and dragging me off to its secluded glen. It's not that I have that great an imagination, it's just that I know what's out there. Thank God there was the gully to follow, or I would have gotten lost immediately. As it was, I had my eyes fixed on the gully so firmly that I actually walked into the fence. Luckily, this little enterprise lacked the funds for razor wire, or I'd be there still.

My heart was pounding as I slid under the fence, but it wasn't as bad as I'd thought it would be. When I was little, and my teachers rousted us out of bed for those midnight games, I hated it. I was fit enough, but I couldn't bear the knowledge that people I lived and studied with were going to reach out of the darkness and snatch me. I loathed the sudden shock when they swung out of a tree or leaped out of a pile of leaves and pinned me gleefully to the ground. I knew they weren't spiteful. It was just part of the game. Still, inevitably I would be caught first. I simply couldn't take the offensive.

On the other side of the fence, the trees were fewer and farther apart. I saw no sign of the guards, so I made my way to the edge of the woods. I wanted to see what kind of facility I was dealing with.

To begin with, it was ugly. Whoever set up this place had picked some prime real estate. But the site was so beautiful that it seemed a dreadful shame to have some no-account architect crap out the blocky structures that squatted on the lawns. One thing that caught my eye was the utter lack of windows in the buildings.

Also, it was small. There were only three or four buildings, and their facilities were pitiful. There wasn't even a cricket pitch. There were, however, several outdoor shooting ranges on this side of the installation.

I waited for a long time at the edge of the trees and shrank back into the shrubbery when one of those guards came zooming by. I thought back to my Estate training and the teacher who'd instructed us in subtle outdoor movement. He'd been in the SAS and had crawled through every kind of terrain known to man. I'd always been a disappointment to him, but he'd concealed his contempt well. If he'd seen the way these guards checked their fence lines, he'd have had them flogged. Maybe they'd grown complacent, secure in their secrecy. Or maybe this place couldn't afford the best.

After the guard passed by, I scuttled carefully across the lawns toward one of the buildings. They didn't even have floodlights! I blended in well in my black, but I wasn't naive—I knew I wasn't invisible. There were some fixed security cameras, but my rudimentary surveillance had turned them up with ease.

I slipped between the cameras and pressed myself against the wall, where a bush had been permitted to grow. Crouching down, I was fairly well concealed. I took some long, deep breaths and tried to calm myself. My heart was about to climb out of my bottom, but I was secretly kind of thrilled. My plan was actually working. I was almost ready to check out the door to the nearest building when I heard a sound—and I froze.

There was a metallic fnikt, *and a light gleamed as a man lit a cigarette, not two meters from me.*

Oh. My. Holy. Fuck.

Just thinking about it, I want to throw up. This guy, with a gun, had come out of the door for a smoke. And I had been about to walk around the corner and bump right into him. I wasn't shaking. I was rooted to the ground, which makes what happened next even more unexpected.

I reached my hand out, around the corner, and brushed my fingertips against his wrist. Electricity coursed between us, and, well, you know how it goes.

In fact, you're the only one who knows.

It was just the slightest of touches, but I reached out from inside and didn't let him feel me or see me. Did you know you can do that? Everybody's eyes have blind spots, and I created a new one that encompassed me. In fact, it wasn't just a blind spot. I cut myself entirely out of his perception. I could have stood in front of him and screamed, but as long as I kept contact with him, he wouldn't know I was there. It took concentration, but I managed it.

Now, I could have forced him to walk into the building, but it's very, very hard to compel someone who's conscious to do something without his knowing about it. And I didn't want him to realize that anything strange was happening that night. So we stood there for several minutes while he smoked and I sweated.

I took the opportunity to examine the guy. He was dressed in a green uniform with no insignia. He did, however, have a name tag that read GUSTAVSON. Finally, he flicked his cigarette butt away, turned, and went back inside. I, having carefully moved my hand from his wrist to the nape of his neck, followed him.

We walked down a long, tedious hallway. The interior designers for this estate, apparently having graduated from the same school as the architect, had elected to go with cinder-block walls painted the color of bile. The walls gleamed nauseatingly under the humming fluorescent tubes, and it was kind of like walking down someone's well-lit large intestine. Now, if you ever get a free moment and would like to set yourself a little challenge, try this. Find somebody who's taller than you (shouldn't be hard), put your fingers on the back of his neck, and then try to follow him as he walks around briskly. You can't break contact with him, and it's not a good idea to step on his heels. So I was trotting along after Gustavson, awkwardly nipping along on my tiptoes.

We passed doorways, but fortunately we didn't pass any other people. If we had, I would have had Gus shoot them and then abruptly reevaluated *my plans. Instead, Gus walked into his office, which turned out to be some sort of security hub. There were some monitors, and for a horrible moment I worried that there might be an alarm going off, that I had missed a camera. But all the outdoor views on the monitors were ones I'd carefully avoided. No alarms were sounding. I was becoming less and less impressed with this place's security. My guard settled back into his chair, spoke an authoritative "All clear" into his walkie-talkie, and peered without any real interest at the monitors. This was not terribly revealing. So I touched his mind and soothed him into a very deep sleep.*

Then I took a closer look around. On the monitors, I saw shooting ranges, a driveway, and a helipad. There were also some indoor views, and it was these I was most interested in. All of them had their lights on, which seemed like a shocking waste of electricity, but maybe this was because there were no windows. I saw a garage with some cars and trucks all painted an uninteresting brown. I saw a large room that seemed to be a distressingly cheap combination of dining hall and gymnasium.

There were two changing / shower rooms that were clearly designed to afford the bathers no privacy whatsoever. No barriers, no cubicles, just a row of showerheads. And the fact that there were cameras in there gave me the absolute creeps. These were for the students? At the Estate we'd each only shared a bathroom with one roommate. It doesn't pay to deprive adolescents of their privacy, especially the genetically variant types. And these chambers were completely spartan. No tiles, no paint, just cement. The closest they came to ornaments was a line of hooks along the wall. At least they kept the genders separate, unless it was a matter of kids with bizarre physical features in one room, and those without in the other.

Then I found the dormitories. Two rooms, with six beds lined up in one and eight in the other. The lights were glaring down on them, but the occupants seemed to be sleeping relatively peacefully. There were no real amenities in these rooms either. No chests of drawers for their clothes, no curtains around the beds to give them any privacy. This was like a prison. I thanked God I hadn't been sent here as a child.

Now, this was all fairly informative, but I needed to know more. There had to be offices, classrooms. Apparently, only the students and the grounds were monitored, but the compound included several other buildings. They had to be keeping the records somewhere. There was a map panel up on the wall, with little glowing bulbs that I realized were cameras and alarm sensors. After a bit of basic orientation, I figured out that I was in what the map coyly referred to as *Admin*. The other buildings were, variously, *Living Quarters, Instruction,* and *Physical Plant*—but the biggest by far was *Medical*. Since I didn't have the time to check out the other three, I went for a little walk around Admin. Plus, I'm a bureaucrat, so I'll always head for the filing cabinets.

My exploration yielded some storage rooms, a little kitchenette, and finally the offices. I was surprised to find that although their surveillance was primitive, they actually bothered to lock the doors. Maybe they worried that the students would wander around. Not that a locked door made a difference to me, since we'd all been rigorously trained in "the ladylike arts of breaking and entering," as my teacher had insisted on referring to them. I peeled off my fingertipless woolen gloves and pulled on a pair of latex ones. Finger-prints, you know. A little twiddling with some picks, and I was in an office like any other. Computers, coffee machine, dying plants. I carefully locked the door behind me—I didn't want one of Gus's friends wandering in.

Some memoranda on one of the desks identified this installation as *Camp Caius,* which to me sounded simultaneously military and recreational. Like a place you might send a fat Roman legionary for his summer holidays. The filing cabinets looked like they had the greatest potential for yielding useful information. Computers are all very well, but I can't pick their locks as easily as I can those on doors. So I let my gloved fingers do some walking. And I came up with quite a few interesting facts, although they seemed to be limited to the topics of finances and the students. The rest of the information must be kept in the archives or in a different office.

The earliest records I could find for this Camp Caius dated back twenty years. I skimmed the financial statements. All I was really looking for was confirmation that this was where those missing funds were going. And it was. I only had to look for those damn account numbers (which I'd memorized by that point, I'd looked over the records so often). I was also curious to see what they were spending their money on, since it was clearly not going toward any luxuries. It turned out that a sizable portion of the funds was *being blown on training fees and surgical facilities. I don't know who they were hiring as teachers at Camp Caius, but they were paying them more than the staff at the true Estate makes, and we get the best. The surgeons were making even more. I jotted down some names of instructors and doctors and then checked my watch.*

I figured I had another half hour before I needed to get out.

What next? I turned to the students' files. This school seemed to hold on to its kids for a while longer than the Estate. Students didn't leave until they were twenty-three, and then they all seemed to be forwarded on to some place called Albion. The only problem was that I couldn't find any information on what or where Albion might be. Still, wherever it was, it wasn't heavily populated. Camp Caius had only produced something like fifteen graduates in five years. Which made no sense. I mean, if they had fourteen students right now . . . Then I found out how many students died here. Quite a few. As in, more often than not—some in training exercises, most under the knife.

The really frustrating thing, however, was that there was no mention of any members of the Court. I couldn't imagine an operation like this opening without one of the elite overseeing it. Only we eight possess the control needed to set it up. The financial access. The procurement of the children. Nobody else in the Checquy wields the necessary power in so many fields. I skimmed through pages and pages, but found no mention of any of us. All reports were forwarded to the Founder, but no explanation was given as to who the Founder was.

I was actually quite interested in the current students. Who were they? How were they obtained? The answers might give me some clues in tracking down the mastermind. I eyed the photocopier in the corner, then decided to risk it. Gus wouldn't be waking up anytime soon, and if I just Xeroxed the front page of each file, I'd have the basic details. I bustled over and tentatively fired up the machine. It was noisy, but it sucked in the papers I fed it and spat out the duplicates. I had just finished putting the last files away in their drawers when someone tried the door. I froze.

Don't panic, I told myself. It's one of Gus's buddies doing his rounds. But did that mean he'd found Gus and tried to wake him? Or was he on his way back to the command center, checking the doors as he went? There were no alarms I could hear. All of these thoughts flashed through my brain before I heard the sound of a key in the lock.

Absolute terror jump-started my thoughts, and those thoughts carried my body three quick steps behind the door. It swung open, and one of the guards came in. He took a cursory look around. It wasn't Gus; I knew it couldn't have been, but I was relieved. This guard was taller and younger. His gun wasn't in his hand, which reassured me a little. He was just beginning to turn away when the photocopier beeped. He spun around, his hand going for his gun, but I tore one of my gloves off, reached out, and made the connection.

I silenced his voice.

I stilled his body.

I poured sensation into his spine.

He never even saw me as I overloaded his system. He dropped to his knees, twitching, mute. I hadn't hit anybody like that since my earliest times in the Estate, before I learned to control my powers. His senses were completely overwhelmed. The London Symphony Orchestra could have been playing in the room. The entire Playboy Bunny Corps could have been doing the cancan right in front of him, and he wouldn't have known.

Then I knocked him out completely. He buckled and sprawled on the floor, and I knelt down and shut his eyes. He would wake in an hour or so with a terrible headache. And soiled trousers. There would be no proof of my coming or going. At least, aside from this poor schmo's being on the floor. Maybe he'd put it down to some sort of seizure. Hurriedly, I shut off the photocopier, taking care to use my gloved hand, and then I left. I risked a look in the office and found Gus sprawled in his chair, just as I'd left him. I paused for a moment, and then went in. It would look rather suspicious, I decided, if two guards were found unaccountably unconscious.

I laid my fingers carefully on Gus's temples and reached in with my powers, rousing and wakening. He sighed and his eyes opened briefly, but his brain was still not taking in any information. He was no longer submerged in the trance I'd put him in, just in a normal drowsy state, so light that he would come out of it without ever being aware that he'd napped. I backed out of the office quietly.

Getting out was just as easy as getting in. When I finally got into the car, Wolfgang looked at me strangely, but I was too busy driving us the hell away to spend any time soothing him. It wasn't until we had gone seventy miles and I had to pull off to the side of the road to go to the toilet that I realized I was grinning like a loon, and humming the 1812 Overture.

So much to think about!

Love,

Me

19

Myfanwy knocked hesitantly on the guest room door, carefully carrying two cups of tea. She and Bronwyn had agreed the previous night that, since they'd both had quite a bit to drink and it was so late, her sister would stay over.

"Bronwyn?" There were the sounds of someone waking up with tremendous difficulty and getting struck by a hangover. "I have tea for you." She heard a mumbling that she interpreted as "come in," so she did. Her sister was lost in the thick covers of a large bed, but a mass of blond hair helped Myfanwy pinpoint her whereabouts.

She sat carefully on the edge. An arm emerged and gingerly took the tea. Finally, Bronwyn managed to get herself sat up, her hands wrapped around the cup.

"This is good," said Bronwyn.

"Val made it," admitted Myfanwy.

"Who's Val?"

"My housekeeper."

"You have a housekeeper?" asked Bronwyn.

"She also cooks," said Myfanwy. "It was either hire her or starve to death in the middle of appalling squalor."

"It is insanely early," said Bronwyn accusingly.

"I know, I have to go to work, and I wanted to say good-bye." Myfanwy paused and took a long sip of her own tea. "So, what's your schedule like today?"

"I have class at ten," said Bronwyn glumly. "So I need to go home and get changed and pick up my notes and stuff. And then to school. And you?"

"Remember my friend Shantay? I have a meeting with her this morning, and then all sorts of paper shuffling throughout the day. And this evening will probably be a formal dinner with the heads of my department to discuss some new developments with the Americans. Tedious. But necessary," she sighed. "Val is cooking waffles, so I figured we could have breakfast, and then I can get a car and driver to take you home."

"I can't believe that you have a driver," said Bronwyn. "You must be really good at what you do."

"Yeah, well, total prodigy at paperwork," said Myfanwy dismissively. "But I really want to spend more time with you. I mean, now that we've found each other—" She broke off awkwardly. "I guess it's kind of abrupt to say I want us to be a family. But friends, at least?" She looked shyly at her sister.

"Absolutely. I can't wait till you meet Jonathan! I'll e-mail him. He gets back in two weeks. Unless, you want to write to him directly?" Bronwyn asked.

"God, I wouldn't know how to write a letter like that," said Myfanwy helplessly. "Maybe it would be better if you wrote it." Bronwyn nodded. "Now, if we don't get downstairs, Val will kill me."

Morning, Rook Thomas."

"Morning, Bishop Petoskey," said Myfanwy to Shantay as she walked into the reception area outside her office. "You're here early. I'm guessing Ingrid has provided you with coffee and pastries?"

"Yes, Rook Thomas," said Ingrid, looking slightly frantic. Ingrid was notorious for being the first day-shift person in the building, but Myfanwy had heard from her driver that Shantay had arrived before her.

"Our office sent the latest reports on that Grafter chick," explained Shantay. "And the minibar in my hotel room was mysteriously emptied."

"By arcane forces beyond the understanding of normal human beings?" asked Myfanwy as she sifted through the in-box. It was the sort of question you learned to ask automatically when you worked with the Checquy.

"No, it was me," admitted Shantay without a shred of embarrassment.

"Oh, okay. Ingrid, what do we have going on today?"

"There are manifestations in Bath and Exeter," Ingrid read from a list. "The city teams were dispatched as soon as they erupted and are taking care of it now. The Elephant and Castle plague team are hoping to present their final findings this afternoon. And the entire Court will be meeting with the Croatoan representatives this evening."

"Dinner?" asked Myfanwy.

"Yes, indeed," confirmed Ingrid. "The Apex House chefs are already working."

"Excellent. Well, then, Bishop Petoskey, won't you come in?" said Myfanwy, concealing a smile.

"Why, thank you, Rook Thomas, I would be delighted," said Shantay, giving her a wink. Once the door was securely closed, Myfanwy burst out laughing.

"What in God's name are you doing here this early, Shantay? Aside from trying to break my secretary."

"I got bored" was Shantay's casual response. "Bishop Morales is still sleeping and there was nothing to watch on the hotel TV. You said that you always get in early, and I wanted to hear how it went with your sister."

"All right, let's go up to the residence," suggested Myfanwy, opening the portrait.

"You get your own apartment?" asked Shantay incredulously.

"Well, I kind of have to share it with the Ghost of Pimping Past," cautioned Myfanwy.

So, she had no Grafterness in her?" asked Shantay after Myfanwy had described the entire evening with the sort of detail men believe women normally reserve for recounting dates. "Definitely her real face?"

"The only surgery that girl has ever had is getting her wisdom teeth taken out," said Myfanwy. "When we hugged, I knew her inside and out. She's my sister—I could almost read her DNA. We connected like magnets."

"So, she has powers like yours?" asked Shantay, raising her eyebrows.

"Nope, she's totally normal. No weird enhancements, no supernatural powers."

"Well, that's good. You must be thrilled."

"I am," said Myfanwy, "but I'm also nervous. What if my brother and sister decide they don't like me?"

"They have to like you," said Shantay. "That's the good thing about having family." They were sprawled on some furniture composed of leather, wire, and chrome, going over the reports from the States. Since Dr. Crisp had not yet arrived in America, they consisted primarily of physical descriptions of the Grafter agent and the details of how she got to Los Angeles. "And you still have to meet your brother?" asked Shantay, throwing aside the file and lazily sliding off her chair onto a bearskin rug that seemed to possess some alarming worn spots. Myfanwy would never have sprawled on it, but then, she knew who'd owned the apartment previously.

"Yeah, and that's going to be infinitely harder. Bronwyn was three when I left; she didn't really remember me. But Jonathan was eleven and I guess we were pretty close. I have no idea what I'm going to tell him," confessed Myfanwy. "I don't remember much of my life before the Checquy. Do you have any ideas?"

"You could tell him that years of being on heavily addictive medication have fogged your memory," suggested Shantay. "Or that when you entered the public service you were obliged to undergo intense sessions of brainwashing. Or that you were hit on the head with a cricket bat and suffered amnesia."

"Oh, yeah," said Myfanwy. "Amnesia, because that's so likely. He'll totally buy that—bravo!" She applauded sarcastically, and both women looked up in surprise as a section of the wall rotated to reveal a heavily stocked bar featuring lots of mirrors. "Huh. Clap-on, I guess."

"Anyway, you know what the really disturbing part of this is?" said Shantay.

"What?"

"You have apparently been pronouncing your own name incorrectly for decades."

"Thanks for that," Myfanwy said dryly. "Regardless, I am not going to change—" The lights above flickered, and she looked up, startled. The phone trilled, and she picked it up. "What's up, Ingrid?"

"Rook Thomas" came the secretary's voice. "I'm sorry to disturb you, but there's an emergency situation in Bath. The manifestation I mentioned earlier has some unprecedented aspects. The local team is having problems, one of the Barghest teams has already been dispatched from here, and they need a Rook to be on-site."

"Oh-kay," said Myfanwy slowly. The prospect of going to an actual manifestation failed to fill her with delight. She'd been reading some of the files and had learned that far more Checquy operatives died by being torn to pieces than from any other cause. The organization provided an amazing retirement plan, but hardly anyone ever got to use it. "Doesn't Gestalt normally do these things?" she asked hopefully.

"Rook Gestalt is concentrating on the Grafter investigation," Ingrid reminded her.

"Rook Gestalt has four bodies. Not one of them can go to Bath?"

"The twins are in the north of Scotland, Robert is in Ireland, and Eliza is in York," said Ingrid.

"Fine," said Myfanwy. "How am I getting there?"

"A helicopter will be on the roof in a few minutes. You can take your private lift."

"Should I wear gum boots or anything? I can't really recall doing this sort of thing before," she said.

"No, what you're wearing will be fine," Ingrid assured her. "After all, you're only there to observe."

"Super," said Myfanwy sourly as she got up off the couch. "Well, call me on my mobile if anything else happens."

"What's up?" asked Shantay.

"There's a manifestation in Bath, and I have to go supervise."

"Oh, that sounds kind of interesting. Can I come?" asked Shantay.

"I don't see why not. Let's roll," she said. They then spent seven minutes looking for the private lift, which Myfanwy explained away by saying she'd never used it before. It turned out to be behind a door that Myfanwy had assumed was a closet.

The helicopter was thwupping impatiently on the roof, and a man in purple held the door open for them. They settled back comfortably in the leather seats and stared out the windows as the city glided down and away from them, like a vast albatross that has seen an interesting sardine. Myfanwy answered her ringing phone.

"Thomas."

"Rook Thomas, this is Ingrid. Background information has started to come into the Rookery regarding the manifestation you're headed toward. I'm zapping it to your phone now."

"Thanks," said Myfanwy. She opened the message attachment and started to read it intently.

PHONE TRANSCRIPT FROM CITY OF BATH
EMERGENCY SERVICES, 01:35–01:37

OPERATOR: Emergency Services.

CALLER: Yeah, hi. Look, I'm sorry to be calling so late, but it's the house across the street. It's what, one thirty in the morning? And they have all these funky purple lights flashing in their windows, without even closing their blinds, and there are people, like, moaning or chanting or yodeling or something, and I don't really feel comfortable going over to complain. I mean, I can't get to sleep and I have an exam tomorrow, and this whole thing is just so weird, you know?

O: Yes, we'll send a car over to take care of it, just as soon as you give me your name and the address of the house you're complaining about.

C: Oh, right. Um, I'm Rowena Lillywhite, I live in thirty-seven Bennett Street, and I'm complaining about the people in thirty-four Bennett Street.

O: Okay, Miss Lillywhite, I'm sending a car around now.

C: Thanks, I really appreciate it.

(End of Transcript)

Myfanwy searched through her memory for any references to purple light and weird yodeling/moaning/chanting. She'd spent a great deal of time reading through the purple binder and the Checquy records, but this didn't ring any bells. She pushed down the first little niggling feelings that were swimming up into her mind. Feelings of chaos and panic.

She snuck a look at Shantay to see if she'd noticed. Shantay was sitting calmly in her seat, checking messages on her phone. Myfanwy shook her head and breathed deeply. She could do this. She turned her attention back to the phone and scrolled down to the next message, which began with a note from Ingrid.

Rook Thomas, this is the working summary that Mahesh Poppat, the head of the Bath Situation Response Team, has written up. It's cobbled together from a variety of sources, but it should give you some idea of the situation.

1:55 a.m. — Constables O'Hara and Parker arrived at 34 Bennett St. They knocked, found the door open, and entered.

1:59 a.m. — Rowena Lillywhite called again, upset about the screams that had started issuing forth from her neighbor's house. In the middle of her call, the screams stopped, and she told the dispatcher that the chanting had started up again.

2:02 a.m. — Richard Drake, the emergency services supervisor on duty, notified Alexander Jefferson, the Bath chief of police, that there was something "bizarre" going on. As per long-standing instructions, Jefferson contacted our Bath office, and the local team was mobilized.

So that's how it all works, mused Myfanwy. *I wonder if every manifestation is begun with something atrocious happening to someone.* The next section appeared to be a hastily typed report by Mahesh Poppat. It was hard to be certain, but something about the report suggested a frantic concern that the Rook not be angry. *He was probably expecting Gestalt,* she thought. *Given that the last time I saw Gestalt get angry he tried to strangle the help, it's probably a reasonable concern.*

Poppat described the precautions they had taken, sealing off the street, setting up a perimeter. He made a great many references to "standard operating procedure," probably in an effort to forestall administrative strangulation. Things had proceeded typically until the Pawns sent into the house failed to emerge. At least, they had failed to emerge in any recognizable form. After a flickering of the violet lights and many subsequent screams, a torrent of viscous, meaty fluid streamed out one of the windows. The fluid was currently being analyzed to see if it contained any of the personnel.

Much to Myfanwy's surprise, this had not automatically bumped the incident up to emergency status. Good old standard operating procedure made another appearance, and a second, larger team of Pawns was sent in, this time with cameras and a protocol of constant radio contact. The camera feed fizzled, radio contact cut out, screams set in, fluid emerged, and the chanting continued unabated. At this point, Poppat (following the manual rigorously and scrupulously, he assured the reader) contacted the Rookery. A special Barghest team was dispatched from there, and Rook Thomas was notified.

And here I am, on the way to Bath, to observe the chanting house that eats people. A word in the précis had caught her eye, and she opened the purple binder and thumbed through until she came to the appropriate section.

The Barghests

In theory, every member of the Checquy is well versed in the art of kicking ass and could be mobilized as an effective soldier. An integral part of our education on the Estate is martial arts and weapons training—as central to the curriculum as algebra (which I was very good at) and music (I sucked; they made me play the French horn). But of course, not everybody is destined to be a fighter. Even those students who don't have hang-ups about confrontation are sometimes just better suited to fulfill some other function within the organization.

Still, an awful lot of Checquy members are soldiers, and they are very good. I want to make it clear that the average Checquy fighter would rank high in the echelons of international special forces. They are identified while still young, so the instructors are in a unique position to build them up as warriors. From a very early age, they embark on the same sort of training that adult career soldiers receive. They become proficient in numerous styles of fighting, are experts with hundreds of weapons, and learn survival, counter-terrorism, and strategy skills. Plus, they possess superhuman abilities.

They are equipped to go to war against the monstrous unknown.

And the very best go on to be in the Barghests.

My research has indicated that the Barghests are what the Checquy grew out of. An elite squad of supernatural soldiers sent in to fight the worst of the nightmares. There's not a person among the Checquy today who would not, were the call given, put down her pen, take up a weapon, and march into the darkness. When we offered our services to Cromwell, we were only fighters. In the centuries since, the Checquy grew into the organization that it is now. Nevertheless, the Barghests stand as the epitome of what we are. They do not exist for research, administration, or record keeping. They are not bodyguards. They are not police. They are warriors.

There are ten teams of Barghests; six are scattered around the globe, and four are based in the United Kingdom. The six international teams are under the command of the Chevaliers: two teams in Canada, one in New Zealand, two in India, and one in Australia. The four UK teams are under the control of the Rooks and are generally used as heavy backup. When bad shit goes down in the Isles and the local forces can't handle it, they call in the Barghests.

But while in theory I possess authority over them, Gestalt is the one who does the on-site commanding, so I don't know them that well. Every three months I have to do one of those reviewing-of-the-troops things, and they're all lined up in their killing uniforms. Gestalt and I walk authoritatively down the line, and it's just so uncomfortable. I'm always aware of how much they do, and they exude this sense of extreme capability, with their eyes straight ahead and every muscle clenched. To be honest, I'm kind of intimidated.

Not to mention that my incompetence in all things martial and physical is a fact of general knowledge in the Checquy. It's a small community, and there are people in the Barghests with whom I was at the Estate. I can't help but feel ridiculous in front of them. I have never dared to stop and stare pointedly at a Barghest's uniform and claim that he is mussed or rumpled or has in some way failed to be the perfect soldier.

Still, I'm the one who approves their entry into the ranks, reviews their files, and takes care of their maintenance. Considering all the training they receive and the enormous amount of money we spend on them, I think it's safe to assume that they should be able to handle anything that comes up.

When Shantay and Myfanwy arrived at the airport, there was a car waiting for them, and they were whisked through the city by a diffident purple-clad driver.

"We'll have to take the waters," said Shantay, who was leafing through a guidebook that had been left in the car.

"Hmm?" asked Myfanwy, who had moved on to the purple binder's section on Bath. According to Thomas, the city had once been a veritable hotbed of manifestations, with every sorcerer, bunyip, golem, goblin, pict, pixie, demon, thylacine, gorgon, moron, cult, scum, mummy, rummy, groke, sphinx, minx, muse, flagellant, diva, reaver, weaver, reaper, scabbarder, scabmettler, dwarf, midget, little person, leprechaun, marshwiggle, totem, soothsayer, truthsayer, hatter, hattifattener, imp, panwere, mothman, shaman, flukeman, warlock, morlock, poltergeist, zeitgeist, elemental, banshee, manshee, lycanthrope, lichenthrope, sprite, wight, aufwader, harpy, silkie, kelpie, klepto, specter, mutant, cyborg, balrog, troll, ogre, cat in shoes, dog in a hat, psychic, and psychotic seemingly having decided that *this* was the hot spot to visit.

In fact, Thomas had found evidence suggesting that Bath was the place where the Checquy had been founded, a reaction to the continuous torrent of bizarre happenings. According to old reports, it had been practically impossible to wander down a dark alley in Bath without tripping over something that had more limbs than it was supposed to. For centuries, Bath was the greatest source of Checquy operatives in the country. Then, about twenty-two years ago, the incidence of weirdness began to diminish noticeably. The local office, which was the largest in the United Kingdom other than the London installations, shrank until it maintained only a token force. It was now the place where new Pawns were sent to get used to things, and where the unsuccessful remained.

So, this manifestation was remarkably remarkable.

"We'll have to take the waters," repeated Shantay.

"Is this some American thing I missed when I was watching sitcoms?" asked Myfanwy distractedly. "Or just a weird euphemism?"

"No, apparently it's an English thing," said Shantay. "After this manifestation gets taken care of, we should go have high tea and take the waters. There are these natural springs that have been fashionable for centuries."

"Sounds delightful. You're really being a tourist."

"Well, I want to have the whole English experience. High tea, supervising manifestations, taking the waters, going to Harrods, discussing possible international conspiracies."

When the car arrived at its destination, the door was opened by a nervous-looking gentleman of Indian ancestry who was dressed in camouflage fatigues.

"Rook Thomas, it's very nice to see you again. It's been a few years." He was about the same age as Myfanwy. She dithered for a moment, trying to figure out how to treat him. Expecting to be patronized, she'd been rallying the icy regality that had served her so well with the twerps at the interrogation. But this poor sod was so nervous that it seemed unnecessary—perhaps even unkind—to bully him.

"Mahesh, it's lovely to see you!" she exclaimed with a broad smile, accepting the hand he offered and stepping out of the car. "How long has it been?" she asked.

"I don't think we've seen each other since we graduated from the Estate," said Poppat.

"Ah, yes, the Estate. Good times," said Myfanwy in a tone that suggested that those times, although good, were not a topic for current conversation. As Shantay stepped out of the car, Myfanwy turned. "Mahesh, this is Bishop Petoskey from the Croatoan. She is here to observe." If anything, this terrified the Pawn further. "Bishop Petoskey, this is Pawn Poppat."

"Pawn Poppat. It's a particular pleasure," Shantay said. Myfanwy shot her a reproving look.

"An honor, ma'am," said Poppat with a nervous little bow. Myfanwy looked around. They were on a perfectly normal-looking street with tidy and respectable row houses, but there was an atmosphere of unnatural stillness, as if the houses couldn't quite believe this whole thing was going on. At either end of the street were massive trucks blocking traffic access. There was an intensely irritating sound reverberating down the street and into Myfanwy's frontal lobes.

The chanting droned loudly and was not constant, shifting from an almost Gregorian invocation to a twisted yodel, as if someone were driving a steamroller over a crowd of Swiss musicians. *If that's been going on all night, I'm surprised more neighbors didn't complain,* thought Myfanwy.

"So, what's the situation?" she asked as Poppat led them toward an enormous armored truck. It seemed to consist of two large trailers conjoined by one of those accordion connectors. They entered at the end and walked through a narrow aisle. On either side, the Barghests sat on low benches, and Myfanwy snuck curious peeks at them. The soldiers were dressed in gray armor made of what looked like dull, hard plastic. They were solemn and had that deadly air of poised stillness that one finds in cocked bear traps. Some were carrying large weapons, and others were carrying nothing at all. As Myfanwy and her companions passed through, the troops nodded their heads respectfully.

They passed into a short section lined with locked cage doors. Behind some of the doors were racks of guns; other cages were empty and would presumably act as temporary restraining cells. Then they went through a medical area, where a Pawn in scrubs was sterilizing her scalpel-like fingernails. Beyond that was the accordion joint, and then finally Poppat opened a door labeled COMMAND SUITE. Myfanwy observed glowing monitors everywhere, ergonomically padded chairs, and nerdy Pawns staring at the screens, tapping away on keyboards, and, in one case, industriously licking a monitor.

Poppat fluttered around Myfanwy and Shantay like a mother hen, ensuring that they were settled comfortably and out of the way of the nerd Pawns. They thanked him and accepted the offer of coffee, which was delivered from the galley (through yet another door).

Myfanwy couldn't help noticing that the nerd Pawns were shooting them—especially her—anxious sidelong looks. It was as if they expected her to zap them if they tried to use the backspace button.

"All right, Pawn Poppat," said Myfanwy, prompting a muffled guffaw from Shantay. "Please fill us in on the situation." He nodded, looking a little perturbed, and gestured toward the many monitors.

"Well, we can be quite certain that everyone on the first two teams is dead," he said with a little wobble in his voice. Myfanwy remembered that those would have been his people—the workmates he saw every day. "As per standard operating procedure"— *There we go again,* thought Myfanwy—"we evacuated the street and coordinated with local police to keep it discreet."

"What explanation did you give?" asked Shantay curiously.

"We told the police it was a religious cult that had been messing with the gas mains, and that it needed to be kept quiet," said Poppat calmly. "We told the neighbors it was a gas leak in a house with asbestos."

"Standard operating procedure," contributed Myfanwy.

"Absolutely," said Poppat, seeming to relax after hearing the magical incantation. "All members of the first team were affixed with vital-sign monitors and were in full environmental gear. They proceeded in through the front door, and Cassie—she's the team leader— reported that the entire inside appeared to be covered in a lumpy coating of purple fungus. They confirmed that the air was breathable and free of toxins. Then we lost contact."

"The transmission just cut out?" asked Myfanwy.

"Like someone shut a door on the radio waves," piped up one of the nerds at the computers, a plump girl with little tufts of leaves instead of hair and eyebrows. "That won't happen this time," she said with satisfaction.

"Oh?" said Myfanwy, a little coolly. She was still trying to construct a credible Rook persona and figured that a Rook was not accustomed to being interrupted.

"Yup," the girl replied. "This team is being sent in with cameras, and they'll be spooling out comm wires as well as being in contact via wireless means. And we're stationing someone at the door to prevent it from shutting."

"Ingenious," remarked Myfanwy dryly. *Thank heavens we're utilizing the very highest of tech. I could check if the budget will stretch to a couple of bricks for propping the door.*

"We should be ready to send the team in very soon," said Poppat hastily. "Lydia," he said to the plump nerd, "check with Barghest FitzPatrick to see if the team is prepared." The Pawn at the computer nodded, the light glinting off the foliage covering her head. "Lydia is our communications specialist," Poppat quietly explained to Myfanwy and Shantay. "She's very accomplished."

"She'd better be, with an attitude like that," whispered Shantay to Myfanwy.

"Pawn Poppat," said Lydia. "FitzPatrick says the Barghest team is ready."

"Excellent. Switch the channel onto the speakers, please." The room suddenly filled with the hushed sounds of professional soldiers. Controlled breathing, the quiet creak of body armor, somebody sucking his teeth. Then a man's deep voice came over the speaker.

"Barghest FitzPatrick awaiting the order." There was a pause; Myfanwy and Shantay stared raptly at the monitors, which had suddenly blossomed with images from all the Barghests' cameras. Then Myfanwy realized nothing was happening.

"Rook Thomas, you're the ranking officer," said Poppat apologetically. "You give the word."

"Oh! Okay," said Myfanwy, flushing with embarrassment, trying to ignore the snort that had come from Lydia. "Begin the operation." The lights in the trailer dimmed, turning red like a submarine's in battle mode. The nerds leaned intently over their workstations.

"I copy that" came FitzPatrick's voice. "Barghest team, let's move."

The light in the trailer shifted as the pictures on the screens changed. The entire team was jogging outside, moving toward the house. It was disorienting, watching the multiple perspectives move around crazily. Myfanwy blinked, feeling a little nauseated. She took a sip of coffee and found that it was terrible. That damned yodeling was building over the speakers. She looked back to the screens and saw that the team was entering the house. As the door opened, the sound grew stronger, and everyone in the trailer winced.

"I'll dial it down," said Lydia. The sound grew less piercing, but it was still present, an irritating background.

"Can you analyze this?" asked Shantay.

"It's being transmitted back to the Rookery labs," said Lydia without looking over. "They'll let us know if they come up with anything."

"Loza, you're holding the door," they heard FitzPatrick say.

"Aye, sir."

The command center dimmed as the team moved into the house. There were no lights inside, and sheer sheets of something purple covered the windows, muting the sunlight. Myfanwy squinted, trying to discern meaning from the shapes.

"I'm switchin' the cameras to night vision," said a nerd with a thick Cockney accent. The monitors slid into a green tint, and what had previously been nebulous outlines sharpened into a bizarre vista. From what Myfanwy could make out, it was as if someone had taken a normal sitting room fully furnished with lamps, squashy armchairs, and so on, and draped a carpet of scummy fuzz over the entire place. The material covered the walls and ceiling and spread through the doorways.

"What can you tell us, FitzPatrick?" asked Poppat intently.

"This stuff is purple, and rubbery underfoot. It smells like . . . what would you say, Turner?"

"It's fungal," said a gravel-voiced Pawn. "Not unlike *Aspergillus fumigatus,* but with a few extra factors I don't recognize. Not synthetics, though."

"Who is this Turner?" whispered Myfanwy to Poppat. One of the nerds tapped rapidly on his keyboard, and Turner's file was up on a monitor. She looked automatically at the heading "Advantage" and saw that Turner had enhanced olfactory senses and an eidetic memory.

"FitzPatrick, any sign of the previous teams?" asked Poppat.

"No, sir, not here in the entryway."

"All right, proceed through the house, staggering your troops."
Poppat turned to Myfanwy and Shantay. "We're placing them throughout the premises, each pair of sentries stationed within sight of the
previous pair."

Myfanwy nodded. It made sense.

The Pawns cautiously spread out over the ground floor, depositing sentries at strategic corners and doorways. The wires the soldiers
were spooling out glistened against the fungus that covered everything. The rest of the rooms gave the same impression of a regular
life hastily covered up with a thick cover of mold. There was even a
vase of flowers on the kitchen table, each petal covered in a lumpy
purple skin.

"Sir, there's no sign of the teams or of any other individuals," said
FitzPatrick. Myfanwy guessed that the background of chanting was
grating on all the Pawns' nerves. Though Lydia had toned it down,
even the hushed version they were hearing in the trailer made her ill
at ease.

"FitzPatrick, this is Rook Thomas. Is there any sign of where the
sound is originating?"

"Upstairs, Rook," said FitzPatrick. "Shall we proceed up there?"

"Is the ground floor secured?" Poppat asked.

"Yes, sir."

"Then call your stationed troops except those necessary for main-
taining sight lines to the front door. And proceed."

"Yes, sir." The Pawns went up the stairs, leaving a pair at the base
and another pair at the head of the staircase.

Lydia cleared her throat. "The Rookery has noted a change in the
chanting; they're analyzing and comparing," she said, still intent on
the monitors in front of her.

"I didn't notice anything," whispered Myfanwy to Shantay. "Did
you?" The American Bishop shook her head. The team of Pawns
came to the first door, which was ajar. Just as FitzPatrick was leaning
forward to push it open with his rifle, several things happened at
once.

The monitor showing the Pawn at the front door flashed as she was jerked inside the house.

All the other pictures moved rapidly too as the Pawns swung around at the sound of Loza's scream. Then a wave of material rose up from the floor and covered the cameras.

There was a brief flurry of screams and gunfire.

The front door swung shut, slicing neatly through the cables the Pawns had brought with them.

Holy fuck, thought Myfanwy in horror. *Holy mother of fuck.*

There was a moment of stunned silence, and Myfanwy took a deep breath. *You are the Rook, so keep calm.*

"Any ideas?" she asked collectedly, though her heart was still pounding. The screams had torn through the room before wireless contact was abruptly lost. The nerd Pawns were typing frantically, licking monitors, and talking with great urgency on headsets and cell phones. It was evident that nobody had yet figured out what was going on or what to do, so Myfanwy sat back patiently and waited for them to come up with answers. A few of them shot nervous looks at her over their shoulders, and she pretended not to notice.

"Any thoughts, Bishop Petoskey?" she asked Shantay quietly, folding her fingers together to keep them from shaking.

"Uh, well, this is certainly not like anything I've ever seen before," replied Shantay with a fair bit of awe. "We don't get these sorts of manifestations that frequently."

"Yes, well, I gather this is quite unusual even for us," Myfanwy said, desperately casual.

"So what do you intend to do?" asked Shantay.

"Oh, I'm sure Pawn Poppat will follow his beloved standard operating procedure," she answered, casting a look over at the Pawn, who was rushing about madly and being very busy indeed. "I don't like to bother him. It must be difficult enough having an emergency occur in front of the boss without having her demanding to be kept entertained." In fact, Poppat was bustling over toward her.

"Rook Thomas, standard operating procedure dictates that at this point we have the house destroyed, either with explosives or with a ring of—" He was cut off abruptly by an excited shout from the other end of the command center.

"They're alive!" one of the techno-Pawns shouted. Everybody froze and watched the monitors as he rapidly brought up the screens that showed the vital signs of the team members. Myfanwy remembered seeing them when she came in while Poppat explained that every Barghest had been fitted with extensive monitoring equipment under his armor.

"They're all alive?" asked Myfanwy intently. *Is this good or bad?*

"Yes, ma'am," said the technician. "All the Barghests. According to these indicators, they haven't had anything introduced into their systems, and while they're all quite excited—heart rates up and so on—they haven't been harmed."

"How unfortunate," said Pawn Poppat.

"Unfortunate?" asked Myfanwy.

"Well, yes," said Pawn Poppat. "Because we still have to destroy the site..." He trailed off. Myfanwy turned to the techno-Pawn.

"Are they...moving?" she asked carefully.

"No, ma'am."

Shit.

"Are they conscious?" she asked.

"Yes, ma'am."

Double shit.

"Ah." Myfanwy pursed her lips and turned to Poppat. "You know, Mahesh, I feel somewhat hesitant about wiping the building off the face of the earth, since we have people alive in there."

"I can understand that, Rook Thomas," Poppat began, "but standard oper—"

"Yes?" she interrupted, with her eyebrows high.

"Well, it is quite clear, and Rook Gestalt has never hesitated to—"

"Yes, quite." There was an uncomfortable silence, broken mercifully and hesitantly by Lydia.

"Rook Thomas? The Rookery has an update on the analysis of the chanting."

"Anything useful?" she asked. *Am I going to have to sign a death sentence for fourteen of my people?*

"I think you need to hear it," said Lydia.

"All right," sighed Myfanwy. Lydia twisted some selector knob. The chanting increased throughout the room, but a part of it had been augmented, amplified. Now layered over the droning was a tense voice, insistently repeating itself.

"Send in the Rook...Send in the Rook...Send in the Rook... Send in the Rook..."

"Figures," said Myfanwy bitterly.

20

Dear You,

Six girls. Eight boys. That's the current number of kids in the Camp Caius stable, and they're an intriguing little bunch of brats, ranging in age from eleven to twenty-two. The pages I copied give me the basic details, but only the barest beginning in describing their powers. The impression I get, however, is that these kids are possessed of nothing in the way of natural power but rather undergo an extraordinary amount of surgery with an eye toward instilling abilities, which is the most disgusting thing I've ever heard of.

This whole endeavor is completely alien to the Checquy style of doing things and it is, as far as I know, almost impossible. I'm not even sure why these kids were chosen. See, the students don't seem to have anything in common. They all come from different parts of the country, and their families are from different social classes and backgrounds. I've researched their families, I've checked their NHS records, I've looked into everything about them, and I can't find a reason that they were plucked out of their homes.

Let's face it. If you want to look at this in as cold a manner as possible, there are plenty of children out there that can be gotten easily. Orphans. Street children. Hell, you can import them. Given how long Camp Caius has been around, you could probably breed them. But these children were taken from private British families — so you have the people of Camp Caius putting themselves to enormous trouble for no apparent reason. Doing this sort of thing is a major task even for the Checquy, so I just don't understand it.

Once in a while, I sit back, amazed at what the Checquy does. From what little I recall of my family life, it was pretty tight. My parents were educated people, relatively well-off, independent. And yet they crumpled when Wattleman and Farrier told them that the Checquy was taking me. You'd expect a fight from them. A word of protest. Even a lawsuit. At the very least, you'd expect them to contact the media. If the government comes and takes your kid, you're going to talk about it. Maybe look for some support group. Instead, families keep it secret. And why?

Well, many of the Estate students are unnatural. Think about Gestalt. Would you want that in your house? So a lot of parents are relieved to have their children taken away. In fact, some are willing to pay. For those whose families do want them, it gets uglier, because the Checquy has been doing this for a very long time and they have become very good at it. They lie, they threaten, they make promises. And they have the law backing them up. I'm still not sure exactly what story Wattleman and Farrier gave my father that last day. I wasn't paying very close attention.

With all of these tools, they can bludgeon people into compliance or deceive them completely. Parents are left believing that their children are deathly ill, have horrendous mental problems, are contagious, whatever. In the end, they know their children are no longer available to them and that the government is taking over their care. A depressing number of families are left feeling that they have been done a favor.

Anyway, I'm still trying to work out what the deal is with Camp Caius.
Regards,
Me

21

"Rook Thomas, at the very least you should wait for the second team of Barghests to arrive from the Rookery," pleaded Poppat.

"No," said Myfanwy, her eyes fixed on the uniform someone had handed her. The outfit she'd worn to the office that morning would not be at all appropriate—she was certainly not going to trip about some haunted house in a skirt and heels.

"But I cannot possibly allow a member of the Court to enter a manifestation site without an escort, and all the local troops..." He trailed off.

"All the local troops have been liquefied," Myfanwy finished for him. "I'm not certain that an escort would do me any good anyway. And if I've got even the smallest chance of helping our people, then"—she took a deep breath—"I have to go in."

Poppat gripped her arm desperately. "Myfanwy, we both know this is not your field. I can't let you go in there alone."

"No" came a firm voice from behind them. They turned to see Shantay zipping herself into a Pawn combat uniform. She'd coiled her hair up at the back of her neck and suddenly looked much more dangerous. "She's not going in alone. I'm going in with her."

"Absolutely not," said Myfanwy. "There may be legal precedents for you coming along to observe, but can you imagine the repercussions if a Bishop of the Croatoan was harmed on a Checquy op?"

"Yeah, but you'll probably be dead too, so it's not like it'll be your problem."

"Well, then," said Myfanwy. "As long it causes me no inconvenience."

"I'm not letting you go in there by yourself."

"You don't get a say," said Myfanwy tartly. "And even if you did, the voice didn't request an American Bishop, it requested a Rook."

"*The voice* can go fuck itself!" said Shantay. "I'm sure the boys and girls you sent in there were good, but I can handle myself, and you need someone to cover your back." Myfanwy wavered and Shantay, sensing an advantage, pressed it. "Honey, don't take offense here, but we live in a small world. News gets around, and our dossiers on you are at least as detailed as yours on us. So I know this sort of thing isn't your forte. You need a strong arm backing you up, and that's going to be me."

It might not have been Thomas's forte, thought Myfanwy, *but I've got a few tricks of my own.* Still, she didn't like the thought of going into that house alone.

"Fine," she said finally. "You can come."

"Like there was ever a question," sniffed Shantay, pulling out an extremely large handgun and checking it over.

"Excuse me, but what the hell is that?" asked Myfanwy.

"What?"

"That bloody cannon in your hand!"

"It's my gun," said Shantay innocently.

"Where on earth did you get it?" asked Poppat. "There's nothing like that in the armory."

"It was in my purse."

"Your purse?" repeated Myfanwy. "How did you get it through Customs at the airport?"

"The airport? Honey, we arrived at the embassy. Why do you think Bishop Morales was so tired? She stepped us between the cities."

"Oh," said Myfanwy, momentarily stunned by the strangeness of the world she'd been born into.

"Now what kind of gun are you going to take?" asked Shantay.

"I am not taking any kind of gun."

"You are definitely taking a gun."

"Is that a fact, Dirty Harry?" asked Myfanwy, eyeing Shantay's weapon.

"Honey, I can punch my fist through a tank if I put my mind to it, and I am taking a gun."

"Fine, I'll take a gun. But nothing that weighs more than I do."

Poppat tried to insist on accompanying them, but Shantay pointed out that it was needlessly cruel for him to leave all responsibility to some poor schmo of a second-in-command.

"Actually, *I'm* the poor schmo of a second-in-command," Poppat confessed. "The head of the Bath section, Pawn Goblet, called in sick yesterday. Flu."

"Talk about sucky timing," Shantay commented. The American Bishop was cracking her knuckles and her neck in a very military manner. Myfanwy was having difficulty bending her arms—the jacket she'd been given was her size but was made out of Kevlar, leather, and plastic and felt like it had been constructed of wood. "You know, it's been years since I did anything like this," remarked Shantay. She and Myfanwy were standing on the doorstep of the house, being given a final check-over by the techies.

"Oh, yeah?" Myfanwy was trying to figure out how she had suddenly acquired two knives and a large pistol. "How many years?"

"One and a half," confessed Shantay.

"Indeed?" replied Myfanwy. "What's this?"

"Pepper spray. Don't you want to put on a pair of gloves?"

"No. What's this?"

"Taser," said Shantay.

"Amazing. Well, I guess we should do this then," said Myfanwy with a palpable lack of enthusiasm. She put her hand on the doorknob, turned it, and they walked into the house.

"Charming," she said, and noticed Shantay looking at her strangely. "Well, aside from the massive blanket of fungus covering everything. But if you look beyond that, it's really not in bad taste." Shantay carried on staring at her. "Oh, shut up. Do you see any sign of the Barghests?"

"No," Shantay said in a stage whisper. She was holding her large pistol in her hand and looking very tense.

"What is wrong with you?" Myfanwy whispered back. "You look like you expect someone to grab your ass."

"I'd be okay with that, as long as it was a person," whispered Shantay. "It's when it's the decor reaching out to cop a feel that I get nervous." She kept turning around, scanning the room.

The air was hot and wet, as if they'd stepped into the lungs of some giant jungle beast. Baroque curves of fungus swept up from the floor and down from the ceiling, and Myfanwy couldn't tell whether they'd crawled up from the cellar or poured down from the upper floors. In some places, the mold was a smooth, featureless blanket that clung tightly to the wall. In other areas, it was jagged and lumpy, as if it had been slapped on like mortar. There were also thick ligneous branches that coiled down and hung oddly in the air.

A thought occurred to Myfanwy.

"Why are we whispering?"

"Because I'm concerned that eldritch forces will rip my face off," said Shantay. "I don't want to disturb anything."

"Oh. Okay." Myfanwy looked around again. "So I should whisper too?"

"Not if you don't want to," said Shantay testily.

"No, it's fine. Well, I suppose we should go upstairs?" Myfanwy suggested. "That's where that damn chanting is coming from. Hold on a sec, though," she said, an idea having just come to her. She went down on one knee, and with her bare fingers spread out, she reached down.

"What the hell are you doing?" asked Shantay in horror. "Don't *touch* it!"

"Trust me," whispered Myfanwy. "I think this will work." As soon as she'd entered the house, she'd sensed the place tingling around her. She could feel the vitality humming through the room, but it was blurry, like a guitar string that has just been plucked. She couldn't focus on it, and it nagged at her. So she laid her hand palm-down onto the floor and connected herself.

Instantly, her senses snapped into place. The sensations she'd been picking up were crisper, more defined.

"I see what the problem is," she said. She had been looking for a single shape when in fact the impression consisted of many patterns merged together. It was as if a dozen layers of transparencies had been laid one on top of the other. They complemented one another but didn't quite match.

It was almost... *choral*.

"What the hell are you doing?" exclaimed Shantay, forgetting in her consternation to whisper. Myfanwy blinked and concentrated on looking out of her actual eyes. From under her palm, little ripples were spreading out through the sheets of mold.

"Sorry." She stood up, wiping off her hands on her pants. "I was getting some very curious vibes off this room."

"Like what?" asked Shantay.

"It's like a lot of voices all together."

"Voices?" Shantay repeated dubiously.

"It's got a distinctly human sound, but there's something else mixed in."

"Great," said Shantay darkly.

"You're a very glass-half-empty person, aren't you?" observed Myfanwy.

"That's experience talking," said Shantay. "In these situations, the glass is always half empty."

"Always?"

"Always," confirmed the Bishop. "Right until it fills up with some sort of spectral blood that grows into a demonic entity."

"It's probably just as well that I went into administration," remarked Myfanwy. "So, shall we head upstairs?"

"Yeah, sounds good." Despite their casual tone, the two women were looking about nervously. Shantay hefted her pistol and flexed the fingers of her other hand. Myfanwy realized that she was grinding her teeth. When they reached the stairs, both paused, waiting for the other to go up. Myfanwy went first, one step at a time, her booted feet sinking slightly into the fungus. The dim violet light cast an eerie glow on their faces. Looking down at her hands, Myfanwy was taken aback. They looked like the hands of a corpse. She and Shantay slowly proceeded, the chanting continued, and Myfanwy found herself becoming hypnotized by it.

"Myfanwy" came Shantay's voice behind her, shocking Myfanwy out of her reverie. She gave a little scream and clutched at the fungus covering the banister, which peeled off in her hands.

"What? What?" the Bishop exclaimed, looking around frantically for some supernatural horror to shoot.

"Nothing! Just...don't *do* that!" snapped Myfanwy irritably.

"Do *what?*"

"Don't suddenly blurt out my name when I'm concentrating on not dying."

"Sor-*ry*," said Shantay, not sounding sorry at all.

"So what did you want?" asked Myfanwy.

"I have a really bad feeling about this place. It's giving me the creeps, and I've been in a lot of weird places."

"*You* don't like it?" said Myfanwy. "*I'm* the one who's going up the stairs first! You've done all these ops. What happened to the chick who was all 'I'm going to kick some ass'?"

"That was before we came into the house that smells like some giant porcino mushroom. How do we know that the landscape isn't going to just swallow us up like it did all those Pawns?"

"It asked for a Rook. Do you want me to give it a warning?" Myfanwy yelled up to the next story. "Hey! You asked for the Rook! Well, I'm here, so don't try any shit!" She turned back to Shantay. "Satisfied? Why are you looking like that?" She followed Shantay's gaze to the wall, where the fungus appeared to have spontaneously remodeled itself. Where previously there had been an irregular surface with bumps where framed pictures had been absorbed, there were now hundreds of growths. Each one was twice as long as her index finger and tipped with a shiny black orb that was unmistakably an eye gazing piercingly at them.

"Should I shoot them?" Shantay whispered out of the corner of her mouth.

"Is that your approach to everything?" asked Myfanwy out of the corner of *her* mouth.

"Pretty much. Maybe that explains why we have so few manifestations in the States."

"Maybe," said Myfanwy. "Let's just head upstairs." Turning her back on those hundreds of giant snail eyes was one of the hardest things she'd had to do in her very short life. But Shantay followed her and they moved much more quickly this time. At the top of the stairs, there was a long hallway with doorways spaced along it on both sides. Every door was open, and more unflattering purple light was spilling out into the hallway. Motes of dust and spores hung in the dim beams. The chanting was oppressive now. They could practically *feel* it hammering the air.

Carefully, they padded toward the first door, checked that their weapons were ready, and peeked inside. The same fungus grew here, but it seemed more intense in color, as if it were closer to the root of it all. The purple had darkened to the shade of an eggplant, and there were thick veins of crimson shot through it. It almost *glistened,* sweating a thick ichor that stank of rotting meat.

Whatever furniture had been in the room had been absorbed, just like downstairs. But it looked as if previous to the eruption of the mold, someone had stacked everything in the far corner of the room so that there was a large space in the middle. Crouching in the fetal position, knees drawn up to chests and chanting monotonously, were two rows of people who had also been covered by the fungus.

The two women drew their heads back around the door and shared a grim moment.

"That's pretty messed up," allowed Shantay. "Did you see their faces?"

"The only parts of them that weren't draped in that stuff. It's like they're wearing robes of gunk." Myfanwy shuddered. "What do you think we should do?"

"Well, I don't think it's these guys who called you in," said Shantay thoughtfully. "They don't seem to be conscious of what they're chanting. They don't seem to be conscious of anything, really."

"Someone else, then?"

"Let's check the other rooms." They made their way down the

hall. Every room had its group of people chanting in unison, staring blankly. There were men and women of every age, arranged in meticulous rows. Even the bathroom had four people crouched in position, their faces ringed by fuzzy cuticles of moss. Myfanwy put a cautious foot inside and moved slowly toward the figures. She ignored Shantay's whispered warnings and crouched down in front of the closest chanter.

It was a boy, a teenager. He had a little pudge hanging off his cheekbones and a little smudgy mustache, one that suggested he was trying to pass for eighteen but failing miserably. His eyes were focused on something that wasn't there, and his pupils were like pinpoints.

"Shantay, this kid isn't more than fourteen. Christ, his voice is breaking even as he's chanting!" She stood up in disgust and looked at the others. "None of the people in this room are old enough to have a checking account."

"Well, they're certainly old enough to be possessed," remarked Shantay. Myfanwy reached out toward the boy's face, took a deep slow breath, then placed her index finger softly between his eyes.

She was suspended in an ocean of sensation—the sum of the boy's self. But where she would have expected a complex torrent of sights, tastes, and sounds, everything was muted. Delicate currents drifted about, wafting a vague acknowledgment of the temperature in the bathroom, the distant sound of Shantay tapping her boot, and the smell of Myfanwy's deodorant. But all that, everything that was the world, barely registered.

Instead, there was the overwhelming presence of the chant, echoing and booming above and below and all around, like thunder. It sucked everything toward it. Through it, she could feel the separate pulses of the people around them. Every person in the house who was chanting was connected to the rest. The pressure of the invocation was surrounding her, pressing on her, trying to pull her in. Myfanwy tensed and wrenched herself out.

"Damn it!" she spat out, lying flat on her back. Shantay was kneeling down beside her, wiping Myfanwy's face with the sleeve of her shirt. "What the hell happened?" Myfanwy asked.

"You zoned out for about twenty minutes, and I developed a

massive new phobia of mushrooms, checked your pulse seven times, and took a phone call from Poppat. Then the chanting got a little ragged and you hurled yourself back on the floor," said Shantay, ticking each development off on her fingers.

"What did Poppat have to say?" Myfanwy asked weakly.

"Just checking in. In an ill-advised bout of honesty, I told him you were in a trance and then I spent five minutes convincing him not to immolate this place with us in it. And I explained about the people chanting and said that you'd call him back."

"Oh, great," said Myfanwy without enthusiasm.

"Are you okay?"

"Yeah, but there's some weird stuff going on in this kid's nervous system. Probably all of them are going through the same thing. Help me up, and let's find out who's pulling the strings. If we survive, then I'll call Poppat."

Shantay heaved her to her feet, and they dusted each other off. There were only a few doors left, but they approached them cautiously, knowing that there was inevitably going to be some sort of unpleasant surprise behind them.

It happened sooner than Myfanwy expected. Common practice and the laws of nightmarish manifestations dictated that it would be the last door along the hallway and that there would be a moment of stark horror. And so as they walked down the corridor, Myfanwy got more and more tense, her gaze focused on that final entrance.

Thus, they almost walked right by the second-to-last room and only just noticed the frantic man inside. A pair of double takes ensued, and then they were standing in the doorway. The man was dressed in a suit that had clearly seen better days, but the house's fungal activities had taken their toll on both his clothes and his face. Dirt, sweat, and spores had created a mottled cover all over him, and he reeked like a mossy log with BO. He was moving rapidly from chanter to chanter, stooping to whisper something to each of them as he passed. What effect all this industry was supposed to have, Myfanwy couldn't tell, but he kept it up, even after he became aware of their presence.

Although he never took his eyes off the fungus-clad people on the floor, the man took advantage of the pauses between each whisper to shout something in the general direction of the door, so Myfanwy and Shantay received his message as a series of short exclamations.

"Thank God, you've come!—They started two nights ago without warning!—I mean, *I* certainly never gave the order—and then the growth manifested!"

He stayed squatted in front of an extremely fat woman, staring fixedly into her eyes.

"I came over yesterday morning to check on the congregation and see what progress they'd made—well, they've bloody well made some progress! The invocation was building in volume—I mean the neighbors were going to hear it eventually, and the light would show up when the sun set. I had to call in sick to the office, and since then I've been trying to quell them here. I would have called you directly, but I put my phone down on a table after I called work, and it got overgrown. And then I couldn't leave, and the whole situation went critical. Once the Checquy showed up, I decided my only option was to let the congregation run through its self-defense routines. I knew you'd be called in after the second team was consumed. Jesus Christ! Do you realize those were *my* people I had to liquidate? My people!"

Myfanwy shot Shantay a horrified look and received an incredulous stare in return.

Could this man actually be the head of the Checquy outpost in Bath? she wondered. She gingerly reached out with her mind, finding the pattern of the man's senses. *And if so, why is he doing this? It can't be a Checquy action, or he wouldn't have liquefied the teams. But if it isn't, then why is he talking to us like we know exactly what's going on?*

"At least I could prevent them from killing the third team—Barghests, right?" He didn't pause for an answer. "I don't understand it! They weren't supposed to be starting this yet, and unless we do something, it'll only spread. They're barely responding to any of the instruction phrases we were given. I could only get my message into

240

the chanting by shooting one of the congregants and briefly grafting myself into the system. We'll have to get someone in to clean me out. I've still got some of that gunk in me.

"Anyway, I knew you'd hear the message. Thank God you shouted up—my vision is so poor through this thing's sensory organs that I was ready to have you cocooned." Myfanwy shuddered at the implications, then wondered where the Barghest strike team was being kept. The man was still talking.

"... no idea how to stop them. I'm running though all the emergency codes and nothing is working. Do you know some backdoor hack to shutting it all down?" He turned around, looking for an answer, and froze when he saw them. "You're not Gestalt!" he exclaimed in a tone of complete shock.

Ah, thought Myfanwy. *Suddenly it all makes a bit more sense.*

They stared at each other for a moment, and then Myfanwy briskly cut him off from the world. *After all,* she thought, *I have no idea what this guy is capable of. For all I know, he can make my spleen eat itself. Better not give him the chance.*

"Don't worry, Shantay, I've got him," she said.

"Are you sure?" asked the tall woman cautiously. She moved forward and relaxed a little when she saw the guy in the suit was frozen in a crouch, breathing rapidly, his eyes glazed and his features fixed in a look of total confusion. Now that Myfanwy had the chance to look the guy over, he seemed vaguely familiar. *Probably one of those hundreds of personnel files I read.*

Shantay waved a hand in front of his eyes and noted that his gaze didn't shift. She leaned forward carefully and flicked his ear. Nothing. "That's very impressive," she said. "How did you do that?"

"I figured it out just now," said Myfanwy, who was looking around dubiously at the chanters. They were still droning along.

"So, am I insane, or is this guy one of your people?" asked Shantay.

"I think his name is Goblet," conceded Myfanwy.

Suddenly the man pulled himself out of his trance and smashed Shantay with an uppercut. The American Bishop was sent reeling back and fell over one of the cultists. The fungus-enshrouded figure kept chanting, undisturbed. "How the hell did you do that?" Myfanwy asked him.

Goblet stood and bared his teeth at her, and a coating of spines erupted all over his body. Myfanwy gave a little squeak as his hair lengthened itself and hardened into a mass of spikes. Bony quills pierced his clothes. His once-distinguished suit was now a perforated mass of wool.

Shantay had rolled to her feet and was rubbing her jaw. Now she stood up and shot a look of absolute loathing toward the porcupine man. "Don't fucking move," she said, bringing her massive pistol up and pointing at him. "That *really* hurt. I thought you said you had him," she said tightly to Myfanwy.

"I thought I did."

"Well, can you do it again?"

"Maybe." Myfanwy reached out with her senses and carefully probed at Goblet, who was slavering in the middle of the room. *How on earth did he get out of my grasp? I disrupted his spine here and here, so he couldn't have just—oh. Well, this is fascinating.* Myfanwy reeled herself back in and looked to Shantay. "No good; he's got, like, seven supplementary spines, all woven together in a lattice. I can't get control of all of them at once—the impulses are strobing between them." The guy had been swinging his head back and forth, following the conversation, but now he again focused on her.

"Rook Thomas, I would never have guessed that *you* would venture out of your little office and get your hands dirty," he said with massive contempt. His fingernails stretched into horny barbed talons and he moved toward her.

"Oh, *please*," said Shantay, and she shot Goblet in the back. He reeled for a moment and then got a grip on himself, swung around, and backhanded her against a wall. His spikes cut the Bishop in the face, and she cracked her head against the fungus.

"I had no idea that we'd sunk so low. Enlisting Americans in the

Barghests? But then, this is the same Court that appointed you as a Rook," he spat out in disgust. "A useless little girl who weeps in corners and fiddles about with the account books."

"No doubt they should have selected some treasonous git who grows spikes out of his arse instead," Myfanwy remarked as she fumbled for the pistol at her side and nearly dropped it in the process.

"Treasonous?" he exclaimed. "This endeavor is for the good of the Checquy, and by extension, the good of the nation!"

"Is that why you didn't feel the need to inform the Court of your activities, Goblet?" she asked.

"Pah! The Court isn't ready for this! At least, not yet." He took a step closer to Myfanwy and she backed up against the door, which had closed silently behind her. Around them, the chanters continued chanting obliviously.

"So, you felt it was your responsibility to set this up?" she asked even as she sidled around a cultist, keeping obstacles between her and Goblet. She surreptitiously fiddled with the gun and tried to figure out how to take the safety catch off. No doubt this was something Thomas had learned in her first days at the Estate, but unfortunately the knowledge did not appear to have stuck. It didn't help that she couldn't take her eyes off Goblet for fear of his gouging them out.

"Ah, Rook Thomas. Such an amateur in fieldwork! You're angling for some information about the plan." Goblet smirked, baring a set of saw-edged teeth. "Shall I give you all the details, like a Bond villain, right before your wristwatch turns out to be some sort of buzz saw?"

"I'm not wearing a wristwatch," pointed out Myfanwy.

"Even better," said Goblet. "I won't have to tear your arms off at the beginning of our little session. I always like to leave them till the end." Myfanwy faltered a little at this prospect, and Goblet noticed. "Oh, yes, Rook Thomas, we're going to have all sorts of fun. But you're going to die without ever finding out what the hell is going on here."

"Goblet, I will find out everything. In fact, you will tell me."

"Indeed?" said Goblet, raising an eyebrow and several quills. "And how do you expect—" He broke off, his eyes crossed, and he slumped to the ground, revealing Shantay, who was wearing shiny metal gauntlets. No, not gauntlets. Her fists appeared to be covered in a highly polished, flawless silvery metal. Flawless except for the flecks of blood and fragments of quills that adhered after she'd bashed the back of Goblet's head in.

"What a prick," the American Bishop remarked. She flicked some pieces of quill off her knuckles with a metallic scrape, and the silver melted back into her skin, except for a few patches that resolved themselves into rings and bracelets.

"That's very convenient," said Myfanwy admiringly. "I wish I could grow my own accessories."

"Yeah? Well, I wish I could get men to shut the hell up," said Shantay. "You want to trade for a while?"

"It's tempting," mused Myfanwy, "but I've only just figured out how to make people sweat profusely, and I still want to play with it."

"Fair enough."

"Anyway, we should probably try to come up with a way to stop this thing." Myfanwy gestured vaguely at the tableau that surrounded them: the mold, the supine hedgehog man, the frantically chanting cultists. "Goblet here seemed to think the lot of them were veering out of control."

"Do we want to call in your boys out in the trailers?"

"Won't they get swallowed up by the slime?" asked Myfanwy.

"Maybe not, with Goblet out of the picture."

"I'm not sure—for all we know, it was him keeping it from eating us and digesting the team that went in earlier," said Myfanwy. She looked around anxiously but was relieved to find that the fungus wasn't inching its way up her boots. "I think we're okay for the moment. All the more reason to resolve this issue quickly."

"Agreed. I could bash all their heads in, if you'd like," suggested Shantay, her jewelry glittering with the promise of unspeakable violence.

"I'm not particularly keen on bludgeoning several dozen British citizens."

"Well, then, what do you propose?" For an answer, Myfanwy

knelt down by the nearest chanter—a terribly thin woman who looked as if she'd been attempting to live exclusively off photosynthesis. The fungus cupping her face was an angry puce and had draped itself lightly over her frame. Myfanwy reached out and spread her fingers over the woman's face. Myfanwy's eyes glazed, and a look of intense concentration came over her.

There was a reverent pause as Shantay watched expectantly.

Then she watched less expectantly.

Then she checked her watch.

Then she looked at her nails and gave one of them a few quick licks with a file she produced from a pouch.

Then she went over to Goblet, and gave him a solid kick in the stomach for good measure.

Then she checked her messages on her mobile phone, listening intently against the chanting.

Then she glanced at her watch again.

Then she hummed a few lines from a popular song and got a good close look at each of the people chanting.

Then her phone rang.

"Did it ever occur to you that this might require a modicum of concentration?" snapped Myfanwy in irritation, breaking out of her trance. "Did the dramatic pose and the look of profound focus not tip you off?"

"Sorry," said Shantay, "but I can't turn my phone off. I'm Bishop for the Croatoan. What if there's an emergency?"

"*Is* it an emergency?" asked Myfanwy icily. Shantay looked at the caller ID and shamefacedly put her phone back on her belt. "Well?"

"Okay, so in this particular instance it wasn't an emergency," admitted Shantay.

"Who was it?"

"My mom."

"Christ," muttered Myfanwy, going back into her trance. Shantay sighed and looked around vaguely. It was a little while before she noticed that Myfanwy had begun to bleed from the nose and that her limbs were trembling.

"Oh, crap!" she exclaimed, dropping to her knees and holding her sleeve up to the Rook's nose. She called Myfanwy's name but got no response. Instead, there was a slight increase in the chanting, and the blood continued to flow out of Myfanwy's nose. Shantay saw a red blush blossoming along her friend's jawline. She peered more closely and saw that it was actually a dusting of spores. It thickened before Shantay's eyes and rapidly grew into a fuzzy coating down Myfanwy's neck and up toward her hairline.

"Oh God, oh God, oh *God*," Shantay muttered to herself, frantically trying to comb the growths out of the Rook's hair. Her fingers became silver, metal curled up over her manicured fingernails, and she clawed along Myfanwy's camouflage sleeves, scraping off the little mushrooms that had suddenly sprung up. Then, remembering, she held part of her own sleeve to Myfanwy's streaming nostrils. "Myfanwy, honey, you need to wake the hell up!" she called into the fungus-covered ear.

Shantay heard a stirring behind her and looked over to see Goblet twitching feebly. He must have had some sort of regeneration ability. Either that or his quills had provided more protection than she'd anticipated. She looked at her silver fingernails and briefly entertained the idea of clawing out his jugular. Instead, she twisted around awkwardly—by this time, she was holding Myfanwy up in her arms—and lashed out with her boot. Her heel connected with Goblet's bequilled jaw, and for that one moment, it was totally worth it.

But then Myfanwy went into convulsions, and in the process of shaking about, she slammed her head back into Shantay's face.

"Ow! God dabbit," she yelled, clutching at her nose and dropping Myfanwy on the floor.

The chanting got louder and more frantic, and Shantay failed to notice that there was a light dusting of fungus along her forearms.

22

Dear You,

Well, this was a day and a half. I'm currently in a limousine on the way back from Whitby, along with Chevalier Gubbins. Bishop Alrich and Sir Henry are flying back in a helicopter, since Checquy policy dictates that no more than two Court members can be on the same aircraft, and I felt that, after today's money- (and staff-) eating fiasco, springing for another helicopter would be extravagant.

It started out early, which is exactly how I don't like my Saturdays to begin. I like to sleep in a bit, have my breakfast cooked for me, sit by a blazing fire, maybe do a little shopping, and then go into the office. But this Saturday I had to wake up at four in the morning so as to get ready to be picked up at quarter to five. My bodyguard for today, Anthony, was waiting at my door when I walked out, and I wondered guiltily how long he'd been standing in the freezing winter wind. He carried my briefcase, garment bag, and satchel to the limo, making sure I was comfortably settled before heaving his ponderous bulk into the front passenger seat. Once I was in the car, I fell asleep, and I only woke up when we picked up Gubbins, who was abominably cheerful.

"Morning, Myfanwy," Gubbins exclaimed as he bounded into the car, jolting me awake. I had been drooling copiously on the armrest. "Gad, but it's freezing out. Still, this is fairly jolly, eh?" His bodyguard, an anorexic-looking black man, sat silently next to him.

"Oh, yeah," I said. Quite jolly when you weren't the one who had to plan all of this.

"I have to admit, I'm not entirely certain of the details—I was in Brasília when the notification came out."

"It's an egg hatching."

"Of course it is," he said, rolling his eyes. "Whenever there's a supernatural event, there's always an egg."

"Eggs are big in our business," I said through a yawn. "Anyway, there's this seventeen-year-old student at the Estate. Noel something, I've got the details written down somewhere. He's not much in the special-abilities department—gets along with animals or some such—but he's enthusiastic about history and research."

"Smart kid?" asked Gubbins.

"They don't give them the option of not being smart," I said. "You think Frau Blümen would let her standards slip?"

"No chance," he said with a snort.

"Anyway, this kid is allowed special access to the archives, and he was digging through some manuscripts when he came across mention of something particularly interesting." I rummaged in my bag and produced a thermos of coffee; I offered it to Gubbins, who shook his head politely.

"So, what was the interesting thing?"

"You won't believe me," I warned.

"I'm in the Checquy," he said. "I'm paid to believe things no one else believes."

"A dragon," I said wearily.

"You're bullshitting me," he said.

"I told you. I didn't believe it either. I mean, there's been no confirmed sighting of a dragon for centuries, and even back then, they were spotted only in places that were cold beyond reason. The beginning of the Little Ice Age was the last time they were here." I was trying not to watch as Gubbins did some strange little isometric exercises. The man was like a yogi on acid. I poured myself some coffee and kept my eyes firmly on my hands.

"Anyway, it seems that some particularly fecund female dragon decided to lay her egg in North Yorkshire. Apparently the area was very popular with dragons."

"Oh?" said Gubbins.

"Yeah, dragons and pterodactyls. For millions of years, something about the place has been very attractive to flying reptiles. People have found entire pterodactyl skeletons, and some bits of dragon skeletons that they thought were a subspecies of pterodactyl. One of our operatives, Yves Tyerman, witnessed and recorded the egg laying. His report was accepted by the Court in London and filed away, not to be seen again for hundreds of years."

"I suppose the civil service is always the civil service," said Gubbins breezily.

"Well, thanks to Noel whatever's research, this dragon egg was brought to our attention. Now, these things take centuries to hatch, but this kid, with freakish attention to detail, calculated the exact date of the hatching."

"The exact date?" asked Gubbins skeptically.

"Don't look at me," I said. "I'm no dragon expert, but it seems they're fairly punctual about this sort of thing. Our little prodigy did some math, got a long-suffering tutor at the Estate to drive him out there, and his powers told him that the dragon in the egg was alive and would be hatching this evening. You and I are going to make sure everything is ready. Which is why we are going up so early."

"And this all happened in the past few days?"

"No, this happened about six months ago," I said wearily. "But I had to authorize the ground scans and excavations."

"Excavations?"

"Dragons bury their eggs pretty deep," I said. "So we have been conducting a discreet archaeological dig."

"And now we are going to witness the hatching of a dragon egg?"

"Uh-huh. But not just the hatching. This kid . . ." I shuffled through my papers. "His name is Noel Bittner. And he maintains that he will be able to establish some sort of psychic rapport with the dragon when it hatches. He says he's already touched minds with it and that they will bond when it emerges."

"Fascinating," said Gubbins.

"Yeah," I said unenthusiastically. "So naturally we have to have half the Court there to witness the occasion. A Rook, a Chev, a Bishop, and the Lord. In addition to all the support staff, and Bittner."

"So, where are the Bishop and the Lord?" he asked pointedly.

"Bishop Alrich will arrive after sundown with Sir Henry," I said bitterly. "They're flying up." He nodded glumly, and we both settled down with our laptops and the many, many papers that are necessary if you are going to run any government department.

By the time we arrived at the site, I was starving and Gubbins was suffering from a bad case of cabin fever. You would think that a man so flexible would do all right in a small, enclosed space. After all, I know for a fact that he can fit himself into a suitcase and remain there for seven hours. I've seen him do it. But within the relatively spacious confines of a Rolls-Royce limousine, he managed to drive both himself and me to the brink of insanity.

Only scrupulous good manners (which we had both acquired at gunpoint at the Estate) and the fact that he was my favorite member of the Court prevented us from coming to sharp words. As it was, we both bounded out of the car into the snow with an enthusiasm that surprised the Pawn waiting for us. Gubbins's bodyguard emerged somewhat more slowly but with even wilder eyes. Anthony, who had been up front with the driver, seemed positively languid by comparison.

"Rook Thomas, Chevalier Gubbins, welcome to the Hatchery," the Pawn said wearily.

"Thank you, Pawn Cahill," I said, looking up at her. She was tall, and dressed in the kind of casual clothes that will let you kill someone easily and won't draw attention from passersby. Khakis are good for this sort of thing. "Gubbins, this is Pawn Breeshey Cahill. She's been overseeing this project since it was brought to our attention by Bittner." She flinched at the mention of his name. From what I'd heard, Bittner had taken his discoveries to mean that he was head of the entire show. For Pawn Cahill, who had been obliged to simultaneously stroke his ego and run a thirty-man operation, it had been somewhat trying.

"It's a pleasure to meet you, Pawn Cahill," said Gubbins, like the gentleman he was. "I understand you've been working under difficult conditions, but I've heard nothing but good about the way you've handled everything." She flushed with pleasure. "Thank you for meeting us," he continued. "I know it's an early morning."

"Coming on the end of an extremely long six months," she said, smiling at him. I marveled for a moment at how she blossomed under his attention. She hadn't brushed me off exactly, but her eyes seemed to slide over me to him. I'd been disregarded, and it chafed. It didn't used to bother me, but since I learned what is going to happen — since I learned about you — I've *been observing myself more. People ignore me. They scan right over me, and they do it because I'm not . . . not what they expect a leader to be.*

I brought myself back to the conversation. Cahill was explaining the details of the facilities that had been installed. I listened and mentally ticked off all the expenditures I had authorized. Checquy archival crew with camera equipment. Scientists with sensory equipment. A huge mobile refrigeration unit for housing the dragon when it hatched. One of our satellites put into geosynchronous orbit above us. Accommodations for the excavation crew. A relatively plush command center. Catering. It had cost an astonishing amount of money, and still Bittner the wunderkind hadn't been pleased. He'd wanted the egg and the entire shebang moved to Stonehenge. When that had been denied, he'd wanted a new Stonehenge created somewhere else. My observers at the site had reported he'd been outraged at some of the other things I'd denied him. If he knew what I had authorized, his outrage would have known no bounds.

". . . and if you'll follow us over to the farmhouse, there's breakfast waiting for you," finished Cahill.

"The farmhouse?" repeated Gubbins.

"Yes, this land was a private farm," she explained. "We acquired it for a handsome sum." I listened silently but mentally added the qualifier that it had been I who vetoed the proposal that we pay the farmer a pittance and use government authority to "scare the living hell out of him," as Bittner had suggested in one of his many memos. Remembering the appalling treatment of my father, I had opted for the kinder side of eminent domain. We had paid the farmer well and provided a cover story calculated to allay concerns and discourage interest.

Pawn Cahill gently guided us through a complex of temporary structures to the farmhouse, where a gorgeous buffet had been set up. I may have scrimped in some areas, but one of the lessons my teachers at the Estate had drilled into me was that an army marches on its stomach. As a result, I always made sure there was a good catering staff at all long-term field operations.

Gubbins, the bodyguards, and I gathered up platefuls of pastries and hot food and poured ourselves brimming cups of coffee, fueling up for a long day of finalizing details. We had all settled down when the door burst open with a bang. Anthony produced, seemingly out of his armpits, a pair of submachine guns, while Gubbins's skeletal bodyguard (whose name was Jonas) turned out to have been hiding a sawed-off shotgun within his robes. (Did I mention he was wearing robes? Well, he was. Bright purple ones.)

"Stop," I said quietly to the bodyguards. The person who came into the room pointedly ignored them.

"So, you're Rook Thomas," he said loudly. I had recognized him instantly as Noel Bittner—something about his overwhelmingly irritating arrogance and the fact that he was still unable to drink alcohol legally. And his glasses. "I have put up with your small-minded limiting of funds. I understand that not everyone can appreciate the astounding opportunities that exist here. The unique forces at work today allow a chance for majesty, pride, and magic to reenter these islands!" He paused for breath, and Gubbins murmured to me out of the side of his mouth, "Should we have them shoot him?"

I shook my head. "Apparently he's the one who needs to bond with the dragon," I whispered back. Gubbins looked as if he wanted to reply, but Bittner had already commenced another rant, armed with more outrage.

"I would expect that a Rook of the Checquy would have an understanding of the raptures surrounding this event and would not have denied the appropriate conditions for the dragon to emerge into this world. I had heard rumors about you, but I could not believe that you would be so inured to the wonder of this occasion. And now! Now I have just learned that you have allowed armed soldiers on this site, not to guard the hatchling, but to stand by to kill it." Bittner leaned over the table, talking in my face. Instinctively, I shrank back, and noticed with disgust that he was spitting on my food.

"I demand that you remove the troops! The dragon and I have already touched minds, and it may sense the horror I feel. I can't promise that I will be able to soothe it, even with my innate empathy." He glared at me. Behind me, Anthony was tensed, ready to crush the boy utterly, and I tried to take heart from his presence.

"Noel," I began quietly.

"I prefer to be called Adept Bittner," he said. Gubbins raised his lack of eyebrows but refrained from pointing out that no such title existed.

"Adept Bittner," I said. "I can understand your concern." He swelled righteously, and I hastily continued. "But you must understand that not everyone can easily comprehend what is going on here. This is an unusual situation, even for the Checquy." I could mangle words with the best of them, and this was a kid who had clearly read too much of a certain kind of book. His righteous swelling changed subtly to prideful puffing. "These men are not here for the dragon but rather to reassure the visitors, who are exceptionally important, as befits the situation." Bittner nodded reluctantly.

"I understand. And it's not as if bullets could harm the dragon; it was the disrespect I objected to."

"Rest assured," I said, "we are sensible of the honor that is being done here." He liked that and nodded in a manner that he probably thought grave and wise. I took a deep breath. "Adept Bittner, will you join us for breakfast?" Beside me, I could feel Gubbins recoil at the prospect.

"No," said Bittner, casting a reluctant look at the buffet. "I am fasting in preparation for this evening. Now I must go to the egg and commune with the dragon." Noel Bittner swept out, and I pushed my plate away with an unsteady hand. He wasn't a scary person, but I didn't like being shouted at by anyone.

"Myfanwy," said Gubbins. "I cannot believe you let that little shit talk to you like that. I don't care how talented he is, you are a member of the Checquy Court, and he is just a student at the Estate." Gubbins was pissed off—not just at Bittner, but at me. I took a deep breath.

"Chevalier Gubbins," I said. "This is the only person who can communicate with the dragon. If we can stop it from doing what dragons traditionally do, which involves flying all around the place burning houses and eating hundreds of humans before heading north, then it will be a good thing. If we can bring it under the control of the Checquy, then it will be a great thing. To that end, I will put up with almost any amount of shit." Gubbins subsided, but I could tell he was not happy. Wordlessly, I stood up and got myself a fresh breakfast.

The rest of the day was spent overseeing preparations for the hatching. It was winter, and although the egg had been moved from its hole, it couldn't be brought inside. Dragons like it cold. Really, really cold. So even though it was below zero, we'd had a huge cooling apparatus set up. There also needed to be special accommodation so that humans could observe closely without freezing to death or being killed by a newborn dragon's temper tantrum. So a ring of viewing chambers had been placed around the egg, furnished with comfortable chairs, heaters, bulletproof glass, brandy, and opera glasses. And heavily bundled snipers on top. All the luxuries of home.

By the time the helicopter arrived, it had been dark for quite a while, and I'd been able to shower in the farmhouse and put on something slightly more formal. After all, it's not every day that you appear at the birth of a dragon. Gubbins and I were both stationed at the entrance to the pavilion, ready to welcome the last witnesses from the Court.

"Good evening, Sir Henry," I said demurely. "Welcome." The Lord crunched through the snow, nodded benevolently, and hurried into the heated room, casting off his heavy coat. Gubbins followed him to make him comfortable, leaving me to welcome Alrich, who came out of the darkness. The guards tensed discreetly. Everyone was cold, and a light snow had begun to fall, glowing in the glare of the lights, but Alrich glided over the ground without a sound. He left no footprints in the snow, and his breath didn't steam. His hair shimmered like burning blood, and he was dressed in thin black silk. Waiting for him, even with the heat coming through the door behind me, I shivered.

"Bishop Alrich," I whispered. He smiled and nodded his head slightly. I was ready for him to glide past me, but he offered his arm, and, gulping, I accepted it. Behind us, the glass doors slid shut, and I began to regain feeling in my feet. Gubbins was introducing Sir Henry to various key members of the site staff.

". . . and this is Noel Bittner," he finished. Bittner swept forward, stepping on my foot. He was dressed in some sort of tailored robe with a hood, which was drawn back. Sir Henry looked at him with an amiable smile that deepened when Bittner made a deep bow. I wanted to roll my eyes, but I had to acknowledge that we all made habitual obeisances before the heads of the Checquy. Though we didn't generally clap our fists to our chests and sink to one knee.

"So this is the young man who has unearthed both the history of the egg and the egg itself," said Sir Henry in approval. I saw Pawn Cahill stiffen, but she kept her mouth shut.

"Actually, Sir Henry, Pawn Cahill oversaw the excavation," I said discreetly, and Bittner shot me a dirty look.

"Ah, of course," said Sir Henry benevolently, clasping her hand and giving it a hearty shake. *"Damn impressed with the setup here. Rook Thomas sent along the reports, and I gather it was a first-rate operation."* She brightened while Bittner looked on sourly.

"Noel," I said, *"this is Bishop Alrich,"* and the little snot stepped back slightly. He'd been drawn to the power of Sir Henry, but Alrich intimidated him. Enough so that he didn't correct me for not using his self-bestowed title. He bowed, another choreographed affair but one that was a little less prostrating. Alrich, to my amusement, said nothing and merely gave a small nod. Bittner rose uncertainly before checking his watch.

"Sir Henry, it's almost time for the egg to hatch," he said. *"If you will excuse me?"* Sir Henry nodded, and Bittner strode off. He slid open a door leading into the courtyard where the egg stood, and I flinched as the wind blew in.

I'd taken the opportunity to inspect the egg earlier in the day. Dark blue, with a faintly pebbled surface and centuries' worth of dirt ground in, it was twice as tall as me and would have taken four or five of me holding hands to encircle it. It was still, a little snow piled up on top of it, and it made me very uncomfortable. Bittner invited me to touch it, but, wary of any possible activation of my powers, I put my hands behind my back and declined. He responded with a contemptuous smirk.

Now the egg was illuminated by spotlights, and the drifts of snow around it had melted. A wooden walkway stretched up to it, and it was along this that Noel Bittner walked, his robe flapping in the wind. In the viewing galleries surrounding the egg, technicians, biologists, historians, and a camera crew were all watching intently. On the roof, a ring of Checquy troops were armed with a variety of weapons. The historical texts were hazy about how to kill a dragon, since no one in recorded history had ever managed it. In our section, we settled back in vast armchairs and accepted beverages from a butler. The lights dimmed overhead, but the lights on the courtyard brightened, so we could see everything clearly.

Bittner was rigged with a hands-free radio so that his every reaction and observation could be recorded for posterity. He was breathing deeply. I suspect *it was on purpose. His stance was, to my eye, overly dramatic—he'd spread his arms, and his thin robe flapped in the wind. I suppose he had thought this would appear striking in the icy cold, but after Alrich's entrance, anything short of actual nudity was unimpressive. Besides, I've never had any patience for posers.*

"It's warm under my hands" came Bittner's breathless report through the intercom. "I'd say we have two minutes."

One of the scientists' voices came through next. "All observers, don your protective eyewear and sporrans." The butler came around with a tray full of glasses that looked like old motorists' goggles. There were also little lead-filled aprony things that we draped over our laps.

"One minute," said Bittner. I smoothed my skirt anxiously and then replaced the lead sporran. Around me, the other observers were tense, and Alrich, as always, was utterly still, no breath stirring his body. All of us were staring at Bittner's white hands on the egg and listening to his voice over the intercom.

"It's stirring. I can feel its movements. Its muscles are flexing within the shell." He was milking the occasion for all it was worth. And why not? After all, this was the sort of thing that could make a career in the Checquy.

Besides, now I could feel it too.

It was there, faintly itching on the edges of my perception. I looked around to see if the others could sense it, but they were all intent on the adolescent prodigy communing with the waking monster. I had a twinge of last-minute doubt. Dragons had ravaged Europe before, killing untold numbers. In front of us was the last of a dynasty that had faded by the fourteenth century. An eleventh-hour surge of the bloodlines, and now we were watching it emerge.

I sensed the movement within the shell. Muscles flexed against their containment, and mine flexed in unconscious sympathy. I felt the stirrings of panic in my stomach. Normally, to use my powers I need to be touching someone. Occasionally, when someone is under major physical or mental pressure, I get hints of that person. But this was different. My fingers hooked into claws, and I strained against my own muscles to straighten them out. I wanted to spread my wings and scream into the air.

Bittner had fallen silent, but we could all see the egg rocking slightly. Then a claw cut through the shell, stabbing like a stiletto. It was neat, controlled, slicing through the egg and peeling off six-inch-thick sections. In a shockingly short amount of time, the egg had fallen away and we could see a mass of brown scales. Bittner spread his arms and the dragon uncurled, limbs stretching, tendons snapping into place. A serpentine neck drew itself out and up. Massive, fanlike wings were unfurled up into the sky. We watched, spellbound.

"My God," whispered Alrich.

Bittner's breathing was ragged over the intercom. We heard him gasp just before the dragon threw its head back and shrieked into the night. Centuries-old lungs were cut by air for the first time. Eyes opened and saw their first light. And I felt it all. It screamed again, louder, and we all clapped our hands over our ears.

"Rook Thomas?" Cahill asked uncertainly, and I saw that she was ready to give the order to the snipers.

"No!" shouted Bittner, whirling around to face us. "You must not! The dragon and I are bonding! We share a unique rap—" He was cut off abruptly as the dragon reached out and languidly clawed his head off.

I clapped my hands to my mouth, but my eyes were glued to the tableau. Around me the room reacted. People stood up, knocking their chairs over. Some shouted. One or two were ill. Alrich burst out laughing. Anthony put his hand on my shoulder as if to guide me away, and Cahill shrieked into the radio, giving the order to attack. In front of us, the courtyard was filled with flashes as the soldiers opened fire. Bullets swept through, and the glass flexed as bullets ricocheted off the dragon. I'd given orders for the strongest reinforced glass possible; these were the kind of windows the pope sat behind. Smoke curled up in front of us, and the dragon was lost to view. Its tail slapped against the glass then disappeared back into the clouds. Then a torrent of fire burst through, illuminating the smoke and the snow.

"Status? Status!" Cahill was shouting. There was no answer, and the smoke slowly cleared. The dragon was rearing back on its hind legs, unharmed, fanning its wings gently. Around the courtyard lay the scattered bodies of soldiers. Some lay on the roof, burning. There were bodies on the *ground, torn apart. Against our window, a man hung down, eviscerated, his insides painting the glass red.*

"Orrrr . . . fuck," said Anthony behind me. The dragon reached out, plucked up half a guardsman, and began to devour it messily. With weak fingers, I opened my mobile phone and dialed.

"This is Rook Thomas. Can you hear me, Monica?"

"Yes, ma'am" came her voice. In the background the wind whistled, and I pictured her, bundled up tight against the cold, her hair tied back, watching the stars wheel above her as she waited patiently, standing on nothing. The dragon's head swung down and around, and through the mirrored glass, it saw us. I felt its muscles tense and its talons slide out.

"It's gone badly. Begin now, please." I was proud that my voice didn't shake.

"Yes, ma'am." Monica hung up, and I turned to Pawn Cahill, who was staring in shock at the various parts of her troops.

"Pawn Cahill, close the shutters please." She stared at me, not processing, and I grabbed her hand. "Close the shutters!" A shock passed through her body; she looked at me with widening eyes and slapped at the controls at her side. Our view of the dragon was cut off as massive iron curtains rolled up out of the ground.

"Thomas, what the hell is going on?" demanded Sir Henry, grabbing me roughly by the shoulder and turning me to face him. "I demand you tell me—" He stopped talking, and everyone else stopped as well because they could hear what was happening. From above us, there was a shrill screaming sound that grew in volume and intensity. It built and built, and we all huddled together as the sound entered our heads and trembled through our bones. Then, with a resounding crack, it arrived. A shock wave struck, vibrating through the shutters and fracturing the glass although not shattering it. There was silence.

I reached out and touched the button Cahill had pressed, and the shutters slid down. In the courtyard, the spotlights had gone out, but we could see the corpse of the dragon lying on the ground. Its head had been severed neatly from its body, and in the gap, standing calmly at attention and covered in steaming dragon guts, was Pawn Monica Jarvis-Reed, who had just arrived from four miles above us armed with only her own indestructible body and some easily laundered clothes.

After that, as you can imagine, the evening broke up fairly rapidly, and if you'll excuse me, I am now going to pass out from exhaustion.

Love,

Me

23

The two women lay on the floor staring blankly into space, dust settling quietly on their eyes. Their clothes were stiff with mildew, and all around them the cultists continued their chanting. A little way off, Goblet the hedgehog man was lying in a way that suggested he wouldn't be going anywhere or doing anything for a while. Under a coating of fuzz, Shantay's phone rang, playing a little electronic version of the *Addams Family* theme song.

Myfanwy sat up with a gasp. She drew deep breaths of musty air into her lungs, and her fingers scrabbled along the floor as her whole body strove to pump oxygen to where it was needed. She fumbled for the canteen of water on her belt and then spent a long time gargling and spitting, coughing out whatever was offending her system. Finally, she managed to look around and answer the phone.

"Hello?" she said hoarsely.

"Myfanwy?" came Poppat's voice; he sounded frantic enough to forget about protocol. "Thank God! We've been ready to have the whole site leveled and torched! We've had that phone ringing for forty-five minutes!"

"Oh, really?" asked Myfanwy absently. "Well, don't do anything to the house, I've figured out the problem."

"Brilliant," said Poppat. "Is Bishop Petoskey okay?"

"Oh, yeah," said Myfanwy, leaning back against the prostrate form of her friend. "She'll be fine in a minute or two, and this whole situation should be resolved in about half an hour." She looked around at the mold coating the room. While she'd lain unconscious, new branches of fungus had grown out from the walls, covering the doorway and weaving a barricade across the windows. "Yeah, half an hour...or so."

"Can I at least send in some troops?" the Pawn asked.

"Probably best not," she said, watching as a new arm of growth slowly stretched its way across the ceiling. "I'll call you back when it's clear."

"But you're certain you're okay in there?"

"Yep. I'll call you back in a bit."

"But what if—" he began, but she hung up.

"Nice guy, but he really needs to have that manual removed from his colon," she remarked to the chanting drones. "Of course, you guys have your own problems, but at least you're not dependent on standard operating procedure." She sighed and looked disdainfully at the mold coating her clothes and skin. It itched and seemed to consist of equal parts black mildew and some virulently orangey-red spores.

Myfanwy called up in her mind a picture of the system she'd mapped out while tapped into the cultists. Once she'd figured out how it worked, the whole thing had proven...well, in fact it had proven to be horrendously complex. But at least now she understood it. With a mental twist, she disrupted all the tiny connections that made the spores a part of something larger. She blew on her skin, and the little flakes fluttered away dead into the air.

Myfanwy then reached out with her fingers and touched the back of Shantay's hand. Under her touch, spirals of silver spread out liquidly across the American's skin, thickening and joining themselves until she was entirely made of metal. Her hair gave off little fizzling and crackling sounds as the metal coiled itself down and over her dozens of braids, like sculpture made by the most dexterous and anally retentive artisan in the world. The mold that had coated her skin was scythed off by the spreading metal, and Shantay glittered in the near darkness.

Myfanwy stared in awe at her friend, a fashion model dipped in quicksilver. Her finger on the back of Shantay's hand was grubby compared to the shining perfection beneath it. But she resisted the urge to draw back and instead sent another little message down through the metal skin and coursing along into Shantay's system. Shantay shuddered, as if she'd been shocked by electricity. Once, twice, and then she sat up, opening her eyes. While her skin was silver, her eyes were hard and shiny, like black gemstones.

"Wakey, wakey," said Myfanwy. "I'm sorry we don't have any coffee or tea, but that's what you get when you elect to take a nap in a manifestation site."

"*That,*" said Shantay hoarsely, "was no fun at all. I feel like I brushed my teeth with a loaf of old bread."

"Yeah, well, not to fret," Myfanwy said with a sigh. "I figured out the problem."

"So you know how to stop all this?"

"Sure, it's as simple as doing *this*." She blinked.

And the chanting stopped.

So what exactly did you do?" asked Shantay. They were sitting in the lobby of a youth hostel waiting for a car to come get them, surrounded by a crowd of backpacking students from Australia and America. Both of the women had insisted on showers after they emerged from the house, but the Checquy headquarters in Bath had been packed full of Pawns, soldiers, and doctors, all of them trying to do fifty things at once. No doubt they would have stepped aside in the face of Myfanwy's superior rank, but their need was greater. There hadn't been a vacancy in any hotels ("There's some sort of convention in town, Rook Thomas. I'm dreadfully sorry") and so it had been the youth hostel or nothing. Apparently they didn't let you use the Roman baths anymore, not even if you were a Rook.

"It's hard to describe, but it involved disrupting the flow of instructions from the fungus to the hosts. The main thing is, I was able to get them to shut up and open all those little pods down in the cellar where they were keeping our troops," said Myfanwy.

"Do we know what they were trying to do?" asked Shantay. "I mean, other than grow something that looked like the back of my refrigerator?"

262

"Well, didn't our friend with the spines say that he was worried about it spreading? Maybe it was going to eat Bath or something. It was growing. It wasn't going to stop."

"A mold bomb?" asked Shantay, looking around in irritation as she was jostled by a college student carrying a backpack twice her size.

"I guess. That's not what's worrying me though," said Myfanwy. Her brow furrowed for a moment as she thought. "There was something funny about Goblet."

"The fact that he's a high-ranking member of your organization who's apparently engaged in treasonous activities?"

"Well, I'll admit that that's a trifle peculiar," allowed Myfanwy. "But that's not it."

"Maybe the fact that he implicated your counterpart in the conspiracy in front of an important representative from a foreign government?"

"Well, not *just* that," said Myfanwy with a bit of irritation.

"How about that we have to go back to London for that dinner thing, and you look like a wreck?"

"You know, you're not helping. Ah, the car is here. Thank God."

"So," said Shantay. "Does this mean we're not stopping to take the waters?"

Norman Goblet

Goblet was inducted into the Estate during a time of change. The original curriculum and philosophy of the Estate had been a combination of the postwar mentality and the traditions of the Checquy—a sort of hybrid military camp/guildhall. It was certainly an improvement on the previous master-apprentice approach, but as the years passed, the Checquy decided that a new system was needed. Drastic changes were made. With this reformation of the Estate and its methods, there were some kinks that needed to be worked out, and, in my opinion, Norman Goblet stands out as one of the kinkiest.

Make that the most kinked.

Drafted in at the age of twelve, Norman Goblet was the darling of his teachers. This new incarnation of the Estate was based on the classic boarding-school model. So the Estate was remade as sort of an Eton with tentacles. In any case, in every such academy, there is always one student who plays the game just the right way, who is made head of house (yes, they had houses back then. Thank God they disbanded them a couple decades back), gets grades that are good enough to keep him out of the bottom set but not so good as to mark him as a swot, and sucks up to the headmaster so hard that he leaves the man a desiccated husk. Such a youth was Goblet. His ability to kick ass was matched only by his ability to kiss ass. Naturally overbearing and pompous, he would be an ideal Court member. So it came as no surprise when he was appointed school captain and earmarked for greatness in the Checquy.

It was a matter of no small satisfaction to his peers when he failed to live up to the promise he'd shown. After some unremarkable performances at the Annexe, he was moved to Bath, which was then the highest action site in the Isles. I gather this was based on the recommendation of his old headmaster, who was keen to see the golden boy thrive. But thrive he did not, remaining in Bath even as the number of supernatural occurrences waned. Eventually he was made head of the region, partly out of the Checquy's sheer embarrassment and partly because it was clear that there wouldn't be a great deal for him to mess up.

I meet with Goblet biannually, once at the yearly review session when all the region heads come to the Rookery and again at the executive Christmas party. To be perfectly honest, he doesn't strike me as particularly noteworthy. Kind of bitter, but I can understand that. He'd been as much as promised a seat on the Court, and it never materialized. Which was good for the nation, but not so great for Goblet.

"Ingrid, are all of Gestalt's bodies coming to the reception tonight?" Myfanwy asked, holding the mobile phone with her chin as she paged through the purple binder. She and Shantay were flying back to London, and she was trying to find the section that described the penalties for treason. She'd browsed through the section at one point and vaguely recalled a long list of punishments culminating with the guilty party being ritually trampled to death by the population of the village of Avebury, which seemed unlikely, or at least somewhat difficult to arrange.

Back in the mold house, she'd spent several minutes figuring out how to make Goblet's spines retract into his body. Then she'd draped his coat over his head and led him by the hand out of the building and into the trailer, taking great care not to let anyone see who he was. Myfanwy was not keen to have everyone know that a high-ranking member of the Checquy had been responsible for the whole thing. She'd arranged for Goblet to be transported to the Rookery and put somewhere where he wouldn't be inconvenient. As it was, it looked likely that the incident was going to enter the realm of Pawn legend. Supposedly there hadn't been any threat in the past four decades that the Barghests couldn't overcome. And now that scrawny Rook—you know, Thomas, the skinny little girl who threw up in the Estate swimming pool that one time? Yeah, she went in after the strike team was eaten and then walked out complaining she needed a shower and a box of chocolates.

When Myfanwy had reached the incident trailer, she'd found her team looking very alert, eager, and keen to follow orders. A contingent of Checquy scientists, who had been standing by in a sterile compartment of the trailer with eagerly poised scalpels, had entered the house cautiously, after she'd assured them that they were no longer in danger of being swallowed up. A Pawn armed with chain saws had gone into the basement and spent a messy half hour slicing open the pods she'd told him would be there. Inside had been the Barghests, all of whom were in justifiably bad tempers. The cultists were being carefully removed from their dead, graying little cocoons and documented, in an effort to figure out who the hell they were. The whole house had been curtained off from the public with big sheets of plastic that were inscribed with dire warnings about asbestos, and samples of everything inside were being collected to be studied under a microscope.

"Yes, Rook Thomas," said Ingrid calmly over the phone. "The Lord and Lady like the effect of all four bodies, and they are quite keen to impress the Americans. They'll expect you to be wearing something formal. Might I suggest the crimson dress? The one that Greek woman made you buy?" There was a long, awkward silence, since Myfanwy had absolutely no idea what her executive assistant was talking about. A crimson dress? How out of character. As far as Myfanwy could tell, everything in Thomas's wardrobe was black, gray, or white.

Ingrid sighed. "Val tells me that it's in the wardrobe in your guest room, along with all those other clothes the Greek made you buy and that you never wear. I'll send over the instructions on how to put it on."

"Christ," said Myfanwy, who'd been paying only partial attention but was now jolted away from her perusal of the administrivia. "I thought it was going to be an intimate gathering."

"Well, it is just the Court members and their entourages," said Ingrid. "And the envoys from the Croatoan and their entourages."

"Hold on a sec," said Myfanwy, turning to Shantay, who was busily checking her e-mail. "Shan, do you have an entourage?"

"Uh, yes," said Shantay in a tone that suggested she was also in possession of a spine, a nose, and various other things that were usually taken for granted.

"So where are they?" asked Myfanwy. "Why aren't they hanging around you? And don't take this personally, but why aren't they entertaining you so that you don't have to come along to manifestations?"

"They had to fly in, so they're still settling in at the hotel."

"Oh," said Myfanwy. "Ingrid, is...*my* entourage going to be ready?" she said hesitantly. Since the day she'd assumed this life, she hadn't been aware of having any specific entourage, as such. Maybe Thomas had elected not to have any.

"I'll be going to the hairdresser in an hour," said Ingrid, "and I've e-mailed them the instructions for your hair, so they will be ready for you when you arrive. Now, will Anthony be an acceptable bodyguard?"

"Yeah, sounds great," said Myfanwy. *So Ingrid and Anthony are my entourage.*

"Excellent, then we shall come to your house a half hour before sunset."

"Sure," said Myfanwy. *It sounds like I'm going to the high school formal.*

I can't wear this!" Myfanwy exclaimed in horror.

Val came trotting into the guest room and stopped short when she saw the dress Myfanwy was holding up.

"You can't wear that!" the housekeeper exclaimed.

"Yes, I know," said Myfanwy, who was shivering in her underwear but much preferred it to the alternative.

"It's like all the material that's supposed to be on top migrated to the bottom," said Val.

"Yes, I know," said Myfanwy, who thoughtfully eyed her own chest and wondered how the thing was supposed to stay up. How could Thomas describe herself as shy and unassuming while owning a garment that would embarrass a Venetian courtesan? It wasn't that it was indecent so much as that it implied a great deal of self-confidence. It was extraordinary and undeniably unorthodox. It would have been striking on anyone, but on Thomas it would be downright shocking.

In fact, all of the outfits in the guest room wardrobe represented a drastic schism in Thomas's apparent fashion sensibilities. Myfanwy had opened the doors and then actually taken a few steps backward, stunned by the clothes she'd found there. Inside, a garden of colors blossomed. A full range of dresses, gowns, and outfits awaited, all beautifully made, and all crying out for attention.

"What kind of party are you going to?" Val asked.

"It's for work," said Myfanwy helplessly.

"Formal?"

"To a certain degree."

"Obviously. You don't see a lot of trains nowadays, not outside weddings." *Any wedding in which this dress appeared on the bride would have to be pretty damn open-minded,* thought Myfanwy. *And might well incorporate the honeymoon on the altar.*

"We're meeting with the Americans," Myfanwy explained.

"Oh!" said Val, obviously doing some mental rearranging.

"Do you think I can pull it off?"

"I should think any passerby could pull it off if he tugged on this bit right here," said Val grimly. "Still, your hair is lovely, and with a bit of jewelry you'll look very special."

Upon learning that this was an international event, Val had clearly filed it in the same category as the Oscars, or possibly World War II. She began fussing around as if Myfanwy were her daughter going off to prom. Obviously more familiar with certain aspects of the house than Myfanwy was, Val produced a jewelry box and drew out a large metal necklace to take the place of whatever material was missing from the top of the dress. In a pinch, it could also be used to bludgeon someone to death over the canapés.

Somehow, together, they figured out how Myfanwy was supposed to fit into the gown and where each strap and fastening was supposed to go. When Myfanwy finally stood in front of the mirror, their breath was taken away.

"Well," said Val. "Well."

It was glorious, in an alien sort of way. Myfanwy looked as if she had bathed in the blood of ten fashion designers. The artists at the salon had known exactly how to do her hair and makeup to complement the dress, which had clearly been made for her. Everything was covered that was supposed to be covered. It held her tightly and swirled around her, and although Myfanwy hated to admit this, it made her look amazing. It was a dress designed to draw attention.

"You look like Cinderella," said Val in awe.

"Yeah, if she'd been into bondage and had Christian Dior for a godmother."

"If only you had a man to walk you in," said Val sadly, reverting to concerned-mother mode.

"I'm just grateful there's no metal or leather in this thing," said Myfanwy. *Or spikes.* They stared at the dress some more and were woken from their reverie only by the sound of the doorbell.

"There! That's your car," said Val. "Now, do you have everything you need?"

"Except for Kevlar and a gun," said Myfanwy, who in the flurry of getting ready had temporarily forgotten about the revelations regarding Gestalt's treachery.

"What?"

"Just kidding."

24

Apex House looked like a fairy-tale palace, the spotlights painting its front pillars vivid colors as the night closed in. Dusk was just departing as Myfanwy's car drew up to the front. Her bodyguard for the night, Anthony, had turned out to be a massively fat Japanese man who spoke with a thick Scottish accent and was dressed in traditional Scottish garb. His kilt could have been used as a tartan slipcover for a settee, and his sporran looked as if it could use some friends to back it up. Still, she'd had the presence of mind to compliment him on his appearance.

An incomprehensible stream of syllables had flowed out of his lips. Myfanwy was unable to tell if it was Japanese, Gaelic, or a bastard hybridization of both. Still, she'd smiled politely in reply.

There'd been a pause at the front while Ingrid had fussed over Myfanwy's costume, ensuring that nothing was crumpled. Ingrid wasn't looking too shabby herself in her purple dress, although she was nowhere near as exotic as Myfanwy.

"I'm so glad you got that dress, Rook Thomas. It's a real departure for you, but it suits you."

"You think?"

"Absolutely. It will certainly turn some heads."

"Oh . . . goody."

They moved through the hallways, and everywhere Pawns and Retainers stepped aside, bowing slightly. Was it Myfanwy's imagination or were the male employees taking the opportunity to get a look at the top half of her dress? Judging by the reactions of the female employees, the news of her attire would make its way through the

Checquy gossip highways quickly. Combined with her escapades in Bath, this meant her corporate image was in for a major change. Behind Myfanwy to her right sailed Ingrid with a look of calm efficiency on her face. On her left, Anthony hulked along. They entered the reception room, and the Bishops and the Chevaliers were already there, with their Retainers, all looking suitably classy and powerful.

Bishop Grantchester was dressed in a tailored tuxedo, with strands of inky mist coiling themselves artistically around his arms and shoulders. They trailed behind him as he moved about the room. Chevalier Eckhart was in military uniform. Chevalier Gubbins wore a tuxedo also, although his was rather rumpled. He appeared to be doing his best not to contort into any undignified poses.

It was Bishop Alrich, however, who made Myfanwy's jaw drop. He was dressed in a kimono of black silk intricately embroidered with threads of a deep metallic crimson. It was so long that it trailed the floor behind him, although not quite as much as Myfanwy's dress did. Massive vanes sprouted from his shoulders, arcing back and up like blades. It was an outfit of bizarre and decadent elegance. His hair was plaited down his back in a loose tail of auburn. He caught Myfanwy's eye and gave her a small smile as he scanned every aspect of her outfit. Apparently he approved, because his smile grew larger.

Gestalt arrived, all four bodies walking liquidly in step. Much as Myfanwy hated to admit it, they looked impressive. The mind behind them had decided to take advantage of the bodies' striking similarity and had dressed them identically in a livery of dark blue. Myfanwy studied Eliza, the female and the only one she hadn't yet seen. She was lovely, with her hair coiled intricately at the back of her head. When the four siblings turned their heads to look at her, Myfanwy tensed, but nothing happened.

The Lord and Lady arrived and were honored, he resplendent in military uniform and sporting so many medals that they practically constituted body armor, she dressed in a classic evening gown. Everyone chatted politely, and no one stared at Myfanwy's dress to an extent that could be considered rude. The Retainers moved around carefully, wary of bumping into anybody who might accidentally destroy them. Alrich's and Myfanwy's costumes in particular posed difficulties, since they projected out in unexpected ways. Finally, the Croatoan envoys were announced.

Bishop Morales entered first, flanked by two men, both of whom appeared to be bodybuilders. A little old woman of Mexican descent, she walked with a cane and was dressed in something black and expensive. Myfanwy was called upon to present the Bishop to the heads of the organization. Farrier and Wattleman greeted her formally, and the rest of the Court introduced themselves. Then Shantay entered, looking as marvelous as might be expected, considering she had access to all the boutiques of Rodeo Drive and the kind of figure that, according to some of the Checquy histories, people actually *had* sold their souls to possess.

Pleasantries were exchanged, and waiters wove through the crowd. Myfanwy had been a little concerned that the ballroom would be decorated as blandly as that hideous boardroom. But it was an enormous space with glittering chandeliers, beautifully sculpted columns, and large arrangements of flowers. The perfect place for a party.

"We'll be moving in for dinner in about fifteen minutes, Rook Thomas," Ingrid whispered to her. Myfanwy nodded her thanks and went back to paying some attention to what one of Eckhart's Retainers was saying. From there she was sucked into a conversation with Shantay, Gubbins, Wattleman, and Robert Gestalt. The chitchat was painfully polite, with all the participants avoiding any mention of the Grafters and instead making cocktail chatter that she could easily coast her way through. Discussion of the Grafter threat would occur the next day, with a formal agenda and minutes taken. And so Myfanwy spent most of her time eyeing the Gestalt brother warily and wondering what would be the best way to expose Gestalt's treachery. She'd just decided to have Ingrid make her an appointment with Farrier and Wattleman the next morning when Gubbins suddenly started chirping about the day's activities.

"So, Bishop Petoskey, I understand you had quite the adventure today, accompanying Rook Thomas out to one of our manifestation sites." Shantay caught Myfanwy's eye and looked a trifle wary, as if she wasn't entirely sure how much she should say. "Of course, it was all perfectly legal, Sir Henry," Gubbins assured the Lord. "Under the terms of the Sororitas Pact, our American cousins are allowed to attend manifestations."

"Indeed," said Wattleman, not looking particularly pleased at the information. "And whereabouts did you go, Bishop Petoskey?"

"Oh," fumbled Shantay, who was the only person besides Myfanwy aware of Gestalt's apparent betrayal of the Checquy. "Well, it was, um..."

"Bath, wasn't it?" prompted Gubbins helpfully.

"What?" said Gestalt suddenly, looking at Shantay and Myfanwy with narrowed eyes.

"Oh, yes," continued Gubbins, cheerfully oblivious to the tension in the air. "Something about a house full of people generating a fungus, wasn't it? I like to listen in on the transmissions whenever the Barghests go out."

Gestalt had gone rigid and then slowly slid one of his hands into his coat. Myfanwy mentally reached out, gently reading his sensations, and realized that the Rook was holding a gun. She took a deep breath and went for it.

"Rook Gestalt, I accuse you of treason against the Checquy and the United Kingdom of the British Isles!"

The entire place fell silent, the conversations dying away as heads whipped around. With lightning reflexes, the Gestalt in front of her drew his gun and pointed it at her face. She saw the murder in his eyes and felt a moment of pure satisfaction when he found, much to his bewilderment, that he wasn't able to pull the trigger.

Oh, yes, that would be me doing that.

She raised her eyebrows at him then focused and made him throw the gun away, into a distant corner of the room.

Then, as an afterthought, she made him throw himself in the opposite direction, straight into one of the large floral displays.

For a moment, everyone in the room was frozen — even Gestalt's other bodies stared in astonishment. Then the place seemed to explode into action. Across the room there was a shriek as a Gestalt twin backhanded Lady Farrier and shoved one of her Retainers into a waiter. A tray of hors d'oeuvres went flying. The other two siblings pulled out guns and a couple of alarming-looking combat knives, and the sister fired a round into a woman pouring drinks. All three siblings opened their mouths and barked out sharp commands. Myfanwy was too distracted by the sight of the waitress falling dead to the floor to catch all the words, although she did hear *uprising* and *take them*.

In response, several of the Retainers who were scattered about the room produced weapons and began to move menacingly toward the members of the Court. Three of them darted at Conrad Grantchester. That corner of the room was abruptly engulfed in darkness as the Bishop poured a torrent of inky smoke out of his pores. Ingrid and Anthony were swallowed up in the fog, and Myfanwy caught a glimpse of them being attacked by two other people in purple. She heard coughing, people crashing into one another, and the unmistakable swearing of Joshua Eckhart, confirming that he'd retained all the vocabulary he'd picked up from his deplorable parents. There was the wild slamming sound of gunfire, and everyone ducked.

Bishop Morales took the hands of her two Retainers and was gone with an abruptness that actually hurt Myfanwy's eyes.

The Gestalt brother whom Myfanwy had directed into a large vase of flowers was getting to his knees, dripping water, decorative ferns falling from his shoulders. *Oh, no,* thought Myfanwy, *you're not getting involved.* She slammed her thoughts down on him and sent him sprawling. Then she pinned his body with her mind, freezing every joint.

Shantay's Retainers were down, shot in quick succession by the Gestalt twins, and Myfanwy saw, to her horror, that some Checquy Retainers had actually turned on their Court members. One of Gubbins's secretaries dragged a wire garrote over his master's head and set about throttling him. Farrier's bodyguard had kicked Farrier in the ribs and was now looming over the older lady with a knife. The room was filled with people trying to kill one another. Luckily, no one had made any moves toward Myfanwy yet, and she drew back a little.

Eliza Gestalt was bringing her pistol to bear on Wattleman, and Myfanwy immediately released her hold on Robert, mentally seized the female Gestalt, and froze her as she was taking aim. Behind Myfanwy, the brother got up and started fighting with one of Wattleman's bodyguards. Myfanwy could feel Gestalt wriggling against her mind, and she clenched her thoughts around the traitorous Rook. Her vision lurched as she looked out of Eliza's eyes.

For a few seconds, she could read Eliza's body. She felt taut muscles, hands callused in unfamiliar ways, and the uncomfortable sensation of her period. Then she drank in even more information. Her legs had been waxed recently, and there were fragments of hors d'oeuvres in the crevices of a back tooth. She could feel the remnants of the injuries the body had picked up over the years: white lines on the knuckles and the backs of the hands, one along her stomach, and the slight ache of scars that had come from claws raked across her back.

Myfanwy held tight until one of Grantchester's Retainers kicked her behind her knees, knocking her to the floor and shaking her grip on Eliza. The Retainer stamped on her ankles and she shrieked and involuntarily released Gestalt.

Eliza blinked her eyes a few times and then turned to the gaping Wattleman and shot him in the head. The old man crumpled, falling into the startled Shantay's arms. A few meters away, Gubbins was struggling against the garrote clutched in the hands of his Retainer. Myfanwy looked back at the man who'd knocked her down and saw him drawing a long knife from inside his coat. She reached out through the pain that was throbbing in her legs, entered his mind, and forced him to stab himself in the thigh and then turn the blade.

Behind her, Alrich was in the process of tearing the limbs off one of his secretaries.

It was anarchy, with Court members and Retainers attacking one another left and right. Gubbins dislocated his neck backward, simultaneously slipping out of the garrote and smashing his attacker in the nose.

Eliza had gone after Shantay and was firing frantically at the American Bishop and the old man she held in her arms. Unfortunately for Gestalt, Shantay had grown a skin of glittering armor and was curled over Wattleman, shielding him. Bullets were ricocheting off her in a flurry of sparks. When the ammunition ran out, Eliza looked at the metallic woman in front of her and apparently decided to find a target that could actually be hurt by a combat knife—also a target that couldn't fold her in half. She turned and went after a loyal Retainer who was defending Lady Farrier.

Not going to happen, thought Myfanwy weakly, and she was about to lock the woman's legs and send her sprawling when she felt hands closing around her throat. The treacherous Retainer who had stabbed himself was powering through the pain, and although he hadn't managed to remove the twisted knife from his thigh, he had dragged himself over and appeared quite capable of strangling her.

Bugger! thought Myfanwy, and in a panic-filled moment, she froze him completely.

With his hands still clasped tightly around her throat.

Oh, brilliant.

All right, don't panic, she thought. *You can still breathe a little. Now, how did you make that fat guy loosen his grip on the briefcase?* She carefully followed the trails of his nervous system and found that it wasn't at all standard issue. *What in the hell? This makes no sense. If I make a mistake, I could end up strangling myself.* Taking very, very shallow breaths, she laboriously began tracing out the nerves, careful not to make him tighten his grasp.

While she gingerly loosened the man's grip, Gubbins dived at a Gestalt twin and began to engage in horrendously contorted combat. The second twin joined in, and Myfanwy suddenly understood how Gestalt had risen to the post of Rook. In awe, she watched one mind coordinating two bodies in flawless martial arts. Then the third brother joined in with lightning-fast blows, all of them timed to strike simultaneously. Myfanwy could tell that Gubbins was hard-pressed, even as he bent his body into impossible positions. He backhanded a brother and received a fist to the stomach for his trouble. Flexing, now standing on one foot, now on two hands, Gubbins was a blur, striking out desperately at the bodies of his fellow Court member.

Teddy Gestalt darted forward and grabbed the Chev by the lapels of his tuxedo. Gubbins locked his hands around his assailant's wrist and elbow and twisted himself backward violently, rolling over his own spine and flinging Gestalt into the air. As Myfanwy watched, Alex Gestalt reached out without looking. The two brothers clasped hands, and, like a trapeze artist, Alex snatched Teddy out of the air. He spun and brought Teddy smoothly to the ground, then whipped him around and launched him back at Gubbins.

The Chevalier lashed out low with a foot, and Teddy somer-saulted over him, distracting Gubbins long enough for the other brothers to grab him and plant two fists in his stomach. The Chev crumpled, and the siblings reared back to strike him dead.

Three fists struck simultaneously, like hammers pounding into flesh, pulping Gubbins's skull.

Behind them there was a roar as Alrich burst out of a crowd of attackers, shaking off a mist of blood. His kimono in shreds, gore streaking his arms, the Bishop looked like an avenging angel engaged in slaughter. He snarled and moved toward the melee, his long, tapering fingers hooking themselves into claws.

Gestalt, in a stunning display of good sense, elected to run.

In four separate directions.

"They're bolting!" shouted Shantay, who was still clutching Wattleman.

"Like hell," croaked Myfanwy. She was finally able to peel the man's fingers off her throat, and she took her first full breath. Then she flung her thoughts out wildly, trying to ensnare all four of them. A migraine blossomed in her brain from the effort, but she held them. Four bodies stumbled, although she could feel a single intellect battering itself against her. She tightened the web and smiled a small smile of satisfaction. She *had* Gestalt. She had him and there was no way the Rook could escape—no body to slide into, no extra sibling to mobilize.

But then, suddenly, the mind was gone, evaporating through her fingers. Mental activity in the brains faded.

"What?" Myfanwy cried out, loosening her grip in shock. She swept the area frantically, but she couldn't detect even the slightest trace of the traitorous Rook. The siblings' knees were buckling, but then they straightened. Wherever Gestalt's mind had gone, it was back now, and the bodies were escaping. Myfanwy wildly spun tendrils out of her psyche and, straining, snared one of the twins. She snapped her mind around him, and then she *wrenched* at his senses, warping his perception so that he ran straight into a wall, knocking himself out.

Eat that, you prick.

The Retainers were also running, and the other siblings got lost in the crowd. Lost, that is, until Alrich launched himself impossibly across the room, scattering people like skittles. The Bishop snagged a brother by the shoulder, swung him up, around, and then down, crashing him onto the floor with tremendous force. The other twin stumbled over a dead secretary but made it to the door. He and Eliza vanished, and the treacherous Retainers—the few Alrich hadn't shredded—blocked the passageway, preventing anyone from chasing the fleeing Rook.

Myfanwy cut the Retainers' legs out from under them, and Alrich looked out the door.

"They're gone," he reported grimly.

"Damn it!" spat Myfanwy, slumping to the ground. She sighed heavily. "Can somebody get this man off me, please?"

Well, Bishop Morales is safely back in Miami," said Shantay, folding up her mobile phone. "Our superiors inform me that I'm supposed to fly back to the States tomorrow and report your decisions of tonight." She sank down on the couch next to Myfanwy, kicking her shoes off. A waiter approached discreetly. "I'll have a gin-gin mule," said the American Bishop. The waiter bowed politely and looked to Myfanwy.

"Yeah, me too," said Myfanwy, trying to ignore the doctor who was tending to her ankles. Immediately after the chaos, she had wondered whether the heads of the Checquy should repair to a secure location. Perhaps the Prime Minister should be informed? Her suggestions had been brushed aside by Farrier "until we've decided what we want to say," and instead, the entire party had migrated into an adjacent receiving room, which resembled the ballroom except for a conspicuous lack of corpses and blood. Now there were ten people from the original dinner party, and four doctors tending to them.

Only three loyal Retainers had survived the battle. Ingrid and one of Gubbins's secretaries were standing uncomfortably against the wall, despite repeated invitations from various members of the Court to sit down. Lady Farrier was seated next to Wattleman's bodyguard, a tall redheaded man, each of them sporting a black eye. They held identical cocktails in their hands and looked identically pissed off.

"I simply cannot believe that more than twenty-five people were killed at an official Checquy function!" seethed Wattleman. The old man had shaken off a bullet to the head and seemed somewhat irritated that others in the party hadn't done the same. "There hasn't been a slaughter of this magnitude on Checquy soil since... since..." He looked to Myfanwy for help.

What, am I also the historian here? she thought in irritation. She searched her memory for any relevant information and came up with nothing.

"It's been ages, sir," she said firmly.

"Exactly!" he exclaimed. "Ages! And to do it when we're entertaining such distinguished guests!" Myfanwy was fascinated that it wasn't so much the attempted assassination of members of the Court that was filling him with rage but more the fact that Gestalt and his people had broken the laws of decorum by doing it during a drinks reception. And in front of the Americans.

"Yes, they seemed surprisingly unconcerned with obeying the laws of hospitality, and of this kingdom," said Eckhart scornfully. In the middle of the battle, Myfanwy had seen him grab a metal drinks tray, melt it in his hands, and form it into poniards. Now he was briskly winding the metal into bracers around his wrists. "After all, that's why Thomas accused Gestalt of treason."

"Yes," said Bishop Grantchester quietly from an overstuffed couch. He sat, his tuxedo unrumpled, and looked dangerously calm as he took sips from a martini. "That is an interesting point. We must follow protocol here. Rook Thomas, what were your grounds for that accusation?"

"My grounds?" echoed Myfanwy incredulously. "What, you think that I accused an innocent man? And that this innocent man led a spontaneous mutiny in the middle of cocktail hour? With weapons that they all just happened to be carrying? *Yes,* I have proof of Gestalt's treachery, but if we're going to be sticking to protocol, I don't think tradition calls for one of the heads of the organization to be eating sausage hors d'oeuvres while I report!" As she finished her rant, she realized that she was shouting, and that everyone was looking at her.

"It looks as if Rook Thomas grew some teeth to go with that dress," said Bishop Alrich dryly.

"What remains of it, anyway," said Farrier primly. "Still, they both make good points. Rook Thomas, *you* are not on trial here. Nevertheless, we would all like to know exactly what Gestalt has been up to, aside from subverting my secretaries and humiliating us in front of our guests."

"And murdering a member of the Court," said Eckhart. "Or have you forgotten that my brother Chevalier is lying dead in the next room?" No one spoke for a moment, their thoughts on Gubbins's battered body, which was currently covered with a blood-spattered tablecloth.

Myfanwy had to think fast. She needed to bring them up to speed, but there were certain things she simply couldn't risk sharing. So she recounted everything that had happened in Bath and mentioned that an attack had been made on her a week before, which had led to the black eyes. She couldn't say for certain that the two events were related, but it *did* seem suspicious.

She also very pointedly avoided mentioning anything about her memory loss.

"And you think it was Gestalt?" exclaimed Wattleman. "Members of my own Court are trying to have each other murdered?"

"And succeeding," pointed out Alrich grimly. "Gubbins is dead, and almost all the Retainers in that room were either killed or treacherous. Or both." The Bishop was sadly examining his shredded clothes but had not bothered to wash away any of the blood that covered him. Nor had he accepted a drink.

"Yes! What about that?" said Farrier. "I am highly concerned with the number of Retainers who proved eager and willing to stab me. God, that *any* was willing to do it—well, it is distressing. But so many! Perhaps the remaining Retainers should be escorted out?"

"Lady Farrier, the fact that these people were willing to put themselves in harm's way to protect us should serve as proof of their loyalty," said Myfanwy forcefully. She had no intention of letting anyone take Ingrid away from her. The two of them had found Anthony lying facedown, dead from over twenty stab wounds, his absurd purple tartan stained almost black from all the blood that had been inside him. They'd had a little weep together and had held hands when the party changed rooms.

"I suppose," said Farrier dubiously. "They have been searched for weapons, of course?"

"It's kind of a moot point now," said Alrich. "And besides, some of them were storing their weapons internally. I saw at least three Retainers pull knives from pouches in their skin, and I felt a couple of their blows. No normal person would be able to strike with such force." Myfanwy thought briefly of mentioning her strangler's peculiarly modified musculature but decided to keep it to herself—she wasn't keen on drawing anybody's attention to her new willingness to use her abilities.

"But surely you screen your Retainers very closely?" Shantay broke in. "The Croatoan's policy was modeled on yours. No Retainers are powered."

"Of course we screen them!" snapped Eckhart. "Inside and out. It's as thorough an examination as we can make it."

"And that's pretty damn thorough," muttered the bodyguard with the black eye.

"Then that must mean later modifications," said Shantay excitedly. "Deliberate changes to their bodies. But no one can make those sort of modifications. No one except..." She trailed off in horror.

"The Grafters," finished Myfanwy. "We have been infiltrated by the Grafters."

There was a horrified pause, during which everyone eyed one another speculatively. *Does every member of the Court expect every other member of the Court to pull a bazooka out of an orifice?* thought Myfanwy.

"If the Checquy has been compromised, then any Retainer could be a traitor," said Farrier in an observation that was simultaneously paranoid and obvious. The woman shot anxious looks at Ingrid and the other Retainers.

"Perhaps we should have them all killed," said Myfanwy flippantly. There was another thoughtful silence, and, much to her horror, Eckhart actually seemed to be considering it. "Oh, for Christ's sake! I was kidding!"

"It might actually be necessary," said Grantchester slowly. "We can't afford to have traitors among us."

"We can't go around killing the Retainers!" exclaimed Wattleman. "The organization would collapse!"

"In addition to any incidental qualms one might have about murdering the staff," Myfanwy muttered to Shantay. She felt as if her parents were embarrassing her in front of her best friend. "Anyway," she said more loudly, "we can't just assume this infiltration is restricted to the Retainers. After all, Gestalt was a traitor. Any powered individual could be working for the Grafters. Any one of us could."

"But not *another* member of the Court, surely," said Wattleman weakly.

"It's impossible to be certain what has happened to this organization," said Grantchester. The air around him shaded itself. Apparently, when he was stressed, his control over his abilities slipped. Curious, Myfanwy gently reached out and read his sensations. Inside the Bishop's body, it felt as though ice water were roiling just beneath his skin, seeping out of his pores. "Who knows how deep this infection goes?" The question hung in the air.

"Well, there is one person who knows," said Myfanwy thoughtfully.

25

"Ingrid, do you realize that today is a Sunday?"

"Yes, Rook Thomas."

"You and I are driving into the barren wastelands of southwestern Scotland to visit a prison on a Sunday morning," said Myfanwy, staring out the limo window. The car was in the middle of a fairly large convoy of bodyguards to protect the Rook while she was in transit. There were two armored limousines, one of which contained her, Ingrid, and two honor guards, the other containing a septuagenarian Pawn with the ability to breathe cyanide and sweat tear gas. There were also four heavily armed men on motorcycles, a van of soldiers, and a satellite tracking them from many kilometers above.

Myfanwy had been a trifle embarrassed at the prospect of traveling with a small army, but Joshua Eckhart and Security Chief Clovis had insisted, citing the need for heightened security. Both had assured her that *these* were men they trusted, partially because the guards were powered and had all gone through the Estate's indoctrination process, but mostly because of the terrible threats Eckhart and Clovis had made to them if something should happen to Myfanwy.

In fact, these were only a few of the security measures that had been implemented in the past two days for the protection of the Court. As soon as Clovis arrived at Apex House on the night of the attack, he'd proclaimed that they would not be permitted to return to their homes for the immediate future but would henceforth be residing in their secure apartments in the three headquarters. Panic buttons had been issued to everyone. The various Checquy facilities around the nation were placed in lockdown mode, and every member of the Court was now under the constant protection of two honor guards whenever outside his or her quarters. Even while the Court members were in their offices, there were always two guards standing outside each of their doors.

"Yes, Rook Thomas."

"Hmm?" Myfanwy said absently.

"Yes, you and I are driving into the barren wastes of southwestern Scotland to visit a prison on a Sunday morning. These are desperate times," said Ingrid.

"Yeah," agreed Myfanwy. "Clovis said we haven't been at this level of security since those creepy blond kids were wandering around in Winshire. He insists every Pawn and Retainer has to be accounted for. And that's nothing compared to what the Americans are doing. In her last call, Shantay said something about shooting anyone who knows the capital of Belgium."

Since the American Bishop had flown back to Washington, D.C., the two of them had talked on the phone several times. Shantay was overseeing the protection details for high-ranking figures in America, and while she'd been joking about the capital of Belgium, a great many security arrangements had been put into place on both sides of the Atlantic. Myfanwy was painfully aware of this, since she'd had to sign off on several measures.

A number of public figures had received discreet Checquy protectors, border security had been upped, and there was a heightened terrorism alert, presumably to the bewilderment of all human terrorists. Even as Myfanwy was driving to Scotland, Farrier and Grantchester were meeting with a secret council that included the Prime Minister, the Home Secretary, the Minister of Defense, the heads of MI5 and MI6, the ruler of the country, and the first in line to the throne. Myfanwy didn't envy them the task of explaining the problem.

She opened up the big purple binder and flipped through the pages to the entry on Gallows Keep Prison.

Gallows Keep

Was the ancestral manse of some obscure Scottish noble family who man-aged to piss off the king. Treason or something. So they were stripped of their lands and chattels and sold into slavery, and the place was handed over to the Checquy. They ignored it for a few decades until it was pointed out that they should probably do something with the king's gift.

It's a dour-looking castle in the middle of nowhere, which makes it the perfect place for the Checquy to store some of its undesirables. Actually, the perfect place would be an island on a different planet. But this was a pretty good second choice.

The reason it's called Gallows Keep is that, prior to the establishment of the current facility, human-shaped enemies of the Checquy were usually stored at the end of a rope. As it is, we still stage a fair number of hangings. And beheadings. And stakings. And burnings. And immersions in vats of distillate of eel. Whatever means of execution are necessary, really. Gallows Keep is more of a temporary holding facility that's used until the Checquy decides that the subject cannot be redeemed.

On the outside, the place looks as if they're expecting the English to turn up and demand that the inhabitants turn over all the virgins and any cattle and coins they might have hanging around. But on the inside it's super-sophisticated, with all the very latest in security cameras and lead manacles.

It's where we store enemies we can't kill.

"I miss Anthony." Ingrid sighed wistfully. Myfanwy looked up in surprise. It was most unlike her secretary to show such emotion.

"He was a good man," agreed Myfanwy. *I only met him the once, but he seemed nice. And Thomas seemed to approve of him. Plus, now that we're in Scotland I could have found someone to tell me what the hell he was saying.*

"Security Chief Clovis is looking for a replacement," said Ingrid. "I asked him if we could have another incomprehensible bodyguard. It made the car trips so soothing." *Is she drunk?* wondered Myfanwy before deciding it was just the mournful countryside and lack of sleep that had brought out the maudlin in her secretary. Ingrid shook her head. "Anyway, we'll soon be at Gallows Keep."

"Yes," sighed Myfanwy. "This should be a pleasant little interview. All I have to do is put on my scary face."

"You have a scary face?" Ingrid sounded skeptical.

"Yes," said Myfanwy indignantly. "I have a very scary face."

Ingrid surveyed her for a moment.

"You may wish to take off the cardigan then, Rook Thomas," she advised tactfully. "The flowers on the pockets detract somewhat from your menace."

Rook Thomas," said Gestalt. The past thirty-six hours had clearly been very bad ones for the Gestalt bodies the Checquy had managed to hold on to. Myfanwy was in the room where the formerly tidy and now somewhat rumpled twin was imprisoned, and a pair of cold blue eyes regarded her with hate. She'd ordered her two bodyguards to stay outside the room and they'd agreed only because the door was made of glass and they could see exactly what was going on. One of them was holding her cardigan, which she'd taken off at the last minute, putting on a blazer that was much more official-looking but also much less comfortable. Restricted as she was to the secure Rookery residence, Myfanwy had had a Checquy courier fetch it from the guest room wardrobe in her house before they left for Scotland. Now she found that it had some sort of corset sewn into it, so she was standing very straight. Hopefully that would also help her appear a bit more intimidating.

"Gestalt, you're looking well," Myfanwy said. "I mean, as well as anyone could look in that delightful apparatus. Which is to say, you look like utter shit." Gestalt was pinioned in stocks, his hands and head poking out through the holes. The stocks themselves were affixed to the wall with thick iron bars. A sphere of chicken wire encircled his head, looking like an attempt to keep out extremely fat bees. "My goodness," she said cheerfully, "but they're certainly not taking any chances with you, are they? All you need to complete this picture is a big iron ball shackled to your ankle and a hockey mask."

"Frankly," replied Gestalt, "I don't know why they bother."

"You mean since you have so many other bodies running about?" Myfanwy asked.

"Exactly" came the flat answer.

"Still, you've lost access to half of them, haven't you? I mean, three days ago there were four siblings walking around, free to do as they pleased, and now there are only two. We've got the Teddy body here, and the Robert body in the next room. Bit of a comedown, wouldn't you say?"

"I've still got twice as many bodies as you have," said Gestalt snidely.

"And you think I feel the lack?" asked Myfanwy. "I assure you that the rest of us do not go about wishing we had a couple of extra bodies. No one is suffering from body envy. But that's not the reason I came to talk to you."

"I wouldn't have thought so. Are you going to ask me where my other bodies are?"

"No, of course not," Myfanwy assured him. "At least, not yet. Dr. Crisp wanted to be flown in immediately to interrogate you. He's never quite forgiven you for attempting to strangle him. And he feels that your unique physiology would offer a *marvelous* challenge. But we still need him in America. And anyway, we have a nice buffet of torturers to choose from right here in this facility."

"Torture!" scoffed Gestalt. "You realize that I could abandon this body, don't you? I could simply slide out of it and into a different one."

"Oh, yes, I know that. After all, you vacated yourself entirely the other night, didn't you? All four siblings, and not a brain between them. Not that there was much there to begin with," Myfanwy added sweetly.

"So then why are you here?" asked Gestalt.

"I wanted to see if there was anything you wanted to tell me of your own free will," Myfanwy said.

"You must be joking!" the body said. "If I wouldn't tell you anything under torture, why on earth would I tell you anything of my own free will?"

"There are worse things than torture," said Myfanwy with a small smile. She'd spent the ride up from London thinking about this, and her creativity had surprised her. "After all, you may have four bodies, but I'm fairly certain you're emotionally attached to all of them. Now, you can choose of your own free will to answer my questions, or you can choose of your own free will to have various limbs chainsawed off."

Gestalt was staring at her fixedly.

"You've never had fewer than four bodies to work with, have you? So I'll bet that having only two is driving you nuts. But at least *our* two are as yet unharmed." She paused for dramatic effect. "How would you like to slide into a body with no eyes, or ears, or limbs?

"Now, of course you wouldn't be present for the actual procedure—you wouldn't feel the pain, so it's technically not torture—but I'm betting just the *knowledge* that we're abusing your body would hurt you. It may be one body of many, but it's still *your* body. We wouldn't have to mutilate both of them. In fact, maybe we could rig it up so that you could watch it going on. See yourself get ruined."

"You wouldn't dare!" screamed Gestalt. "You touch me and I'll kill you!"

"I'll kill you first," promised Myfanwy in a cold voice. "I'll kill you twice if I feel like it."

"I hate you! I hate you!" the body screamed until she reached out and shut it up.

"You need to be quiet for a moment," she said. For a minute, she worried that Gestalt would leave, unable to tolerate her manipulation of its body, but the blue eyes still glared at her. "Now, let's think." She pursed her lips thoughtfully.

"I wonder how many people are involved in this little mutiny of yours. I know it wasn't just the Retainers at the reception the other night. After all, I had the pleasure of meeting Mr. Goblet the other day. So why don't you tell me a little more about your operation in Bath?" Myfanwy unzipped Gestalt's mouth and was treated to a string of obscenities.

She shut him up again. "Charming. And then there's the alarming evidence that you've been fraternizing with the Grafters. Given the punishments for Checquy officers committing treason, do you want to talk about *that?*"

Apparently he didn't, but at least this time there was no swearing. Gestalt did look a bit nauseated, but Myfanwy couldn't blame him. She'd read up on the penalties for treason and for fraternizing with the Grafters and felt a bit ill just thinking of them. They actually made her threats seem a trifle merciful. *No wonder Gestalt almost strangled Crisp when we caught that first infiltrator,* she thought. *He must have been terrified that the Grafters were about to be exposed.*

"Perhaps," she mused, "there is the possibility of leniency. If you talk, that is. The Court does not want to see one of its own tortured, let alone undergo the agonies for consorting with the Broederschap. But there cannot be any secrets held back, Gestalt. For instance, where *did* you go for that moment last night?" she wondered. "Some little spiritual bolt-hole? A psychic holiday home? It was foolish of you to do it, because now we know that there's more to you than meets the eye."

"I'm not the only one with a secret," snapped Gestalt. "Do you think no one noticed that you were affecting people all the way across the room? As I recall, we all thought you had to be touching someone to make them do what you wanted. Not that you were ever supposed to have the guts to do so. That was one of the reasons we worked so hard to get you into the Court!"

Ah, thought Myfanwy. *Now we're getting somewhere.*

"Yes!" crowed Gestalt triumphantly. "Now they know about your powers, and they'll find out all your secrets when they cut you open!"

"You wanted me in the Court?" asked Myfanwy.

"A weak, sniveling little girl who could never look beyond the figures? Of course we wanted you in there. And it wasn't easy either."

"Well, thank heavens you worked so hard," said Myfanwy. "Now I'm here, and you're... Well, you're wearing something that looks like a guinea pig hutch mated with a bear trap."

"Not for long. We'll change places, and then it'll be you who needs to worry about chain saws. And you've only got the one body!"

"I'm trembling," sneered Myfanwy with contempt. "Look, I've gone all fetal. Only not."

"Remember, I am in here, but I'm also out there," Gestalt said. "Walking free. I could come to your house and have all sorts of fun." Myfanwy kept her face calm, but inside she felt a stab of fear. Despite all of her predecessor's warnings, she still kept thinking of Gestalt's bodies as separate people.

"It may be that you harbor some dream about overthrowing the Checquy," said Myfanwy coldly. "Getting your bodies back. Whatever." There was a sudden hunger in Gestalt's eyes. "Let me assure you that at the first sign of trouble, I will have these two bodies shot. I'll do it myself. The only way that Teddy and Robert will see the sky ever again is if you work with me. We'll talk again. When you've had some time to think it over.

"But," she cautioned, "think fast, Gestalt. The torturers are putting together their agenda, and they're aiming to start tomorrow. Time is running out." She made a little buzz-saw sound and mimed slicing off her own hand at the wrist, raising her eyebrows at Gestalt. At that, fury overtook the twin, and he hurled himself about frantically in his bonds. His eyes locked on Myfanwy's, and she seized the opportunity to seize him.

Through one set of eyes, she looked intently at a computer in a darkened room. Her cheek ached dully, and her knuckle smarted. There was a glass of gin in her hand, and a plate of cheese lay on the desk.

"Get..."

Through another set of eyes, she slept. An electric blanket soothed her muscles, and soft sheets caressed her skin.

"...out..."

Through the third set of eyes, she stared at herself, and felt cold iron around her neck and wrists.

"...you..."

Through the fourth set of eyes, she saw a door. She sat on a hard bed, with her knees pulled up to her chest. The lights overhead were dim, and the strip of light under the door burned the eyes.

"...fucking..."

Through the last set of eyes, she watched television. The room was bright and comfortable, with windows looking out over a river. She ate a carrot and glanced up when a tall woman with piercing blue eyes walked into the room.

"...bitch!"

Contact was broken, and Myfanwy took a faltering step backward. She felt like she'd run several miles. She was sweating profusely, her heart was pounding, and her knees were weak. Instinctively, she'd bent over, and the prongs of her corseted blazer dug into her ribs. She drew in a gasping breath and forced herself to stand up straight. She and Gestalt stared at each other, both panting slightly. Neither said anything, and then Myfanwy backed warily out of the room. Gestalt's eyes were locked on her, smoldering with rage.

26

"Did you get anything out of him?" asked Ingrid over a bowl of soup. The warden had insisted on providing them with a dining room for lunch and had diffidently excused himself after Myfanwy asked him for a bit of privacy. Outside the door stood the toxic Pawn and the two honor guards, and three of the bodyguards hung outside the windows, suspended by climbing ropes. On Myfanwy's insistence, they were facing out.

"Maybe," said Myfanwy.

"Did he get anything out of you?"

"I like to think not."

"Did he figure out that you lost your memory?" asked Ingrid casually. Myfanwy looked up at her, shocked. She slammed her mind down around Ingrid's body, cutting off everything but voice, sight, and hearing.

"I suppose I should have expected that," said Ingrid. "The word around the office is that you can now seize control of people without touching them."

"You didn't see it yourself?" said Myfanwy. "I did make a man stab himself with a knife in front of the whole Court." She put a little steel in her voice, hoping to get across the idea that if she so desired, she could make Ingrid do the same thing. Admittedly, Ingrid was currently holding a soupspoon, but Myfanwy felt sure she could improvise.

"Well, keep in mind that I was choking and flailing around in the cloud that Bishop Grantchester had produced," pointed out Ingrid.

"Of course." Myfanwy nodded.

A pause ensued, during which Myfanwy felt uncomfortable and Ingrid seemed quite content with herself, despite the fact that her muscles were frozen.

"So, anyway, about that little item you brought up..."

"Your amnesia," said Ingrid helpfully.

"Yes, that," said Myfanwy. "Although I prefer not to think of it that way."

"You prefer not to think of your total lack of memory as amnesia?"

"Does that sound unreasonable?"

"I'm only striving for accuracy, Rook Thomas," said Ingrid.

"And yet you call me Rook Thomas," said Myfanwy.

"*You* call yourself Rook Thomas," Ingrid clarified.

"Let's not get caught up in minor details," said Myfanwy. "How long have you known?"

"Since the evening when I came into my office and found Rook Myfanwy Thomas curled up on the floor, weeping and muttering about how she could feel her memories evaporating." Myfanwy gaped at her. "This was the other Myfanwy Thomas, of course," added Ingrid helpfully. "The one that was you before *you* were you."

"Uh-huh," said Myfanwy.

Ingrid looked at her levelly and heaved as much of a sigh as her body would allow her.

"Very well," said Ingrid. "This is what happened."

It was late, and Ingrid was not pleased to be in the lift of the Rookery. Her eldest daughter, Amy, was coming in on the train from York—back from university for the weekend—and Ingrid was eager to get home. It was only when she'd pulled out of the underground parking lot and swerved around a late-night protester that she realized she'd left her daughter's gift in the desk drawer. Just one last irritation in what had been an exceptionally long and irritating day.

First, there'd been the frantic covering up of an escaped harpy in downtown Stoke-on-Trent. Then, there'd been the last-minute discovery that a report due to the Prime Minister that day contained several major errors and would have to be rechecked in minute detail. Ingrid had felt guilty leaving Thomas alone in the office, since the little Rook was still scanning the final version of the report, but her boss had known about Amy's arrival and urged her to leave.

"Honestly, Ingrid, go," Thomas had said. "I'm almost done going over this. Once I'm finished, I'll give it the okay and the Rook's Messenger will courier the hard copy right over to Number Ten. And then I'll just go up to the residence and sleep there. You've canceled my car, right?" Ingrid smiled and nodded.

"Have a good night then, Rook Thomas," Ingrid said. "And do try to get some rest over the weekend."

"Hmm?" said Thomas, already re-engrossed in the report. "Oh, yes. You too, Ingrid. Have fun with your family." As Ingrid watched, the Rook turned her complete attention back to the paper in front of her, absently brushing her hair away from her face. The executive assistant shook her head, knowing that much of her boss's weekend would be spent in the office. She felt a stab of pity but left with a spring in her step. Most of the staff had already gone for the day, and she enjoyed the dim quiet of the hallways.

On the way down, she'd passed the publications department and seen that there were still lights blazing and several heads bent over papers, reading frantically. Now, as she walked briskly back to her office to get Amy's gift, everyone was packing up and leaving. Clearly Rook Thomas had approved the report and it had been sent off, safe in the protective gullet of Toby, that evening's Rook's Messenger.

If that woman hasn't already gone up to the residence, *thought Ingrid,* if I find her reading over something new, I am going to confiscate her highlighters and send her to bed. *There was no light coming from under the door, which probably meant that Rook Thomas had retired to the residence, where, in all likelihood, she was still working.* "Well, at least she's out of the office," *Ingrid murmured to herself, but she was brought up short by a sudden, unexpected sound. Movement where there should have been none.*

Ingrid was an executive assistant who had entered the Checquy, not after years of rigorous training at the Estate, but after sixteen years in the civil service. She possessed no inhuman powers apart from an abundance of common sense and an ability to keep things organized. But a decade in the Checquy had taught her how unpredictable life was. This sound could be anything. Ingrid stepped carefully to her office, listening intently for further sounds before opening the door warily.

"Rook Thomas?" Ingrid whispered. The lights in the office were off, and when she fumbled at the switch and turned them on, she was half relieved to see that there was no one there. She peeked guiltily into her boss's office, but it was similarly empty, and the portrait door leading to the residence was shut. Sighing, Ingrid tried to think of what to do. Had she been certain about the sound? Was it worth bothering Rook Thomas?

A noise from the Rook's private bathroom drew Ingrid away from her dilemma. She moved carefully to the portrait door that featured a past Rook with a large powdered wig and compound eyes. It crossed her mind to do something sensible. She could leave the office and lock the door behind her. She could call security or find a powered member of the Checquy to help her. The only problem was that when you worked for the Checquy, you learned that conventionally sensible ideas often turned out to be unconventionally foolish. Like the story of that cleaning lady who opened the closet because she'd heard plaintive cries for help coming from within. Or Declan the accountant, who had thought it best to back away quietly and try to summon help when the escaped Portuguese land squid came squirming down the corridor. No doubt at the time the moves had seemed wise, but the cleaning lady had been rendered sterile and blind, while Declan's whispered phone call had made the land squid feel threatened. As a result, the accountant had been permanently stained purple and obliged to learn how to operate a calculator with his tongue since he no longer had any arms.

Now Ingrid could hear a pained whispering coming from inside the bathroom, and she immediately recognized the voice. She turned the knob and opened the door. Lying on the floor in front of the sink was Rook Thomas, curled up with her knees to her chest, her body shuddering uncontrollably. Ingrid stepped back in shock.

Thomas's eyes were wide, and her lips were blood-red. No, Ingrid corrected herself in horror, those frantically whispering lips weren't just red but bloody and raw. It looked as if someone had given the young Rook's mouth a few licks with some fine sandpaper.

"It's all collapsing," Thomas moaned. "I'm breaking up."

"Oh, Myfanwy," Ingrid breathed in horror. "What happened to you?"

"My thoughts," Thomas whispered desperately. She looked up at Ingrid, and the horrified secretary saw threads of blood slide down her lips. "They're drifting away. He licked them out of me, and now they're fading."

"What? Who did this to you?" asked Ingrid, going down on her knees and reaching out a trembling hand. Thomas flinched away. "Myfanwy, I'm going to get help. I'll call security, and the medics—" Ingrid broke off when her boss grasped her arm with a surprising strength.

"You can't, because that's not how it's supposed to play out," said Thomas frantically. "Today's the day, and I have to leave. Besides, I can't trust anyone, they might be sent to kill me. There's a traitor. There's—" Her brow wrinkled. "It's gone already." She buried her face in her hands. "It's gone. I finally knew. I finally knew who it was and . . . God damn it!" she shrieked. Ingrid jumped at the sudden sound and saw that Thomas was now looking at her with burning eyes. Thomas looked around desperately. "Did you hear that?"

"We've got to get you out of here," said Ingrid briskly. "Whoever it is will know to look for you here."

"There's a door," said Thomas. "A door in the office." She struggled to her knees, although she was still shivering terribly.

"The one to the residence?" Ingrid asked.

"No, that's where they came from," said Myfanwy, her eyes rolling in panic. "Some of them are dead now, and the others are stunned, but I know more can get in." She stiffened. "More have come into the residence, I can feel them. The door's locked, but it won't stop them."

"There are dead people in your residence?" asked Ingrid.

"Please, help me to the office," insisted Myfanwy, ignoring Ingrid's question. With a visible effort, she used the wall to stand herself up. She swayed, and Ingrid hurriedly reached out to support her. Ingrid felt her own muscles tense and then relax abruptly as Thomas's powers coursed through her. For a moment, Ingrid looked through the younger woman's eyes and

saw herself. Her lips burned, and pain tore through her head. And then it all snapped back.

"Sorry," mumbled Thomas weakly.

"It's fine," said Ingrid. "Don't worry about it. Now," she said briskly, "into your office?"

"Hurry," said Thomas. "They're coming."

"Are you sure?"

"I can feel them."

Ingrid stared levelly at her boss. Though nominally composed of secretive people, the Checquy was a relatively small community. The nature and limitations of Thomas's talent were a matter of common knowledge.

"You can feel them?" She looked at Thomas and saw dark bruises rising up around her eyes. "Oh, Jesus."

"Hurry." Together, they managed to make their way into the office, and Ingrid moved expectantly toward the portraits.

"No," said Thomas. "Not there." She tottered over to a corner of the room and drew back the carpet. Built into the floor was a metal hatch with a keypad set into it. The Rook knelt down awkwardly, punched in a code, and the metal door slid up smoothly, revealing an extremely steep and narrow spiral staircase that disappeared into darkness.

"Where does that go?" asked Ingrid. She was a trifle taken aback by the discovery of a hidden hatch in an office she'd been in hundreds of times. But on this night, it didn't rank as the most startling thing to happen.

"Garage," said Thomas. "Private section in the parking garage across the street."

"As in cars?" said Ingrid incredulously. "You can't drive like this! You can barely stand up!"

Thomas opened her mouth to say something, and then gave a little jerky nod of acknowledgment. She shrugged Ingrid's hand off her shoulder and swayed a little, but she stayed upright as she put her hands to the sides of her head and took a deep, shaky breath. Then, under Ingrid's horrified gaze, the Rook's eyes rolled back in their sockets. Ingrid bit her lip but assumed that this part was deliberate.

A couple of minutes passed, during which Ingrid kept looking anxiously over her shoulder, waiting for whoever had done this awful thing to Rook

Thomas to emerge from behind a portrait, brandishing dreadful weapons. Then, without warning, the Rook began convulsing. Her hands were still locked to the sides of her head and she stayed upright, but it seemed as if every other muscle in the woman's body was jerking violently. Ingrid stood by helplessly, afraid to touch her in case Rook Thomas's powers zapped her. Finally, the seizure stopped, and Thomas brought her hands down from her head.

"All right," said the Rook, breathing heavily. Her eyes were focused, and she seemed to be much more in control than she had been before.

"All right?" repeated Ingrid. "All right what? What was that?"

"I did some stuff to my brain," said Thomas. "Which is something I've never done before, and was probably a really bad idea. But I think I've got a bit of time before I lose it completely."

"Lose what?"

"All my memories," said Thomas. "So I've got to go. Now. While I still can."

"Wait! Don't forget your jacket," said Ingrid. "It's pouring rain out." The Rook caught her gaze, and the two women smiled at each other, thinking of all the times that Ingrid had reminded her to wear her coat.

Thomas let Ingrid help her on with the jacket and then began easing herself down through the hatch, but she looked up when Ingrid grasped her wrist.

"You said you knew who did it," said Ingrid urgently. "Who did this to you?"

"I'm sorry, but I have no idea what you're talking about," said Thomas, her forehead wrinkling. She stared at Ingrid for a moment. "Thanks," she said awkwardly. "For everything." Then she turned her attention to the complicated task of negotiating the steps. She disappeared, and the hatch swung down over her.

Outside, the rain beat down more heavily.

And that was the last I saw of her," said Ingrid. "I left the office immediately and ran down the fire stairs to the parking garage, got in my car, and picked my daughter up from the station. Then I spent the entire weekend with the doors and windows locked, waiting for a phone call. Nothing came, so that Monday I went into the Rookery. When you walked in, I didn't know what to think."

"And you didn't say anything," Myfanwy said warily.

"No."

"Why not?"

"To whom should I have spoken?" asked Ingrid defensively. "To you? I didn't know what had happened, although the lips and the eyes looked like Rook Thomas's. She'd said that her memories were going—I thought that maybe you were her, and you'd just lost the past few days. I certainly wasn't going to say anything to Rook Gestalt. And anything I could have said to the Bishops or the heads of the Checquy would only have led to more problems for Rook Thomas."

"And you cared about Myfanwy Thomas that much?" asked Myfanwy.

"Apparently I did," said the secretary. There was a strange little pause. "I do." The two women smiled cautiously at each other.

"So, she just disappeared down a spiral staircase," said Myfanwy finally.

"Yes."

"I think I'll have to check that escape route," said Myfanwy thoughtfully. "There may be some clues down there as to what happened."

"What did happen?" asked Ingrid. "I've been dying to know."

"Well," said Myfanwy, who had made a decision. She unclasped her powers around Ingrid, and the older woman slumped a little as her muscles were unlocked. "I opened my eyes and I was standing in the rain..."

It was a selective retelling, and all mention of Bronwyn was edited out. Myfanwy was also careful not to reveal how much information had been left behind by her predecessor.

"So you're not some plant," said Ingrid. "In the beginning I was a little worried that there might be some sort of invasion of the body snatchers happening in the office next door."

"And what changed your mind?"

"No plant would have done such a spectacularly obvious job of not being Rook Thomas. Especially since—let's face it—she wasn't that difficult to impersonate. All one would need to do is keep one's head down and look meek. I was fairly sure within the first four hours of your appearance. I knew for certain at the reception. The Rook Thomas I knew would never have worn the crimson dress. That was why I suggested it."

"So do you think anyone else suspects anything?" asked Myfanwy carefully. She had also kept to herself the fact that Farrier knew who she was, and who she wasn't. Ingrid sighed, and rubbed her eyes.

"I really don't know," the secretary said wearily. "It's such a difficult time. I've been reading up, and the Grafters are the only force that ever came close to *really* defeating us. But they came very, very close. And now suddenly they're here, and it looks as if they've been among us for a long time. Richard Whitlam, did you know him?" Myfanwy shook her head slowly. "Well, the old Rook Thomas would have known him. Everyone knew him. Lovely chap. He was one of Bishop Alrich's aides for thirty years. Recruited right out of university, and he was always very kind to all the new Retainers. Went out of his way to make us feel welcome."

She smiled. "My first day, he came down to the office and gave me a cactus—the one that's still on my desk. A lovely fellow, really kind, and utterly devoted to the Checquy." Ingrid sighed. "The news around the office is that at the reception he unsheathed a stiletto made of bone and tried to stab the Bishop." Ingrid looked at Myfanwy helplessly.

"If a man like that—a man who watched over a Court member while he slept, a man whose loyalty was never in doubt, a man who was *loved*—can be a Grafter, then I don't know what we can do. Because, Rook Thomas, I don't know if the Court members realize this, but *the Grafters already know our secrets.*"

Myfanwy felt a sudden sense of doom wash over her. Ingrid was right. In their shock over being attacked at the reception, the Court had failed to look at the big picture. They were afraid their secretaries and cleaning ladies would stab them. But all the secretaries and cleaning ladies needed to do was unlock the front doors and usher the Grafters in.

Correction: the *rest* of the Grafters, because they were already here.

"These people aren't infallible, Ingrid," Myfanwy said, making a tremendous effort to be calm. "That thing at the reception wasn't planned. They weren't prepared for a full insurrection."

"You don't think smuggling weapons into the Apex represents a fair amount of preparation?" Ingrid asked. "They could have killed us all!"

"Maybe if we were talking about the House of Commons, but this is the Court of the Checquy," said Myfanwy. "Going up against Eckhart armed with a dagger and a pistol is like going up against a tank armed with a stick of butter. I can't believe that a centuries-old organization was about to infiltrate us and decided to stage a coup using the equivalent of feather dusters. Maybe they are getting ready for it, and that's why they had weapons on them. But if they are planning a putsch, then the reception was not the way it was supposed to happen. No, that happened because I outed Gestalt."

"So you think Rook Gestalt was behind it all?" asked Ingrid. She perked up a little. "If Gestalt was the head of the Grafter infiltration, then..."

"Then several centuries haven't been long enough for the Grafters to develop any talent-spotting abilities. Gestalt is lots of things but nowhere near sophisticated enough to head a coup. I read the files, and I know Gestalt was promoted to the Court for its extraordinary combat abilities."

"Of course, and that's why they also promoted you, to balance him," said Ingrid, apparently forgetting for the moment that an entirely different person had been promoted. "Everyone knew they needed someone to take care of actually running the Rookery and the domestic operations."

"Yes, well, they also needed someone who wouldn't assert herself in inconvenient ways," said Myfanwy dryly. "Gestalt let that little tidbit slip while I was wearing my scary face. The Grafters put me on the Court."

"One person wouldn't be enough to get someone promoted to the Court," said Ingrid. "Not even one person with four bodies."

"So what are you saying?" asked Myfanwy with a sinking feeling.

"I'm saying that there are more Grafter agents in the Court."

27

"Rook Thomas?" Ingrid's voice came hesitantly through the intercom.

"Yes?" Myfanwy yelled from her desk, where she was intently working on an analysis of the Grafter investigation and the greater implications of Gestalt's treachery.

"Your mobile phone is ringing on my desk, where you left it for me to recharge," said Ingrid accusingly.

"Can you answer it, please?" asked Myfanwy, who was aware that this report would be scrutinized by the Courts of two nations and didn't particularly want it to sound like it was written by a moron. She ignored the heavy sigh that came over the intercom.

"It's a Miss Bronwyn?" There was an unspoken implication that if Myfanwy had been willing to trust her secretary with the secret of her amnesia, she should have been willing to tell her about anyone who'd be calling to ask for "Ms. Myfanwy Thomas."

"Oh, yeah, I'll take it." Myfanwy saved her document, got up from her desk, and went to retrieve the mobile phone, stepping gingerly between the teetering stacks of papers that covered most of the floor. Since getting back from Scotland, she'd been sifting through the personnel files of the traitorous Retainers, looking for some insight. So far, there had been no blinding revelations, but there had been some memorable avalanches of documents. Ingrid flatly refused to bring any more pieces of paper into the office, and a member of the cleaning staff had almost gone into hysterics when asked to dust.

"Hullo, Bronwyn?"

"Heya! How're you doing? I got your e-mail about your job crisis."

"Well, things are a little more under control, but people are still pretty stressed."

"So it's a big deal, then. I mean, it's been five days since you went to Scotland."

"Five days?" repeated Myfanwy. "Seriously?"

"Uh, yeah. It's Friday. That's why I called. I was wondering if you wanted to come out tonight. A few of us are going clubbing and I thought that if you weren't busy, you might want to come."

"Clubbing? Clubbing what?" asked Myfanwy.

"What?"

"Do you mean self-defense?"

"What are you talking about?" asked the girl whose world did not consist primarily of supernatural security.

"What are *you* talking about?" asked the girl whose social life consisted primarily of occasionally going out to lunch and visiting sites filled with paranormal malevolence.

"Going clubbing—dancing."

"Oh...hmm," said Myfanwy warily.

"You don't seem very enthusiastic." Bronwyn sounded a bit hurt.

"Oh, no," said Myfanwy hastily. "It's just that I don't think I've ever actually been clubbing."

"Really? Oh, right," said Bronwyn, remembering the backstory Myfanwy had given her. "Well, you should come, then. I mean, it's a good time, and Mum always said that Thomas girls are born to dance. Unless..." She trailed off uncomfortably.

"What?" asked Myfanwy.

"Well, I just remembered that you said you were...kind of nervous about going out."

What? thought Myfanwy confusedly. *Oh, right. My purported agoraphobia.*

"No, I really should try and go out," said Myfanwy definitely. "Let me just check on a few things." *Like finding a way to actually get out without an escort.* "I'll get back to you." The sisters agreed that

Myfanwy would make the call later in the day and that if she *did* come out, Bronwyn would not have any unrealistic expectations about Myfanwy's ability to dance.

Ingrid, do I have any meetings scheduled for tonight?" Myfanwy asked over the intercom.

"You know, Rook Thomas, all appointments are supposed to be made through me" came the tart reply.

"I *am* making an appointment through you," said Myfanwy.

"Well, you are supposed to call Bishop Petoskey of the Croatoan this evening."

"I'll e-mail Shantay and let her know that I'll call tomorrow," decided Myfanwy. *She would kill me if she knew I blew off an actual social opportunity in order to talk business on a Friday night.* "And please let Security Chief Clovis know that I'll be staying in the residence tonight, so he won't need to prepare any bodyguards for me. Oh, and see if you can get me a flashlight and a gun."

"Security Chief Clovis is already on his way up to discuss internal security with you."

Ingrid shifted into hyperefficient mode. By the time Clovis arrived, the desk and chairs were stacked high with a bizarre array of firearms. Myfanwy was peering intently at her computer, a tower of files on her lap.

"Good afternoon, Rook Thomas," Clovis said. Standing among the teetering stacks of paper, he was a figure of exquisite stillness.

"Good afternoon. Could you please shut the door so that Ingrid doesn't burst an eardrum trying to hear everything?" There came an irritated snort from the antechamber. "How are you, Clovis?"

"Busy, Myfanwy. We have just finished designing the new security protocol. We'll be examining every member of the Checquy Group for Grafter implants."

"Oh, well, that's good," said Myfanwy.

"Yes, except that it means subjecting every member of the organization to unpleasant, time-consuming, and highly intrusive physical examinations. This has to be done in-house, and our medical staff is going to be heavily overworked for the next several months. You see, until we have examined all the doctors, we will have to place random groups of three observers in the examination rooms to ensure that the examiners aren't doing any tampering. And every doctor in the organization, plus a randomly selected civilian medical practitioner, has to concur on the verdict of every test. As a result, we are going to be sending results to thirty-five doctors located around the world. We think it's highly unlikely that every doctor in the Checquy is a Grafter mole. And if all of them are, well, then we have the civilian doctor."

"Hell," said Myfanwy dubiously, "it sounds like a huge amount of work."

Clovis nodded curtly. "We're trying to be as thorough as possible. Of course there's no guarantee that every Grafter agent is going to have Grafter implants, but all of the traitors at the reception did have them, so that's where we're starting. And before we check all the doctors, we'll be screening the members of the Court. Starting tomorrow. So please prepare yourself."

"Great," said Myfanwy with a profound lack of enthusiasm. "Nothing says Saturday like unpleasant, time-consuming, and highly intrusive physical examinations. Schedule mine in the afternoon, because I want to catch up on some sleep."

"Very well. There will, of course, still be guards on the doors to your office until then."

"I feel safer already," said Myfanwy wryly. "Coffee?"

"Thanks, but I have to get back to work. Everyone has been on edge for the past week, and I have to supervise the examinations of your doctors. Now, do you mind telling me why you have all these guns lying around? Are you afraid the paperwork will rise up against you?"

"Oh, no. I'm going to use the guns as paperweights."

After Clovis left her alone in a roomful of weapons, it was time to take the plunge. Carefully, she set the huge pile of folders down on her desk and belted an Ingrid-supplied holster around her waist. She dubiously picked up her selected gun and, after hastily reviewing a firearms instruction booklet (also Ingrid-supplied), crept over to the corner of her office that Ingrid had pointed out to her earlier that week.

A quick scan of the directory of secret passages in the purple binder had confirmed that there *was* a passage, and a little cautious poking around had revealed how the corner of the carpet peeled back. But Myfanwy had been so busy researching treacherous Retainers she hadn't had a chance to explore Thomas's escape route. Now she peered dubiously at the intricate-looking hatch in the floor. She noticed, with a little thrill of dismay, that there were drops of blood on the keypad.

She typed in *230500,* and the door swung up, revealing a very narrow spiraling staircase, like the sort one would find in a church tower. Myfanwy looked carefully, hoping for some sort of light switch. Nothing. Well, it figured. That was why she had gotten the flashlight. Still, the prospect of climbing down into a deep·dark hole was not particularly enticing. Myfanwy couldn't help but remember that the last time anyone saw Thomas, she had been vanishing down this same deep dark hole.

Between the moment Thomas pulled the hatch closed behind her and the moment Myfanwy opened her eyes in the park, Thomas had left the building, fled halfway across London, and been attacked by highly trained operatives. Myfanwy thought of the bruises she'd found when she inspected her body in the hotel room that first day. Thomas had been savagely beaten. Had it happened in this passage, down in the darkness?

I have to go down there, she thought. *I have to see. If there's anything left, any clues, they may give me an answer as to who attacked Thomas.*

Plus, this might enable me to go out and play with Bronwyn tonight.

Once again she checked the pistol holstered at her hip and the flashlight dangling by a strap from her wrist. Myfanwy steeled herself, then clambered down into the narrow stairwell. It was clear that the shaft had been added to the building well after its construction, and there was barely enough room for her to stand straight. Anyone less slight would have had to turn sideways to descend. She took a breath, willing herself not to develop sudden claustrophobia, and then started down into the darkness.

What wanker designed this?" Myfanwy wondered aloud as she climbed carefully down the staircase. She was uncertain how many stories she had gone down, but she had to be running out of Hammerstrom Building to descend through. Her legs were killing her, and she had scraped her back several times as the shaft narrowed. It was obvious that it had been made to accommodate the vagaries of the building rather than the comfort of the person using it. By the time she reached the bottom, Myfanwy was dusty, abraded, and deeply annoyed. She was partially mollified, however, by the discovery of a light switch to the side of the stairs.

"Lovely decor," she said as fluorescent lights hesitantly flickered on. The corridor was perfectly square and led away in both directions. The walls were cinder block, and the floor, under a covering of dust, was unfinished concrete. Myfanwy saw with a little thrill of dread that there were scuffed footprints in the dust leading away from the base of the stairs. She drew the gun. Then she set off down the passageway, following in her own footsteps.

It was clear that, despite her self-performed brain surgery, Thomas had been deteriorating as she stumbled down this corridor. Here she had fallen to her knees and had to put her hands down to push herself up. Myfanwy paused and put her hand down in the print contemplatively. Farther along, there were small patches of blood on the floor, and Myfanwy lightly touched her own knees, recalling how they had been skinned when she first saw herself in the mirror. She searched her mind, looking for some feeling of déjà vu. Nothing.

As she walked along cautiously, the silence bothered her. How deep had she gone? It felt like she had climbed down the stairs forever, but without any indicators it was impossible to know. Still, according to Ingrid, this bizarre passageway led to a garage. So she moved forward.

Aside from the mustiness, there was something unpleasant in the air. *What is that smell?* wondered Myfanwy. It tickled a place in the back of her head—not a memory, but something instinctive. The tunnel ahead bent at a sharp right angle, and she slowed cautiously. The smell grew stronger, and she felt her throat tighten in a manner that suggested vomiting was a distinct possibility.

This is ridiculous, she thought. *I'm possessed of terrifying powers. Why am I relying on a ridiculous little gun that I picked because I thought it was cute? I don't need this thing.* She threw it contemptuously over her shoulder. *Damn right! I took out a house of weird fungal cultists that had devoured three teams of supernatural SWAT teams. I am a badass.* She paused and expanded her senses outward, searching for any kind of life. *Okay, nothing. At least,* she thought uneasily, *nothing that I can detect. But then why does it smell so bad down here? There's something foul wandering the underground tunnels beneath my office, something that's invisible to my vaunted powers.*

Crap.

Where's my gun?

After backtracking, Myfanwy picked up her gun from the dust and listened carefully. Deathly silence. Feeling slightly absurd but still scared, she held her gun in two hands and jumped smoothly around the corner, landing in a position that implied she was prepared to open fire on whatever she saw.

"Oh, thank God." *Not to worry, it's not a weird monster. It's just three rotting dead people,* she thought as she threw up on her cute little gun. After wiping her mouth and then shaking the pistol to clear some vomit off it, she approached the corpses cautiously. All of them were dressed in purple garments, though they were now sodden in body fluids. *Nasty.*

One of the bodies lay a little way off from the other two, and Myfanwy could see from the two large holes in his chest that he had been shot. *I guess he was shot by the other guy. The one who appears to have—yes, he seems to have shot himself,* she thought. *Judging by the massive handgun he is holding against the side of his head. The half of the head that is remaining.*

Oh-kay, so let me think this through. Thomas is trying to get away through this corridor. Then these guys appear, coming from the other direction. They think she's going to be completely out of it, all drugged up or whatever. Plus, she's notoriously powerless. So they grab her, and she makes one of them shoot the other two and then shoot himself. Thomas continues on to the garage, leaving those footprints leading on down the corridor.

Gosh. Well, good work, Thomas. And with that mental tip of the hat to her predecessor, Myfanwy stepped gingerly over the corpses and set off along the tunnel.

Despite the rotting bodies, Myfanwy was feeling markedly more cheerful as she went. The air was getting fresher, and if Thomas's footprints still skidded awkwardly, and if there was a dropped hair clip lying on the ground, well, Myfanwy already knew how Thomas's story ended. Right now she was interested in the details. *I really should see if any of those Retainers were carrying ID. Though I'm definitely not touching them without gloves.*

Finally she came to a metal door with a keypad, and she punched in the code again. The door swung open, and she entered the garage and looked around with interest. Like the tunnel, it was well lit, but there was no dust on the ground here. An automatic door took up most of one wall and beyond it, the binder had told her, was a public parking garage, from which she could drive out easily and without attracting notice.

She turned her attention to the contents of the garage. There were five cars, draped meticulously with dustcovers. *That's Thomas's work all right,* Myfanwy thought, remembering the dust sheets that had covered the furniture in the safe house she'd gone to. *Always taking care of the details.* Myfanwy smiled ruefully, thinking of her own work as a Rook. Ingrid had confirmed that she had the same talents as Thomas—the same eye for minutiae and the same ability to immerse herself in information.

She peeled back one of the sheets and caught her breath. *It doesn't matter what kind of outfit I pick for this evening, this car would be enough to get me laid.* It was red and had all the curves she herself lacked. *Who would have thought that under Thomas's flower-embroidered cardigan there beat the heart of a car freak? I wonder if they're all in this vein?* In fact, they weren't, but they were all quite clean and nice. A sedan. A Mini. A Land Rover. A truck. A motorcycle. *I see, a vehicle for every situation. So I guess this means I don't need to get a cab,* Myfanwy thought as she opened the red car's door and saw that the keys were in the ignition. *Let's see if I can still drive a manual.* She pushed the button on the remote, and the automatic door to the private garage rolled itself up.

Just before she drove out into the public area of the parking garage, her eye was caught by an open space and a discarded dustcover—the place where a car had been until it was driven away by another woman in her body.

28

"Hey, babe!" Bronwyn said enthusiastically when she opened her apartment door to find Myfanwy. "You look great! Except for what you're wearing." The sisters hugged, a little awkwardly.

"What can I say? I came straight from the office, and this outfit is only this good because it was a casual Friday." In fact, Myfanwy had been dressed in a suit, but she'd dug up a pair of neatly pressed jeans and a black T-shirt in the residence wardrobe.

"Your office must be really dusty. I suppose the jeans will cut it, but we're going to have to find you a better top. Come in." Bronwyn ushered Myfanwy into the flat, which proved to be fairly untidy and was obviously a place where two very different people lived together. "Sorry about the mess. With Jonathan away, I've been free to throw my stuff around." Myfanwy noticed some bolts of fabric on the couch, and a sewing machine on the kitchen counter.

"I'm just going to finish getting changed," said Bronwyn as she disappeared down a hallway. "And I'll find something for you." Myfanwy looked around curiously. If not for her being drafted into the Checquy, this might have been her life. She wandered across the room, absentmindedly trampling her sister's creations underfoot, and peered at the photos on the mantel. There were several pictures of a couple who were obviously their parents, and others of Bronwyn and a guy who must be their brother, Jonathan.

"Okay," said Bronwyn, "I've got some stuff for you." Myfanwy looked over at her and cocked an eyebrow. Bronwyn was dressed in the kind of outfit that heiresses wear to clubs in order to get their pictures in the tabloids. It actually pushed attention away from itself and onto all the skin it wasn't covering. Myfanwy opened her mouth to object, various genetically built-in big-sisterly protests arising. *But,* thought Myfanwy, *I wore the crimson dress, so who am I to judge? Plus, if anyone tries to molest my little sister, I'll make them kick their own ass.*

"All righty," Myfanwy said, "what are you suggesting I wear, because—oh, hell no. That is not going on my body." *I'm only willing to wear something as risqué as the crimson dress once a season.*

"Why? What's wrong with it?" asked Bronwyn in an amused tone. Compared to Bronwyn's outfit, it was quite modest, but compared to Bronwyn's outfit, outright nudity was quite modest.

"Because it suggests that I'd gladly trade sex for a cocktail. In fact, it suggests that I might even trade sex for eye contact," said Myfanwy. "Plus, won't we freeze to death when we go outside?"

"I think you're overreacting," said Bronwyn. "Now, how about this?" Myfanwy rejected several options before Bronwyn declared that she was the one studying fashion, the one who knew where they were going, and the one who would decide what Myfanwy would wear. Accordingly, several minutes later they strolled down to the place where Myfanwy had parked the car, Myfanwy clad in something a friend of Bronwyn's had made at school.

"Holy shit," said Bronwyn. "This is what you drive when you're not being ferried about in a government car?" They both looked at the red sports car, which had attracted a few awestruck admirers. "Maybe I should go into the civil service."

Myfanwy, who was beginning to worry that taking the hot rod out for a spin had been a mistake, muttered something about leasing and performed the complicated maneuver of getting into the car, which was so low-slung she was practically sitting on the street.

"We're not going to be able to park this car near the club," warned Bronwyn. "It'll get scratched or stolen or something."

They maneuvered through the traffic, Bronwyn chatting away on her mobile phone, making arrangements with her friends, and giving directions to a secure garage for the car. Eventually, with the vehicle guarded by the good people at a familiar-looking five-star hotel, the sisters joined the queue for a club that Bronwyn assured her was *the* place to be seen getting drunk and dancing.

When they were finally admitted, Myfanwy looked around with interest. Inside, the club was far less impressive and louder than she'd expected. Bronwyn took her by the hand, led her to the bar, and yelled over the music to ask what she wanted to drink. *Whatever!* Myfanwy mouthed to her sister and slid a banknote into the girl's hand. Bronwyn winked and then squirmed her way through the press to the bar. Myfanwy wondered briefly how Bronwyn was going to get a drink in that crowd but then remembered the top she was wearing. *If it's a male bartender, he'll probably give her a keg.* She tried standing on her tiptoes to see if she could catch a glimpse of her sister, but the rest of the people in the crowd were of a normal height.

When Bronwyn finally emerged from the mass, she held two large glasses filled with an ominous amount of liquid. They moved cautiously with their beverages to a grouping of chairs where Bronwyn's friends were seated, looking tall, pretty, and normal. Myfanwy smiled politely, listened to them gossip, and amused herself by surveying the crowd. *All these people, and none of them know the secrets I know.* She took a cautious sip of her cocktail, followed by a long drink, then settled back into the cozy chair and looked at the dance floor through the filter of her powers. Sensory patterns of the crowd rippled before her. Hearts beat in rhythm with the music. Lungs gasped in the air, and sweat shimmered on skin.

I need to clear my head, she thought. "I'm going to get some water," she told Bronwyn. As Myfanwy walked across the club, she tensed her mind and subtly directed the movement of the dancers. The crowd opened up in front of her and closed behind her. She walked up to the bar and people moved aside, not even realizing they were doing it. *Damn, but I'm good,* she thought. She ordered a glass of water, and as she tilted her head back, her control slipped. A big-arsed guy jostled her, and she stumbled awkwardly into someone. "I'm very sorry," she apologized as she turned around and came face-to-face with Bishop Alrich.

Two reactions warred within Myfanwy. The first was fear at the thought that Alrich must be the traitorous member of the Court and that he had stalked her here and would kill her. The second was outrage that the universe would do this to her on her only night off.

Bewilderingly, and possibly as a result of the unaccustomed alcohol, the second reaction won.

"Oh, come *on!*" shouted Myfanwy, slamming her glass down on the bar and spraying water and ice everywhere.

"Rook Thomas?" said Alrich, looking completely composed in the face of her anger.

"What in the hell are you doing here?" she raged. "And where are they?"

"Who?" asked the Bishop calmly.

"Your bodyguards!" She looked around frantically for people dressed in purple who were possibly ready to produce Grafter weapons and kill her.

"Myfanwy, I do not have any bodyguards."

She stared at him. "Say what?" she said weakly.

"I do not have any bodyguards with me."

If there are no bodyguards, then he's out here, in the night, with no backup. Myfanwy reached out toward Alrich with her powers and was not terribly surprised to find they did not work. *Of course they wouldn't,* she thought. *Not on him. He doesn't need backup to dispense with me. Even this club full of civilians probably wouldn't stop Alrich. He could shred them all in a few moments and think nothing of it. Still, he hasn't torn me in half yet, so can I assume he's not the traitor?* She evaluated her options.

Option 1: Fight.

Without powers that work on him, it's pointless. He could punch a hole through my torso without spilling his beverage.

Option 2: Flight.

Even if I could make it to my car, he could still probably catch me. And if he's not the traitor and I run away, it will make for some embarrassing staff meetings later.

Option 3: Scream for help.

If Alrich is a traitor, see violent results from Option 1. If Alrich is not a traitor, see social awkwardness from Option 2.

Option 4: Engage in polite conversation.

It may help me gather information as to whether Alrich is the traitor. Also, possibly buy me more time to stay alive.

Myfanwy elected to pursue Option 4.

"So, um, Alrich, what are you doing here?" she asked.

"I was out in the city," said Alrich carelessly. "And I smelled you in the air."

"You *smelled* me," said Myfanwy weakly. She resisted the urge to sniff her pits.

"Yes," said Alrich. "Your scent was hanging in the air, and I was curious as to what Myfanwy Thomas would be doing out tonight. I was especially intrigued when I tracked you to a nightclub of dubious reputation."

"I don't understand. You're out and you don't have any bodyguards. And something's different about you . . ." She stared in shock at the curtain of hair that hung over his shoulders. "Did you dye your hair *blond?*" Myfanwy took a step backward, suddenly noticing Alrich's getup. "And what *are* you wearing?" she asked, looking at the tight leather trousers and the mesh shirt. "You look like sex in boots."

"*This* from the girl who wore that crimson gown to the reception," said Alrich, raising an eyebrow in amusement.

"Yes, well, um," Myfanwy floundered. "At least I didn't wear it tonight," she shot back, and he burst out laughing.

"Let me buy you a drink," he said.

"All right, but make it something weak. Apparently, I have a terrible head for alcohol."

Bishop Alrich

Is a vampire.

Despite this, I would urge you not to brandish any holy symbols at him during Court meetings. Quite aside from the fact that they won't work, it's very bad manners and would make for an inconvenient break from the meeting agenda.

With that key point of etiquette established, I can move on to the dossier.

Alrich emerged into this world in 1888, in a mansion in London.

Picture a room draped with tapestries, with thick carpets on the floor. There is a massive fire burning in the fireplace. The wood burns with a sweet, foreign smell. In the center of the room, standing on a plinth of gold and copper, there is an egg. Big enough to hold a grown man in the fetal position, the egg is made of a semitransparent material that is a dark brown-red in color. Its surface is not smooth but jagged and bumpy. In fact, as you look at it, you are put in mind of nothing so much as scabbing. If you look closer, you can see that there are the marks of fingers on it, suggesting that it has not been laid but sculpted. If you peer very closely, with the firelight shining through the egg, you can vaguely see a figure inside.

More logs are added to the fire, and the heat in the room rises until you can feel the sweat prickling your shoulder blades and trickling down the small of your back. Soon the air is hot in your throat, and then you see that, like yourself, the egg has begun to sweat. Beads of ruddy fluid, like dirty blood, are materializing on the surface, and the shell itself has become a little more transparent.

As you watch, you notice that the egg is softening, changing shape. It is flexible. And then, near its top, a hand tipped in talons tears through the shell, sending rivulets of blood and albumen leaking down the surface and onto the pristine carpets.

All the while, you know you cannot make a sound.

The hand rips the now-leathery shell down, pulling chunks back inside. The material tears entirely, and a torrent of the fluids spills out. The thing inside emerges awkwardly, its mass of hair tangled, and its skin dyed bright by the birthing fluids. It slips, its limbs giving it problems, and falls to its knees on the carpet. As you watch in horror, it throws back its head and screams.

The sound is not human.

After long minutes, it finally stops screaming. And then, unbelievably, it begins to tear at the egg and eat the pieces. You have stood strong throughout this whole occurrence, but this is too much. You can feel your gorge rising, and you have to get away. You move out of your hiding place, and it cocks its head at you, then moves hesitantly in your direction. You tear away one of the tap-estries, behind which a window is concealed, and throw yourself desperately through the glass, out into the snowy night.

As you flee, you risk a look back through the falling flakes and see a figure standing in the window, watching you.

These were the circumstances of a vampire hatching as described by Elea-nor Thurow, an agent of the Checquy who was gifted with chameleonlike abilities and an inquiring mind. It was not actually Alrich's hatching but that of his sibling, Pitt. Alrich was born one week later.

At that time, the Checquy did not officially believe in the existence of vampires. The organization's formal position was that vampires were nothing more than the villains of gothic novels, poorly adapted from Eastern European folktales. Pawn Thurow, however, had spent some time in Eastern Europe among the folk, and while she had not actually seen a vampire, she'd heard anecdotes. Very convincing anecdotes. When she returned to Britain, she had asked some mild questions and received sharp responses.

One Rook had actually sneered in Pawn Thurow's face, declaring in front of several witnesses that "only the most credulous and naive of minds could believe such ridiculous and unlikely fantasies," which must have been pretty rich coming from a man whose entire lower half consisted of a sort of sparkly fog. In any case, Pawn Thurow was undaunted by the scorn of her (nominal) superiors, and she embarked on a private project to track down an example of a vampire.

What Thurow had done was in the best traditions of the British Empire: she had simultaneously discovered a species and gone to war with it. Thus, the official position of the Checquy on vampires went almost instantly from "Don't be ridiculous, you silly girl, there's no such thing!" to "Right, they do exist, and they appear to be killing us."

Thurow had tracked down Alrich and Pitt's creator after months of detec-tive work. I've read her journals (which is where I found the above descrip-tion), and she appears to have been a very dedicated and clever woman. She was also no stranger to dangerous situations, since her abilities and tempera-ment had made her ideal for infiltration and close surveillance. This was a woman who had stood unseen and watched, disapprovingly, as the head of a cult that worshipped emotion tried to sire the personification of hatred with an *adoring disciple. After shooting both the would-be parents (in flagrante delicto), she slipped through the congregation of horrified onlookers and opened the gates of the compound to the Checquy soldiers.*

Also, earlier that year, she had spent several months on the street pretending to be a prostitute. This had been done as part of a loaner program with the Metropolitan Police, who at the time were seeking the notorious murderer of several unfortunate sex workers. It's worth noting as an aside that even the Checquy never figured out who Mr. The Ripper was or whether there was some sort of supernatural aspect to the whole thing.

In any case, Thurow's secondment to the Metropolitan Police Service had sharpened her investigative skills. Her discovery of the vampire involved a great deal of patient, camouflaged standing in private rooms and offices listening to the conversations of those who would notice the effects of a vampire. Her research took her from local police stations to the chambers of Episcopal palaces to a boarding school whose students were suffering from a peculiar strain of anemia.

Eventually Thurow's investigation led her to a mansion near Regent's Park. She entered and found the house bare except for the two rooms that contained the aforementioned eggs, which were housed in palatial splendor.

It was clear to Pawn Thurow that there was something peculiar going on in the house, but she was not immediately certain what it was. Remember, most of her ideas about vampires were based on fiction and folklore (Dracula would not be published for another nine years), and nothing added up. She searched all the rooms and found neither coffins nor anything sleeping upside down in any closets. There was no freshly turned earth in the cellars. To her bewilderment, she found a cross hanging proudly on the wall in the mansion's chapel. Despite all her searching, she could find no sign of whatever creature had produced the eggs. So she made the decision to remain, cloaked, within the house and wait for nightfall.

It's not the decision I would have made, but then, I'm not habitually armed with a pair of revolvers and a quiet determination to prove my superiors wrong.

I also know a little more about vampires than she did.

In any case, Thurow selected one of the rooms that contained an egg, activated her camouflage ability, and waited patiently. Seven hours later, the sun

320

having vanished, a tall man entered the room and carefully laid a fire. Thurow described him in her diary as "striking, with long white hair and a face that seemed drawn back from his nose."

The man lit the fire, piled it high with aromatic woods, and scattered sweet-smelling oils upon the flames. And then the hatching described above began. I have no idea why the parent vampire at the window did not pursue Thurow when she fled the house—perhaps it needed to tend to Pitt; perhaps it thought dawn was too close. Whatever the reason, it gave Pawn Thurow time to return to Francis House (then headquarters for the Rooks) and frantically report that she had found a vampire, had seen another one born, and believed there would be a third born soon.

Only when she mentioned the neighborhood this was all taking place in were her superiors moved, worried that some influential and wealthy families might be at risk. Checquy forces were dispatched skeptically to the mansion, only to find it on fire. Pawn Thurow was eyed warily, patted on the head, and told to go home.

Eleanor Thurow went home fuming and wrote furiously in her journal.

She failed to turn up at work the next day.

A Retainer was sent to Thurow's home, and found her nailed upside down to her bedroom wall.

An immediate search of her house was conducted. Her journals were discovered and brought back for inspection. Her corpse was taken down carefully, examined, and found to be missing more blood than one would have anticipated, even taking into account the . . . drippage. Upon this discovery, the Checquy operatives pounded a stake into her heart, cut off her head and crammed it full of garlic, and then gave her a good Christian burial.

I would love to know how that jackass of a Rook was going to explain to his troops that the woman he'd sneered at had been right, but the next day his body was found sliced in two, lengthwise. It seems that Thurow's intrusion upon the hatching had prompted some sort of vendetta, and by bolting back to the headquarters, she had given the vampire a trail to follow to the Checquy. With that began a nighttime war of attrition.

At first, it was one death each night. Not in any pattern—one night it was a Rook, the next a Retainer, the next a Pawn who worked as a clerk. As a means of sowing panic, it was very effective. Checquy operatives in London were petrified and became unwilling to leave the organization's strongholds. The facilities, however, proved not to be as secure as everyone believed. Corpses were found, some of them drained of blood, inside Checquy buildings. One per night.

Eleven days later, the number of killings doubled. Despite the increased security, every night two Checquy corpses were found. People began sleeping in groups and rules were instituted, obliging Checquy members never to be alone. Every morning, there was a frantic head count, and every morning, two people were found to be missing. Sometimes their bodies were found together, sometimes in different rooms, sometimes in entirely different buildings. Corpses were found in hallways, in offices, and in the most secure chambers of the Checquy. The unpredictability only increased the fear.

Seventeen days after Eleanor Thurow witnessed the birth of Pitt, the death rate went up again. Three deaths every night, and this time the deaths were different, more calculated. People would wake up to find that the person they had been sleeping beside was staring at them with dead eyes. Guards would turn to ask their partners a question, and find them lying on the ground with their throats torn out. One woman was drowned in the blood of her secretary.

Then one morning, the head count revealed that no one in any London facility had died. It was checked and double-checked. The relief must have been overwhelming—there were spontaneous celebrations in the hallways. But over the course of the day, panicked messages came from the Checquy offices in Cardiff and Cheltenham, and from an inn in St. Bees where a Checquy researcher was on holiday.

For the next week, Checquy operatives all over the country were killed.

Finally, after thirty-three days and seventy-two deaths, the Lord and Lady of the Checquy woke up in their heavily fortified bunker to find their bodyguards mesmerized into comas and a vampire looking down at them. Heller, the parent vampire, introduced himself and stated that over the previous few weeks, his younger spawn had become quite impressed with the scope of the Checquy. In the course of acquainting himself with the reach and purpose of the organization (and, although Heller didn't say it, killing its members), his younger spawn, Alrich, had become somewhat enamored. Would the Lord and Lady be willing to accept him into their service for a time?

Are you startled by this abrupt change in direction?

So were the Lord and Lady.

But you don't rise to the head of the Checquy if you can't adjust your thinking fast.

Alrich entered into the Checquy as a Pawn amid a labyrinthine mass of agreements and arrangements. Of course, the killing of Checquy operatives ceased, and the other two vampires vanished without a trace. Alrich's sleeping place was unknown to the Checquy, and each evening he would present himself at Francis House for his assignment. Initially, it was awkward, partly because no one knew exactly what his capabilities were and he was not obliged to submit to any sort of testing, and partly because no one knew how many Checquy colleagues he had killed. There was also the not unreasonable fear that he might suddenly decide to resume chomping down on people and draining them of blood. By that time, there wasn't anyone in the organization who hadn't lost an acquaintance to the predations of the vampires. There was a fair amount of hostility toward the new recruit as a result of this, although no one was stupid enough to try to take revenge.

For the first few months, Alrich worked alone, mostly in combat situations. Some assassinations, handed out by a recently elevated and extremely nervous Rook. A few outbreaks in which he was sent in to quell monsters. He was a weapon—one that people were afraid to use. And then he was assigned a partner, a man named Rupert Campbell who bled fire and who had recently lost his wife (to childbirth, not to vampires—even the Checquy isn't that tactless). Campbell had been a very good operative, but now he was lost, almost suicidal, and a drunk. Two embarrassing agents, together. I've no doubt the Court rather hoped they would destroy each other. Instead, Alrich found a friend and mentor, and Campbell found something to distract him from his despair. Together they accomplished outstanding things.

If you want the details, you can read Alrich's official file, but I feel it is enough to say that, as a result of their exploits, both of them rose to the rank of Bishop. And Alrich has stayed there, while Campbell died in 1929.

Alrich possesses a deep and detailed knowledge of the Checquy and the nation—after all, he's been working for us for well over a hundred years. He is a terrifying and effective combatant, but it is his formidable intellect that makes him the organization's most valuable asset. He represents a vast body of corporate knowledge (I've been prevailing upon him to commit it to paper for several months), and he handles his role brilliantly.

Practically everything we know about vampires is the result of having Alrich on staff, but he is famously close-lipped, and he has still never been tested. We don't even know how vampires are made—it was one of the conditions Alrich set for his entry into the Checquy, that he would never be questioned about the procedure and that he would never be asked to create a new vampire. I mean, we know they come out of eggs, but that's it. We don't know where the eggs come from, or what material is inside them. Is something put in there to be changed? A corpse? A living person? A baby? Maybe there's nothing put in there, and Alrich just grew. Maybe he was a normal person once. He will not say.

As for other vampires, well, the other two—Pitt and Heller—have never been heard from again. We have no idea if they are still alive or if they are in the United Kingdom. Two vampires have been found since Alrich joined us, and both have been killed (one notably by Gestalt). Their bodies have yielded no clues to us, having dissolved away into blood and water upon their deaths. Their possessions give no indication of their origins or whether there are others. I wonder if the two the Checquy killed were related to Alrich somehow—could he perhaps be using the Checquy as his private army, manipulating us in a master game of vampire politics? It is a disquieting theory, and one without any real basis beyond my own paranoia.

Within the Checquy, Alrich is regarded with a peculiar mixture of fear, pride, and blasé acceptance. He is a vampire, and some people are distantly aware that he was once an enemy of the Checquy. But he's our vampire, and besides, he's been here forever. Longer than almost anyone. Newcomers are taken aback at first, but it's almost a mark of pride to ignore his inhumanity or to think it unimportant.

And, after all, none of us are normal.

Alrich is the personification of charm, and so it is easy to forget that he is a predator, a predator of human beings. He does not need to kill his prey, and his ability to mesmerize his victims means that they need never know. However, I have noticed that those who work under Alrich tend to die younger than they should. His staff also suffers from a higher rate of sick leave than any other section of the Checquy. If this were brought to the attention of the organization, there would be a substantial reaction. Is Alrich feeding on his staff? Is he modifying their memories? I don't know for certain, but a formal inquiry would be a very bad thing for the Checquy.

Already, within the Court there is wariness. Alrich will never rise above the rank of Bishop, that is understood. Does he chafe at that? What are his priorities? Will he remain with the Checquy forever, or is this simply an apprenticeship, an adolescent phase? Perhaps one evening he will open his eyes and simply leave. His motivations are alien to us.

If Alrich is our enemy, then you face a foe who has power on every level. His strength means he could shred you like a dried leaf. His mental abilities can prevent you from taking any action. His speed can outdraw your fastest reflexes. His cunning and authority will prevent you from mustering any support within the organization. And his lack of humanity means that he will not hesitate to destroy you if he deems it necessary.

However, his predatory nature means he might play with you beforehand.

"So, what *are* you doing here without any bodyguards?" asked Myfanwy. "Because Security Chief Clovis has two people following me around, and they're incapable of blending in anywhere, so I had to ditch them." *Although at this exact moment that doesn't seem like the wisest decision I ever made.* "Thank God Clovis can't see the two of us right now. He'd be furious," she said, sipping delicately from the apple martini Alrich had ordered for her. *If Alrich were going to kill me, surely he wouldn't have bothered to buy me a drink. Although that doesn't mean he's not the traitor.*

"My personal habits mean that I require a certain amount of privacy," said Alrich, looking everywhere but at Myfanwy.

"Your personal habits?" echoed Myfanwy. "I don't underst—Oh!" *I guess it's hard to pick up a fresh piece of meat when you work the night shift for the Checquy.* "But a nightclub? With your hair dyed platinum blond?"

"It's not dyed, I'm just hungry," said Alrich. "In any case, I don't really need bodyguards. Plus, it's hard picking up sweet young things when I'm being watched. Not everyone approves of my lifestyle."

I'll bet, thought Myfanwy. "So, how about *him?*" She gestured discreetly with her chin toward a handsome young man who actually looked very much like Alrich, although without the glorious length of hair and with a much smaller wardrobe budget.

"Oh, yes, he looks suitable," said Alrich softly.

"Go for it," said Myfanwy. "I have to rejoin my party anyway, or they're going to start wondering where I am." Alrich put down his untouched beverage, turned to her, and bowed elaborately.

"Very nice, but I'd be more touched if that move wasn't subtly calculated to show your arse off to the entire club."

Alrich winked and moved smoothly over to the dancing blond. He whispered into the boy's ear, and a broad grin spread across the young man's face. He took Alrich's hand and led him off the dance floor toward the exit.

Damn, that's impressive, thought Myfanwy. *That kid has no idea what he's getting himself into. He's going to have a night he would never have forgotten if it weren't for the mesmerism.* She wandered back over to Bronwyn's party, where a few hopeful young men were engaging the fashion students in conversation.

"Who's the guy?" asked Bronwyn. "He's super hot."

"Friend from work," explained Myfanwy. *And possible murderous traitor.*

"Charisma thought he had to be a model."

"I'd have introduced you, but he was here with a distinct purpose."

"Yeah, I noticed. Too bad. Until he left with that bloke, I was kind of hoping that he was hitting on you. Why are the hot ones always gay?" she asked.

"Yeah," said Myfanwy. *Or vampires.*

"You want to go dance?" asked Bronwyn.

"Not at all," said Myfanwy.

"Great, let's do it," said Bronwyn, gulping down the bottom half of her beverage and standing up abruptly.

As it turned out, Myfanwy was not a natural dancer. Bronwyn and her friends were swaying around in a manner that Myfanwy recognized vaguely from the few music videos she'd seen. But much to

326

her surprise, Myfanwy was enjoying herself. She was as relaxed as she could recall being since she had opened her eyes in the park and wondered who she was. She had a few cocktails floating around inside her, and she was dancing (badly, but less badly than she had been at first) with her sister and her friends. The music was throbbing, and she watched the pulse of the people around her. Myfanwy closed her eyes and let the beat move her. Then a hand tapped her shoulder and she swung around. Startled, she opened her eyes, and looked into a chin.

It was a good, strong-looking chin, attached to a strong, good-looking man. He was dancing awkwardly and looked slightly embarrassed about having bothered her. He spoke, but his words were lost in the beat of the music.

"I'm sorry, what?" she yelled, rather pleased that a decent-looking guy had approached her in a club. Myfanwy watched his lips carefully, looking for something about a drink being bought for her, and managed to miss everything he said. "What?"

He peeled back his lips, and revealed a smile full of razors.

Well, naturally.

29

Dear You,

Today has been a very stressful day.

It was actually supposed to be a fairly tedious day. I had a mountain of paperwork to work through, reports to report on, and, miraculously, all the other members of the Court were far away doing things that were pressing but didn't constitute dire emergencies. I had settled myself in comfortably and was reading about the talking mice that had infested Lewisham before they were disposed of by our regional office. The extermination had taken months and had resulted in a massive amount of bills and records, all of which I was obliged to trawl through.

I had just started on the accounts for the third month and was attempting to figure out why the genocide of some vocal vermin required fifteen million pounds and the requisition of a Saracen armored car from the Second Armored Regiment when I received a frantic call from Heretic Gubbins, who was in New Delhi putting down a would-be potentate. He was talking very quickly, but as best as I can recall, the conversation went something like this:

Me (distractedly): Yes, hello? Hello?
Him: Hello?
Me (still distracted): Hello?
Him: Hello?
Me: Hello, I can hear you.
Him: Rook Thomas?
Me: Yes.
Him: Yes, this is Heretic Gubbins in Delhi.

Me: Hel—

Him: I'm terribly sorry, but it turns out that the Greek woman is coming a week sooner than expected, so there's no one to meet her except you.

Me (trying to figure out why we'd even needed to take the mice out): *Uh-huh. Right. What?*

Him: The Greek woman.

Me (still not really paying attention): *Yes.*

Him: She is coming in, and you will need to meet her and entertain her today.

Me: Oh, okay. Wait, what Greek woman?

Him: You know the one, I can never remember her name, but she does that thing, and is thousands of years old.

Me (beginning to panic): *Does what thing?*

Him: Oh, she turns people into livestock.

Me: She does what?

Him: Turns people into—

Me: I heard! And what am I supposed to do with this woman?

Him: Oh, you know, the usual.

Me: I don't know what the usual is! That's not my job! That's your job! If you want to switch jobs, then you can come over here right now and balance the extermination budget in London while (shuffling through papers) *figuring out why the hell a two-door wardrobe in the spare room of a country house is considered to be a matter of national concern!*

Him: Rook Thomas, all you need to do is pick her up at Heathrow, escort her around London, and have dinner with her.

Me: I can't do that!

Him: Why not?

Me: Because . . . I don't eat dinner. (Mortified pause.) *Because I don't do well with people.* (Snapping completely.) *Especially people who turn other people into farm animals!*

Him: I'm sorry, I didn't get that, I think we're breaking up . . .

Me (shrieking): *No, we're not! You're just saying that to—*

(Phone goes dead.)

Now, I've managed to cultivate a reputation as the person who knows everything through the simple expedient of having no social life. But the world we live in is strange enough that the description "Greek woman who is thousands of years old" is not enough to identify a specific individual. It didn't even ring any bells. I had Ingrid ring up Gubbins's secretary, who had the woman's name and the time of her arrival at Heathrow. Which turned out to be half an hour from then. Fortunately, we hire extremely good assistants, so in less than ten minutes these two women had managed to rustle up two limousines, some drivers with no discernible personality, an itinerary for a day of entertainment, and my hulking sumo Scot of an honor guard.

"Ingrid, who is this woman?" I asked as our car stuttered through traffic. We were crushed together on a seat so that Ingrid could point out details from her files; Anthony sat across from us, having been dragooned into serving as an easel for a large strip of paper that illustrated the timeline of the Greek woman's life. Thus, I was facing backward (which makes me carsick), and Ingrid had her documents spread out over my lap.

"She is currently known as Lisa Constanopoulos."

"Currently?" I repeated, trying to examine my skirt through several layers of files. Was I imagining things or had I put it on backward?

"The name is a recent acquisition — these ancient ones hold on to names about as long as they hold on to suits," said Ingrid.

"Is this skirt on backward?"

"Yes. Now, bear in mind that Ms. Constanopoulos has a confirmed age of at least three and a half thousand years," continued Ingrid. A shower of files fell to the floor as I tried to swivel the skirt around. Anthony and I leaned forward simultaneously and smashed foreheads.

"Ow!" we both yelled, and I reeled back into the seat.

". . . past century she is notable for having kneed Joseph Stalin in the groin during a drinks reception, and she played a large part in the South African diamond industry," Ingrid went on. "She also cured one member of our royal family of cancer in the 1950s, and infected another with syphilis in the 1960s."

"Sweet Mother of God, my head!"

"Hmmrgmmmrg, Rook Thomas," rumbled Anthony across from me.

"What did he say?"

"I don't know," replied Ingrid.

"How long until her plane lands?" I asked, pressing hard against my bruised forehead.

"Five minutes," said Ingrid.

"How long until we get there?"

"Twenty minutes."

"Oh, hell."

As we trotted through the bowels of Heathrow, Ingrid gave me further details on my lunch date.

"She was a close friend of Eva Perón and was briefly implicated in the Great Fire of Chicago. She may be in possession of a quail that lays golden eggs, and she is responsible for four earthquakes over the past two centuries."

We were ushered into the special reception room that important people go to so they won't have to endure Customs. It's luxurious and private, and you don't have to mingle with the public. It's the room that you wait in if you are very, very powerful and once got shitfaced with Joseph of Arimathea. Or if you are Mick Jagger.

Naturally, the Greek was late. We arrived half an hour after her plane landed, but I suppose when you have all the time in the world, you can afford to wait for the other party to settle in. Also, you learn the art of making a good entrance. Ingrid was in the middle of describing the three modern cults dedicated to the worship of the woman when she came into the room.

This chick had just arrived from Milan, where she'd been picking up designer outfits and lovers, and she was wearing one of each. Her arm was looped casually through the elbow of an Adonis type who looked to have the intelligence quotient of an ironing board, and behind them were two people, an elderly woman and a large Australian Aboriginal man.

I had been expecting a glorious beauty, a goddess who carried herself with all the dignity and confidence of the ages. After all, this was a woman who'd dickered with lamas and dueled with a pope. So I was taken aback to see a woman of my height (which is not great, as you well know) with bouffant, peroxide-blond hair. Blood-red lipstick. Massive sunglasses. A cigarette in one hand. And long, crimson fingernails.

Still, she looked like she was in her forties. No small feat when you've lived longer than Methuselah.

"My darling Rook Thomas!" She swooped across the room, leaned down to me, and planted a kiss on each cheek, leaving massive lipstick smears. Her accent was liquid, sliding smoothly around Europe and South America. She wore enough rings on each finger to bludgeon Anthony to a standstill.

"You are very pretty!" she lied to me. *"I am so pleased to meet you! Did you know your skirt is on backward?"* I muttered something inarticulate about how it was my honor to welcome her to the United Kingdom on the unknowing behalf of the monarch and also about Chevalier Gubbins sending his regrets. My tongue was completely tied, and I managed to turn my skirt only halfway around.

"Oh, yes! Harry! I saw him in Kuala Lumpur a few years ago."

"Ten years," said the elderly woman behind her with a sigh. The male model, who'd been jettisoned as soon as Lisa caught sight of me, shot her a dirty look. From the files, I knew that the elderly woman was Lisa's personal secretary and that the Aborigine guy wasn't her bodyguard but her IT expert.

"Ten years?" repeated Lisa vaguely. *"Really? Anyway, I hope he's doing well, but I am quite confident that you and I will have a pleasant time."* Then, to my intense mortification, she added, *"And I think we can quite definitely help you in the wardrobe department. Tell me, are all your clothes so . . . gray?"* Behind me, Ingrid made a sort of muffled snorting sound. I can only assume she was choking on a breath mint. I shot her a look, hoping she hadn't heard anything, and saw that she was wearing a poker face, which could only mean that she'd heard everything.

Bugger.

Lisa bustled through the hallways of Heathrow, a Rook of the Checquy and a cover boy flanking her. It was like hanging out with a woman who was simultaneously my grandmother and my personal shopper. She reeled off names of clothing stores and tailors we would have to visit. Her elderly secretary jotted them down, while behind them hustled Ingrid and Anthony, listening in increasing dismay as their schedule, meticulously created to ensure political correctness and impeccable security, was jettisoned in favor of a sort of supernatural makeover.

I attempted to protest, citing variously my salary hindrances (a lie), Checquy policy (another lie), and the fact that I didn't know any of my sizes *(which was true, but I really didn't like having to admit it). All these were swept aside when Lisa promised to pay for everything, assured me that nobody in the Checquy wanted to offend her, and informed me that when you pay the amount she was intending to pay, they make the sizes fit you.*

Three hours later, my wardrobe had expanded by a factor of five, I was now the owner of several tins of makeup, and Anthony and Ingrid were both carrying armloads of shopping bags. From personal aide and honor guard, they'd been quickly demoted to luggage monkeys. Their shell-shocked expressions matched mine, and Ingrid later confessed to me that she was pathetically pleased that Lisa had deemed her restaurant selection worthy. Given the topic of lunchtime conversation, I was grateful that Lisa had asked for a separate table for our entourages.

"You see, Myfanwy Thomas," she said, gesturing with her glass of wine, "I do not think that you are enjoying life enough. Of course, that peculiar Estate they sent you to seems to have this effect on many." She took a long drag of a cigarette.

"Well, ma'am—"

"Lisa! I told you, I have to get used to being called Lisa!" She drained her glass and beckoned the waiter, who'd been hovering in fascination.

"Right, yes, Lisa. You see, we are taught—"

"I know this school thing is the modern craze, but I learned at my grandmother's knee, and it has obviously served me well."

"Obviously—"

"The woman taught me how to use my strength, but the most important thing she taught me was how to enjoy life."

"And how long did that take?" I asked, only to be ignored as she barreled on with her lecture.

"You do not know how to enjoy life. I can tell. You need to find yourself a man, and use him."

"Excuse me?" I squeaked. I could feel the blood rushing to my face.

"Young girl like you, you need to be out dancing with boys, that's what my grandmother would say about you."

"But—"

"Find a nice boy, lead out him out to the bushes . . . ," Lisa continued, eyeing the young man-slut she'd brought along with her. "Of course, this

whole future betrayal thing is no doubt weighing heavily upon you. Thank you, waiter, I'll have a Perrier and so will my friend." Lisa checked her nails critically, and then took my hands and looked at mine.

"Of course," I agreed, wondering absently if my nails would pass muster until I processed what she'd said. "What did you say?"

"Darling, you must have some water. My grandmother always said that a glass of water for every two of wine would lead to long life and clean bowels. Although I notice you've had only one glass of wine."

"Lisa—"

"How are your bowels?"

"Lisa!" I exclaimed, and our aides at the next table looked over in consternation. I continued in a quieter voice. "What do you mean, a future betrayal?"

"Myfanwy Thomas, you will be betrayed in the future by a member of your Court. You know it. I know it. You will stand in the rain, and all around you will be dead men."

"How do you know?" I whispered.

"I can see it all around you, my little precious," she said, still holding my hands. Although her voice was calm and quiet, her grip was firm. "I see it clearly."

"What else?"

"Hmm?" she said, staring at my fingertips intently.

"What else can you see?"

"I can see that you need a manicure."

"No! What can you see in my future?"

"I can see that you'll need an evening gown. Fortunately I know just the man to make it for you."

As it turned out, the man she knew had died thirty-two years ago, but his granddaughter was also a dressmaker and she presented some sketches of a scarlet creation that I was too embarrassed to comment on. She also jotted down some measurements that were markedly different from the ones the other tailors had recorded. When I demurred, Lisa called over her elderly secretary and boy toy to ask what they thought. They were encouraged to visualize me wearing it, which meant that for several minutes my chest was ogled by two strangers.

"You should be proud to show off your breasts, Myfanwy Thomas," Lisa declared loudly in front of everyone.

"Sorry?" Just kill me.

"They're fine! A little small, but with a lovely shape. You should be nursing babies! Giving suck!" She gestured elaborately.

Kill me now.

"You know how many babies have suckled at these breasts?" she asked. *"Yes, and some grown men too!"* she added, briskly slapping her boy toy on the bottom. He gave her an oily smile and then his eyes slid back to my chest.

Finally, we got Lisa to the hotel and escorted her up to her suite. As I said good-bye at the door, she gripped my wrist, pulled me close, and whispered in my ear in a hoarse voice. Cigarette smoke and French perfume filled my nostrils, but that wasn't what made my flesh crawl.

"Myfanwy Thomas, bad things are headed your way. As bad as ever I have seen in my life. You will lose everything. You will end in the rain, and beyond that I cannot see. So enjoy yourself while you can." Her eyes burned into mine, and I could see the age within her. Centuries and centuries, stretching back to an unimaginable beginning. And then she shut the door, leaving me shaking in the hallway.

Ingrid and Anthony deposited me back home. And now I am sitting in the dark, alone except for my many, many shopping bags.

30

Razormouth's breath stank of chemicals, and Myfanwy jerked her head away reflexively. Something about the odor brushed a memory far in the back of her mind. She had stopped dancing, and now she tensed in preparation. Her powers were primed, but she hesitated to use them in such a public setting. *How am I going to explain this to Bronwyn?* she thought frantically. Razormouth had made no move to hurt her, and she dared a quick glance at her sister, who was still dancing obliviously with her friends.

The guy looked normal once he closed his lips over his teeth. Well, maybe not completely normal, but certainly more normal than a lot of the people Myfanwy worked with every day. Shaved head, pointed nose, pale lips drawn back in a tight smile. She was braced for any movement, but he simply stood there, swaying slightly. Myfanwy raised her eyebrows in a question, and he gestured toward a table that was a little away from the speakers and miraculously free of people. She hesitated, and he slowly lifted up one hand, holding a mobile phone. He discreetly offered it to her so that Bronwyn and her friends could not see it. Myfanwy sighed, took it gingerly from his fingers, and followed him to the table.

"Hello?" she hazarded. An indistinct voice came through, drowned out by the music. "You'll have to speak up, I'm in a nightclub and they're playing some sort of, I don't know, fornication music." The voice spoke louder now but was still impossible to understand. Myfanwy looked at the man with the sharp smile and made a face that indicated that she couldn't hear the person on the other end of the phone. He rolled his eyes and made a face that indicated this had not been his idea and that his protests had been ignored. He jerked a thumb forcefully over his shoulder toward the exit.

"You've got to be kidding!" she said loudly to him. He gestured again to the exit. She leaned close to his ear and spoke clearly. "My friends might think it strange if I leave with a man one minute after I meet him." He looked at her blankly. "Clearly, you're not familiar with the whole 'girls going out as a group' phenomenon, but unless you're prepared to cause a scene, I'm not leaving."

"I am prepared to cause an *exceptionally* upsetting scene," he whispered in her ear. He had an accent that she couldn't quite place. European. Scandinavian?

"I'm willing to bet I can cause an even more upsetting one," Myfanwy whispered back. "Unless you can out-awful the idea of you plucking out your own eyes with your thumbnails." He stepped back warily. Myfanwy raised an eyebrow at him and froze his joints. Instead of being alarmed, however, he smiled his razor smile and looked suggestively toward Bronwyn and her friends.

"You wouldn't dare!" she spat, and tightened her mental grasp on him, clenching her mind around his lungs. He tensed, his eyes widening, but didn't lose his smile. Instead, he gestured with his chin back toward the girls. She turned around and saw that the girls were fine, dancing unconcernedly. Bronwyn caught her eye and waved, her eyebrows rising to ask if everything was okay. Myfanwy forced a smile and nodded. Bronwyn took another quick look at the man with the teeth (currently concealed by his lips) and made a face indicating that he was kind of cute.

Then Myfanwy noticed with a growing sense of unease that the girls were surrounded by particularly bad dancers. Several of them were wearing clothes better suited to committing grievous bodily harm than picking up girls. Hesitantly, she cast out her awareness, trying to bind the dancers. *No good,* she admitted to herself. *The girls are in the way and everyone is moving, and I just had a beverage that had six kinds of vodka in it.* Defeated, Myfanwy turned her attention back to the man with the dangerous teeth.

"You know, I really hate being coerced by means of a cliché," she said. He looked at her without comprehension. "Come with us or we'll kill your friends? Man, you might as well have just jammed a gun in my ribs during the strobe."

"Would that have worked?" he asked.

"I doubt it," said Myfanwy. "Now, if we're not going to make a scene, what am I going to tell my friends about why I'm leaving?" He blinked nervously. *This is clearly a person experienced in the realms of supernatural warfare but who has had practically nothing to do with normal people. Especially girls.*

"That you would like to see my car?" he asked. She restrained the urge to laugh in his face.

"Does that mean that I will be coming back?" she asked.

"I don't really know," he fumbled. Despite the seriousness of the situation, she was beginning to feel a little sorry for him.

"I am not telling them that I want to see your car. I am not sixteen, and we are not in the musical *Grease*. I'll tell you what. You leave. I will go back and dance for five minutes, and your goons can keep an eye on me. Then I'll pretend to receive an urgent message from work and I'll step out to talk to your friend." Razormouth considered the matter and then nodded and left. His friends kept dancing badly.

Five minutes later, Myfanwy left the club. She'd shrugged off her conversation with the toothsome bald guy and, seized with a sudden reckless fatalism, had danced briefly with one of the goons. Now outside, she looked around and saw neon light glinting off a shaved head.

"Rook Thomas," he said, smiling his smile.

"Nameless Irritating Man with Aggressive Teeth," she said, smiling hers. "So, where's your friend?"

"Just across the street, if you'll follow me." He offered her his hand, and bowed slightly in a manner that would have been normal in the Rookery but which drew whistles and cheers from the line of people waiting to go into the club.

"Go for it, luv!" shrieked one girl. Similar (if more specific) words of encouragement filled the air, and Myfanwy felt herself blushing.

They walked hurriedly across the street, and he opened the door of his car for her.

"You've got a pretty shit job with this, you know," she pointed out to him. He flushed uncomfortably, and nodded. "Still, you were very polite. Are you Belgian, by any chance?" He nodded awkwardly. "Thought so." And she got into the car.

Myfanwy settled back into her seat and took great care to compose herself before she raised her eyes to look at her host. *That will impress them,* she thought with satisfaction. *I am calm, cool, collected, and I have already mollified their flunky.* Then she saw what was occupying the rest of the limo.

I am not going to scream, she thought desperately. *I am not going to throw up. I am not going to faint. Even though these would all be exceptionally reasonable reactions to what is lounging in a tank of slime in front of me.*

The thing in front of her looked as if it had been flayed right before she got in the car. It was shiny with fluids that usually flowed exclusively beneath several layers of skin. The eyes were mismatched, one of them glinting a bright Teutonic blue that would have done Hitler proud, and the other so bloodshot that it was a stomach-turning orange.

Chitin plates trailed delicately through the angry flesh, seemingly placed with calligraphic care. Rangy cords of muscles wrapped around limbs with alarmingly irregular ridges and spurs.

In the mouth, there were white nubs of teeth that, although technically perfect in themselves, were just *wrong.* They jutted out, twisted in their sockets, and sometimes seemed to be in the process of migrating around the mouth. Shiny white canines snarled where incisors normally grew; a molar had been replaced with a bicuspid. The front teeth were missing, but as Myfanwy watched in horrified fascination, little white edges slid out of the gums. When the thing peeled back its lips in a horrible smile, the whole effect was jarring.

But more than anything, it was the biological *presence* of the thing that turned Myfanwy's stomach. She had not sought to probe it with her powers, but her senses spread out from her unconsciously and then recoiled violently when they touched the thing in the tank. In this creature, the connections that lay within every human being were marred, hideously twisted. Nerves had been rerouted, arteries and muscles torn out and fused to places they should not have been. It was a deliberate perversion of biology. Myfanwy could no more touch that thing with her mind than she could deliberately drink sewage.

The creature reclined, partially submerged in a waist-high tank that had replaced a row of seats in the limo. The tank was filled with a viscous fluid that shimmered with oily rainbows. The skinned thing rested its arms on the rim of the tank and laid its chin on the back of its hand. As she watched, a canine twisted itself into place with an audible click. She winced slightly.

"Good evening, Rook Thomas," it said. She nodded and smiled politely, pressing her lips together so hard that the blood rushed away. Her powers were tightly wound back into her center, cringing away from everything in front of her.

"I am Graaf Gerd de Leeuwen of the Wetenschappelijk Broederschap van Natuurkundigen," it said to her. "I apologize for my current appearance. A new skin is being grown for me, but I did not want to wait. Once we heard that you were unattended, I knew this would be the perfect opportunity to meet with you."

Myfanwy nodded sharply, not trusting herself to speak.

"Let me begin by stating that, regardless of our discussion's outcome, neither I nor any of my people will touch you this night. Nor will we hurt your friends. I am letting you know this without offering any conditions. This is a courtesy I am extending to you because you have something I want. And because I have been told you have power."

Well, that was a well-constructed introduction, thought Myfanwy. She made a mental note that the Grafters didn't know who Bronwyn was.

"They are civilians," said Myfanwy. "Touching them, following them, or investigating them would be extremely undiplomatic. I would find it difficult to have a productive meeting if I thought they were going to be harmed, this night or any other night." She watched the blood flush through the cheeks of the thing in front of her. Or at least, through the capillaries that lay where the cheeks would be.

"You do not make demands of me," it said shortly.

"I wouldn't think of making any demands," said Myfanwy. "But let's change the subject. I gather that I have something you want." *Whatever it is.* The thing's muscles jerked in vexation along its neck, and tendons tightened in its fingers. She gritted her teeth as tiny platelets of chitin scraped along the metal rim of the tank. She watched in nervous fascination as it controlled its rage.

"Very well," it said through clenched teeth. "Now we will talk."

"Fine," she said.

"I do not like being in this country," it said peevishly.

Myfanwy waited expectantly. She was guessing that what it wanted was not a Eurostar ticket out of the United Kingdom.

"I would still be in België, but unfortunately circumstances have dragged me here."

"That must be trying," said Myfanwy with as much false sympathy as she could muster. *How tiresome, to have to come and invade a country,* she thought. She was beginning to lose her patience. The skinned man in the tank looked at her with his head cocked to one side.

"Yes," he said dubiously. "It displeases me that I am obliged to speak with a member of the Checquy. I have not forgotten the Isle of Wight." Myfanwy gaped as she realized what this man was saying. He had been there when the Grafters invaded. The thing in front of her was over three hundred years old. In her shock, her defenses wavered, and she began to gag. *I can't stay near this thing for too much longer or I'm going to be sick all over him. We need to wrap this up,* she thought. With an effort, she fought back the nausea and attempted a smile. It was more of a rictus, but it served.

"I can understand how vexing it must be for you, but I don't believe that the first official communication between you people and the Checquy since the War of Wight is that you want them to know you're angry about being here. So, let us talk plainly. What do you want?"

"You do not talk to me like this!" he shouted, and he spasmed in his tank, sending fluids splashing. "And you do not play games with me!" His eyes were burning with rage as he leaned forward out of the tank toward her.

"I am not playing games!" she shouted back at him, all thoughts of diplomacy vanishing. He jerked in surprise, but did not move. "What do you want?"

"You know what I want!" he screamed. Yellowy foam sprayed from his lips onto her cheeks, and she flinched. Aghast, she scrubbed at her face.

"What the hell—look, I have no idea what the fuck you want, but you better talk now or I'm getting out of this car."

"I want my *deelhebber!* I want Ernst von Suchtlen!" he snarled.

Genuinely bewildered, Myfanwy blinked. "What?" she asked.

"*What* what?" he spat.

"What are you talking about?"

"*What?*" he yelled.

"I don't understand," she said, trying to calm him down. "What is it that you want?"

"I want you to produce Graaf Ernst von Suchtlen!"

"Who?"

"The other leader of the Wetenschappelijk Broederschap van Natuurkundigen," he said through teeth that would have been clenched if they'd lined up.

"I'm sorry," she said carefully. "But we don't have this person."

"Don't patronize me," he said, sneering. "He vanished from our *fabriek* months ago, leaving instructions for the continuance of our strategy here and for the concealment of his absence. From *me.*" He clenched his fingers on the rim of the tank. "Both worked so well that I was not aware of his disappearance until a few weeks ago."

"He's been gone for months, and you didn't realize?" asked Myfanwy.

"Time passes differently for us than for you," he said with contempt. "Once I discovered he was missing, I tracked him. We found a record of a piece of mail sent to Myfanwy Thomas, who is a Rook of the Checquy. Our mortal enemies. It is the only thing that indicates where he has gone. I sent my personal agent to find him, and you promptly took him and tortured him! Now"—and here he took a deep, controlling breath—"where is Ernst?"

"I'm sorry, but I have no idea," said Myfanwy. *Hell,* she thought. *Thomas didn't even know the Grafters were active. If some Grafter guy had turned up on her doorstep, that would have been the first thing mentioned in her first letter.*

"If you fuck with me, I will start killing right now!" he yelled. "Do you want murder in your streets?" He was thrashing in his tank, sending waves of the goop sloshing everywhere. In horror, Myfanwy watched as her jeans from the knee down became soaked. *Is he having a seizure?* she wondered. The windows were splattered, and when he swept his arms in her direction, gobbets were flung onto her face and her top.

"*Listen to me, you flayed fuck,*" she shouted in his face. "I have no idea what you are talking about, but you need to calm down."

"If you do not produce him in three days, I will release a wave of horror upon your people that will blight your country!" he screamed. The tank tore under his fingers, and the remaining fluid began to pour out onto the floor. "I will drown this city in bile and blood!" In his flailing, he was actually doing himself damage. She saw minute tears open up on parts of him, and trickles of red. "Now out, Rook! You have only the time I give you!" He was still raving as Myfanwy opened the door and a wave of his fluids poured out onto the sidewalk. She stumbled getting out, dropping her purse and spilling its contents into the goop. *Great, just great,* she thought as her cell phone emitted a piercing squeal and died in the slime. The bald man was standing by the door, looking anxious. When he heard the shouting from within the car, he paled.

"Get him out of here," said Myfanwy shortly.

"Did you do what he wanted?" said the man frantically, as he got into the front seat.

"Does it sound like it?" she asked. He cringed, shut the door, and the limousine peeled away, leaving her covered in a pungent slime, standing across the street from the club and a crowd of gawkers.

I can't believe this is the second time I've walked into this hotel looking like an abused wife, Myfanwy mused as she walked up to the doormen. To her surprise and irritation, this time they did not leap to open the door for her.

"Excuse me?" she said, blushing angrily.

"Sorry, dear, but we don't allow the homeless in here," said one. He was apologetic about it, but also quite firm.

"Homeless?" she squawked. "I am not homeless! I . . ." She frantically sought an explanation for her appearance. "I'm a rock musician."

They looked at her dubiously.

"I have credit cards," she said.

They carried on looking at her.

"I tip generously?" she hazarded

"You're going to need to move along, miss," said one of them.

"I don't believe this!" she yelled. "Last time I walked in here I had two black eyes, bloody lips, and was sopping wet! And I had no problem getting a room. What kind of business are you people running? I have a car parked in your security garage right now, and I don't want to get slime on it!"

"Miss, it's three in the morning, and if you don't move along, we're going to have to move you along."

"If you put one finger on me, you will regret it!" she said coldly.

"No doubt," said one. "These uniforms are dry-clean-only." Myfanwy was stupefied. Since settling into her position as Rook, she'd grown used to people doing what she said. She briefly considered using her powers to hurl them out of the way, but realized that no power on earth could make a hotel clerk check her in if he didn't want to. *But what can I do? I can't take Bronwyn home like this.*

"Fine, then I want my car from the garage," she said angrily. "I have the stub here somewhere." She tried to scrape some of the slime off her fingers and opened her handbag.

"Clear off," said one of the men forcefully. "Now."

Shooting the doormen a filthy look, Myfanwy walked down the footpath and got a perverse pleasure out of watching a couple of pedestrians jump out of her way.

Okay, my mobile phone is coated in slime and no longer works. I can't let Bronwyn see me like this, even if I could get back into the club, which I sincerely doubt. The slime was beginning to itch, and it was viscous enough that she couldn't simply scrape it off. *What the hell is this stuff?* Then she had an idea, and abruptly turned a corner.

Thank you, God, she thought. In a breach of security that would have had Clovis tearing out his hair, the rear entrance to the hotel had one person behind a desk, and that person was dozing. Apparently, it was the entrance for conventions and functions, and there were few of those taking place at three in the morning. The doors slid open and she stepped inside. In his sleep, the receptionist wrinkled his nose at Myfanwy's appalling odor. She waved her hand at him and he settled into a deeper sleep. Taking a breath, she walked quietly past the desk.

No outraged shouts stopped her. No irritating calls of "I say, excuse me!" The fact that she left a trail of evil on the floor as she padded down the hallway to the swimming pool prompted no threats to call the police. Myfanwy walked through the courtyard and looked around warily. The pool was steaming in the cold night air, and an electric light glowed under the water. Fortunately, there was no one in the courtyard, and the windows overlooking it were all curtained or dark. She laid her slime-covered handbag on a deck chair and gloomily regarded her filthy clothes. For a moment, she contemplated stripping right down, but then eyed the many balconies that looked down on the pool area. *Probably not the best idea,* she decided. *Plus, if angry hotel staff appear, I don't want to have to make a break for it while naked.* Sighing, she walked down the steps into the water. She ducked her head under and felt a delightful warmth glide over her skin.

Myfanwy kept her eyes clenched shut and scrubbed frantically at her body. Globules of muck sloughed off into the water, and an oily haze spread out from her. She raked her fingers through her hair and felt the sludge slide away. She kicked away from the mess and swam back toward the steps.

Well, now I'm soaking wet, she thought grimly, *but it's a definite improvement.* Fate had smiled upon her in the form of a towel left on a deck chair, and she took her shirt off to wring it out. There were some ominous-looking brown-black stains on her clothes, but her skin and hair were no longer caked with crud. She briskly toweled off her hair and arms and briefly considered taking off her jeans before noticing a man looking down at her from a balcony.

"Oh...hi," she said, a little self-conscious about wearing just a bra.

"Evening," he said. "Must have been a hell of a party." She glanced back at the pool and saw that it looked as if someone had dumped toxic waste in the deep end.

"Yes, indeed," she said, suddenly ecstatic. She'd come safely through that manifestation in Bath and escaped relatively unharmed from the battle after she accused Gestalt of treachery. Hell, she'd even endured the interview with that Grafter thing. And now she was pleased with herself for sneaking into a snooty hotel and befouling their swimming pool. "It was quite an event."

"I don't suppose you'd fancy a drink?" the man asked with a smile. "I could bring something down."

"It's a delightful offer," said Myfanwy, smiling back. "But I have to go find the rest of my party. That said, I don't suppose you could lend me a shirt?" She gestured at the large stains on her top.

"A shirt?" he asked. "Certainly." He disappeared into his room and came back onto the balcony carrying a folded blue business shirt. "It may be a little big on you," he cautioned as he dropped it down to her.

"It's infinitely better than the alternative." She put the shirt on, noting with amusement that it reached down to just above her knees. "Well, I must away. Thanks for the shirt."

"I'd tell you to party responsibly, but I think it's a little late," said the man wryly.

"Don't worry, I'm fine," she said. "Have a good night."

"You too," he said, watching as she walked out the way she had come.

Myfanwy would never know whether the club would have let her back in covered in gunk, but it turned out they had no problem with a girl who was soaked from the waist down. The club seemed far more mundane after the events of the previous hour, and Myfanwy eyed it thoughtfully. *How on earth did the Grafters find me* here? she wondered. *It's the last place I would have expected to find myself, so how did they know?*

Maybe they tailed me from the garage, she thought doubtfully. *Which would mean that they've been staking it out since before I knew it existed. That's quite a while to wait.*

But Alrich knew I was here, she realized with a chill. *Could he have tipped them off?* Her speculations were cut off by her own enormous yawn, and she shrugged mentally. *I'll think it out in the morning.* Across the dance floor, even Bronwyn and her friends were starting to look tired.

"What happened to you?" Bronwyn asked incredulously. "That is definitely not the top I gave you, and—you're soaking wet!" She picked anxiously at her sister's clothes.

"I got splashed by a passing car," Myfanwy explained. "And a very nice man gave me his shirt."

"He just took it off?" Bronwyn asked.

"Yeah," said Myfanwy, inventing madly. "He didn't seem to miss it."

"But where's the shirt I gave you?"

"It's in my handbag," said Myfanwy. "I'll have it laundered and get it back to you." *If it's salvageable,* she thought. *Who knows if you can get weird biological stains out?*

"And your work thing?"

"It was a dire emergency, which I solved over the phone," said Myfanwy. "At three in the morning. Are you ready to go?"

"Are you good to drive?" asked Bronwyn.

"Oh, sure. But I think you'll need to be the one who gets the car out of the garage. The guys at that hotel don't like me very much."

31

The phone in the flat was ringing, and Myfanwy was not inclined to answer it. She reached out fully intending to pick it up and hang up, but some sadist (probably her, but possibly Grantchester) had placed the phone on the other side of the room. She flailed at the bedside table, hoping to find a lamp, but instead managed to activate the device that set her round bed to rotating. By the time she had escaped the bed, wandered across the room, tripped over the sodden jeans she had jettisoned two hours earlier, cursed them to the depths of clothing hell, untangled herself, gotten up, and answered the phone, she was still not fully awake.

"Yeah?"

"Rook Thomas, it's Ingrid."

"Yeah?"

"It's six thirty."

"Yeah?"

"You have your medical examinations in half an hour."

"Yeah."

"So, shall I have breakfast waiting for you in your dining room?"

"Yeah."

Rook Thomas?"

"Hmm?"

Rook Thomas?"

"Yeah?"

"It's been fifteen minutes, and you haven't come out yet."

"Yeah."

"Are you dressed?"

"Nah."

"Are you naked?"

"Nah."

"So I can send these large bodyguards into your room right now?"

"Don't you dare! I'll be out in five minutes and there had better be coffee. And once I'm done, send someone up to figure out how to turn off my bed."

Who are they?" asked Myfanwy dully, jabbing a thumb over her shoulder at the two massive men flanking the door to her office.

"Those are today's large bodyguards," said Ingrid brightly.

"Where's the coffee?"

"Oh, there's no coffee," said Ingrid. "The doctors said it was best for you not to have anything to eat or drink until after the tests."

"But...but didn't you say there would be breakfast when I got down?"

"That was just to lure you out of bed," said Ingrid. Myfanwy thought briefly of bursting into tears, but instead nodded a weary assent.

"I'm going to need a replacement phone," said Myfanwy flatly, dropping her slime-encrusted mobile on the desk. Ingrid eyed it silently as some of the vile liquid began to ooze onto her blotter. An infinite number of awkward questions hovered in the air, begging to be asked, and Myfanwy wondered how her executive assistant was going to address this.

"Consider it done, Rook Thomas," her secretary said finally. "Now, did you shower?"

"Yeah, but someone had taken all my soap and shampoo," said Myfanwy.

"Yes, that's because they'll be comparing your scent to preserved ampoules of your sweat," said Ingrid.

"Groovy." She glanced over as two bespectacled men came into the office, looking expectant.

"Now, Rook Thomas, this is Dr. Burke and Dr. Leichhardt." The two doctors both had mustaches and looked like photo negatives of each other. They bowed awkward little bows, which she acknowledged with a nod and a yawn.

"Good morning, gentlemen. Now, I sincerely hope that I'm not going to have to do anything difficult this morning?" she asked, trying to open her eyes.

"Pardon me, Rook Thomas?" asked Dr. Burke.

"I won't be, you know, running laps or anything, right?"

"Oh, no, Rook Thomas," said Dr. Leichhardt. "Our tests are quite passive on your part. Although I feel I should warn you, some of them are quite—"

"Unpleasant, time-consuming, and highly intrusive, I know," interrupted Myfanwy. She turned to Ingrid. "Didn't I ask to have these done in the afternoon?" she said piteously.

"Security Chief Clovis randomly reassigned the appointments," said Ingrid as they walked to the lift. "He seemed to feel that randomness was the key to preventing the Grafters from evading our detection methods."

From what I've seen, thought Myfanwy, *the Grafters are pretty comfortable with randomness,* but she restrained herself from saying anything. "And is Security Chief Clovis awake and at work at this hour?" she asked bitterly.

"Oh, no," said Ingrid, pushing the button for the medical floor.

The doors opened and the two doctors ushered Myfanwy, Ingrid, and the two large bodyguards into the medical center. "And weren't there supposed to be three doctors? To ensure something?"

"Yes, and here is Dr. Wills," said Ingrid, introducing a tall icy blond woman, who was pulling on a pair of latex gloves that reached up to the elbow.

"Good morning, Rook Thomas," said Dr. Wills without a trace of a smile. "Please take off your pajamas and slippers, put on this paper gown, get on this bed, and put your feet in these stirrups." Myfanwy nodded with a deep lack of enthusiasm and looked around for a place to change. The three doctors looked at her expectantly, and she had a grim realization. Ingrid at least had the decency to look away. The large bodyguards tactfully stepped outside to take up positions guarding the door. *Maybe it's better I didn't get any coffee,* she thought. *This isn't something I would want to be fully awake for.* Someone would pay for this.

"Well, gentlemen, shall we get started?" said Dr. Wills, "Ingrid, would you like some coffee?" Myfanwy narrowed her eyes.

Someone was *definitely* going to pay.

Ingrid, I need to know if—ow ow *ow ow!* What the hell are you doing down there?"

"Sorry, Rook Thomas" came an unrepentant voice from between her legs. The two doctors flanking Dr. Wills smiled apologetically.

"Not as much as you're going to be," she muttered to herself, and she beckoned Ingrid over to her. "Ingrid," she said quietly, so none of the audience could hear, "could you check my schedule for the past six months? I need to know if I had any meetings with a Graaf Ernst von Suchtlen."

"Now, Rook Thomas?"

"Please." Ingrid nodded and turned away to scan through records on her tablet computer. Myfanwy yawned, and then gave a little shriek.

"Sorry, Rook Thomas. Your body tenses when you yawn," said Dr. Wills. Myfanwy looked down at her suspiciously and was blinded by a flash of light.

"That didn't come out of *me,* did it?" she asked.

"Oh, no, we're taking some digital photos."

"What?"

"Don't worry, Rook Thomas," said Dr. Burke. "It's not like we're going to post these on the Internet. They're for the outside doctor." There was another jab of exceptional discomfort.

"That *really* is not pleasant," said Myfanwy tightly.

"I'm sorry," said Dr. Wills, "it's not normally so crowded in here."
"What?"

"I mean crowded in the examination room," said Dr. Wills.

"Gentlemen," snapped Myfanwy. "Please try not to jostle my interrogational gynecologist!"

"We'll be careful," said Dr. Leichhardt soothingly. "Now, this may be uncomfortable in an unorthodox way, but whatever you do, don't clench." Myfanwy closed her eyes in horror and thought of England. She was just coming to the conclusion that England was totally not worth it when Dr. Wills snapped her gloves off. "Rook Thomas, we're just about done here. Now, I know you haven't been interested before, but perhaps we should take this opportunity to talk about whether you'd like to start on birth control?" Ingrid looked at her with a raised eyebrow.

Maybe I should lie and say that I'm a Grafter, she thought desperately. *Or Satan. They'd probably stop this if I were Satan.*

Aaaand with that taken care of, we'll be handing you off to the dentists," said Dr. Leichhardt. "These are Doctors Weiss, Engel, and Olivier."

"It's nice to meet you," said Myfanwy. "Can I put my pajamas back on?"

"I'm afraid not," said Dr. Olivier apologetically, "but we do have a new paper gown for you."

"Oh, rapture." Myfanwy sighed.

"And if you'd please get into this chair," said Dr. Engel. "We have this thing we'd like to slide into your mouth. It will prevent you from closing your jaws."

"Isss theya an eshti-ate on how lung this iss gowingh tuh take?"

"I'm sorry, no. Of course, Rook Thomas, we want to be as thorough as possible. Now, we're just going to close these vises around your head, shoulders, and upper torso. Would you like a comfort bear?" asked Dr. Weiss. He held up a small tartan teddy bear.

"Yesh, leesh."

"Rook Thomas?" came a new voice.

"Yesh?"

"It's Ingrid."

"Sh'up?"

"I checked through your appointment book for the past year, and there's no record of that name."

"Shit. Ut alowt ennee un elsh?" Myfanwy asked.

"I beg your pardon?" Ingrid's brows knit. Myfanwy looked to Dr. Olivier imploringly. Apparently, he spoke fluent "can't shut your jaws."

"She said, 'What about anyone else?'" Myfanwy tried to nod her head in agreement but was limited to blinking emphatically.

"I'm sorry, do you want me to check your schedule for anyone else's name?" asked Ingrid, confused.

"Oh!" said Myfanwy, shaking her comfort bear in impotent frustration. "Hngh!"

"Rook Thomas," said Dr. Engel reproachfully. "We have placed sharp blades inside your mouth. It might be best if you didn't shake." Myfanwy rolled her eyes.

"You want me to check other people's schedules?"

"Esh."

"Very well, Rook Thomas."

"Rook Thomas," said Dr. Weiss. "Do you know how you got these scars on your throat?"

"Oshils?"

"No, you still have your tonsils," said Dr. Olivier. "Oh, and a cavity!"

"Well," said Dr. Engel. "As long as we're in here, we might as well take care of that."

Did you get any sleep in the MRI?" asked Ingrid as they walked slowly down the hallways of the Rookery. The two large bodyguards marched behind them, filling the corridor and bumping the pictures on the walls. Midway through the examinations, Myfanwy had realized that they weren't just there to protect her. They were also there to kill her, or at least secure her, if she turned out to be a Grafter plant.

"For some of the time," said Myfanwy testily. "So, the name never appeared anywhere?"

"No. And it wasn't easy, but I arranged to have all the non-personal diaries of the Court members analyzed as well."

"And nothing?"

"No Belgians," said Ingrid apologetically.

"Figures." Myfanwy sighed. "Now, how many more of these tests do I have to undergo?"

"Blood tests, urine tests, sputum tests, stool tests, hair tests, fingerprinting, eye exams, ear exams, DNA scrape, and a few minutes inside something the techies referred to as 'the swarm of bees.'"

"Why is it called that?" asked Myfanwy suspiciously. "Because it buzzes?"

"Oh, probably," said Ingrid evasively. "After that, we have to have the dogs sniff you . . ." She trailed off as she scanned her list.

"You know, the dogs didn't react to the Grafter that Shantay's people pulled in," said Myfanwy. "They walked her past them and there was no growling at all."

"True," said Ingrid. "But Security Chief Clovis feels that since the dogs picked up Van Syoc, the chance is worth taking. Now, after the dogs we have three gentlemen who are going to lick you."

"Lick me?" Myfanwy asked in horror.

"Yes. Actually, we're very lucky. We only had two men who were qualified to lick, but we were able to bring one of the students in from the Estate. Really, you have to pity them, because they're the only three lickers we have and so they're going to have to lick every member of the Checquy."

"But how old is this student?" asked Myfanwy desperately.

"He's seventeen."

Myfanwy's stomach turned at the news. "And where is he going to lick me?"

"In the examination room," said Ingrid.

"What? No, what I mean is, whereabouts on my body will they be licking me?" demanded Myfanwy.

"The tip of the index finger of your right hand," said Ingrid, as if it were obvious.

"Oh, thank God," said Myfanwy, limp with relief.

"Honestly, Rook Thomas, what were you thinking?" asked Ingrid with amusement. "That they were going to lick every inch of your body?"

"Stupid, I know." Myfanwy laughed weakly.

"Very stupid," agreed Ingrid. She checked her list. "We don't have anywhere near the amount of time that would take."

32

Dear You,

I really think I deserve much more credit for not developing a drinking habit in light of the repeated prophecies of my doom. But then, I've always been cautious of alcohol. At the Estate, booze was strictly forbidden. "A clean mind and a clean body make for a perfect weapon" was what one of the teachers used to say. Of course, there was always something available if you really wanted it. Once in a while, a group of kids would sneak out to the nearest village, or try to. I mean, we were on an island, so it wasn't easy. Plus, as you can imagine, our teachers had been well trained in the art of surveillance.

But for those who wanted a little kick, there was that girl whose hair would get you high if you ate it.

Or that guy who could trip you out if you let him touch your eyeballs with his fingertips, which I was never willing to try.

But I digress.

Several weeks after my shopping spree with the immortal Greek fashionista, I was sipping my coffee and watching the sun come up. Generally, Ingrid is the first person in, but I had somehow managed to beat her into the office by a few minutes and was taking advantage of the opportunity to do my most favorite of tasks: go through the mail. It's probably the result of my years at the Estate, where no one ever got any letters, but I adore getting mail. Normally Ingrid gets to it first, but this time I did, and so I was the first to see that intriguing little package.

Most of the post wasn't particularly interesting. A couple of scientific journals on the nervous system and neuroanatomy (I do a lot of studying). Interoffice memos from the Estate, the Annexe, Gallows Keep, and Apex

House. A couturier in Gloucestershire had been imprisoned for using rodents as indentured servants. That damn mobile forest had been told in no uncertain terms that it should stop mobbing lonely farmhouses. The accounting department was going to review the R & D department's requests for Clydesdales. And there was an invitation to the annual Court Christmas party, to be held at the house of Conrad Grantchester. All the members of the Court had been invited, along with their families.

Of course, since I don't have any family to bring, I generally find myself pounced upon by a Court member's wife who wants to hook me up with someone. I don't know whether their husbands go home at night and tell them all about the spinster at the office or if it's that obvious I'm single. The only consolation is that they do the same thing to Gestalt.

Oh, well. At least this would give me a good excuse to wear one of those dresses Lisa had picked out for me. Not the red one, of course. Nor the purple thing with the straps and the mini-bustle. And certainly not that one with the feathers. Mentally going through the list of garments and crossing a line through each of them, I reached for the package. That one black dress might do, if I found someone who could figure out how all the ribbons braided through each other. I absentmindedly cut the tape on the box. To be honest, I was quite keen on wearing the necklace with the opals. But the dress that Lisa said I should wear it with was cut quite low. Both in the front and the back. And on the sides. In fact, it was really just a skirt with straps. Sighing, I opened the box.

Inside, raw and bloody, was a human heart.

Now, Rook Thomas, I can assure you that we will get the blood out of your carpet," said Ingrid.

"And we're having it tested for anything unfortunate," said Dr. Crisp as he swabbed up a minute amount of gore from my desk with a Q-tip. A multitude of his assistants were swarming over the table and carpet where the blood had spattered. As soon as I had clapped my eyes on the thing in the box, I'd flung it away with what I later heard Ingrid describe to one of her friends as "the squeal of a terrified piglet."

"*And we're scanning both the heart and the box for any dangerous devices,*" *said Security Chief Clovis, taking a break from talking busily on his mobile. "See if we can't trace it through the courier company," he said to a subordinate who was hulking behind him. "It probably won't work, but I want to cover every possible base."*

"*Rook Thomas, are you sure you won't come out of the corner? I think you'd find the sofa more comfortable." Ingrid turned away and spoke quietly to Dr. Crisp. I saw her cast a concerned look back over her shoulder at me.*

"*Trauma?" Crisp said bemusedly. "I shouldn't think so. She probably just needs a nice strong drink."*

"*Or a good slap!" said Teddy Gestalt as he walked into the room. The Pawns and Retainers scattered out of his way as he swept past the trail of blood and looked down at me with undisguised disgust. "Look here, Thomas, this is not acceptable behavior from a student, let alone from a Rook of the Checquy! Now stop that shaking, get up, and quit making a fool of yourself in front of the staff." He cast a final look at me, rolled his eyes, and turned on his heel. "Dr. Crisp, Chief Clovis, I expect a copy of the reports on this development. And try to figure out why anyone would bother sending a heart to Rook Thomas." He said this last in a tone of withering contempt and then strode out of the room, leaving a horribly awkward silence.*

33

A ching, sore, and in dire need of caffeine, Myfanwy sat gingerly
at her desk. She wore soft, gentle pajamas and a dressing gown.
Hours of unpleasant, time-consuming, and highly intrusive examinations combined with only a few hours' sleep had left her in a foul
mood. This condition was exacerbated by the feeling that she shouldn't
go back to sleep because she had to find Graaf Ernst von Suchtlen
and the fact that the office coffee machine had broken and she didn't
know how to work the one in her residence.

While Ingrid had gone off to beg coffee from some other department, Myfanwy had combed back through Thomas's purple binder
and found nothing that mentioned a meeting with any of the Grafters. She was now beginning to regret that she had left the letters at
home in her study. In desperation, and in the throes of caffeine with-
drawal, she was now reclined in her chair with her eyes closed. The
phone rang, sending a blast of agony into her skull.

"Yes?" she said tightly into the phone.

"Rook Thomas, there's a call for you" came Ingrid's voice.

"Did you get me any coffee?" she asked hopefully.

"Yes, there's some being sent up from the kitchens."

"Great. Let me know the second it gets here," said Myfanwy, and
then she hung up and closed her eyes once more. A moment later,
the phone rang again.

"Excellent, is the coffee here?"

"No, I'm sorry, Rook Thomas, but you actually did have a call
waiting for you."

"On a Saturday?" said Myfanwy plaintively. "Oh God. *Fine.* Who is it?"

"Someone named, let me see, I had to write it down phonetically. It was a . . . Gerd de Leeuwen."

"Are you serious?" asked Myfanwy.

"You do not put me on hold!" screamed a voice in her ear. Myfanwy flinched, inadvertently hurling the phone away from her, into the ornamental roses in the corner of the room. Clutching at her ear with one hand, she fumbled the phone onto speaker setting.

"Hello?" she said.

"I am Graaf Gerd de Leeuwen!" shrieked the unmistakable voice of the skinless Belgian she'd met the previous evening.

"How did you get this number? *I* don't even know what this number is," said Myfanwy, too tired and cranky to be polite. This man's organization was the cause of her recent bout of examinations. In addition, her fear of him was much diminished by the fact that she didn't have to look at him.

"Do not question me! I possess the knowledge of the ages!" he gargled.

"Big deal," said Myfanwy with a snort. "You know, fifteen minutes before I met you I had drinks with a vampire. The man has been dead since the eighteenth century, and he still manages to be quite well mannered." She paused, waiting to see if her mention of Alrich would elicit an incriminating reaction from the Grafter—perhaps some evidence that the Bishop was the traitor.

"Where is Ernst von Suchtlen?" demanded the voice, apparently willing to ignore her remarks.

"Are you on crack?" asked Myfanwy. "You said three days! And you said that ten hours ago."

"Where is he, that you need three days to produce him?" came the triumphant voice down the phone.

"Oh God." Myfanwy sighed as the Belgian launched into a long-winded diatribe. "Look, hold on a moment, I have another call coming through." She pressed the button, cutting off a scream of impotent rage. "Hello?"

"Rook Thomas, I have your coffee."

"Excellent, Ingrid. Bring it in." Myfanwy switched back to the Grafter's line and rocked slightly from the blast of seventeenth-century Belgian abuse. The bodyguards opened the doors, and Ingrid came in with a large mug of coffee and a new mobile phone and froze when she heard the torrent of shouting. Even though he was speaking in an unintelligible language, the caller was clearly neither polite nor businesslike. Ingrid cautiously approached the desk.

"Does this have anything to do with that Graaf Ernst von Suchtlen you were asking about?" whispered Ingrid, wide-eyed at the language spewing out of the speakerphone.

"No, this is his partner, who has no skin," said Myfanwy, pushing the mute button and looking longingly at the coffee. "They're the leaders of the Grafters. This guy waylaid me last night and demanded to know where his partner was."

"You're talking with the Grafters?" exclaimed Ingrid. "Why don't you have the call traced?"

"We can do that?" asked Myfanwy in surprise.

"As long as you keep them on the line," said Ingrid.

"...and I shall unleash the terror now!" screamed de Leeuwen, breaking into English and then hanging up.

Well, what do you want from me?" snapped Myfanwy. "I'm a genius in administration, not telecommunications."

"So now what are we going to do?" asked Ingrid.

"I don't know, wait for fungus to carpet the Cotswolds?" said Myfanwy with irritation. Then the phone rang and Ingrid went to answer it but hesitated over the empty cradle.

"Where is the phone?" she asked.

"I threw it into the roses," said Myfanwy, hitting the speakerphone button. "Hello?" she said wearily.

"This is Graaf Gerd de Leeuwen," said the voice of the skinless Belgian.

"Oh, hi," said Myfanwy, gesturing frantically to Ingrid and knocking the coffee over. In her haste, Ingrid slammed her shin into a footstool before limping out of the office to her own phone. The precious caffeinated nectar spread over Myfanwy's desk, saturating various documents of national importance and engulfing her new mobile phone. She gave a little anguished moan and tried scraping some of the coffee back into her mug using her laminated security pass.

"I have been advised that I may have acted rashly," said de Leeuwen. "With that in mind, the original offer of three days is reinstated."

"Three days from now?" asked Myfanwy, pausing in her coffee-reclamation efforts. *You bloody bipolar Belgian bastard.* "Or three days from the time of the original offer?" She looked through the doors to Ingrid, who was talking rapidly on the phone and making frantic gesticulations to keep him on the line. Myfanwy made a face indicating she had no control over the conversation, and then tried in vain to catch up with the thread of the Belgian's diatribe, which unfortunately had just ended with the phrase "do you understand?"

"Well, frankly, sir," she fumbled. "Today is Saturday, and although we have many people working over the weekend, we may not have enough." *Yes, that makes complete sense,* she thought, and tried to interpret Ingrid's expression.

"What have you done, that you need more people to get him?" came the suspicious question. Myfanwy's head had begun pounding again, and since the tender ministrations of Dr. Wills and Dr. Engel had turned out not to be so tender, her own tender bits were aching. She took a sip of reclaimed coffee and winced. *Diplomacy isn't working. Good manners aren't working. Hell, even sanity isn't working,* she thought. *I'm just going to have to talk plainly with this thing.* She took a deep breath.

"Think back to last night. I know it may be lost somewhere in the centuries of accumulated material in the filing cabinet of your brain, but it *was* just last night. You were floating around in a fish tank of sewage, and I was there looking like I was going to throw up. You were shrieking unintelligibly, and you might remember that I said that we…*Did. Not. Have. Him.* Now, we will do our best to help you, but if you've misplaced one of your men, then you have only one person to blame, and it's not me." Myfanwy looked up and saw that Ingrid and the bodyguards were staring at her incredulously. *Maybe that was a little too plain,* she thought guiltily. "Plus, as you may know, I am the most junior member of the Court. There are other people you may wish to speak to regarding your endeavor."

"What endeavor?" came the suspicious question.

"The whole, I don't know, 'We exist, and we're sneaking agents into England and America' thing."

"Not only will I not speak to other members of your Court about this, but you will not do so either," said de Leeuwen flatly.

"I beg your pardon?" said Myfanwy.

"You have been contacted because Ernst sent something to you, the general of our greatest enemy. If I did not think you knew where he was, you would be flayed, your sister would be dead, and I would be watching troops vat-grown in Mechelen rape your Prime Minister in Trafalgar Square on a pyramid of Cockney skulls." Myfanwy felt ice water bleed into her veins.

"What?" she whispered.

"That is right," the Belgian confirmed in a tone of deep satisfaction. "So, I suggest you drop this little pretense that you do not have him because now you understand exactly how serious this is."

"You said they would not be touched or investigated," she said in horror.

"Do not be naive" came the reply.

"You motherfucker. Where do you get off threatening my family?" Myfanwy shouted into the phone. "You make one single move toward Bronwyn and I will have your country carpet bombed. I will track you down and seize control of your body, and you will tear your own guts out of your *arse*. You fucking corpse!"

"You do not talk to me like that!" the Belgian shrieked. There was the sound of splashing in the background, and she realized that he was still in his tank.

"I'll have one of my large bodyguards shit in that tank of yours, and you'll rub it into your flesh like it came from the Body Shop," Myfanwy continued. "All those little modifications of yours? Well, you'll pick those out with your fingernails, you reject carcass from a butcher-shop window." Over the speakerphone came the sound of someone having a fit of apoplexy in a swimming pool.

"Now, Mr. Graaf Gerd de Leeuwen, call me in three days and we shall see what the situation is. If my sister feels even the slightest bit of discomfort before then, you'll be receiving your partner in the form of a set of matched luggage. Good-bye," Myfanwy said, then she disconnected the phone with shaking hands. She turned to Ingrid, who had entered the room again. "Hi."

"So, in addition to telecommunications, you're also not much of an expert on diplomacy, hm?" said Ingrid weakly.

"I need a drink," said Myfanwy.

"I think we both do," said Ingrid, swinging open a portrait that concealed a well-stocked bar. She poured each of them a shot of something amber while Myfanwy shook the coffee off her new mobile phone.

"That guy's not stable," said Myfanwy. "It was bad enough when we thought the Grafters were planning an invasion, but I assumed that at least they were sane."

"Yes," said Ingrid. "Rook Thomas, you have a sister?"

"Yeah," said Myfanwy defensively.

"How can you have a sister?" She lowered her voice. "You've been *you* for only two weeks."

"This body has a sister," said Myfanwy. "It is just as much my body as the person's you worked for before, so, yes, I have a sister. She tracked me down."

"How?"

"Tax records."

"I see, and how do the Grafters know about her?" asked Ingrid.

"I was out with her last night," said Myfanwy guiltily.

"You went out last night?"

"We went clubbing" came the reply.

"Clubbing?" Ingrid exclaimed.

"Yeah." Myfanwy felt herself blushing. "That's how my phone got all slimy. What did you think happened?" With a visible effort, Ingrid calmed herself.

"Rook Thomas, I am not your mother, nor am I a member of the Court, and I know that you are a clever woman, so of course you do not need me to point out how abominably stupid that was. You don't need me to point out that you put your life, your sister's life, and the well-being of the nation in danger. And now we've got lunatic Grafters on the line."

"I know," said Myfanwy in a small voice.

"What is your sister's name?"

"Bronwyn."

"And her birthday?"

"Why is that important?" asked Myfanwy, confused.

"I'll put it down in the book so that you don't forget to get her something," said Ingrid matter-of-factly.

"That's a lovely thought, but shouldn't we be worrying slightly more about the Grafter's insane threats and slightly less about updating my birthday book?" asked Myfanwy, wondering if perhaps her secretary had poured herself too much therapeutic alcohol.

"The comms department said that they'd let us know when they had a successful trace," said Ingrid. "Do you have a plan?"

"Well, since I don't know anything about this Ernst von Suchtlen that I'm supposed to have in custody, I figure we'll trace the call, track down the man with no skin, unleash the might of the Checquy upon him, and you and I can kick him once they've got him down. That should take care of everything. Except for the traitors in the Court, but I'm sure that will all be sorted out once we have the Grafter head honcho," outlined Myfanwy. She took a contemplative sip of her amber fluid.

"Do you know how long it takes for them to trace a call?" asked Myfanwy.

Ingrid shrugged helplessly.

"Okay, well, I guess I should get back to the business of running domestic operations," she said. "Is there anything new from the Court?"

"You need to get your nominations in by the end of Friday," said Ingrid after checking her tome of an organizer.

"Nominations?" repeated Myfanwy blankly.

"Replacements for Rook Gestalt and Chevalier Gubbins," said Ingrid.

"Right, of course. Um, so what's the process for that whole thing?" asked Myfanwy.

"Actually, I'm not too familiar with the procedure," said Ingrid. "I gather that it's one of the things only the members of the Court are supposed to know, although I'm fairly sure it involves the Prime Minister, the Minister of Defense, and the ruling monarch." Myfanwy gaped at her, and Ingrid looked a trifle embarrassed. "The secretaries talk," she said. "But I *do* know that you have to come up with a list of five possible people from within the Checquy, for both the Rook position and the Chevalier position."

"Gosh," said Myfanwy anxiously. "Ten people. Well, I'll have to give that some thought. How about Colonel Hall? I like him, and he seems very knowledgeable. I looked over his file at one point, and he's exceptionally qualified. Do you know he oversaw army troops in Northern Ireland? And various peacekeeping missions overseas?"

"He's very nice," agreed Ingrid. "His secretary adores him and his team worships him, but I'm afraid he can't be a member of the Court."

"Why not?" asked Myfanwy as her secretary flushed.

"Well, because he isn't a Pawn," said Ingrid.

"No powers, huh?"

"No powers," agreed Ingrid. "It's a law of the Checquy that only those who are powered can rise to command."

"I'm not comfortable with the fact that you have to have bizarre powers to be a member of the Court," said Myfanwy. "I mean, I never use mine. Or at least, hardly ever, and almost never for Courtly duties."

"Yes, but in theory, you could be called out to supervise operations. Frankly, you're lucky that you haven't been called upon more often since Gestalt was exposed last week. Speaking of Gestalt, are you allowed to tell me what the situation is?"

"Well, apparently, there's not going to be a trial or anything. Gestalt has never argued its innocence, and trying to kill everyone at that party was proof enough of its guilt. But I spoke to Sir Henry and Lady Linda, and they agreed that it was inappropriate for me to supervise the interrogation, since we were the same rank. So we've turned that responsibility over to the Bishops. I gave them my ideas for ensuring Gestalt's cooperation, and now I just have to wait and see if they come up with anything good." Alrich had been absently licking his lips when he'd accepted the responsibility. She shuddered slightly at the memory and had another drink of amber liquor.

"Waiting for the phone trace, waiting for the torturers," mused Myfanwy, scratching at a place where blood had been taken with an alarming-looking triple-pronged needle wielded by a midget on a stepladder. "I really hate waiting. Is there anything I can do in the meantime? Anyone for me to talk to?" she asked plaintively. "No section heads or project leaders?"

"It's the weekend, Rook Thomas," Ingrid reminded her gently.

"Of course," said Myfanwy testily. "And people shouldn't be at work on the weekend, because that would be ridiculous."

"Well, the twenty-four-hour office is functioning," clarified Ingrid, "and the Grafter situation means that the watch office is open. And of course, the medical staff is here conducting tests. A strike team and two pilots are on call. The security guards are here, and the cleaning staff, and—"

"Fine," said Myfanwy. "I will just squint at all these documents with my laser-scanned eyes and sign everything with my well-licked fingers."

"Now, Rook Thomas," said Ingrid reprovingly, "you know they

apologized. Apparently, your touch numbed their tongues and they had to try all your digits."

They looked up when a young man clutching a piece of paper ran into Ingrid's office. He caught sight of Myfanwy and Ingrid through the door, colored, and then rushed toward them. One of the massive guards stationed at the door thrust out an arm, and Ingrid and Myfanwy were treated to a glimpse of the soles of the young man's shoes as his body rotated in the air around the axis of the guard's forearm.

"Ooh!" Myfanwy and Ingrid flinched at the same time. The other massive guard stepped into the room, nodded to the two women, and placed his foot delicately on the young man's throat. The supine man was gasping and desperately waving the piece of paper around.

"Don't kill him!" exclaimed Ingrid. "Rook Thomas, this is Pawn Summerhill from the communications section." Myfanwy nodded to the guard, who reluctantly lifted his boot, letting Summerhill sit up.

"Rook Thomas, Mrs. Woodhouse..."

"What is it, Alan?" asked Ingrid. "Have you traced the call?"

"Not yet," he said. "We're still working on it, but this fax came through. It's addressed to Rook Thomas." Myfanwy took the paper from Summerhill's hand, and he put his head between his knees. The fax paper was covered in ornate copperplate, and she had to squint at it to see past the curlicues and flourishes to the message.

Rook Thomas of the Checquy,

I have unleashed a small horror in Reading, simply to demonstrate our capabilities. Unless you hurry, there may not be much left of John Perry's home. I look forward to seeing Graaf Ernst von Suchtlen on Tuesday.

Regards,

Graaf Gerd de Leeuwen

Myfanwy read the words in disbelief, and then they all jumped as the lights flickered overhead and angry chimes sounded. The phone started ringing frantically on Ingrid's desk, accompanied by a red light flashing.

"What the hell is that?" asked Myfanwy with a sinking feeling.

"Incident," said Ingrid grimly, heading to the phone. Myfanwy, the two hulking guards, and the wheezing kid from the communications department watched as Ingrid answered the call. "Right. Right. All right. Yes, she'll be there. How long? Fine. Thanks, Jennifer." She hung up. "Well, Rook Thomas, I'm afraid there's been an outbreak in—"

"Reading," said Myfanwy tiredly.

"Yes," said Ingrid, raising her brows in surprise.

"The Grafters," hissed Myfanwy, and realized that the guards and the kid were staring at her in horror. "None of you heard that, and I mean it," she said in as deadly a tone as she could muster up in her pajamas. *That skinless piece of shit said that if anyone knew he and I had been speaking, he'd kill Bronwyn. Obviously, I can't expect him not to kill her anyway, but I don't want to take any more risks than I have to.* "In fact, you two are my bodyguards for the foreseeable future. No replacements. And you," she said to the quaking communications kid.

"Pawn Alan Summerhill," said Ingrid discreetly.

"Pawn Alan Summerhill, how vital are you to the tracking of this telephone call?" asked Myfanwy.

"Well, it's my fourth day," he ventured.

"Are you some sort of indispensable wunderkind whose presence would make a profound difference to the call tracing?"

"No . . ."

"Fine. Then you'll be accompanying us to Reading," said Myfanwy. "You will speak no word of what you have heard in this room to anyone, and you will not leave my sight without permission. Is that understood?"

"Yes, Rook Thomas," he said, trembling.

"Good. Ingrid, is the incident contained?" asked Myfanwy. "Is it discreet?"

"It's a police station" came the answer.

"Fuuuuck," said one of the security guards, and everyone looked at him. "I used to be a cop," he said defensively.

Ingrid went on. "The police station is in the middle of the town and they have had the good sense to seal off the building. The portable operation centers should be ready by the time we get there."

"Any other details?" asked Myfanwy.

"The Barghests are mobilizing, and we'll rendezvous with them at the site," said Ingrid. "Gentlemen," she said to the bodyguards, "you'll be acting as on-site security for the Rook." She went to her desk and came back holding her coat and a laptop in a case.

"What are you doing?" asked Myfanwy.

"I'm coming with you," said Ingrid. "The helicopter will be here in seven minutes."

"Okay, but—"

"Rook Thomas, you're still in your pajamas. You may want to go upstairs and change. And don't forget to bring a jacket."

"Fine," said Myfanwy with a sigh, swinging open another portrait and going up to the apartment. Behind her, one of the large bodyguards had trouble squeezing up the stairway and had to be pushed by the other one.

It was very different being in a helicopter with Ingrid, a terrified neophyte Pawn, and two large bodyguards, as opposed to just Shantay. People's knees kept bumping and Li'l Pawn Alan (as she'd taken to calling him in her head) was crushed between the large bodyguards, both of whom looked as if they were about to be violently ill. Ingrid was reading rapidly off her laptop. Myfanwy was wearing a pair of large sunglasses and listening to the appalling reports that were coming in.

"The Reading police have set up cordons at a fair distance," said Ingrid.

"And beyond the cordons?" asked Myfanwy.

"Let me see," said Ingrid, scanning through reams of text. "Okay, yes. Well, there are a few people hanging around, but not many. They can easily be dispersed, either with official announcements or, if necessary, tear gas."

"Well, that's something. What's the cover story?" asked Myfanwy.

"Hostages, but no one's used the T-word."

"No one is to use the T-word at all!" exclaimed Myfanwy. "Jesus Christ, do you have any idea how complicated that would make everything? Plus, the heads and the Bishops would skin me alive. I do not want the T-word to pass anyone's lips."

"Bishop Grantchester did alert everyone in the organization that the T-word was never to be used," Ingrid reminded her mildly.

"Yes, because he had a very long conference with the Prime Minister and the Minister of Defense, and then the Rooks had to listen to a lecture for four hours," said Myfanwy. *Which thankfully I did not have to attend. Thomas was so pissed off that she wrote thirteen pages of single-spaced diatribe.* "In any case, Ingrid, make sure the Rookery Liars are coming up with a rational excuse for what's going on."

"A rational excuse, like crazy people?"

"A rational excuse," said Myfanwy firmly. "Now, does anyone know who this John Perry person is?" She would normally have referred to her purple binder, but in her haste, she had forgotten it. She looked hopefully around at the various people crammed into the helicopter, but none of them seemed to know. Ingrid looked up from her laptop and confirmed that no one of that name was a member of the Checquy. Googling the name had led to a variety of people, none of whom were from Reading or seemed to have anything to do with the situation at all.

"Okay," said Myfanwy. "Well, that's a mystery for later. Now, do we know if anyone has been harmed?" *Please, God, let them just have been taken hostage. It is going to be bad if that skinless piece of shit has started harming civilians. I must be cold, calm, and collected.*

"There are seven police officers, three clerical staff, and a couple of dozen civilians caught in there," said Ingrid grimly.

"Damn!" said Myfanwy. She slammed the armrest in frustration.

"This was so completely unnecessary. I told de Leeuwen that I would find his damned partner!"

"But you didn't mean it," said Ingrid gently. "You were tracing his call, planning to hunt him down before your time was up."

"Yes, but he didn't know that!" snapped Myfanwy. "So why would he feel compelled to do this?"

"You called him a reject from a butcher shop and threatened to make him torture himself in a tub full of feces," said Ingrid.

"You think he did this because of something I said?" said Myfanwy.

"Well, he didn't strike me as the most stable of individuals," replied Ingrid. "He might have done this because of the way you said hello, or because it's Saturday, or because one of his aides didn't bow deep enough, or who knows what."

"It's still Saturday?" said Myfanwy exhaustedly. "You know, I don't generally do this. Rook Gestalt was the one who took care of situations in the field."

"Please, Rook Thomas," squeaked Alan, the little Pawn. "Back at the Estate we all heard about how you handled the incident at Bath." The large bodyguards nodded, and even Ingrid smiled at her confidently.

Oh, brilliant, Myfanwy thought dismally as the helicopter began its descent. "Ow!" she exclaimed as they landed roughly, jarring everything that had been investigated by the Rookery doctors. The two large bodyguards, looking profoundly relieved to be on the ground, got up and surveyed the landing pad. There was a limousine waiting for them, flanked by two formidable off-road vehicles. Clustered around the vehicles were several large people, all of whom were antsy and heavily armed, which was never a good combination.

"Rook Thomas, we'll just make sure these people are secure," said one of the large bodyguards. As they left, Alan slowly unfolded. Myfanwy watched through the window as the bodyguards hulked over to the collected Checquy staff, weaving slightly as they recovered from airsickness. Ingrid's phone rang and she answered it, then nodded as she listened.

373

"We're cleared to go, Rook Thomas," she said, getting up. "Alan, get those cases, please."

"Where are we?" asked Myfanwy. The helicopter appeared to have landed in a recently vacated cow field. "We couldn't find an airport? Or a helipad? Or a place that wasn't mined with—damn it! Now I have cow shit on my shoes."

"At least you're not wearing heels," retorted Ingrid as she sank into the soil. Behind them, Alan struggled with the cases.

"Rook Thomas, this is Pawn Cyrus West. He's site manager for this incident," said one of the large bodyguards.

"Good to see you, Cyrus," said Myfanwy, trying not to notice how hesitantly he took her hand. She remembered Ingrid saying that word had gotten around about her making that guy stab himself.

"Ladies. Gentlemen." She acknowledged the Checquy team members with a nod and eye contact. "It's good to see you all. Cyrus, I'm certain you're eager to get back to the site." She stepped into the car and was joined by Cyrus and her team. The large bodyguard inspected an extremely large gun that he'd taken from one of Ingrid's cases.

"That thing has the safety catch on, right?" asked Myfanwy anxiously.

"Uh...absolutely, Rook Thomas," said the large bodyguard uncertainly, peering at the side of the gun.

"He's not really a gun person," whispered Ingrid to Myfanwy. "But he does have the ability to make people's skin burst off their torso."

"Oh...good," said Myfanwy. "Anyway, Cyrus, could you fill me in on the situation in the police station?" He nodded and began to speak in an incredibly soporific droning voice. Myfanwy, already hungover, low on sleep, having been probed, drained, injected, scanned, and scraped, found her eyelids drooping. But she managed to extract several key facts from the lecture. According to various reports:

(a) A nondescript man walked into the station and, with his bare hands, broke the neck of the person closest to him before turning and locking the door he had come through. A large constable had gone after him with a collapsible baton and had his head actually punched off his torso for his trouble. At that point, the entire station had mobilized, weapons were fetched, and in a few moments the man was looking down the barrels of a number of guns and some Tasers. He surveyed the room with a raised eyebrow and gave a snort of amusement. Then,

(b) after ignoring instructions to drop his weapon, he shrugged off the many, many bullets that thudded into his body. Regarding the blank stares of the cops with a smirk, the man raised his arms, and, with a grunt of effort (according to the emergency call of the frantic police chief),

(c) "he made these sort of fleshy tentacle things just *explode* out of his arms, reach out, and impale the people around the room. There was blood splashing everywhere, and then he reeled the people in, and his skin started eating out over them, pulling them into his body. And now he's growing all lumpy because they're inside of him, and he's getting huge and—oh my God, no! Send help! Please!"

(d) The Checquy mobilized immediately and arrived to find the streets around the station nearly deserted, since the good people of Reading were not accustomed to hearing barrages of gunfire emanating from the police station on a Saturday afternoon. The sounds of the firearms, combined with unearthly screams and blood spattering on the windows, had served to drive a large portion of the populace away. The Reading Checquy's Situation Response Team arrived almost immediately, isolated the area, gently ushered the remaining onlookers away, and deterred the media.

"With your approval, Rook Thomas, I will be retaining command of the operation. The Barghests were automatically called in and you were notified because we're at some color crisis level," finished Cyrus.

"Chartreuse," said Pawn Alan helpfully. Everybody looked at him, and he shrank a little under their regard.

"I'm sorry, who is this?" asked Pawn Cyrus.

"This is Li'l Paw...I'm sorry, this is Pawn Alan...something," fumbled Myfanwy.

"Summerhill," ventured Pawn Alan.

"Pawn Alan here heard something that I am going to need to tell you," said Myfanwy to Cyrus, "and which no one in this car is going to tell anyone else. Now, you know how everyone in the organization is scheduled for these medical examinations?"

"Yes, I heard that they're not pleasant," said Pawn Cyrus. "Should I be worried?"

"Oh, no, they're great," said Myfanwy. "But the reason we're having them is the same reason we have people getting shot and, er, impaled in Reading."

"I'm not certain I understand," said Pawn Cyrus.

"It's the Grafters," said Myfanwy, and she watched as the blood drained out of his face. Her focus was disrupted, however, when the large bodyguard dropped his gun and everyone in the car flinched.

"Now, Cyrus," Myfanwy said, after the large guard had shamefacedly picked up his gun, "the information I have given you cannot be shared with anyone. I can only hope it will help you with the approach you take to this operation, which you will, of course, retain command of. The Barghests will be yours to unleash. I am here just to observe." She tried not to think of the last time she'd appeared just to observe. From the expression on his face, Cyrus was trying not to think of it either.

"Is this the beginning of another invasion?" he asked anxiously.

"No," said Myfanwy. "At least, I don't think so. I gather that this is more of a warning. But of course, there's always the possibility the Grafters might take advantage of a moment of weakness, so we need to subdue this quickly." Cyrus was looking ill, and Li'l Pawn Alan looked like he was going to burst into tears. Myfanwy felt a headache coming on in the very front of her head.

"So," she said, "Cyrus, do you happen to know anything about a John Perry?"

"Of course," said Cyrus.

"A John Perry from Reading?" she said suspiciously.

"Of course. John Perry from Reading," said Cyrus. "Rook John Perry."

"*Rook* John Perry?" repeated Myfanwy.

"Rook John Perry, the most renowned Checquy operative ever to come from Reading," said Cyrus. "Rook John Perry, one of the most renowned Checquy operatives ever."

"Oh," said Myfanwy, shooting dirty looks at everyone else in the car who did not have amnesia and so had no reasonable excuse for not being able to identify Perry. "Refresh my memory," she directed.

"He was key in stopping the invasion of the Isle of Wight by the Grafters," said Cyrus.

God, this skinned Belgian really holds a grudge, thought Myfanwy as she and everyone else who wasn't from Reading sank into a guilty silence, and Cyrus managed to look simultaneously insulted by their ignorance and concerned about the prospect of the Grafters in his town. He placed a call on his mobile phone and began speaking in a tone that was both hushed and frantic.

"Rook Thomas, are you all right?" asked Ingrid suddenly. Myfanwy looked up in surprise and realized that she was pressing her knuckles against her temples.

"I'm getting a headache right in front of us."

"Right in front of us?" repeated Cyrus.

"It's highly specific," Myfanwy said shortly. "Do we have any aspirin in this car?" Everyone looked around vaguely.

"We have Johnnie Walker Blue Label," said Ingrid, who was examining the minibar.

"*Really?*" asked the large bodyguard with unseemly enthusiasm.

"I am not going to drink whisky on an empty stomach on the way to a manifestation," said Myfanwy. "Nor are any of you," she added pointedly as the large bodyguard cast a wistful look at the bar. "Now, Ingrid, you have nothing in your purse?"

"I'm sorry, Rook Thomas," said Ingrid. "Perhaps there is some sort of first aid kit. Would you like us to check with the driver?"

"No...yes...I don't know," said Myfanwy, wincing in pain. "This is not normal. It feels like, like..."

"Like what?" asked Li'l Pawn Alan, excitedly.

"Like it's coming from outside my head," said Myfanwy.

"What?" asked Alan. "Where?"

"There!" spat Myfanwy, pointing ahead of them to a large building surrounded by Checquy troops and vehicles. "Right there!"

34

Dear You,

The heart wasn't much of a lead. They ran it through every scanning device known to man and got that anorexic girl who claims to be psychometric to try a reading, but even she got nothing. So the heart is now down in one of the locked fridges, and I am without a clue as to why it was sent to me. If I were in a better mood and had a shit sense of humor, I'd suggest that it was a valentine, but I shall restrain myself and instead talk about our latest acquisition — and how I got stuck with a hasty cover-up operation.

There has been a rumor going around the community for years that there was some sort of animal out there, in private possession, that could tell the future. Now, the Checquy sees its share of precogs, psychics, and ball-gazers (both crystal and otherwise), and they are, without fail, absolute crap. Usually we get an irritating prophecy that will, inevitably, rhyme but not scan and that is so metaphor-laden as to render it completely incomprehensible. Or else it's some twit who wants his epilepsy to have a greater meaning. So, while we feel somewhat obliged to keep looking for psychics, we don't pay too much heed to what they say.

You can see why we would be quite keen to get our hands on any creature that could accurately predict the future — an animal would be much less likely to be faking it for attention. A team of agents had been tasked with finding and acquiring it through fair means or foul. They followed hundreds of leads, scoured the kingdom, and managed to spend an astonishing amount of money. (I know, because guess who did the accounting and administrating of this little fiasco.) Agents retired and were replaced. Several times they thought they had found the beast — although the rumor had never been clear on what species it actually was.

As a result, over the course of the endeavor, I received several swine, a goat, a rabbit, a Jack Russell terrier, and, my personal favorite, a cardboard box containing what the finder proudly declared were "the prophetic snails of Beccles." Each of these had been unveiled, with great fanfare, to the members of the Court. Needless to say, none of these specimens were able to see the future. Or if they could, they were unwilling to communicate their findings to us. All that came of the endeavor was professional embarrassment. Oh, and I got to keep the rabbit.

This ridiculous exercise in futility was one of the things I inherited upon becoming Rook, and I would gladly have dropped it, but it is one of Wattleman's pet obsessions, and so I was obliged to keep it up.

But this morning it was confirmed. The team had finally acquired the animal, and exhaustive tests by our top scientists had been conducted. And so I found myself laboriously penning formal invitations to the members of the Court to come dine at the Rookery tonight before observing the unbelievably magical amazingness of the United Kingdom's only oracular duck.

Of course, I couched it all in slightly more impressive terms.

I sent the invitations out via the Rook's Messenger and tried to get on with my work. Generally, it consumes all my time, but today I couldn't focus. Hours passed with me staring blankly at my computer, unable to concentrate. Eventually, I realized that I was having doubts about the duck.

If you think about it, quite aside from the unlikelihood of a duck being able to tell the future, the odds that our motley crew had finally found the one and only psychic animal in the kingdom were not good. And frankly, I did not relish the prospect of whipping off the cover and presenting the Court with a non-oracular duck. After so many awkward mistakes, the search team had assured us that this time they'd definitely found the right animal, but it didn't do much to settle my nerves. So there was really nothing for it; I was going to have to go down there and check out the duck for myself.

I wanted to see the duck so I could test not only whether it could communicate its predictions clearly, but also whether it could predict accurately. A duck intelligent enough to communicate with people might (I thought) be intelligent enough to lie about telling the future. But I was in a unique position to test its skills because I already knew what my future held. So, down I traipsed to the labs, walking through the corridors, keeping my eyes firmly on the ground. As always, I tried not to make eye contact with the staff. I'm always so embarrassed by those little bows and curtsies I get, and besides, who knows what they're thinking? Everyone here knows who I am, and I realize they hold no great respect for me.

Still, they do respect my position, and so when I asked for some time alone with the subject, it was hurriedly arranged. The staff paused in their tests and their grooming of the feathered fortune-teller and ushered me into a soundproof white room, where I sat with a duck and a laptop computer. Well, the duck had the computer, with an oversize keyboard that the boffins had rigged up for it (apparently, there had been problems with beak-to-key-size ratio). Dr. Crisp had just explained the details of how the duck worked.

"We're talking old-school fairy tales, Rook Thomas," he had said genially. "Only three questions per person. Ever. And it has to be done in one sitting. Yes or no answers."

It's actually kind of alarming to see a duck in person. They're taller than you would think, and more . . . immediate. We stared at each other, the duck and I, and I hate to admit it, but I blinked first.

"Yes, well. I am Rook Thomas," I said to the duck. "But perhaps you already knew that?" The duck gave no response other than nuzzling at its feathers with its beak.

"So, do you have a name?" I asked, trying to strike up some sort of rapport. The duck looked over at me and promptly shat on the table. Clearly, this was not going to be a conversational meeting. I turned my attention away from small talk and got down to asking about the future.

"Duck, will I be attacked by operatives of the Checquy?" I asked. Its neck straightened abruptly, and it pecked the Y button on the keyboard. Its answer displayed on the monitor.

Since my fate had already been predicted by, among others, a schoolboy, a homeless man, and a thirty-seven-hundred-year-old oracle, this wasn't the greatest revelation in the world, but I was impressed with the duck's rapid response. I tried to decide what to ask next. It was a unique opportunity to gain an advantage.

"Duck, um, will I be attacked in my house?"

N.

I heaved a great sigh of relief. I'd been imagining that I would be jerked

*out of my sleep or have to watch as my rabbit was killed in front of me,
and I could dismiss those fears now. But I could still ask one question.
What did I need to know? I felt horribly weary, aware as always of
everything that needed to be done before the end came. Did I have
time?*

"Duck, will I . . . will I lose my memory within a month?"

Y.

*I put my hands over my face for a good minute, and the duck just sat
there, each of us thinking our own thoughts. I appreciated that it ignored me.
It left me free to frantically recalculate my schedule. I'd never known when it
was going to happen—when I was going to "lose everything," as Lisa had
put it—but I'd always assumed that there would be time to prepare. And
now, now I know that I have weeks at most.*

*Lost in thought, I absently thanked the duck and left the room. The
other members of the Court would be arriving soon. And besides, the smell
of duck shit was not terribly pleasant.*

*W*hat the hell were you doing in there, Myfanwy?" Teddy Gestalt
demanded. Dr. Crisp's team of scientists looked up in surprise. "The rest of
the Court will be here in a couple of hours, and I come back from Stirling to
find you meddling with this new acquisition instead of making the necessary
preparations for a formal reception and presentation."

"All of that has been attended to, Rook Gestalt," I said mildly. "I just
wanted to make sure that the duck was working properly. You may not
recall, but we've actually had several false starts in the pursuit of this
particular item, and—"

"Are you implying that I am ignorant of what goes on here?" exclaimed
Gestalt in a poisonous tone. "That I have not been spending enough time
here in the Rookery? Because if you would like to start going out to the
various field operations, Myfanwy, then you are more than welcome." He
stared triumphantly at me, secure in the knowledge that I would never want
to do such a thing. For one brief, shining moment I wished I could casually
accept. Just to shut him up.

Then I remembered you, and the preparations that still needed to be *made. I'd never finish everything in time if I started traveling around the country.*

"No, Rook Gestalt, that won't be necessary," I said in a small voice.

"Very well, then. You will probably want to wash your face and get changed," he said. "This is going to be a very important evening."

"I know that it's important, Gestalt. I do. That's why I have asked the subject three questions in order to confirm that it can indeed provide accurate predictions of the future. I'm sure you also want to be confident that we don't deliver a bogus oracle to the Lord and Lady." Gestalt licked his lips nervously. Wattleman's fascination with the project was infamous, and the potential for humiliation was very real.

"What about the tests that Crisp and the others performed?"

"I preferred to verify for myself," I said carefully. "The prospect of Sir Henry Wattleman, VC-Enshrouded Co-head of the Checquy, posing vital questions to an ordinary waterfowl and receiving nothing but some crap on the table does not appeal to me. I don't think it would do either of our careers much good."

Gestalt grimaced and I continued, keeping my tone level and uninterested.

"I have asked three questions about this evening. The duck's answers should be confirmed by the time we are supposed to reveal it to the Court. If it has been proven wrong, then we shall simply say so, and exchange humiliation for embarrassment."

"Hmm," said Gestalt thoughtfully. "Perhaps that is not a bad idea. In fact, maybe I should also—" Whatever Gestalt was going to say was cut off when a meek-looking aide appeared and whispered that the members of the Court were going to be arriving early. "Never mind," he said, and I was relieved that he hadn't thought to ask what questions I had posed to the duck. "How long do we have?"

"The first car is on its way now," said the aide cautiously, wary of Gestalt's infamous temper.

"Now?" we repeated in aghast unison. The aide looked surprised and decided to include me in the conversation.

"Yes, and Sir Henry just called to let us know that he is bringing a special visitor."

"A special visitor?" we again said in unison.

"Yes, an important visitor who is to be seated to Sir Henry's right at the dinner table," said the aide, wilting under our fixed stares. Gestalt and I turned to each other.

"An important visitor?" he said to me. "The duck didn't mention this?"

"What? No!" I said. "I didn't waste a prophetic-duck question on the possibility of unexpected dinner guests. Do you even know how the duck works?"

"No," said Gestalt. "And I don't care. But a special visitor... presumably one who is not in the Checquy—"

"Who is to be seated at the table next to Wattleman," I said. "And—"

"Who has been invited to a secret unveiling," said Gestalt.

"The secret unveiling of a major supernatural find that could influence the future of the nation," I said.

"Prime Minister?" asked Gestalt.

"Or royalty," I suggested.

"Fuck!" we said together, and we bolted, leaving behind us a team of scientists who had been privy to our dialogue and were now rushing back into the soundproof room to groom the duck and get it ready for its big performance. When important personages are brought into an equation, everything gets more complicated. Everything needed to be perfect.

At the very least, Gestalt and I wanted to be there to greet whoever it was with a proper show of respect.

United by desperation, we sprinted through the corridors of the Rookery, Gestalt pulling me by the hand. We knocked several Retainers out of our way, sent stacks of paper flying. Gestalt and I ricocheted off someone made out of concrete, and I lost a shoe.

"No time!" shouted Gestalt. He tugged on my hand and we kept running. "Leave it!" he said. I kicked off the other shoe.

"You," I yelled at a woman ahead of us. "Call Ingrid, and let her know that someone important is coming to dinner and will be sitting next to Sir Henry." She was nodding frantically as we passed her.

"Out of the way!" shrieked Gestalt as we rounded a corner and came upon a group of secretaries. They moved back just in time.

"No siblings?" I gasped out. Maybe one of them could meet the guests.

"They're all in the field," Gestalt said, panting. It was, I admit, slightly encouraging to see that Gestalt was also out of breath. "Hold the lift!" We paused in front of the doors. It was crammed full. "Everybody out," Gestalt wheezed. The staff stampeded out in the face of his authority, or possibly in the face of the fact that I looked about ready to have a heart attack. We tumbled into the lift and Gestalt pressed the override button, allowing us to go directly to our floor. I leaned against the wall as we descended. I looked at the mirrored wall, and my heart sank.

"My hair looks like shit," I said. "I'm in my least impressive suit, have no shoes, and we may have the ruler of the nation coming for dinner—oh God! Will dinner be ready?" I fumbled for my phone and then realized I'd left it in my office. "Do you have a phone?" Gestalt was leaning over, his hands propped on his knees, but he shook his head nonetheless. "Can your other bodies put a call through to the kitchens? Or to Ingrid?"

"I'm doing it now," he said.

"And ask her to bring me a pair of shoes."

"Right, shoes," he agreed from between his knees. "Come here."

"Why?" I said suspiciously. In the headlong sprint I had forgotten that I had, at most, a month. At most. Suddenly, I wondered if I was going to be attacked in a lift.

"I'll fix your hair," he said, pulling a comb out of his inner coat pocket and holding it up.

"Oh," I said. He unbent and stood behind me, carefully rearranging my hair.

"You're good," I said, eyes downcast. He smelled delicious. I remembered for a moment my crush on his brother, and felt my cheeks flush.

"I have a female body," he said briskly. "All right, you look fine." Actually, though I hated to admit it, I looked quite good.

"Thanks. And here, your tie is crooked." I straightened it self-consciously, and smoothed his collar. It was while we were in this pose, with me up on tiptoes, him looking at me, and both of us flushed with running, that the doors opened. Ingrid was there. Anthony was there. Gestalt's executive assistant and his bodyguard—a slim Chinese chick with lots of facial piercings—were there. Everyone was staring. "Stop that," I said. "Ingrid, how long do we have? Ingrid!" She blinked and then snapped back to herself and handed me a new pair of shoes.

"The first car is just pulling in now, Rook Thomas."

"And whose is it?"

"Sir Henry, with his guest," she said apologetically.

"Damn it!" exclaimed Gestalt. We moved rapidly toward the entrance, though not running now. "Do we know who his guest is?" he asked over his shoulder to the retinue.

"No, sir," said his secretary.

"How long has it been since a prime minister came to the Rookery—hell, since they visited any Checquy installation?" Gestalt wondered.

"Thatcher came once, at the beginning of her career," I remembered.

"And royalty?"

"Well, only the ruling monarch and the first in line are aware of our existence," I said. "But the last two monarchs haven't come more than the once required after they've been crowned. I'm certain of that."

"And they give us five minutes to prepare." Gestalt seethed. He calmed himself as we arrived at the reception area, which was actually very nice for all that it was in the garage. There was a carpeted area for people to be disgorged onto from their cars, sliding stained-glass doors that led to the elevators, and Ingrid had assembled some impressively tall honor guards to line the area and greet the arriving guests. Gestalt and I bustled past the guards and hit our marks just as the garage door was opening and Wattleman's car was pulling in. My attention was caught by several people shouting angrily by the car.

"What the hell is that?" demanded Gestalt.

Anthony rumbled some syllables in an indeterminate language.

I nodded sagely. "What?"

"We have protesters outside the building," said Gestalt's bodyguard with a musical chime of her lip piercings.

"When did they start?" I asked as the car slowly drew closer to us.

"Half an hour ago," said Ingrid.

"What ridiculous thing are they protesting?" asked Gestalt, clearly vexed by the inconvenience. "Are they complaining about the bank?"

"No, they're protesting the covert government operations being run out of this office," said the bodyguard.

"What?" Gestalt and I exclaimed in horror.

"I'm arranging a meeting with Security Chief Clovis," said Ingrid calmly. "He's said not to worry."

"It's not going to look good," I murmured as the car drew up in front of us. "Thank God the windows are tinted. Oh, and egg-proof." The door opened and Sir Henry got out. All of us made the proper welcoming gestures while craning to see who the other person in the back of the car was.

"Ah, I see you are all eager to meet our visitor," said Sir Henry jovially. "And of course, it is a great honor for us all that he has deigned to visit us on this historic day. Roo—Miss Myfanwy Thomas, Mr. . . . ." He paused, obviously trying to figure out which first name belonged to which Gestalt sibling. I took pity on him and whispered it. "Ah, yes, Mr. Theodore"—he winked broadly—"Gestalt, may I present Rupert Henderson."

"Huh?" said Gestalt, and I would have snickered except that I was also trying to figure out who this person was. He was dressed in some sort of hessian muumuu, and his hair looked as if it could do with some styling by Gestalt. I was pretty sure he was neither the person who sat on the British throne nor the Prime Minister.

"You may not know him by sight, but I am sure that his reputation has preceded him," said Sir Henry proudly.

"Absolutely," said Ingrid smoothly while Gestalt and I tried to recover our poise.

"Sir Henry, Mr. Hessian—I mean Henderson!" I began.

"What?" barked Mr. Henderson loudly. "Speak up, girl!" I faltered and could feel my eyes filling. I ducked my head and blinked furiously.

"You mustn't shout at our Myfanwy, Master Henderson," said Wattleman genially. "She's got a soft voice"—patting me on the shoulder—"but she's marvelous behind the desk." As Gestalt led us to the lifts, I could hear Wattleman talking in what he thought was an undertone to Mr. Henderson. "Terribly shy girl. We try not to upset her—she goes to pieces."

"Always has," added Gestalt quietly. Walking right behind them, I could feel my cheeks burning, and I sniffed surreptitiously. Ingrid discreetly handed me a handkerchief.

Once we were settled in the reception room, we waited for the rest of the Court to arrive, which took a remarkably short time. Apparently, the other members had received the same vague message Gestalt and I had gotten, because each one appeared looking expectant and quickly tidied, only to find to their confusion that they were meeting a strange man dressed like the prophet of the god of compost.

The others made small talk and I stood there awkwardly silent. When we were finally ushered into the dining room for a hastily cooked dinner, I discreetly asked Ingrid to see what she could find out about Rupert Henderson. She nodded and hurried away while the waiters served beverages. Under the pretense of pushing my chair in, Gestalt quietly asked me if I had received confirmation.

"What?" I asked.

"The duck! Have its predictions come true yet?" he asked frantically.

"Oh, right." I was suddenly filled with a spirit of pettiness. "I've only gotten the answer on one. I won't have all the answers confirmed until the end of the dessert course."

"The dessert course?" Gestalt repeated, aghast.

"Yes, and one of the questions relates to you," I added sweetly. He paled. "But don't let that bother you. After all, if it's true, then you can't help but fulfill the prophecy." He walked unsteadily to his seat.

Dinner tasted delicious, and I made a mental note to thank the chefs for coping so well with the altered schedule. Gestalt sweated profusely throughout the entire meal.

Finally, just as we were finishing our raspberry bread-and-butter pudding with drunken fruit ice cream, Sir Henry rose.

"Ladies and gentlemen, my colleagues and friends. Today is a great day—the culmination of years of effort, research, and tireless fieldwork. I hope that we can all take pride in this accomplishment. It speaks well of our organization that we can summon the strength and dedication to pursue a project for so long, and in the face of so much adversity." I put my hands up to clap then awkwardly put them down when no one else applauded.

"Of course, you all know of Rupert Henderson," he continued as we smiled blankly. "His reputation is enough, I feel, to justify his presence here tonight. Without a doubt, his insights into the future and his knowledge on all matters prophetic warrant his active participation in this great event."

We all nodded thoughtfully, although we'd never heard of him before. Ingrid tiptoed behind my chair and placed a sheet of paper in front of me.

Rook Thomas,

There's very little in the files. He was born in Brighton. He is forty-five. Vague murmurings about psychic ability, but nothing concrete enough to warrant his being drafted into the Estate. Nevertheless, he became popular among certain groups in the government and managed to impress some people high up in intelligence. We had no indications that Sir Henry knew him, although Henderson has been consulted several times by other members of Sir Henry's club.

I thanked her quietly and looked across the table as, with a whisper, Gestalt declined a waiter's offer of coffee. That'll do, *I thought.* I caught his eye and gave a significant nod. He froze, cast a worried glance at the waiter, and then looked back at me. I nodded again. He paled.

Yeah, it kinda sucks when you think your future is written for you, doesn't it? *I thought. I watched with mild amusement while he made a visible effort to turn his attention back to the speeches, in which Henderson was volubly thanking Sir Henry while touting himself as the greatest psychic ever.*

It was clear that Henderson didn't know exactly what kind of organization the Checquy was. He seemed to be laboring under the (not entirely inaccurate) assumption that we were involved in military intelligence and had stumbled onto a relic of unsurpassed mystical value. He told us patronizingly that no matter what we might believe, there was more in the world than what we saw on the street. That mysterious forces were all around us, and our mundane assumptions vastly underestimated the supernatural power that existed in the world.

Incredulous, I looked around. Bishop Alrich was regarding the "psychic expert" with a look of utter contempt and sipping from a glass of red. As I watched, the color of his hair deepened to a darker auburn. Chevalier Eckhart was absentmindedly braiding his cutlery into a plait. Lady Farrier looked as if she wanted to stab Henderson with her dessert fork. With the exception of Sir Henry, who looked as if the Sermon on the Mount had simply been the opening act for this speech, the entire Court looked ready to commit murder.

"Thank you very much, Master Henderson," said Sir Henry, clapping pointedly and jolting the rest of us into profoundly unenthusiastic applause.

"Master Henderson has confirmed, through his native clairvoyance, that the acquisition is indeed the creature we have sought for so long."

"Well, thank God we pay Dr. Crisp several hundred thousand pounds a year," I muttered under my breath. "Apparently, that's just to mind the ducks and give us all checkups." From the opposite end of the table, Alrich caught my eye and gave a slight commiserating smile. It was clear that he'd heard me.

"Master Henderson has informed me that the revelations that will emerge from the creature will be of great significance and will need to be kept highly secret," continued Sir Henry. "So Lady Farrier and I feel that only we, as the heads of the organization, should be present when Master Henderson draws the prophecy forth. We shall attend the process, and then confer as to what answers it is safe to share. Rest assured, your discretion is unquestioned, but you also understand that some secrets must be kept as secret as possible." With a face like a thundercloud, Bishop Grantchester led the applause this time, little spurts of inky smoke popping out from his hands.

"Well said," he managed through gritted teeth. Wattleman looked on with his eyes shining as Henderson continued to expound on his powers. Apparently, only he could draw out every nuance of the prophecy, through his natural talents and his studies. By the time Dr. Crisp entered from a side door, amnesia was actually looking like a pretty good option. The scientist came over to me, bent down, and spoke quietly.

"Rook Thomas, the duck is ready in the next room. Now, I've been advised that not everyone in the Court will be witnessing its prophecies?"

"Yeah," I said. "Just one in a series of delightful changes in plan. Here, let me introduce you to our new expert." I cleared my throat, and, for a wonder, Henderson actually paused in his lecture. "I'm sorry to interrupt you, but I've been advised that the subject is ready for you. This is Dr. Crisp, our in-house expert on, well, essentially everything," I said. "He'll give you the details that they have already gleaned about the creature." Dr. Crisp moved forward, smiling politely, and Henderson took his hand.

"Thank you, Dr. Crisp. It is very pleasant to meet you, but I have quite a bit of experience in these things, and I've found it best not to clutter my impressions. I'm sure you understand."

"*Well, research—*" began Dr. Crisp, but Henderson was already ushering the heads into the room where the duck sat. I was slightly gratified to note, just before the door shut, that the duck looked supremely unawed at the sight of them.

"*I'm very sorry, Dr. Crisp,*" I said in an undertone. "*This has always been an important project for Sir Henry, and so we must respect his decisions.*"

"*I quite understand,*" said Dr. Crisp. "*Do you know how long he has been working on this?*"

"*I'm not quite certain,*" I said.

"*Around forty years,*" said Dr. Crisp.

"*Forty years?*"

"*Yes.*"

"*Forty years?*"

"*Yes, that is how long the rumor of the duck has been going around the country.*"

"*Dr. Crisp, I understand that the world is a strange place. I've just spent the better part of a half hour being told in an offensively patronizing manner how strange the world is. But you are telling me that this duck is older than me?*"

"*That duck has been in the same family for three generations,*" said Dr. Crisp.

"*The duck is immortal?*" I squeaked. People looked around in surprise, and I flushed.

"*The duck is . . . long-lived,*" he said.

"*I'll say.*"

"*We don't know how long-lived it will be. The only way to know if the duck is mortal is to stay alive until the duck dies.*"

"*That's very scientific,*" I said. "*But that duck could drastically alter the way this organization is run. Finally, we'll have clear insight into upcoming events. And as far as we know, it will be an asset forever. Think of the good we'll accomplish!*"

He smiled, and then the door of the duck's room slammed open. Everyone's head jerked around in shock.

Henderson stood in the doorway, his hands soaked in blood, feathers in his hair.

"This duck tells me nothing!" he shouted.

For a moment, we all froze in horror. Behind Henderson, Lady Farrier looked as if she was going to throw up, and Sir Henry was holding his head in his hands. Henderson took a deep, shuddering breath, and spoke again, this time quietly.

"This duck tells me nothing."

"And so you felt compelled to kill it?" asked Bishop Alrich dryly. Henderson looked at him, his hands shaking. He took a step toward Alrich and then, showing the first sign of genuine insight all night, elected not to take another.

"What did you do to the duck?" asked Gestalt in a tense voice.

"I followed all the traditional procedures," said Henderson. "I used a purified blade. I invoked all the beneficent elements . . ."

"You cut the duck open?" I squeaked.

"How else does one examine its entrails?" he snapped.

"How about an MRI?" proposed Eckhart, lighting a cigarette. Henderson shot him a look.

"The auguries are only revealed in the creature's death," said Henderson.

"Or not, as the case may be," said Alrich.

"I can't understand it," said Henderson. "Everything was done as prescribed. That is how you take information from waterfowl."

"You unbelievable cretin," said Gestalt. "We'd already verified that the duck could provide accurate answers to spoken questions."

"What?" said Henderson weakly.

"What?" said Wattleman, looking up.

"I don't believe this," said Farrier.

"Should we kill him?" wondered Eckhart.

"That might be best," mused Farrier. "Bishop Alrich?"

"I just had dinner," Alrich murmured.

"We were just thinking about killing him, not draining him," said Eckhart.

"And then perhaps we could try reading his entrails?" proposed Grantchester.

"Now, wait just a moment!" shouted Wattleman. *"Clearly, this was a horrendous mistake, but what's done is done, and we must adapt to these new circumstances."* He spoke firmly, using every shred of authority he could muster. At that moment, he was not a man who had just seen the dream of decades messily and unnecessarily killed in front of him. He was a general. Our leader. It was impressive, I admit, and we all settled back warily. Henderson surreptitiously mopped his brow with the sleeve of his hessian garment.

"So . . . not killing him then?" asked Eckhart. I let out a snort of laughter, and everyone looked at me.

"Sorry," I said in a small voice.

"Mr. Henderson," said Wattleman (I noticed that he'd dropped the *"Master"*), *"has signed all the usual confidentiality declarations. In light of this debacle, we will impose additional restrictions upon him. Rook Thomas, I am certain that you can arrange this."*

"Yes, Sir Henry," I said, wincing as he called me Rook. I had no idea how much Henderson knew, but using Checquy titles in front of him could only further prove our strangeness. Beyond our doings with an oracular duck. And our apparent eagerness to kill him.

Aaaand the guy with the condor on his head who'd just walked by the door to the hallway, which some waiter had left open.

"Good girl," said Wattleman, and he proceeded out of the dining room, followed by the rest of the Court.

It was now up to me to take Henderson up to my office and nod as he signed sufficient forms to ensure that he never spoke about the Checquy, the duck, or anything he'd seen.

So that was my day. I must admit that although I feel bad for the duck, I also feel pretty bad for myself. Now I know how little time I have left, and there is so much to get done.

Love,
Me

35

Someone here has got to have a fucking aspirin." Myfanwy groaned. "I mean, I once read that these incident vans are equipped to reconstitute people who have been dissolved by acid."

"Well, actually, I don't think——" began Cyrus, but Myfanwy waved him quiet.

"I don't care, I don't *care!*" said Myfanwy. "I am seeing spots, and if this doesn't stop, in a few moments *everyone* is going to be seeing spots. Somebody get me an aspirin, *please.*" Various flunkies were dispatched as Myfanwy was ushered to the trailer. The dim sunlight was blinding, and she covered her eyes with her hands and allowed herself to be gently guided by Ingrid and one of the large bodyguards.

The pain grew greater the closer they approached the police station, and the sensations reminded her of the skinned Belgian in his tank, the effect his warped biology had on her. *Grafter work for sure,* she thought bitterly. However, whereas the encounter in the car had turned her stomach, whatever was in that police station was grinding on her thoughts.

"Rook Thomas?" came a deep but hesitant voice that reverberated through her skull. The large bodyguard's hand tightened on her shoulder.

"Yuh?" she snapped. She peeked through her hands and caught a glimpse of gigantic gloved fingers.

"I'm Pawn Steele" came the diffident voice. Through her migraine, the name stirred a memory.

"Pawn Steele. You were at Bath, right? You were the one who went in with the chain saws and cut everyone out of the pods in the basement." Myfanwy remembered him well. A gigantic man whose ancestors had clearly come to England by means of some boats with dragons on the prows. Since today's society frowned on the family trade of pillaging, he'd been drawn into the Checquy, where his potential for directed mayhem was appreciated.

"Yes, sir."

"What can I do for you?" she asked, trying to ignore the *sir*.

"Well, I don't know if you've noticed, but this site smells the same as the incident at Bath," said Steele.

"Smells? No, I hadn't."

"Well, one of my gifts is a heightened sense of smell," said Steele.

"Really? Take my hand," said Myfanwy, ducking her head away from the sun. As soon as she felt his skin against her fingertips, she reached out through his senses. The smell of chemicals and fungus swept through the scent centers of her brain, bypassing the inconvenient route of her nose. "Oh, yeah. It's the same." What had Shantay called it? "Like a gigantic porcino mushroom — only this time it's like it's been doused in formaldehyde."

"Exactly," said Steele. "Is that . . . is that your headache?" Myfanwy hastily broke contact.

"Sorry about that," she said. "Yes, it's the same smell, and the events are linked. But I'd appreciate it if you kept that information to yourself."

"No problem, Rook Thomas. But I was thinking that if you like, I could just go in. I could get all armored up and hack those people out." His voice was enthusiastic, and even through the pain, she could feel his heartbeat increasing at the prospect.

"I see what you're saying, Pawn Steele, and don't even think about it."

"Hells, yeah! I'm on it! Wait, what?"

"I'm sorry, Steele, but in my last operation, the manifestation ate three Checquy teams, including one team of Barghests, before we went in, and I almost had my brain broken down for fertilizer. Now that police station over there is giving me a bitch of a headache, so no one is to approach it. I don't want any more members of the Checquy to be sucked into amorphous entities, especially since we can't guarantee that it will treat them as gently as last time." Belatedly, she recalled her observer status. "Is that all right with you, Pawn Cyrus?"

"Yes, ma'am."

"Okay. Now, will somebody please get me a fucking aspirin!" The noisy bustle of the control room died as Myfanwy and her entourage entered, and everyone took on a hunted expression. For a moment, Myfanwy was ashamed, but then she decided they could probably all bear to shut the hell up and turn off the lights for a few minutes.

A Checquy doctor came in and ran her ungloved hands over Myfanwy's skull and down the nape of her neck. She muttered to herself about node sensitivity and then injected Myfanwy with something that fizzed in the syringe and had the effect of draping a soft wet blanket over Myfanwy's brain.

"You'll feel some fogginess for a few minutes," rasped the doctor. "And then you will need to urinate for a few more minutes."

She moved away as the workers resumed chattering and Myfanwy waited for her feet to touch the ground. Everyone seemed to acknowledge that she would not be making any contributions for the moment, so she settled back with her eyes closed to listen to those around her and try to prevent the top of her head from unscrewing itself and letting her brain glide away on cotton wings.

"Pawn Carmine has a variant of millimeter-wave vision," someone was saying. "He says there's a cube of flesh in the front room and no other life forms in the building."

"So they've all been absorbed?" asked Cyrus.

"Presumably" came the answer. "That cube fills the entire room. We can't see through the windows because the flesh is pressed up against them."

"Do the doors open inward or outward?" asked Cyrus.

"I'll ask Carmine to check."

"He doesn't get closer than twenty meters," warned a woman with a Scottish accent.

"He's also telescopic."

"Or he could just use binoculars," said the Scot. The intercom crackled.

"This is Pawn Carmine," said a calm voice over the speaker. "The doors open inward—they're made of wood with windows."

"Wasn't there furniture in there? A counter or something? Chairs?" asked the Scottish Pawn.

"Yeah, but it looks as if it's all been shoved out of the room or crushed against the walls by the expansion of the cube."

"Is the cube, I don't know, doing anything?" asked Cyrus.

"It's pulsating gently."

"How big is it? I know it fills the room, but can we get measurements, please?" said the Scottish woman, who appeared to be Cyrus's second-in-command.

"It's five meters by four meters," said a little drone at a computer. "And two point five meters high." *That's a pretty big cube of flesh,* thought Myfanwy.

"Pawn Motha is just arriving from Wells," said the little computer nerd. "She's equipped with magnetic resonance. We're setting her up with some binoculars twenty meters from the police station. If you want to wait a moment, she'll be able to give you some idea about what's inside the cube."

"Pawn Carmine, you can see through walls but you can't see through skin?" asked Cyrus.

"Yes, sir."

"Ingrid, I need to go to the loo," said Myfanwy quietly. "Where is it?" They excused themselves and Myfanwy found herself in a cubicle smaller than an airplane toilet. It did have a connection to the intercom, however, so she was able to listen to the report of Pawn Motha with the MRI eyes.

"Okay, I'm getting some interesting structures here. We've got some layers of extremely dense muscle on the outside, but it's not uniform."

"What do you mean?" asked the Scot curtly.

"Well, Pawn Watson, it's a patchwork. I can see where different sheets of muscles have been fused together. The seams aren't bulky, but they're definitely welded together from separate sources."

"You say it's dense?" asked Cyrus.

"Yes—and a good half meter thick. I don't know whether it could stop a bullet, but it could handle quite a bit of force without rupturing. I'm guessing that it's been taken from a few sources and merged together. The strength of any section is going to depend on the sources." Myfanwy frowned, tensed some muscles to stop any incriminating sound effects, and flicked the intercom button.

"This is Rook Thomas. Cyrus, I would anticipate that some extreme muscle-strengthening agents could be present. We've seen them in effect before." She was thinking of the alarming transformation of Van Syoc. "Please continue." She clicked off the voice switch and listened to the commentary proceed.

"I can see a couple of tattoos," said Carmine. "There's a little distortion on two of them, and one of them is really stretched out. I think it used to be an anchor."

"Check the police roster for former naval men" came Cyrus's voice.

What was that medicine? Myfanwy wondered, still in the cubicle. *I don't think I've drunk this much. There was the coffee I scraped off the desk, that amber liquid Ingrid poured for me, that goop they made me drink before they scanned my stomach in those delightful medical examinations, the water I had when I got in last night, and that weird layered drink . . .* She tallied beverages and then called to Ingrid through the door.

"Yes, Rook Thomas?"

"I'm going to need a bottle of water when I get out of here," she said loudly before turning her attention back to Motha.

"All righty, so beneath the muscle strata we have a cage of bones. It's asymmetrical," Motha reported. "There's a pattern, but there are gaps. It's really quite fascinating, like a mosaic."

"So it's like armor?" Watson asked.

"No, the structure probably does provide some armoring, but the flesh isn't compacted within. It's honeycombed. It has pockets of air and pockets of fluids, which are providing some internal support. It's brilliant," she said breathlessly.

That's centuries' worth of Belgian alchemy for you, thought Myfanwy, who was coming to the end of her bladder and wondering if her brain had been drained. The headache was completely gone, and the fogginess felt like it had been peed out as well.

"Anyway, if I'm right, the bones have been scattered around inside the mass," said Motha. "I think they've been disassembled within the cube and redistributed."

"Organs?" asked Cyrus.

"They're in there, all right. Strung together and fluttering away. They're packed in very efficiently, and cushioned by more fluids. And the brains are hooked up!" Motha sounded entirely too enthusiastic, thought Myfanwy. "Well, actually, there're only parts of the brains; it looks as if some slicing and dicing has been done."

Who is this woman?

"Anyway, they're surrounding a central brain, which has had considerable modifications as well. And there's some metal and ceramic stuff in there—appliances, I'm thinking." Myfanwy remembered the satellite phone they'd found in Van Syoc's brain and spine. Odds were that skinless bastard from the limousine was listening in on the police station.

"Eyes?" asked Myfanwy as she washed her hands.

"I'm not seeing any," said Motha. "Carmine?"

"Nothing on the surface" came the contribution. "Nor ears. Nor hair. Not even body hair, so far as I can see." Myfanwy came out of the lavatory and accepted a bottle of water from Ingrid. One of the large bodyguards was waiting outside the bathroom, while the other lurked about at the end of the hall. The entourage walked back to the command center, and Myfanwy looked around for Li'l Pawn Alan, her eyes finally settling on the corner of the room where he seemed to be hiding, far out of everyone's way. Myfanwy nodded to him absently and retook her seat.

"The press has begun asking questions," said Watson, the Scottish woman. "Do we have anything planned out? Any instructions from the Rookery communications section?"

"They're still working on it," said an Indian woman at a monitor. "Because of the gunshots, they can't use a nonviolent excuse like they did in Bath. And since we're not allowed to mention ter—"

"Don't say it!" exclaimed Myfanwy, Cyrus, Ingrid, the two large bodyguards, and Li'l Pawn Alan. The Indian woman blinked under the onslaught, and shrugged.

"In any case, reports are beginning to pop up on the Web, though thankfully not from any reputable sources," she finished before turning back to her monitors.

"Rook Thomas, I don't think there's a way we can retrieve those people," said Cyrus to her seriously. "The ones in the cube."

"I concur," she said gravely. "The only thing we can get out of this situation is the end of it. And that must be done as quickly as possible." The thought of the civilians who had been plugged into the Grafter war machine turned her stomach. And she seriously doubted that the human block had been placed there simply to fill up space in a Reading police station. "I want to see the cube obliterated as soon as possible. In fact, I think the entire site needs to be cauterized. What are our options?"

"Well, ordinarily, Rook Thomas, I would think about standard demolitions or some sort of fire agent. However, taking into account the, uh, information you shared in the car, I'm not sure how successful those would be."

Man, the stories of the Grafters really took hold here, didn't they? thought Myfanwy, eyeing Cyrus. He was a decorated Checquy operative of high rank, but now he was sweating and red-faced.

"In these circumstances," continued Cyrus, "I'd think it would be best if we combined explosives, napalm, and the abilities of Harper Callahan. Do I have your authorization to summon him?"

"If I recall correctly, Harp Callahan is nine years old and is still at the Estate. He has not yet risen to the rank of Pawn, right?" asked Myfanwy, already knowing the answer. The purple binder had taken care to lay out the details of the Checquy's deadliest weapons in its early pages.

"Nonetheless, his abilities have been presented as effective and discrete obliteration options since he was six," said Cyrus.

"But young Harp's powers will leave nothing but a crater. Covering that up would be rather difficult," Myfanwy said. Who was she kidding? Covering this up was going to be a nightmare regardless.

Cyrus's eyes bored into her. "Rook Thomas, I think that this situation may warrant extraordinary measures."

"Very well then. We will summon Harp."

"I think it's wise," said Cyrus. "And look, there's an even chance that Callahan will survive." Myfanwy's stomach clenched. It hadn't occurred to her that using the little boy's powers might kill him. From what she could recall, his file tended to emphasize the amount of real estate that could be disposed of without any troubling side effects such as radiation, pollution of nearby ley lines, or inconvenient paperwork to fill out. Had there been anything about its harming the boy? She couldn't remember.

"He might die?" she asked faintly. Cyrus looked at her soberly.

"Rook Thomas, take into account all the information you shared with me. As a Rook of the Checquy, think of your responsibility to the people of the United Kingdom," he said in a hushed, flat voice. "You do not have time to mull this over."

"Quite right," said Myfanwy, calling the formulaic sentences to memory. Thomas's instructions had insisted that she memorize them.

"I, Myfanwy Alice Thomas, Rook of the Checquy, Hidden Sword of the Crown, First Raven of Scotland, Herald for Eire, and General of Britain's Secret Army, do hereby invoke the presence of Harper Callahan, ward of the Estate, to serve the unknowing populace of the United Kingdom with all his strength and capabilities, that our islands might endure."

It was a ridiculous, archaic statement, but it made everything nice and legal and officially shifted responsibility for the entire operation onto her head. Only the Rooks, the Bishops, and the Lord and Lady of the Checquy could authorize the use on British soil of an agent classified as a Force of Physical Obliteration. Fortunately, there were only three individuals at that power level in the UK. In fact, one of them was maintained in a vault in the Shetland Islands. Utilizing them required that the Prime Minister, the Minister of Defense, the ruler of the country, and all members of the Checquy Court be informed. Even as Myfanwy finished speaking, she could hear the fingers of the crew dialing phones to communicate the information and call forth the student from the Estate.

This has to be done, she reminded herself. *And if that little boy gets killed, well, that will be one of many terrible things I've set in motion since opening safe-deposit box 1011-B.*

And if anyone demands to know why I unleashed a child who could possibly turn this entire town into a slick of molten rock, then I'll be obliged to tell them that my powers indicated the cube was a Grafter weapon. Which it happens to be.

"The cube is moving!" came Carmine's excited voice.

"Peripheral guards ready," barked Cyrus. Little monitors lit up all over the room, and Myfanwy squinted in the sudden brightness. She stared at the pictures and realized that they were from all the little cameras that were slung under the guns of the Checquy troops around the building. "What's happening inside, Jasmine?" Cyrus asked.

Motha's voice came through, surprised. "Those coils of muscle are flexing, and bones are being shifted around."

"How?" asked Watson.

"I don't know, but it's not being done for reinforcement. I'm seeing holes open up in the cage, like shutters being drawn back."

"There's a split in the epidermis!" exclaimed Carmine. "It opened for a second. It's on the side facing the front of the building."

Where we are, thought Myfanwy grimly.

"This doesn't bode well, sir," said Watson to Cyrus. "If something comes out, we're right in the way."

"But we're armored," pointed out the little computer nerd Pawn.

"And we have soldiers on our roof," said Cyrus.

"Some of the bones are being driven down through the floor," reported Motha.

"Why?" asked Watson, her brow furrowed.

"Anchoring," said one of the large bodyguards, and everyone looked at him.

"Anchoring for wh—?" began Watson before the trailer was

rocked by a sudden blow. "Fuck!" Those lucky enough to be sitting down were thrown back in their ergonomic chairs while those standing found themselves lying abruptly and painfully on the floor.

"Status?" barked Cyrus as the trailer trembled again.

"Several muscle tentacles just whipped out of the cube, went through the police station wall, and have latched onto the incident trailer!" came the horrified report from Pawn Motha.

"It's actually pulling you toward the building!" exclaimed Carmine, his panicked voice over the radio almost lost to static. Another massive jerk sent those who had hesitantly gotten up on their hands and knees tumbling back down onto their supine companions.

"Yes, thanks, we can feel it," snapped Myfanwy. "Let's get the hell out of here! Everyone out! Checquy troops, open fire on those tentacles! Where's Steele with his chain saws? Get him on them!"

They were all staring at her. "Now!" she shouted, and she galvanized them with a mental prod to their nervous systems. It was crude and short, but it got them moving.

The large bodyguards acted in marvelous coordination. One picked Myfanwy up like a doll and slung her over his shoulder. Various parts of her that had been examined by doctors earlier in the day protested loudly.

She thought briefly about struggling but decided that acting like a recalcitrant five-year-old would do her no good. The structure juddered over a curb, and they were all flung against a wall. The guard who was carrying her swiveled, protecting her with his body. The other bodyguard stomped along in front of them, shoving the hesitant techno-geeks out of the way. Ingrid and Li'l Pawn Alan held on to the harness of Myfanwy's bearer and were dragged along in his wake. Myfanwy, dangling as she was, managed to make eye contact with Ingrid, who was looking disheveled for the first time ever. They exchanged grim looks, and then Myfanwy, still gasping for breath, craned her neck up to see that the staff of the command center were, with difficulty, following them. Watson was there, shouting, but Myfanwy couldn't quite hear her over the racket of the trailer squealing across the concrete.

"What?" she shrieked at the Scottish Pawn, straining to hear her voice.

"You're going the wrong way!"

Myfanwy tried to twist around in the large bodyguard's grip. They appeared to have come to the end of a hallway, and it was not one that led to any of the exits. She rolled her eyes and prepared to deliver some sort of withering observation to the bodyguard who'd led the way when he turned and called Li'l Pawn Alan forward.

"You're up, laddie," he said firmly. Licking his lips nervously, the lanky Pawn placed both his palms flat against the steel-armored wall and tensed. There was a crackling sound, and when he took his hands away, a mottled gray streak stood out against the metal. The large bodyguard gestured for the young Pawn to move back, and then he wound up his fist and punched the flaw Alan had created, shattering a hole in the wall. Myfanwy's bearer put her down gently and began to help his friend tear away the rest of the wall. The screech of ripping metal drowned the racket of the trailer's journey backward, and everyone watched in awe as a rough but perfectly serviceable exit was created. Then the large bodyguard picked her up again and leaped through the opening.

Myfanwy had forgotten how tall the trailer was — it was mounted on those big tires that could drive over a Volvo and had been jacked up on heavy metal legs. It felt as if they floated for a full five seconds before she was slammed against her bodyguard's shoulder, flashing her undergarments at the gaping Checquy onlookers. The bodyguard slid her out of his arms and deposited her roughly on her feet. She took the opportunity to hike her trousers up before another security operative took her by the arm. Behind her, the large bodyguards were helping people out of the trailer, one guard simply picking each staff member up and tossing him down to his partner, who placed the person politely on the pavement. Ingrid and Alan had been the first to be passed down and were now being ushered away by some brisk-looking Pawns in camouflage.

Myfanwy looked back. The trailer had been dragged much farther than she'd expected, almost to the steps of the police station, and was now being rocked back and forth. The din was horrendous, but what really caught her attention were the two flesh tentacles that had wrapped around it. Myfanwy shook off the guiding arms of the Pawn in camouflage and got down on her knees to peer under the trailer.

"What did it get caught up on?" she shouted at the soldier, who was trying to figure out how best to lay hands on his commanding officer without getting court-martialed or becoming the victim of her infamous powers.

"Some concrete bollards," he said right in her ear. She nodded thoughtfully and became aware of a loud mechanical droning sound between the crashes. She looked up and saw Pawn Steele, clad in some sort of plastic armor, perched precariously on the roof of the trailer and hacking away at a tentacle with one of his infamous chain saws. As she watched in awe, he swept his arms up and brought down churning metal in a glorious motion that sent fluids spattering everywhere. The tentacle parted, and the banging of the trailer ceased immediately. Steele raised his head and gave a triumphant howl.

"Brilliant," said Myfanwy, but the word died on her lips. Instead of hanging limply like any right-thinking unnatural flesh-weapon tentacle would, this thing was shuddering. Before her horrified eyes, the wound *blossomed* and sprouted a mass of writhing tendrils that flailed about. Several of them whipped around Steele, slammed him down onto the roof, and flung his chain saw away. Myfanwy drew in breath to scream, but before she could make a sound, dozens of fingers writhed down to entangle her. As she was mummified, she saw one of her large bodyguards get snared, and then she was being whiplashed into the air and pulled toward the police station.

Myfanwy's skin burned, and she could feel the return of her headache as she was reeled in by the cube. Her breath was crushed out of her as the tendrils constricted. She tried to focus, to reach out with her powers and grab some control, but she could feel herself slipping away. In some quirk of happenstance, there was a gap between the tentacles, and it was situated over one of her eyes. The sky was rolling crazily in front of her, and then the wall of the police station was there with a gaping hole punched in it, and she was being pulled into a crevice that had opened in the cube. Heat and unimaginable pressure enveloped her, and then there was no more light.

36

Dear You,

It is now, much to my chagrin, the holiday season. The time of year characterized by the highest suicide rate within the Checquy. We've already started to see the annual spikes in poltergeist incursions and chronological abductions—but those aren't the things that usually push our operatives to end themselves. It's the fact that we all suddenly remember who we are. And who we aren't. I mean, sure, there are office parties, and gatherings of friends, and a few of us manage to build relationships with significant others—either inside or outside the Checquy. But when most of us walk down the street and see the normal people, we get a little down. The staff therapists get busy.

In spite of my total lack of a personal life, I generally do pretty well at Christmastime. Which is to say, I ignore it as much as I can. Someone has to work over the holiday period, so I usually volunteer, and one of the Chevs does too (usually Gubbins, since he and his wife don't have any kids). Together, we supervise the skeleton crews, drink some sherry via teleconference, and then I go home. Another year taken care of, with barely a taste of the depressing yuletide spirit.

But there are two seasonal social gatherings that are simply unavoidable: the executive Christmas party and the Court's Christmas party.

I had already endured the executive party, to which all the station heads around the nation are invited. It's always terribly awkward, with various people seeking to ingratiate themselves to the Court in an effort to advance their careers. As a result, I had spent most of the party trying to avoid people who wanted to tell me how marvelous they were, and why they should be *promoted. With that delightful obligation fulfilled, there was still the Court party to attend.*

So two days before Christmas, I found myself knocking on the very lovely door of Mr. and Mrs. Conrad Grantchester's very lovely house by the river. Snow had begun falling lightly, and I was glumly sniffing at the flowers I'd brought when the door was opened by a subdued-looking maid.

"Please, come in," she said.

"Emily, are the guests arriving already?" came a call, and Mrs. Conrad Grantchester sailed into view, carrying Grantchester Junior—an adorable little blond child who looked like he should be toddling around naked with a bow and arrow and a set of fluffy little wings. "Myfanwy! Lovely to see you, do come in out of the snow." Caroline Grantchester, thirty-nine years old, was wearing a cocktail dress the color of champagne, and she was beautiful, with dark hair, the bluest eyes in the world, and a figure that proved beyond all doubt that the baby was adopted. Well, that and the letterpress announcement we'd all gotten in the mail that the Grantchesters were adopting a baby.

"Myfanwy, have you met little Henry?" she asked as the maid took my coat and flowers. "Henry, this is your auntie Miffy." Henry regarded his newly acquired auntie Miffy with a moment of disconcerting focus, and then blew some bubbles. I smiled politely and allowed myself to be drawn into the sitting room. Grantchester had married himself a lovely lady whose family went back to the Conquest and had done their share of Conquering. Her social connections, combined with his (always unspecified, but obviously exceptionally important) role in the government, meant that they enjoyed a rich and active social life.

"I love what you're wearing," she lied enthusiastically. Even I didn't particularly like what I was wearing, but it had been in my closet for ages, and it had looked depressed on its hanger, as if it deserved a day out. Unfortunately, it now looked depressed to be on me.

"Conrad tells me you've been working very hard," continued Caroline, and looked to me for some sort of response.

"Oh, well, you know," I stumbled. "It's got to be done." The cover story given to spouses is that we work in the intelligence field, which implies a high level of discretion. So she knew I couldn't really talk about my work, which left me little that I could talk about. I knew that I had three weeks of

408

consciousness left at the most, and this party seemed a tremendous, if unavoidable, waste of my time. Fortunately, I was saved by a knock at the door. Unfortunately, this led to the depositing of little Henry in the horrified arms of his auntie Miffy.

This was pretty much the youngest person I'd ever come in contact with, ever. There had been infants at the Estate, but we didn't interact with them until they were five. This thing was a year old. It didn't seem able to talk, and it regarded me with that same steady look as previously and then started oozing copiously from its nose and mouth. I tilted it away from my top and looked around helplessly.

The knock at the door had turned out to be Chevalier Joshua Eckhart, his round and comfortable wife, Phillipa, and their four children. Two of the boys were twins in their midtwenties, and strapping lads they were, strapping enough to make me regret my clothes. And hair. Then there was a teenage daughter, who looked at me with a certain amount of contempt, and a twelve-year-old boy, who ignored me entirely. I hoped fervently that Phillipa would sweep over and liberate me from the baby-holding, but she just clucked politely when Mrs. Grantchester pointed out little Henry and dispatched one of the twins to bring her a champagne cocktail.

"So, Myfanwy, she saddled you with the baby, did she?" Mrs. Eckhart observed. "I'm not surprised, given that she's wearing a dress worth the gross domestic product of Fiji. You'll want to wipe at his face with the receiving blanket," she said helpfully. "Frankly, I don't know why they haven't gotten a nanny."

"Actually, I think they have one," I said. "I don't know where she is." I looked around hopefully.

"I would have killed for a nanny," Phillipa mused. "Or a Taser. The number of times the twins almost set the house on fire . . ."

"Really?" I said in surprise, and I struggled for a comment. "They seem so, I don't know, calm. And now that they're adults, do, um—oh, thank God—Conrad, do you want to take little Henry?"

"No." He looked at me in disbelief and moved on.

"Oh," I said. Meanwhile, other members of the Court were arriving. I didn't actually want to join them, but at least if I did maybe someone would take the child off my hands.

"Myfanwy dear, Josh has never actually made it clear to me. Do you work together in the office?" Phillipa asked with genuine interest.

"Oh, well, not exactly. We both head up sections," I fumbled as the baby started making noise and fidgeting in my arms.

"Really? You're so young; how old are you?" Before I could answer, we were distracted by one of the twins bringing us both champagne cocktails. "Thank you, Richard—you remember Myfanwy, don't you? She works with your father. Myfanwy, this is Richard."

"Hi," he said sympathetically. "Do you want me to take the baby?"

"Thanks," I whispered. He took little Henry with an ease that surprised me until I realized that he had younger siblings and so was probably used to holding them.

"I'm so impressed," said Phillipa as Richard expertly dandled the baby. "Richard is still at university, and you're so high up in the service at such a young age."

"Well, um, you know. I'm very good at management," I said. "If I were a superhero, that would be my superpower. That, and nothing else," I added hastily.

"Still, it must be difficult," she said. "Josh has to work so hard, and spend so much time away from his family. But I knew I was going to be in for that sort of thing when I married a soldier." At that moment, the soldier himself came over.

"Well, our two youngest children are traumatizing Conrad and his wife suitably," he said with a smile at his wife. "I rather think they were expecting little Henry to remain as conveniently pliable as he is now. Five more minutes with a surly teen and a hyperactive twelve-year-old should leave them fearing the future. Hullo, Myfanwy. Merry Christmas."

"Merry Christmas, uh, Joshua," I said awkwardly. I was used to addressing him by his title, which would have put a damper on the artificial spirit of Christmas. "Are you going away for the holidays?"

"Oh, no," he said. "After all, we need to have the office up to full strength the day after Boxing Day." Phillipa and Richard both rolled their eyes.

"That's very true," I said, frantic not to contradict anything he had told his family. "And thus, there are no opportunities to go away. Unless it's on *business. In which case, you have to go away. Because, you know, the country needs you to."*

"Myfanwy, relax," he said with a laugh. "You needn't worry about covering every base. This girl," he told his wife and son, "is the most thorough person I have ever met." They looked at me with something akin to awe, and I felt myself blushing crimson.

"Oh, look, Alrich is here," I said, pointedly distracting them from the business of looking at me. Alrich had arrived dressed in an uncharacteristically sober suit, but his marvelous complexion stood out all the more against the drab color of the jacket.

"He looks extraordinary," said Phillipa. "I only see him once a year, and I could swear that he looks exactly the same each time. Myfanwy, do you know if he's had work done?"

"Uh, probably, yeah."

"Oh, he must have, more even than Mrs. Grantchester, and yet"—her voice turned thoughtful—"you really can't tell. No wonder she's always so unhappy to see him." It was true, our hostess's posture was as taut as a violin string, and the smile on her face was a triumph of will over the effects of cosmetic Botox.

"She really is all about the life beautiful, isn't she?" remarked Richard. "Frankly, I'm surprised they got a kid—their house is so lovely, and not at all child-friendly." He smoothly decanted little Henry into the arms of a startled-looking maid.

"Well, it was probably the one accessory they didn't have," said Phillipa. "I just don't know how a baby is going to fit in with all the gracious living. I can't see either of them reacting well when the kid throws up on the carpet after eating his birthday cake."

"I apologized for that, you know, Mum," said Richard. "And it was fifteen years ago."

"I know, love, and I forgave you almost immediately, but the stain is still there. Now, Myfanwy, we'd love to have you over for dinner some evening."

"Oh, gosh, that sounds really nice," I fumbled, taking a sip of champagne cocktail to conceal my surprise. There's very little socializing among the Court members; in fact, it's almost entirely limited to business lunches and

the Christmas party. And I wasn't entirely sure how it would fit in with my scheduled amnesia.

"We should invite Alrich for dinner as well," she said. "He looks too thin." I almost spat my drink out at the thought, but settled for choking uncontrollably. Phillipa patted me on the back and handed me a napkin. After that, I cautiously sipped my beverage, listening to normal people dissect the lives of my very unusual peers. Richard remarked that the Gestalts were peculiar, and they both agreed that Gubbins was a lovely man. Then Richard's twin, Luke, came over, and I somehow found myself cocooned in the heart of the Eckhart family. As I listened to them squabble and chatter, I grew increasingly maudlin.

It was inevitable, really, that the party was going to be awkward. At least for Gestalt, Gubbins, and myself—the three members of the Court who had been raised at the Estate. Wattleman predated it. Farrier, Grantchester, and Eckhart had come into their powers late in life. And Alrich, well, he'd been doing this dance for more than a century. They all knew what it was like to be a person rather than a tool. But those of us who had been brought up to be assets first, warriors second, and people if there was ever some spare time scrambled to make normal conversation.

What could we talk about, other than work? That one of Gestalt's bodies had recently finished a yearlong leave of absence to America to get a certificate in administration while the other three simultaneously ran operations all over the British Isles? That Gubbins had been suffering from massive depression since he'd sent five men and seven women to their deaths in an apartment in Vatican City? As for me, there was always the fascinating topic of the impending death of my personality—as machinated by someone in this very room!

I looked at these people and envied all of them, even the leaking baby. No, especially the leaking baby. Normal people were free to go about their daily lives, with their petty trials and tribulations, secure in the knowledge that the supernatural wouldn't bother them. Christ, they didn't even have to believe in the supernatural. That was for us to concern ourselves with. And the other members of the Court—the ones who sat there, drinking their beverages and eating their canapés—even they had more freedom than I did.

So far as they knew, the future would be good—better even than the present. But I knew that my life would end soon, in the rain.

The Checquy is not a family. Even in the most dysfunctional of families, you don't send your brothers and sisters off to dangerous places and make them face atrocities, knowing that they'll probably die in pain and fear. You don't take the bodies of your older siblings and have them dissected—every piece cataloged and destroyed—and then leave them with no more memorial than a name in a file.

No, we're not a family.

But we are supposed to be a team. We may not like one another, but we should respect and be loyal to one another. When you go to the Estate, that's the only thing they promise you. That within the Checquy, you can trust those around you.

Looking around at my comrades, I felt more betrayed than ever. I'd always known that gatherings like these were a pleasant fiction, but tonight's pleasantries were an outright lie. As we smiled at one another and chatted about the weather, one of my colleagues was planning to destroy me.

Who would it be? I wondered, as I watched them. Who had the power to take my memories?

Farrier? Could she have me erased? Her ability to stroll into one's mind and tinker as she pleased made her the most likely candidate, but she owed me. My research into her life had turned up some fascinating loose ends, which I'd pursued. She'd made dire enemies in the last British military conflict, and recently they had succeeded in tracking her down. In the past week, they had tried to have her family killed, and I had stopped them by unleashing the Barghests on them. Illegally. She'd acknowledged her debt to me, and since I'd so recently proven my loyalty to her, I didn't see why the old bird would want to attack me.

Alrich? No one knew exactly what his powers consisted of or what their limits were. We know vampires have strange mental capabilities, including mesmerizing their prey. But why would he bother with me? The files on him were enormous, and his fingers were delicately placed in any number of dirty little pies, but his actions had all been in the interests of the Checquy. There was never a hint that he was involved in anything treacherous.

It was the same for all of them. Crimes might have been committed and subsequently well hidden, but I could not find any indication that they were motivated by anything other than the normal nastiness of humanity. For all my research, I'm not finding any answers.

Love,

Me

37

Myfanwy didn't even have the breath to scream, although she wanted to, very badly.

It's like being born, only in reverse, she thought before panic began to set in. Around her, flesh and muscle pulsated, crushing her. Her skin burned, and her senses, not the ones everyone else had but the ones that came with being Myfanwy Thomas, were overwhelmed.

The impulses of dozens of nervous systems screamed in her brain and fought against one another. It was reminiscent of the colony in Bath, but there the minds and bodies had been anesthetized so they were relatively willing. Here, they were being lashed, enslaved, forced together. And the cube was trying to do the same thing to her.

Stay calm, she thought. *Don't panic.* She tried to remember what she had done in Bath. She'd probed, hadn't she? Delved into the mass and read what it was. Right, so she should center herself and do that again now. With a ghastly effort, she cut the screams and conflict out of her perception and delicately, cautiously reached out with her consciousness to touch and assess the enemy.

It was like putting your lips to a straw and having a river poured into your mouth. Just before Myfanwy was washed away, she realized that she was sensing not just what the bodies were doing but everything they had ever done. Pent-up memory, agonizing in its desperation, flooded into her.

Every inch of Myfanwy's body was suddenly subject to all the sensations that the people in that police station had known. She felt fire licking her fingers while they had ice pressed against them. Her hair was torn out, and her scalp lovingly massaged. She strained to see light, and she was dazzled. Every color permeated her rods and cones. Her lungs took their first breath, and she drowned. Hands and cotton and silk and mouths and leather and water and fingernails touched her skin, and she took a fist to the jaw and a slap to the cheek and a caress along her flank. She tasted spice and sugar and peaches and vomit and the bitterness of burned steak. She choked, and smelled perfume. She made love while she was fucked.

Anyone else might have lost themselves entirely, but she was Myfanwy Thomas, and she had been born abruptly into herself. She knew everything she had experienced in her brief life, and she could separate her own sensations from what was being foisted onto her. Her thoughts floated on top, and she wrenched herself out of the morass.

Okay, so I won't be doing that again. The whole dizzying experience had taken maybe a second, but in that moment Myfanwy had lived a few lifetimes. Without thinking, she opened her mouth, gasping for air, and felt something squirming against her lips. She clamped her jaws shut.

This jolted her into action. *Fuck this!* she thought, outraged. She couldn't scream or strike out with her fists, but her mind launched a wave that would have frozen an army in its tracks. Around her, muscles rippled in shock and lay briefly quiescent. She probed, hard and fast, and found something that made sense. She silently blessed Pawns Motha and Carmine. Thanks to their descriptions, she knew, vaguely, the layout of her surroundings. The fact that she had little air left in her lungs made thinking difficult. It meant that she'd have to work fast, especially since the mind controlling the cube seemed to be recovering.

It wasn't like touching a normal person, or a great number of normal people. Conflicting impulses and the patchwork welding of body parts made for a confusing space to navigate. Still, Myfanwy managed to pinpoint the place where all the instructions were coming from and did her best to cut it off from everything else. She remembered a trick Thomas had described and tried to pay the organism back by flooding it with sensations. She now had a fairly ample library to draw upon, and so she gathered up her strength and pushed out a rush of impressions, straining to overwhelm her enemy. But the brain absorbed the information easily, channeling it and distributing it among the array of lobes it had harvested from the victims. *Damn it!* she thought. That attack, combined with her efforts to isolate the brain, had exhausted her, and she felt her defenses faltering.

Myfanwy's lungs were burning. *Oh God,* she thought. *Help me! Help help!* Soft tendrils stroked against her ears and eyes, and she felt something pushing up into her nose. She was fading away. *Help!* There was no help. And she was out of breath.

As she lost consciousness, she could distantly feel her body convulsing. Her nervous system was being invaded. And then, just as she had lost command of her limbs, she lost command of her powers. They roared out of her, chaotic, wild. A torrent of a thousand different orders and impulses, projected from her panicking brain and tearing into the meat that held her.

All around her, flesh juddered and changed its grip, levering her body up into a standing position. The tendrils stopped shoving into her nose, and the hideous pressure eased somewhat. Distantly she heard a sizzling noise, and then she was no longer being held up by the cube but was taking her weight on her own legs. She was drawing in air that smelled of blood. Her eyes fluttered open, and she could see a dim pink light that brightened as the walls of meat peeled away.

The cube was dissolving around her, breaking down into fluid with a sizzle like shaken-up Coke. The smell of acid burned her nose and slapped her back into full consciousness. There was a clatter as a framework of bones fell to the floor. She saw a mass of gray tissue that she recognized as brain just before it dissolved away into slime. She heard a sound behind her, and, dazed, she looked over her shoulder.

"Rook Thomas," said her large bodyguard, the one who had not been yanked into the cube. He was standing in the doorway of the police station and behind him were some wide-eyed members of the Checquy team, including Ingrid and Li'l Pawn Alan.

"Rook Thomas, take my coat," the bodyguard said.

"Hmm?" she said, before realizing that she was naked and covered in body fluids. *Thank God I didn't turn around,* she thought as the bodyguard splashed toward her and draped his coat around her shoulders.

"Rook Thomas, I think I should carry you out before my shoes dissolve," he said gently. Myfanwy looked down and saw that she was standing barefoot on a little islet of muscle mass. All around her, there was a broad pool of caustic fluid that was wrinkling the leather of the bodyguard's boots. Clumps of skin and bones were scattered about the room, along with a few bleached corpses. She nodded and he scooped her up like a baby, cradling her. He walked hurriedly, and after they emerged from the building and went down the steps, someone else took her while the bodyguard shucked off his boots. A trickle of fluid was coming down the stairs, but the image that stayed in Myfanwy's mind was the tiny little island that had kept her free of the acid, perfectly placed under her feet.

Things were a blur for a little time after that. A new incident trailer was on the way, but the emergency room of a local hospital had been commandeered, and Myfanwy received a gentle but thorough shower and resisted the suggestion that they shave her head bare. Instead, the Checquy doctors washed her hair with strange chemicals and warned that it could lose its color and might need to be dyed. Any other day, Myfanwy might have balked at being showered in the presence of several interested people, but the medical tests of the morning had kind of inured her to being looked at. She had then been installed in yet another backless paper gown—her fourth of the day. She pulled it down to her waist while a Checquy nurse very gently swabbed her skin, which was itchy and peeling.

"Rook Thomas, we've still got the area cordoned off and are in the process of contacting the families of the civilians," said Pawn Watson. Cyrus was still at the site, overseeing the release of a massive cloud of black smoke. By the time the forensic team finished with the scene, Cyrus would have created a very controlled, intense fire that would cover up a multitude of sins. It would also explain why the civilians' bodies could not be provided to their relatives. At the moment, Checquy scientists were wandering around with various pieces of equipment, changing their waders at regular intervals when the rubber began to melt.

"That's great," said Myfanwy dreamily. She looked down and saw that the nurse was carefully rubbing off the dead skin and putting it away in test tubes.

"The Rookery is saying the fire will probably need to be explained as the work of some sort of lunatic arsonist," said Watson. "But they will make it very clear that he was unaffiliated with any group and that he had a long history of mental illness. No mention of anything that is unmentionable." The dour Scottish Pawn did not smile exactly but managed to look at Myfanwy in a way that suggested she was amused by the cover story.

"Marvelous," said Myfanwy. "Oh, and don't forget to get this coat back to my large bodyguard." She looked around for him, but it turned out he was outside the door with Li'l Pawn Alan so as to give her some privacy. Which left her with just Ingrid and Pawns Watson and Motha, a new female bodyguard who was plump and in her sixties, and the Checquy nurse.

"He's not going to want it back," said Ingrid.

"Why?"

"Um, it seems that the acids you were covered in were exceptionally corrosive," said Watson. "They ate large portions of the leather."

"They ate the coat, but they didn't eat me?" asked Myfanwy.

"Yeah, that's why they're collecting all the skin samples," said Motha. "And they kept all the water they used to wash you. The doctors are hypothesizing that your powers protected you from the enzymes in the acid—it was organic, and you were actually in the process of denaturing it."

"How?" Myfanwy said, confused. She hadn't even thought of attacking the acid—she'd been too busy trying to kill the brain. Oh, and dying. That had taken up some of her attention.

"It looks like your immune system kicked in to protect you," said Watson. "And not even that fully—which is why you look like you've gotten sunburned."

"Amazing," marveled Myfanwy. "So—wait a minute! What about the other Checquy members who were dragged in? My body-guard? Steele?" Everyone suddenly looked grim. "What happened?"

"They didn't make it," said Ingrid in a quiet voice. Myfanwy remembered the horribly bleached bodies lying in the remains.

"Oh God," she breathed, and stared at the images on the inside of her head. "They were eaten."

"It's only through the sheerest of luck that *you* survived, Rook Thomas," said Motha gently. "To be honest, much longer and the acid would have started to do some real damage. If you hadn't destroyed the cube from inside, well…" The young Pawn trailed off in awed silence.

Well, Christ, it's not like it was easy, thought Myfanwy. *I was on the very brink of getting broken down for spare parts.* She didn't feel any real triumph over her survival, just a melancholy over the deaths of all those people, people whose memories she had experienced.

Then another, insidious thought occurred to her. Who knew if the women in this room were all loyal to the Checquy? Even Ingrid had not yet been examined for Grafter implants. This was a crucial development. If it was communicated to the Grafters that Myfanwy could destroy their weapons, they would waste no time in terminating her. They wouldn't need to risk using their own biological weapons on her. A perfectly mundane bullet from a perfectly mundane gun would do the job. Regardless of the skinless psycho's threats against Bronwyn, she would need to communicate to the Court the truth about the Grafters' involvement in these two attacks. But first she needed to know whom she could trust.

"Ingrid, how far have the medical tests of the Court progressed?"

"Let me check," said Ingrid, and she turned away with her mobile phone. While she checked up on the details back in London, Myfanwy had another thought.

"Pawn Motha, you saw the internals of the cube—can you tell

me how much of the civilians' brains were left? I remember your saying that some parts had been excised." The Pawn closed her eyes, remembering what she had seen.

"Well, they'd been truncated, obviously," said the Pawn. "As far as I could tell, there'd been some selective lobotomizing—designed to remove the parts of the brain that deal with initiative. I'm thinking the idea was to leave the central brain with all the storage capacity without having to deal with individual impulses. The crew back at the site are examining the remains, but the acid is hampering any meaningful study."

"But you're saying that most likely the personalities of the civilians were erased or destroyed before I got reeled in, right?" said Myfanwy intently.

"I don't know for sure," confessed Motha. "But that would make sense."

That's definitely the kind of thing I would expect from the Grafters, thought Myfanwy. *Especially that skinless bastard. But I like to think it means I didn't kill those people. And if there was still some part of them in that thing, then I hope they are at peace now.*

"Rook Thomas," said Ingrid, covering the mouthpiece with her hand. "Security Chief Clovis is on the line. He says that Chevalier Eckhart has been tested and came through with flying colors. He won't tell me who's being tested now."

"Give me the phone, please. Clovis, this is Rook Thomas," Myfanwy said impatiently.

"Good afternoon, ma'am" came Clovis's voice.

"Yeah, hi. Now, what's this about not telling us who will be tested next?"

"I'm sorry, Rook Thomas. In order for this to work, everything must be kept completely random. And secret."

"Fine," said Myfanwy. "Has anyone other than Eckhart and me been tested yet?"

"Not yet, no."

"Will they be done tonight?"

"No," said Clovis. "The end of the weekend."

"That's great, but at this rate, we'll have to be leaving instructions for our descendants."

"There are four more Court members to test," said Clovis reasonably. "We're working as quickly as we can."

"Fine," said Myfanwy. "Thank you." She hung up and handed the phone back. "Ingrid, set up a meeting of the Court for tomorrow evening." *By that time, the entire Court will have been screened for Grafter implants.*

Gestalt didn't have any Grafter implants, part of her brain reminded her. *At least not in either of the bodies we have in custody.*

"When can I leave for London?" she asked the nurse.

"An hour?" said the nurse hesitantly.

"Fine," Myfanwy said, crossing her arms. "In the meantime, somebody see about getting me some clothes that have a back to them."

The drive to the helicopter field was silent. Everyone was painfully aware that one of the large bodyguards, whose name turned out to have been Ronald, had been replaced. The new bodyguard, Emily, was knitting placidly. Traffic was not good, and the limousine crawled along. Myfanwy eyed the wet bar and ruefully came to the conclusion that although she certainly deserved a stiff drink, it probably wouldn't be a good idea. There was still too much to do. Meanwhile, Li'l Pawn Alan was looking at her with the kind of awe that young guys reserve for powerful women whose bottoms they have seen.

I should probably call Bronwyn, Myfanwy thought. *Just to make sure she's okay. And should I arrange for her to receive some sort of discreet bodyguards? That skinless tool has proven he can't be trusted.* But she quickly realized that any guard she placed on Bronwyn might be secretly working for the Grafters. *I don't know what to do next,* she thought. *All I can do is try to track down this missing Grafter, and that's going to have to wait until I get back to the Rookery.*

You know, I'm just going to call her. She reached automatically for her new mobile and then realized that it had probably been eaten by the cube, along with her comfortable shoes. The fact that she was now swathed in a camouflage jumpsuit and combat boots that were too big did little to improve her humor. She looked over at Ingrid, who was talking on *her* mobile, and thought about borrowing it before remembering that she didn't know Bronwyn's number, and wasn't keen to call directory assistance in front of all these people. Myfanwy leaned back and shut her eyes wearily. Ingrid finished her call and shut her phone with a snap.

"The meeting has been set up, Rook Thomas," she said.

"Thanks, Ingrid," Myfanwy replied, kicking off the boots. She didn't bother opening her eyes when the phone rang. Ingrid's voice was soothing when one didn't actually listen to what she was saying.

"Rook Thomas? It's the head of the communications department." Myfanwy opened her eyes and took the mobile, pulling herself up into a sitting position.

"Hello?"

"Good evening, Rook Thomas. This is Carruthers" came a diffident voice.

"What's happened?" she asked urgently.

"We still haven't been able to trace the phone call," he said apologetically.

"Keep trying. I have utter confidence in you," she said.

"Thank you, Rook Thomas. However, we have succeeded in tracking down the origin of the fax," he said, jolting her out of her disappointment.

"Are you serious?" she exclaimed. Everyone in the car jumped. "Where did it come from? Do you have an exact address?"

"Uh, yes, Rook Thomas. It's in London."

"Hold on a moment," Myfanwy said; she put the phone down and lowered the privacy barrier that separated them from the driver. "Excuse me, but how far are we from the helicopter?" she asked.

"I'm sorry, Rook Thomas, but the traffic is bad," said the driver, gesturing helplessly at the mass of cars in front of him.

"Do we have some sort of siren or flashy lights?" she asked.

"Sorry, no."

Myfanwy nodded reluctantly and raised the barrier.

"Rook Thomas?" said Ingrid.

"They've traced that fax," said Myfanwy. "It's in London and needs to be attended to now, but as you can see, we're stuck here. So I'll have to delegate. Who else has a phone?" As it turned out, everyone did. "Fine. Someone get me Chevalier Eckhart." She turned her attention back to Carruthers, who was waiting on the line. "All right, what can you tell me about—*what?*"

"Rook Thomas, mine is the only phone that has Chevalier Eckhart's number, and that's the one you're talking into," said Ingrid.

"*Fine*. Carruthers, call your new boy Alan," said Myfanwy testily before tossing the phone over to Ingrid. "Get Eckhart now." A phone rang, and Alan handed it to her. "Carruthers, tell me the address. Wait a second, is it ringing?" she asked Ingrid. Her assistant nodded. "Give it to me. Carruthers, give the address to Ingrid." She passed one mobile over and held the other to her ear.

"Eckhart residence" came a female voice.

Shit, what is his wife called? wondered Myfanwy. She remembered Thomas writing about that Christmas party, but couldn't remember the name.

"Oh, hi, Mrs. Eckhart. It's Myfanwy Thomas."

"Myfanwy! Darling, it's lovely to hear from you. Joshua's asleep after all those dreadful medical tests. Did you have to do them too?"

"Early this morning," said Myfanwy, flustered. "Um, there's an emergency—can you wake Joshua up, please?"

"Of course, I'll get him right away!" There was a pause, and Myfanwy looked over at Ingrid, who had finished taking the address from Carruthers.

"Is he still on the line?"

"Yes, Rook Thomas."

"Great, keep him there. Alan," she said, looking around at the Pawn, "get hold of the watch office in the Rookery. I want the status of the Barghests that aren't in Reading. Now!"

"Rook Thomas, Mrs. Woodhouse has my phone," said the Li'l Pawn.

"Use mine," said Emily hastily, shoving it into his hands. Myfanwy nodded her approval. There was sound coming from the other phone, and she put it back to her ear.

"Thomas, what's the situation?" came Eckhart's voice. She had to give it to the man: he'd only just woken up, but he sounded ready to go into action.

"Eckhart, it's the Grafters," she said, ignoring the sudden squeak from Emily. "One of the leaders is in England, and he faxed me a threat. We've traced it, and the source is in London. I'm stuck in Reading, so you'll need to oversee the strike team."

"Very well," he said. "Have you activated them?"

"Just a second," she said. "Ingrid, let me talk to Carruthers." The assistant passed over the phone. "Carruthers, there's no reason we can't strike at the source of the fax now, right? This isn't going to turn out to be the basement of a boarding school or the Belgian embassy, is it?"

"No, it's a private residence, Rook Thomas" came the reply. Myfanwy looked at Li'l Pawn Alan, who had called the Rookery. The Pawn nodded and held out the phone.

"This is Rook Thomas. What's the ready status of the London Barghests?" she asked.

"Team two is still mopping up in Reading; team one is on standby here at the Rookery" came the answer.

"Activate team one. They'll be working under Chevalier Eckhart. We'll need to be discreet—we're staging an attack in a residential area. Carruthers in the comms department will contact you with the address in a moment."

"Yes, ma'am."

She hung up.

"Eckhart, the strike team is ready. I figure that even if any members of the Barghests are traitors, they won't be able to take you. Call me if you need anything further."

"Nicely done, Myfanwy" came the reply. "I'm impressed."

"Thank you, Joshua. One more thing: not a word to any other member of the Court. Only you and I have been cleared of Grafter implants. I have reason to believe that at least one more member is a traitor and we can't afford to have the Grafters tipped off about this strike."

"Agreed. But won't any mention of the Grafters have been communicated automatically to the Bishops and the Lord and Lady?"

"Only you and the people with me now know that the strike is against the Grafters."

"Then I'll keep you abreast of any developments," said Eckhart. "Good-bye."

"Good luck." Myfanwy closed the phone and sat back with a sigh. *I'm a general,* she thought to herself. *I have to send others into battle.* Then she thought of something else.

"Ingrid, we canceled the summons for Harp Callahan, right?"

"Yes, Rook Thomas, right after you melted the cube," said Ingrid. "He was able to return to his cricket match."

"Oh, well, that *is* good." *I suppose. Now, just one more thing.* "Emily," she said to the bodyguard. "Of course I don't need to tell you that everything you hear is to be kept absolutely confidential. But this is really, *really* important..."

38

Myfanwy woke up twice: once when they arrived at the helicopter, and again when they landed. They all squashed into the Rookery lift, then made their way to the main lobby. Everyone was exhausted except for Pawn Alan, who looked to be having the time of his life.

"Ingrid, I'm going to go get changed," said Myfanwy as they entered the assistant's office. "See if there've been any developments, please, and can we get some food sent up? The rest of you please wait outside my office," she said to Emily, Li'l Pawn Alan, and the remaining large bodyguard. Her hand was on the door when Ingrid called to her.

"Rook Thomas, Chevalier Eckhart is on the line."

Myfanwy rushed over to the desk.

"It's me. What's happening?" she asked intently.

"Thomas, we're about to go in" came Eckhart's hushed voice. "Any last things we should be aware of?"

"We're dealing with the Grafters, so don't take any chances. If anybody starts to swell alarmingly, then kill them thoroughly—the last guy ended up eating me. And don't try and preserve anything for sampling."

"All right," he said, sounding surprised.

"I'm not kidding here, Joshua. Destroy them utterly, except for that prick with no skin. See if you can't bring him back."

"Man with no skin; I'll pass the word."

"I'll be waiting to hear from you. Good luck."

"Thank you." And then he was gone.

Myfanwy put the phone down, hoping that Eckhart would come out of it okay. She entered her office, swung open the portrait that led to the stairs, and wearily thought of the climb up to her flat. Suddenly, the big squashy chair behind her desk looked like a much better proposition. *Just for a few minutes,* she thought, stepping out of the combat boots and padding across the room. She stumbled in her oversize coveralls and bumped against the desk, knocking over one of the teetering stacks of documents. It sent an avalanche of paper across her blotter. *Great,* she thought, settling into her chair.

She leaned back and put her feet up on the desk. *If they don't get the flayed Grafter, then what the hell am I going to do? How on earth am I supposed to track down this Ernst von Suchtlen?* Suddenly irritated, she shoved with her feet, pushing all the stacks of documents off the desk.

"Rook Thomas, are you all right?" came the hesitant voice of the large bodyguard.

"Yeah, I'm just doing some filing," she called back.

"Well, the food's here. They've laid it out in the reception area."

"Okay, I'm coming," she said, standing up with a sigh. Her glance fell to the floor and the overturned stationery.

Myfanwy got down on her knees and scooped up the pile. These were not the secret dossiers Thomas had left behind, but personnel records. Her eyes grew huge as she stared at a piece of paper, then she scrabbled through the files frantically.

In Ingrid's office, Emily and the large bodyguard looked at each other. High-pitched squeaks were coming through the door, and they could hear a large number of papers being shifted. Emily nodded toward the door and raised her eyebrows. The large bodyguard shook his head tightly and pointed at her with his chin. The silent debate continued and might have gone on for much longer, but then the doors burst open and Myfanwy walked out, her face cold and set. Behind her, the office was littered with papers she had flung about in a fit of rage. Ingrid looked up in surprise, and Li'l Pawn Alan squeaked in his chair.

"Convene the Court, right now," she said to Ingrid.

"Rook Thomas? I—yes, right away. What about Chevalier Eckhart? He's at that assault."

"Don't pull him off it," said Myfanwy. "That needs to be taken care of. But everyone else. Keep it quiet, though. This can't be like every other meeting, where their entire staff knows, and then the entire Checquy knows. There can't even be a call log for someone to see."

"If you're really worried about no records," said Li'l Pawn Alan, "you should use the secure command suite in the basement. The phones there are encrypted and aren't connected to the regular switchboard. And there's an armed guard on the door at all times." Everybody looked at him.

"What?" he said. "I'm in communications. I just got the big orientation lecture about it this morning."

"Well, that sounds good," said Myfanwy. "Frankly, I like the idea of you two being in a secure place. Head down there and make the calls. But first, please get a car ready for us right away. You two are coming with me," she said to the bodyguards.

"Yes, Rook Thomas," Ingrid said, "but you may want to put some shoes on."

"Shoes?" repeated Myfanwy incredulously, her wrath momentarily subdued. "Right."

"And a jacket. It's chilly tonight."

"Okay, fine."

"Rook Thomas, what…?" Ingrid trailed off helplessly.

"You remember what we talked about in Scotland?" asked Myfanwy quietly. Ingrid looked blank. "The infiltrator in the Court?" The blood rushed from Ingrid's face as she nodded. "I've figured it out." She looked hesitantly at Pawn Alan, Emily, and the large bodyguard, and then leaned close to her assistant's ear and whispered a name. Ingrid cringed at the news as Myfanwy spun on her heel and walked away, with Emily and the large bodyguard following her closely.

Myfanwy was sitting in the car, lost in thought, as the garage door rolled up. Emily and the large bodyguard watched her with wide eyes as she kneaded her temples with her hands and ran through her accusations.

This person is a traitor to the Checquy and the country.

This person embezzled massive funds, and in conjunction with the Scientific Brotherhood of Scientists started a private army within the Checquy and abducted non-powered British children to be troops.

This person . . . this person can tell the Court that they stole my memories.

This person can point out that I'm the amnesiac who woke up and claimed a position of power that she didn't know anything about. They can prove it.

This person can destroy my life.

"What am I doing?" she asked herself. "What am I going to—what the hell is going on?" The car had stopped abruptly, and there were rumblings outside. It proved to be the protesters, who had gathered around the limousine that they saw as tangible evidence of a secret conspiracy, or at least of somebody worth irritating. "I don't believe this."

Myfanwy opened the sunroof and stood up, poking her head out and risking the possibility of having eggs or rotten vegetables thrown in her face. "You people, just bugger off! We have a woman in here who is going into labor. We have to get her to the hospital!" The protesters quieted for a moment. "And she's a lawyer!" Myfanwy added triumphantly, pulling out Ingrid's mobile phone and taking photos of monumentally bad quality. The group scattered, and the car drove on.

"Unbelievable," she said, breathing heavily. The bodyguards made muted sounds of wary agreement, and she closed her eyes. With an effort, she calmed herself and returned her thoughts to where she was going.

Am I going to do this? Am I really going to confront them with this?

This person can destroy my life.

She thought of Gallows Keep and the terrors that waited there for a person the Checquy could not trust. Of the penalties that would be inflicted on an infiltrator.

And then she thought of all the letters she had read. She recalled the despair and the hope and the effort that Thomas had put into them.

Into *her.*

This person can destroy my life. But they already destroyed Thomas's, and by God, they'll pay for that.

She turned her attention to Emily and the large bodyguard.

"We're about to go accuse a member of the Court of treason," she said. "And there may be some tension and unpleasantness. Are you two ready to fight?" The bodyguards exchanged startled glances. "Are you ready to die? I'll level with you—there's treachery afoot, and I can't afford to call in anyone else, since you already possess astoundingly sensitive information. I can't really be certain I can trust you, but at least I know you can't make any calls to warn anyone, because I'm watching you."

"Rook Thomas, I am loyal to the Checquy. I swear to God," said the large bodyguard seriously.

"As am I," said Emily.

"I appreciate that, but I've already had some disappointments," said Myfanwy. "Which is why my powers will be reading you every moment. And I say this with all due appreciation for your willingness to take a bullet or a blade for me: If either of you makes a move against me, then you'll be shooting yourself in the head. And that is *not* a metaphor." Myfanwy stared at them fiercely and was pleased to see that they both met her eyes without flinching.

She spent the rest of the journey making sure that they were appropriately armed. Both were carrying sidearms—in fact, they each had two, in addition to a rather intimidating array of knives, pepper spray, and telescoping batons tucked away under their dark purple coats.

"Yeah, that's very impressive," she said. "No crucifixes or silver bullets?"

"Those don't work unless you're a priest or being attacked by the press," said the large bodyguard. "What kind of weapons are you carrying, Rook Thomas?" Myfanwy blinked in surprise.

"Um, nothing," she confessed. "The members of the Court aren't really supposed to carry weapons. I think it's a ceremonial thing."

"Would you like one?" asked Emily. "There's a small arsenal in the trunk of the car."

"That's a nice thought," said Myfanwy. "But I'd feel even more awkward with a gun in my hand." *And I'm not sure it would do much good anyway,* she thought, grimly remembering how incompetent she had been when confronting Goblet with a gun. Even Ingrid's little book of instructions was unlikely to be helpful.

Outside, it began to rain.

"Rook Thomas, will your opponent be carrying a gun?" asked the large bodyguard.

"I...don't know," she said. "But we're going to a boardroom. And the rest of the Court will be there with their bodyguards."

"Going into battle, you want every advantage you can get," said Emily gently. The bodyguards exchanged looks and set about rolling up the right leg of Myfanwy's coveralls. "We're going to give you a nice little piece in an ankle holster."

"Groovy," said Myfanwy, distracted by a sudden terror. *What's going to happen to me?* she thought. She stared out at the rain, envying all the little cars that zipped by on their way to things that weren't this.

"Rook Thomas, we're here," said Emily, and Myfanwy looked up, surprised. She had slipped into a reverie, and now she gazed up at the Apex. Inside that building was the traitor—the enemy who had conspired to obliterate her identity. She thought of the original Myfanwy Thomas, the shy young woman who had written letters filled with her hidden fears and small pleasures. Myfanwy closed her eyes and sent out a prayer, for Thomas and for herself. Then she let the rage build up inside her.

"Let's go," she said, and stepped out of the car. She flinched against the rain but climbed the steps of the complex resolute, even in her ridiculous fatigues. Her bodyguards flanked her. The doors opened before them. For a moment, Emily ducked behind Myfanwy, but a quick read of her body reassured Myfanwy that it was simply for security.

They were met in the foyer by an imperially slim Retainer with impeccable posture and a greasy manner.

"Rook Thomas, welcome," he said with a smirk.

"Thanks, it's lovely to be here," she said, pausing unwillingly because he was standing in front of her. *Is this one of those tools who still think they can push Rook Thomas around?* "Now, move." She stalked to the lifts and stabbed at the button. While Myfanwy waited, Emily spoke quietly.

"Rook Thomas, that Retainer is talking on a telephone and looking at us." Myfanwy nodded. "Would you like us to kill him?" Emily asked, and Myfanwy shot her a shocked look. "So that's a no."

"As far as they know," said Myfanwy carefully, "I am simply in a foul mood after the tests this morning and the incident this afternoon. He's probably just letting the Court know that Rook Thomas has arrived." They entered the lift, and before the doors closed, Myfanwy shot a hard look at the Retainer, who had hung up and was staring at them. He smiled obsequiously and nodded. *Remember, Thomas didn't always get a lot of respect,* thought Myfanwy.

Maybe I should have let Emily kill him.

Myfanwy and her bodyguards proceeded to the executive conference room. Outside the doors, standing at attention, were two Apex guards, each fully as large as Myfanwy's own.

"Good evening, Rook Thomas," said the guard on the left. "The Court is assembled and waiting for you. You and your bodyguards can go on in."

"Thank you," Myfanwy said with a curt nod. "Long day?"

"Always," said the guard ruefully.

"Well, have a good evening," said Myfanwy. All these good manners were draining her fury—and that was dangerous. She looked back at Emily and her large bodyguard. "Okay, let's go." They walked through the doorway and turned a corner into the boardroom.

Myfanwy stopped short. The room was empty except for the person she'd come to accuse.

"Good evening, Myfanwy."

39

Dear You,

The end of me is nigh.

That was a little gallows humor. I'd like to be able to say that I've attained a Zen-like calm. That I have accepted my upcoming obliteration. But the fact is that my time has just about run out. The duck said I had a month at the most (God help me, I'm pointing to a duck as my authority), and that month is almost over. I just can't stand it.

I don't know if you will get this letter. I don't know if today's the day it happens. Maybe the door will burst open and I'll be dragged away, and they'll find the remains of this letter, and, and . . . I find myself having these little panic attacks. Every loud noise freaks me out. Every knock at the door, every screech of tires or car horn from outside. My hands shake.

I know every day has been a gift, and I know I'm supposed to be grateful, but it's so hard. I hate it. I hate whoever it is who will betray me. I'm coming to the end of my allotted time and I still don't know why this is going to happen to me. That's the part that grates the most. I know I'll lose all my memories, and that's terrible. But the possibility that I might die without ever knowing the reason is even worse.

I've turned up lots of things in my research. Vendettas. Misappropriation of funds. But what does it have to do with me? Why would anyone want to kill me?

I've learned so much about my colleagues recently. Farrier's being cut out of her father's will. Gubbins's regular communications with a woman in Mongolia. The fact that Grantchester's wife miscarried three times in three years. I look at all these little factoids and wonder if they are important. What have I missed?

In the back of my mind, I thought I could prevent this future from coming. I thought that if I found an answer or learned in time not to say or do something, then I could sidestep Lisa's prophecy. The frantically whispered warnings of that little boy at the Estate would be proven wrong. The duck could be dismissed.

I didn't dare stop doing my job, for fear that it would lead to questions being asked and that those questions might be the catalyst for my death. So I worked hard, even as I conducted my private searches. I worked until I almost broke. But in the course of trying to cover every base while still doing my duty as Rook of the Checquy, I ran out of time. I never made it back to Camp Caius, and I never found out who is behind it. I don't know who will attack me, and who will kill me. I can't tell you who your enemies are.

I'm sorry I can't provide you with all the answers.

This is the last letter I will write.

Me

40

"Good evening, Bishop Grantchester."

Something has gone very, very wrong, Myfanwy thought, taking in the boardroom with its conspicuous lack of witnesses and non-traitors. *No time to hesitate.*

"Shoot him," she said to her bodyguards. They unholstered their weapons, and she closed her eyes as two shots rang out on either side of her. When she opened her eyes, Grantchester was still seated, unharmed and looking sardonic.

"I'll give you points for quick thinking," he said. She looked to her bodyguards and saw that they were both lying on the floor, gunshot wounds in the backs of their heads. Behind her, standing several cautious feet away, were the two guards from the door, their guns pointed at her. Myfanwy sliced out with her powers and in unison the gunmen pointed their weapons away from her and shot each other. *"Very* quick thinking," said Grantchester, and the calm smile on his face became a little more dangerous.

Myfanwy reached out carefully with her powers. There was a torrent of sensation seething beneath his skin. As she watched, his eyes shifted color, trails of ink wafting across the whites. Darkness covered his irises. She narrowed her eyes and clasped her mind around his body. His reservoirs of chemicals and enzymes were churning, trying to vent themselves. His pores—minuscule fluttering apertures—were not permitted to fulfill their function, thanks to her. Grantchester gaped, and she realized that her reflexes had outdrawn his.

And yet, Grantchester's attack system was so intricate, with so many redundancies, that curbing it took all of Myfanwy's concentration. If she relinquished even a little control, the room would be filled with some cocktail of organic chemicals. She couldn't spare the effort needed to stop the Bishop from moving, and he jerked to his feet, gasping heavily.

"Damn, but that's unnerving," Grantchester rasped. "I suppose I should have taken your new capabilities into account. The last time... well, the last time you exceeded expectations too. But this is simply amazing."

Well, this is a fun little standoff, she thought tightly. *Neither of us can use our powers to take out the other.* She thought of her gun in its ankle holster and wondered if she dared go for it, though dividing her concentration seemed like the worst thing she could do.

Suddenly he called out in a loud voice, "Norman, Miriam, come in, please!"

More large guards, to break the stalemate, she thought. A side door into the boardroom opened, and two people emerged. They were, however, much smaller than she had anticipated. One of them was shorter than Myfanwy. The other was taller, but terribly thin and gangly.

What kind of secret agents does Grantchester employ? Myfanwy wondered before she got a good look at them. *Oh... young ones.* The short one was a girl of about eleven, and the taller was one of those teenage boys made up exclusively of elbows and Adam's apple. *And scales,* she noted. Both were toting guns, but that was not all that caught her attention.

The gangly youth was covered in flesh-colored scales that glittered in the light. Long scars sliced up his face from the corners of his mouth. The little girl had massive talons coming out of her fingers. Both of them stared at Myfanwy with dead eyes.

Graduates of Camp Caius, I suppose, she thought with increasing dread. *So what do I do now? If I release Grantchester to take them on, he'll be able to use his powers. Although he wouldn't gas his own troops, would he?* she wondered, and then rapidly came to the conclusion that he most certainly would. *What do I do?* At that point, the decision was made for her by the Bishop.

"Take her," he ordered. The youth smiled and moved toward her, opening his jaws. He hissed, and the inside of his mouth was bloody red.

"No!" Myfanwy exclaimed in panic, wrenching her powers off Grantchester. Before she could slam them at the young man, however, the little girl dashed forward, moving with inhuman speed, and leaped up, smashing her in the jaw with an uppercut.

Myfanwy reeled and fell back on the floor, struggling to stay conscious. Distantly, she heard Grantchester's voice and forced her eyes to open.

"She's not dead, is she?" asked the Bishop.

"No, my Lord," said the little girl. "Would you like her to be?" The talons on her fingers grew and began to drip a viscous black fluid. She peeled her lips back and flashed a mouthful of fangs.

Myfanwy reached out feebly with her hands and her powers to ward off the little girl, but the scaly youth was there. His dry fingers closed around hers, and she felt her commands disrupted. The girl twitched a little, but that was all. And Myfanwy could feel a creeping numbness spreading through her, dulling her perception of those around her. She pushed against it, but with a jolt, her abilities went still.

Oh, what the hell is this? she thought. She could sense her abilities but couldn't actually use them. Was it her imagination or could she *feel* her synapses snapping ineffectively?

"That took a little longer than usual, Norman," said Grantchester mildly.

"She put up a fairly good fight, Lord," said the scaly boy in a defensive tone.

"Don't whine," said Grantchester sharply, and both his acolytes straightened up.

"Yes, my Lord," they said in unison.

"Sit her up," said Grantchester. The young man kept his fingers tightly on hers, but with his other hand, he helped her up into a sitting position. She gently moved her jaw and flinched. Much to her surprise, it felt like it was still connected to the rest of her skull. *That little bitch has a good right arm,* she thought foggily.

"Myfanwy." She brought her gaze up to the Bishop. "Now that we have these formalities out of the way, and you're a bit more pliable, perhaps we should move to a more comfortable setting?"

Without waiting for her to respond, he turned and walked away. The Camp Caius kids stood her up. Her limbs were almost as uncooperative as her powers, but she was able to shuffle along awkwardly as Grantchester led them through the side door and down a corridor to his office.

The pain from getting punched in the jaw was fading a little, and she gazed around curiously. The office was nice—nicer than hers. Wealth had been splashed around here, and it showed. Flames crackled in the fireplace. The walls were covered with warm wood paneling and large portraits, similar to the ones that decorated her office. Heavy drapes framed a huge window, but the eye was drawn automatically to a massive desk, behind which Grantchester had settled himself. He gestured, and Myfanwy was guided over to the chair in front of the desk. The scaly guy maintained contact, moving his hand to rest on the side of her neck. The little girl moved to take her place behind the Bishop.

"Well, here we are," said Grantchester. "We have a lot to talk about, but before we begin, would you care for a drink? It's late enough, and the day's been long enough that a cocktail is certainly warranted." He got up and opened a cabinet that revealed a well-stocked bar.

So we're going to pretend this is just a regular conversation? thought Myfanwy. *Okay; I can play polite if he can.*

"That's very kind of you, but I'm fine," said Myfanwy coolly. She wanted as many of her wits about her as possible. She watched as Grantchester mixed, stirred, and poured his drink. He was such a handsome man, she thought. Tall and well built, with beautifully cut dark hair. He was dressed in a tailored suit, and smelled nice. Such a shame that he turned out to be the traitor.

"I heard about the events in Reading," Grantchester remarked over his shoulder. "Was it honestly so bad that it required the presence of young Callahan?"

"At the time, it seemed like the best option," she said. "It was only through luck that the entity was destroyed before he arrived."

"How fortunate that you emerged relatively unscathed," said Grantchester as he settled himself back in his chair. "Now, to business. I expect you've figured out that the rest of the Court isn't coming? They never got your summons." Myfanwy's heart sank. It hadn't been much of a hope, but she'd have given a lot to see Alrich walk through the door. Or even the Lord and Lady. "Wattleman is asleep in his secure residence, Farrier is spending the night reviewing the dreams of all the students at the Estate, and Alrich is in Scotland. And thanks to the heightened alert and the need to screen people, Apex House is functioning on a skeleton crew this weekend."

"But how did you know that I was going to reveal you as the traitor?" Myfanwy asked in bewilderment.

"Your office and that of your assistant are bugged," he replied carelessly. "I've had listening devices there ever since it was my office. You'd be astounded at the kinds of things people say while they're waiting to meet with you. I actually hadn't used them for years, but after recent events I've had someone listening constantly." He smiled and took a sip of martini.

"So," continued Grantchester, "when I heard you say that you knew who the other double agent in the Court was, I put a call in to one of my people in the Rookery. He was serving as the guard at the Rookery's command suite, and I ordered him to stop your assistant and that young Pawn. Well, stop them and shoot them," he corrected himself. Myfanwy felt a horrendous wrench of grief at his words, and blinked to keep the tears from forming.

"In fact," said Grantchester, "all the troops who have guard duty at the command suite are mine. You've got to be strategic with your people, you know. Why were you dragging that young Pawn around anyway?" he asked curiously. "If you don't mind my asking."

"He just got caught up in things," said Myfanwy softly. "He heard me talking about the Grafters, and I didn't want to risk his telling anyone else."

"I know exactly what you mean," said Grantchester. "After all, I couldn't let you tell anyone else about my divided loyalties, could I? Which brings me to the same question. How did you know?" Myfanwy thought about providing him with some creative instructions on where he could go and what he could do with himself when he arrived, but she restrained herself.

Talk it out, she told herself. *Buy yourself some time. Something may emerge, some opportunity.* She took a deep breath.

"Well, you may remember that immediately after Gestalt was exposed as a traitor, I went up to see him at Gallows Keep," she began.

"Yes, but he assured me that he hadn't told you anything very useful," said Grantchester, taking an easy sip. *What?* thought Myfanwy. *Oh, right, the other bodies. Naturally he's been in contact.*

"Actually, he told me a few things that I found *very* interesting," said Myfanwy. She felt a jolt of satisfaction as Grantchester's face turned sour.

"Indeed?" said Grantchester. "What exactly?"

"Well, one of the little facts he let slip was that there was another traitor in the Court," said Myfanwy. *Maybe at the very least I can get Gestalt in trouble.* "And I had no problem believing it," she added, staring straight into his eyes.

"I'm not certain I understand."

"I'd stumbled across a few things that didn't make a lot of sense," said Myfanwy, leaning back in her chair and counting points off on her fingers. "To begin with, there's a secret training camp for a private army, established under Checquy auspices. Camp Caius." At her mention of the name, she felt the scaly youth's hand move on her neck, and the girl behind Grantchester shifted uneasily. "It's down in Wales, a little remote and a little spartan, but it's got some very nice medical facilities. And of course, it's illegal as anything.

"Second, there is the painfully obvious fact that Gestalt could never work such a complicated piece of administrative flimflammery. Financial sleight of hand designed to drain substantial funds while evading all but the most meticulous of forensic accounting. Legal justifications to acquire children who had absolutely no unnatural abilities—children expressly outside the purview of the Checquy. Now, we both know Gestalt was elevated to the Court for his outstanding ability to kick ass, not his intellect.

"Then I had a little tête-à-tête with a high-up from the Broederschap. He tracked me down, despite the fact that I departed secretly from the Rookery through an underground passage. Someone must have tipped him off.

"And *then*, well, there's the tiny little matter of the attack on me. Not the attack this afternoon, you understand, though that was a complete bitch too. The delightful incident in Bath was not particularly pleasant either. But I'm talking about the attack that ended with me standing in a park surrounded by the corpses of Retainers and with no memory of who I was."

"And you were going to tell this to the entire Court?" Grantchester asked.

"Well, I was hoping to keep the memory issues to myself," said Myfanwy. "But I was willing to disclose them if it meant bringing you down." Grantchester was staring at her, his handsome face expressionless.

"Anyway, while Gestalt could not possibly have pulled the strings," she continued, "you could have, easily. You were Rook for many years, with dominion over finances. You and I have both set up enough covert operations to know how it's done. You could have established a little school and maintained it once you rose to the rank of Bishop. After all, you were responsible for revamping the finances of the whole organization. All sorts of things could have been concealed during that restructuring."

Grantchester regarded her with level eyes, his hands forming a pyramid on his desk, but Myfanwy continued, undeterred.

"Gestalt also said that I was placed on the Court deliberately, that the Grafters wanted it. But I'll bet you put the idea forward. You, with your reputation for making unorthodox promotions that prove to be brilliant. You, who can measure people's strengths and weaknesses. You knew I would make an excellent Rook. That I'd keep the organization running smoothly. And that I'd compensate for

Gestalt's obvious lack of ability in that regard. That I'd be kept far too busy to investigate any inconvenient anomalies and that I was too reticent to stand in your way even if I did stumble across one.

"Now, when it came to the meeting between me and Graaf Gerd de Leeuwen, well, I'll confess that I thought it was Bishop Alrich who had set me up. I mean, I was in a nightclub with some friends, and there he was, looking for a few hot bodies to drain. We ran into each other, and then immediately afterward I was surrounded by a bunch of large, uncoordinated Belgians. I figured Alrich had drained his date and then made a quick call to a Belgian mobile phone.

"It may also interest you, Conrad, to know that after I was attacked two weeks ago, I snuck through a passage that leads from my office to a private garage. And there, in the midst of whatever mental breakdown I was experiencing, I was ambushed. Only Rooks can access those tunnels. And all four of Gestalt's bodies were out of town that night.

"I'm willing to bet you have a few private entrances, and maybe even some surveillance, which is how you got into the Rookery and had my memory violated. It's also probably how you knew I was going out last week and arranged to have me tailed."

"Now, that's hardly conclusive," said Grantchester. He sounded amused, which infuriated Myfanwy.

"No," said Myfanwy. "And that's why I didn't say anything. But recently I had cause to sift through all the correspondence files—official and personal—and I came across the announcement that you and your wife sent out when you adopted your baby." Myfanwy took a breath and calculated how she would continue. "I was particularly interested in the family portrait. You see, your wife looked familiar—and not just because she's Mrs. Grantchester. During my interview with Gestalt, I had the opportunity to see through Gestalt's eyes. *All* of Gestalt's eyes," she added darkly.

"It turns out that Gestalt has a fifth body—a smaller body—and that body was in the company of your wife, with her unforgettable blue eyes. So I did a little research and found that Eliza Gestalt took long service leave some time ago—and returned just before you adopted your baby. And there are other things. I know that she has a scar across her stomach and that she has been withdrawn of late. In short, I think your adopted child is Gestalt's baby. I think your child *is* Gestalt.

"You work for the Grafters, don't you, Conrad? No wonder you wanted every scrap of new information sent to the Apex for your strategic risk analysis. You wanted to be certain that you knew everything we knew."

"Well, that's very impressive," said Grantchester. He smiled in a way that made Myfanwy want to break his nose. "You've got it all listed very methodically. That's some very good detective work."

"You must have been amused," she said coldly, "watching me scrabble about, trying to conceal my amnesia."

"Well, in fact," he said easily, "we weren't at all sure how much of your memory was gone. It's nice to know that it actually worked."

Oh, he can't be serious, thought Myfanwy. *He didn't even* know?

"What actually worked?" she asked.

"Well, it's a long story," said Grantchester. "Are you sure you wouldn't like a drink?" Myfanwy remained silent. "You needn't glare at me, it's just good manners to offer. Although really, I'm guilty of an appalling lapse in etiquette. Before we go any further, do allow me to introduce my protégés. This is Norman, whom you have met previously and seemingly do not remember." Myfanwy shook her head. "Well, at least he did that much correctly. You see, Norman here is responsible for your current amnesia." Myfanwy shot a look over her shoulder.

"Oh, yes," Grantchester continued. "He accompanied me, along with a few Retainers, to the Rookery in order to seize you, excise your personality, and remove you from the premises."

"For what?" asked Myfanwy.

"There were a number of possibilities," said Grantchester. "I was actually a little spoiled for choice. You'd be astounded at how malleable a person with no memories can be. If you put them in the right situation, they can be very open to suggestion."

"You were going to have me work for the Grafters?" she asked in horror.

"Or fulfill various recreational roles," said Grantchester carelessly. Myfanwy felt a dreadful nausea open up in her stomach, and it must have showed in her face because Grantchester burst out laughing. "I'm joking," he said, wiping his eyes. "Don't be ridiculous. No, no, we were going to run a battery of tests on you, and then dissect you."

"I see," said Myfanwy, taking deep calming breaths.

"Or at least something along those lines—it was all a rather sudden decision."

"And why did you suddenly decide to do this?" she asked. "Wasn't it risky? Did you think no one would notice I was gone?"

"There would have been an investigation, of course," said Grantchester. "The disappearance of a member of the Court would have been probed in depth. Why, a Bishop would even have volunteered to pursue it personally, accompanied by a handpicked team. And such an offer would have been gratefully endorsed by the remaining Rook. I can assure you, any evidence left after your hasty removal would have been swept under the rug.

"But it had to be hasty, because that evening it was brought to my attention that Rook Myfanwy Thomas had entered Camp Caius a few weeks earlier. One of the guards had been found having a seizure of some sort. All such events are examined closely for fear that one of the Caius subjects might be having unforeseen effects on those around them. Extensive blood work, CAT scans—you get the picture. Eventually they found evidence that you had controlled him—your psychic fingerprints, if you will. Remember all those years of testing you received at the Estate? Well, those results were shared, unofficially, with the staff at Caius, and one of the staff members recognized the hallmarks of your powers.

"I'll admit, I was incredulous at first. Little Myfanwy Thomas's nose was always in the books. She was far too deeply enmeshed in the day-to-day domestic operations of the Checquy to have time to do any extracurricular research. Or so we thought," Grantchester added.

"And then, suddenly, it seemed we had been discovered. All that was keeping us from being completely destroyed was your inexplicable reticence. Fortunately"—and here he smirked with self-satisfaction—"I've always been quick in a crisis. One thing I learned in the field was that if someone has a knife against your throat, you don't hesitate.

"I immediately mobilized a team. I keep several graduates from Camp Caius here at the Apex in a discreet bodyguard capacity, and we proceeded to the Rookery. As you guessed, there are several concealed entrances to that building known only to me. One of these leads to the private quarters of the Rooks. I waited for you to enter the residence and greeted you there.

"I will say this for you, Myfanwy, you were far calmer about the whole thing than I anticipated. I don't believe I shall ever forget the look in your eyes. A girl who usually squeaked if someone spoke unexpectedly, who cringed when someone stood abruptly. Well, not that night. You walked in and saw me seated on the couch, with Norman at my shoulder. Your eyes widened, but otherwise there was no change in your expression.

"Then my other aides stepped in behind you and closed the door. You just walked across the room and stood facing me. You were absolutely still, and your eyes were so cold." Grantchester broke off and shook his head with a bitter little smile.

"I wanted to ask you questions, to know how you'd found out about Camp Caius and why you hadn't said anything. But you just stared at me, and I confess, I found myself a trifle unnerved. I started to speak to you, and you said, 'Just shut up and do it, you filthy traitor.' That's what Myfanwy Thomas, the most pathetic Rook in the history of the Checquy, said to *me*." His voice tightened with rage, but then he controlled himself.

"And so," he said lightly, "I stood up, slapped you in the face, and then set my Retainers on you while you were still reeling.

"Priya and Mark had you by the shoulders, holding you still for Norman here to attend to you. They were wearing gloves, of course, and had you pinned, but I suppose a little of that old Estate training came back to you. You kicked out and managed to throw them off balance. You touched Mark on the cheek and he was suddenly blinded—it turned out that you'd made his pupils close themselves completely.

"Priya was even more unlucky. Using a level of power you'd never shown at the Estate, you somehow forced her facial muscles to turn against her. Apparently, they fractured her skull." He stared intently at Myfanwy, and she shrugged. "Fortunately, by that time, Norman was able to get his hands on you.

"Norman is one of the products of Camp Caius, which you apparently know all about. It's quite remarkable, really. A perfectly mundane infant can be radically enhanced—if you're willing to crack open its skull and torso on a regular basis and do a little tinkering. And inject it daily with various cocktails of nastiness. And suture a new system of canals and reservoirs into the body. And graft some protective insulation onto its epidermis. And provide it with some new probative members." Myfanwy shot a horrified look over her shoulder at the scaly youth, who stood there, unperturbed, as Grantchester listed the modifications that had been performed on him. Myfanwy shuddered and turned back to the Bishop.

"You have to take care of them, of course. They're very delicate. Norman here doesn't eat actual food anymore, do you, Norman?" Grantchester didn't wait for an answer. "He just sleeps with seven intravenous drips plugged into him, trickling in various nutrients, hormones, and chemicals to make sure his system remains in balance. It's a great deal of work.

"The result, however, is a soldier with highly specialized abilities. Not telepathy, unfortunately," he said with a sigh, "but once he establishes physical contact, Norman gains a certain amount of control over the brain. It's only very basic, of course—knocking people out, preventing them from activating their powers, that sort of thing. Once he has more intimate contact, however, he can work with a great deal more finesse. At that point, he can begin to affect memories."

Myfanwy fidgeted uncomfortably in her seat at the thought of Norman's probative members gaining intimate contact with her.

"Yes, Norman's tricks have proven very useful in our little endeavor," said Grantchester. "We would have been revealed several times if some selective editing had not taken place. Rarely anything on your scale, of course. If people had started popping up with amnesia all over the place, well, questions would have been asked. But sometimes a person sees or hears something they shouldn't, and you can't just kill them. That's when Norman steps in and erases a few incriminating memories. It's a pity that the process of creating this sort of operative is so difficult or we could have had several instead of just the one. But Norman's work has proven quite sufficient for our needs—with one notable exception." Grantchester stopped, and looked at her piercingly.

"That evening, Norman was going about his duty—with relative ease, correct, Norman?" The gangly boy nodded his head. "He'd canceled your powers and was wiping out your personality. We felt that you'd be much less likely to strike out at anybody if you had no memories. He finished, and you were laid out on the sofa, with your eyes fluttering away (as they do in these circumstances), and we were tending to the shattered Retainers and getting ready to transport you to a laboratory facility when the most extraordinary thing happened.

"You sat up, shrieking.

"Generally, Myfanwy, those who have been subject to Norman's manipulations are unable to do anything afterward. Especially in the case of complete erasure. The mind is too busy reacting to its forcible deletion to muster up an actual response. The personality is dissolving and continues to do so for an hour before a new, more pliable person emerges. So we were shocked at your actions. That screaming was, well, uncanny. But not so uncanny as the psychic assault that slammed down upon us. It was like a hammer smashing my head. When Norman and I roused ourselves, several minutes had passed, and you were gone—presumably shambling around the halls of the Rookery.

"Obviously, this would not do. The odds of your being able to communicate what you knew before you lost it were slim, but still unacceptable. We could not take the risk that you would encounter any members of the Checquy, so I dispatched my team of loyal Retainers to the passages within the Rookery.

"As it turned out, none of them ever came back," said Grantchester tightly. "Several were found dead in a park in Pinner, and I was obliged to send a cleanup crew after them. Oh, we have your car, by the way. Several other operatives simply never reported in, and I assumed that you had eliminated them as well." Myfanwy thought of the rotting corpses down in the tunnel that led to the garage but said nothing. "And then there was the disastrous incident in the bank. Those poor souls have had to undergo extensive therapy—both physiological and psychological—as a result of your attack on them. It was a pity too, as they were the most able infiltration team in my possession. They had tracked you to the hotel after, in a stroke of brilliance, you used your card in the hotel's ATM to check your bank balance. They listened in on your driver's radio in order to get to the bank before you, after you took a bewilderingly convoluted route."

"I happened to be taking in some of the sights," said Myfanwy with dignity. "And how do you know what route I took?"

"This *is* London," said Grantchester. "The ring of steel? We have enough cameras in the city that I could have put together a mini-series on your trip to the bank. We lost you after that, however. Our attention was on that team you left comatose.

"We had never been certain of the extent to which you had lost your memory. Norman swore up and down that he had done the job thoroughly—that all vestiges of your identity had been denatured, leaving us with a blank slate. You would retain your skills and some of your education, but the thoughts and memories that made you Myfanwy Thomas were gone. He was positive.

"However, he'd also been certain that after he was finished with you, you'd be completely incapacitated. And the corpses scattered liberally around London definitely disproved *that* assertion."

He sighed, seeming rather put out.

"In any case, you turned up at work that Monday looking like you'd been through a war. And I'll admit, I had a little bit of a panic. I immediately activated the listening devices in your office and had you monitored constantly. If you'd done anything that indicated you remembered—if you'd made any accusations—well, there are contingency plans for seizing control of the Checquy ahead of schedule. It would have been messy, and risky, but I think we might have carried the day.

"But you did your job and never brought up anything unfortunate. You seemed a bit confused by things, a little hesitant when it came to routine matters, but I thought that you might have lost only a few days of memory, or perhaps even hours. After all, you knew who you were and did your job competently. Gestalt, who did not know about your memory modification, had no idea anything was going on, although he noticed that you were more assertive than usual."

"You didn't tell Gestalt?"

"The fewer people who know secrets, the easier the secrets are to keep," said Grantchester. "And besides, I wasn't certain. But thanks to your little exposition this evening, I now know that Norman was right—you are not her. And whoever you may have grown to be—well, you have already proven that you know too much." Myfanwy was again conscious of the long fingers on her neck. "It's a pity, in a way. We should love to find out the whole story, but at this point, I'm inclined to cut my losses."

"You're going to erase me?" Myfanwy asked shakily. "Just like you got rid of Thomas's personality?"

"Or lack thereof," said Grantchester. "And yes, we shall. But obviously it's not going to be done the same way. Before, we wanted a cooperative, malleable mind in your body. One that could communicate effectively and prove useful. Clearly, that's a risk we cannot take again. This time, Norman will clear out your brain entirely. The next person to look out of those eyes will be a complete newborn. We'll keep you alive for some tests—tracing some impulses, seeing you react in a laboratory setting. And then later, they'll saw you up into pieces suitable for viewing through a microscope."

"Excuse me?" she said.

"We were always going to make a thorough study of you," said the Bishop expansively. "You terrify the Grafters. A woman who can control living matter. Their great advantage—the weapons with which they can smite the Checquy—are all biological. They wouldn't be able to shoot their guns if you decided that you didn't want them to. Any enhancements their agents possess could tear themselves out at your command. You, my dear, are their worst nightmare. And also their greatest possibility. You're our uranium. If we can reverse-engineer you, there's nothing we can't achieve."

"The Estate scientists couldn't," pointed out Myfanwy tensely. Norman's fingers were tracing their way down, inside her coveralls to her shoulders.

"The Estate scientists are children with Legos compared to these people." Grantchester snorted contemptuously. "The Grafters have been doing this for centuries. They mapped the human genome when Queen Victoria was still on the throne. They surveyed the territory of the human body and built skyscrapers!" His eyes looked beyond her. "Ah, perhaps you would like to speak with my other guests before we have you obliterated?" Out of the corner of her eye, Myfanwy saw two figures passing around the desk to flank Grantchester.

Eliza and Alex Gestalt eyed Myfanwy with utter loathing.

"Of course, Eliza might not appreciate some of the comments you made about her postpartum depression, but you might like to congratulate the parents of my child," he said with an amused look. "I shall leave now, but Gestalt has expressed a desire to watch as Norman does his work. Good evening," he said, getting up. Myfanwy could hear his steps as he walked through the room, opened up a portrait, and climbed the stairs hidden behind it.

"So, bitch Thomas," said the Gestalt siblings in unison. "I can't tell you how pleasant it is to see you pinioned this time. I shall definitely enjoy this after a week of having to hide in Grantchester's residence."

"Do you know what it's been like?" the Gestalt sister demanded. "Afraid to go into my other bodies in case the Gallows torturers are mutilating them? In case I open my eyes just at the moment that they put them out?" She leaned forward across the desk and punched Myfanwy awkwardly in the side of the head.

"This is going to be *so* satisfying," the brother said.

Myfanwy didn't say anything, not even to lie to them about what had happened to the other bodies. In point of fact, nothing had yet been done to Teddy and Robert. Currently, they were restrained, with blindfolds, in soundproof rooms. Alrich and some of the scientists and torturers were attempting to work out an approach that would let them take advantage of Gestalt's hive mind and torture all four of the bodies simultaneously. Myfanwy had smiled weakly at their enthusiastic ideas and resolved not to have anything to do with it. Now she was rather wishing she'd chipped in.

Norman kept his hand in contact with Myfanwy as he turned her chair toward him and then drew her up to her feet. His eyes stared into hers, and she flinched away. Her skin was numb where he touched it, and he pulled her closer. The cold spread down to the tops of her arms as he grasped them within her clothes so that she could not struggle. If she were to kick, it would only be a blow on the shins, like a child throwing a tantrum. Myfanwy resisted the urge to scream as he opened his mouth and leaned over her. His breath wafted into her face, and she wrinkled her nose at its chemical odor. He smelled just like the Grafter in the club.

Norman's tongue, a pallid purple, suddenly bristled with long white fibers. The hairlike tendrils pressed against her lips like a half-remembered nightmare. His lips grated against her own as he shoved his tongue into her mouth. She gagged as it scraped down her throat.

Myfanwy's eyes rolled around, adding images to her memory that she knew would soon be dissolved. To one side stood the girl, watching them impassively. Behind her were the simultaneous breaths of Gestalt. Her attacker's scaly cheeks lightly grazed her own as he greedily probed her mind.

It's coming, she thought. *The end of me.* Her mind hyperfocused, and every detail gained significance. The warmth of her shoes, the coarse chafing of the ankle holster, the smoothness of her coveralls, and the comfortable warmth of her coat. Her fingers caressed the softness of her clothes. *It's all going to be gone,* she thought, and then she felt something under her hands.

She dug her right hand into her coat pocket and came out clutching something. *Do it!* she thought desperately. *Fight! It's worth a try!* She could feel the boy drawing himself back, getting ready to smash forward with all the force of his vile powers. Frantically, she shifted her hand to get a better grip on the object. Norman felt her movement and hesitated. She clenched her fist and, staring into her attacker's eyes, stabbed his thigh with the epi-pen that Thomas had put in the pocket of every coat she owned in case she was stung by a bee.

There was a click.

A spring-loaded needle glided through the membrane in the tip of the epi-pen, piercing the cloth of Norman's trousers. The needle slid through his skin and delivered 0.3 milligrams of epinephrine into his system.

The medication roared into Norman's bloodstream, binding itself to receptors in his body. Myfanwy watched as his pupils dilated. She could hear his heart rate increase. Chemicals shifted, and the man-made additions to his body screamed. His grip on her powers loosened, then failed entirely. She reached out with her mind and punctured the shields around his consciousness. They both stood, unmoving, joined in a horrible kiss, and Myfanwy felt him dying. All the delicate systems that the Grafters had stitched into him were failing, the fragile balance destroyed completely. *Not yet,* she thought. Under her command, his heart kept beating, and his legs held him up. His tongue, with all its fibers, retracted into his mouth, but their lips were still locked. *Don't want to give the game away just yet.*

First things first.

The little girl raised her gun and, against her will, fired at the Gestalt siblings. Alex was hit in the shoulder and fell to the floor with a startled cry; Eliza was struck in the head and neck, and she stumbled back against the glass. Cracks spiderwebbed out around her, and then she was gone, falling back through the glass and into the night. A low horrible wail rose up from her brother, who was flailing on the ground.

The little girl was staring stupidly at the gun in her hand when Gestalt's remaining free body, screaming with rage, clawed his way up the desk. He drew a gun and emptied the clip into the little girl. She crumpled to the ground. Gestalt scrabbled weakly at the desk but seemed to be going into shock and fell back. Myfanwy made sure he couldn't stand up, and then turned her attention to the next matter at hand.

Okay, now you can die, she thought, and let Norman's heart stop beating.

"Oh," she sighed, and there was a hint of a moan in that sound as the body of Norman fell away from her. She rubbed the back of her hand against her mouth, and it came away with traces of blood. She could feel the skin around her eyes swelling and bruising. *This is familiar,* she thought wearily, and leaned against Grantchester's desk, gasping.

"You bitch" came a despairing voice, and Myfanwy looked around at the floor behind the desk.

"Oh, hey, Gestalt," she said wearily.

"You fucking bitch—do you realize what you've done?" he asked. "She was the only one who could bear a new child, and now I'll die."

"What?" she asked, dully, taking deep breaths.

"I can't get any new bodies! For a new child to be part of me, both parents have to be my bodies, and now..." He started to weep brokenly. "Now, the only body that could carry a child is dead, and I'm going to *die!*" Myfanwy stared at him in horror at the implications of Gestalt's words. Her eyes fell to a Grantchester family photo on the desk. It had been bad enough knowing that the blond baby held Gestalt's mind, but that it was a product of incest, with one mind forming both parents and the new child—her stomach turned at the thought. *My God, Gestalt could have been immortal—an army.* She stared down at the weeping, bleeding individual on the floor and didn't know what to feel.

I'll have to bring the baby in and let the Court decide what to do with it. And Gestalt doesn't know about the amnesia... But fuck! Grantchester! She picked up Norman's gun and eyed the portraits before picking up the phone to call for help.

"Myfanwy" came Grantchester's voice over the line.

"Conrad," she breathed.

"I was watching on the camera," said the Bishop. "I'm very impressed—you are clearly far more capable than your predecessor. I don't suppose you would care to join me?" His effrontery took her breath away, and Myfanwy didn't trust herself to reply. "No? Well, I suppose I should have expected that. But in any case, it is evident that I have been beaten in this particular battle. Accordingly, I am withdrawing from the Apex and heading for a slightly more relaxing clime. I made plans for such a possibility long ago." *Looks like Thomas wasn't the only one who liked to be prepared,* thought Myfanwy.

"But rest assured, Rook Myfanwy Thomas or whoever you think you are"—and here his voice became hard—"I have spent years within the Checquy paving the way for the coming of the Grafters. They will come, and they will triumph, and then you and I shall have words." There was a click at the other end of the line, and he was gone.

Myfanwy put the phone down with weak fingers. In a minute, she would alert security and have Gestalt (or what remained of Gestalt) arrested. She would find out how Eckhart's raid had gone, and summon the Court to hear what had happened. She would check on Bronwyn, and call Shantay with the news. And she would mourn for Ingrid and Li'l Pawn Alan.

She would do all those things, but first she needed a minute to collect the thoughts she'd come so close to losing.

41

Wait, so Li'l Pawn Alan can kick arse?" said Myfanwy incredulously in the back of the car. "Against a soldier with a gun?"

"Li'l Pawn Alan can break down the composition of inorganic material, rendering it brittle," said Ingrid primly. "If he's touching the material, he can affect a portion the size of your torso. If he's *not* touching it, then he can only affect a very small amount. But it's enough to cause a trigger to shatter. Fortunately for us."

"Yes, you look fortunate," said Myfanwy, eyeing Ingrid's arm sling and swollen black eye.

"I'm not complaining," said Ingrid.

"You got shot!" exclaimed Myfanwy.

"It didn't hit bone," said Ingrid. "And while getting belted in the face and then shot in the arm is not a treat, it's certainly preferable to getting executed."

After Myfanwy had caught her breath in Grantchester's office and called security, she'd found the watch office in an uproar. Apparently, a Rookery graphic designer working overtime had walked past the entrance to the command suite and seen an adolescent Pawn fighting with a security guard while the Rook's executive assistant bled, unconscious, on the floor. Uncertain of which side to take, the designer had elected to cover all the bases, and she'd shocked both combatants into unconsciousness with her electricity-casting abilities before calling security.

"I'm just glad that they were able to patch you up so quickly that you could come for part of the Court meeting!" said Myfanwy.

"Some medic plugged the bullet hole with a resin that he extruded out of his glands," said Ingrid darkly. "*Directly* out of his glands."

"Ew," said Myfanwy. "Which glands?"

"I don't want to talk about it," said Ingrid. "The meeting was interesting though."

"It was one of the most awkward meetings I've ever had." Myfanwy yawned. "I thought they all took it pretty well, considering."

"The Court has been subject to a number of shocks recently," pointed out Ingrid. "They were all fairly pliable, especially after Chevalier Eckhart produced the photographs of the Grafter bodies."

"Well, yeah, but the revelations about Grantchester—I mean, he was a member of the Court!"

"So was Rook Gestalt."

"True. But Gestalt was a member of the Court whom no one actually liked," amended Myfanwy.

"I always rather fancied Bishop Grantchester," confessed Ingrid. "He used to flirt outrageously whenever he came to the Rookery."

"He *was* hot," admitted Myfanwy. She looked out the window. It was nearing dawn, and London was quiet, with only a few stray cars out. The convoy of limousine and attendant motorcycles was a tiny parade of movement in the streets. The coffee she had finally been permitted at the meeting of the Court was fighting a losing battle against the cumulative effects of a night of clubbing, a morning of testing, an afternoon of being absorbed by a flesh cube, and an evening confrontation with a traitor.

As it turned out, the bureaucratic rehashing of events had taken almost as long as the events themselves. Eckhart's account of his assault on the Grafter home base had included a clinical description of his killing the skinless Belgian. Myfanwy had listened, open-mouthed, as Eckhart explained that the Grafter leader had grown blades of bone from his arms and that the two of them had fought in a chamber in which giant sacs and cocoons hung from the ceiling.

Pods had burst open, warriors had sprung forth, and the Barghests had fought them off while Eckhart and Graaf Gerd de Leeuwen dueled, metal scraping against bone. Two members of the

Barghests had been traitors, and they turned on their comrades. Their Grafter enhancements had not saved them. Finally, without any emotion, Joshua told them how he tore down a chain from the ceiling, shaped it into a javelin, and placed it with great precision through the skinless Belgian's head.

After Eckhart's description, the conversation had turned to Myfanwy's adventures in Reading, followed by Myfanwy's adventures with Grantchester. At that point, she'd done some rapid thinking and come to the conclusion that perhaps she could avoid admitting to the memory loss. She'd had to walk a narrow and confusing tightrope to explain what happened, and in the end she'd gotten out of giving a fully detailed exposition only by feigning light-headedness. The bruises around her eyes had everyone looking at her strangely, but they'd all been too distracted by the revelations about Grantchester and the Grafters to draw any incriminating parallels between her current injuries and those of two weeks ago. Myfanwy had been deliberately vague about Norman's capabilities, and no mention had been made about anyone's losing his or her memory.

Finally, it had been agreed that a full debriefing would take place the next day after everyone had gotten some sleep.

"And you never thought of telling the Court about your amnesia?" asked Ingrid. "After all, there are only four other members left. Farrier already knows, and Eckhart and Alrich seem quite fond of you. Would it have been such a terrible thing?" Myfanwy paused for a moment and remembered the end of the meeting.

As Myfanwy was leaving, Lady Farrier had caught her arm. Throughout the report, the co-leader of the Checquy had been silent, her eyes narrowed in thought. "In the beginning, I was worried," said the Lady. "I thought that in paying back my debt to your predecessor, I might have made a horrible mistake. Might have put the realm in danger." She hesitated. "If I had observed anything in your performance that was harmful to the Checquy, I would have had you terminated. But I can see now that, even though it was done out of a sense of obligation, I did the right thing in permitting you to take the place of Rook Thomas." She shook Myfanwy's hand. "I look forward to working with you in the future, Rook Thomas." Myfanwy smiled awkwardly. "And who knows? You may soon rise beyond the rank of Rook!" She laughed a laugh that had no humor in it and swept away, leaving Myfanwy staring after her.

"It was tempting," admitted Myfanwy. "It can be exhausting, you know, hiding the truth every minute. And I'd been prepared to tell everything when I exposed Grantchester."

"So why didn't you?"

"Because I like the job," said Myfanwy. "And it appears I can do it quite well. But the Checquy is an organization of hundreds of people. There are those who have been trained all their lives to do this sort of thing. Lots of them are older than me, with more experience. I just don't believe that if all the Court members knew the truth, they would let me keep my job. No matter how much they like me."

"I think you bring an advantage by not having all the familiarity and indoctrination," said Ingrid. "You think outside the box."

"Thank you," said Myfanwy. "And if it reaches a point where it comes down to risking the Checquy's security, then I'll tell them about my memory loss. Or maybe just step down." The two women smiled at each other.

"I'm surprised that Security Chief Clovis is still providing you with such intensive protection," Ingrid mused, looking at the motor-cycles accompanying them.

"Joshua Eckhart may have killed my skinless friend with a steel javelin to the face, but there may still be Grafters in the city—to say nothing of their endeavors throughout the country. And Grantchester got away neatly, although we have his wife and that little Gestalt baby in custody." Myfanwy shuddered as she remembered when the appre-hended Gestalt body was brought before the Court. She was not going to forget the malice that had stared out of those baby eyes or the high-pitched, slurred obscenities that had come out of a soft infant mouth.

"Did Mrs. Grantchester know what her child really was?" asked Ingrid.

"She says no," said Myfanwy. "And I believe her. Grantchester was insanely secretive—he didn't share anything with anybody unless he had to. And besides, would *you* take a Gestalt baby into your life knowing what it was?"

"It would be well behaved," mused Ingrid. "And toilet trained from day one. But no. So I suppose not everything is wrapped up neatly."

"Absolutely not. Plus, there's still Camp Caius to worry about," pointed out Myfanwy. Even as they spoke, the Barghests were planning an assault on the facility; they had orders to take as few lives as possible. *I don't know how we're going to rehabilitate those children,* she thought, *but I'm going to try.* She could not bring herself to pity Norman, but the memory of the dead girl with the talons was dark in her mind.

. "And you're all right?" said Ingrid. When she'd arrived at the Apex and seen Myfanwy's black eyes, she'd panicked. But at least this time Myfanwy's lips hadn't picked up too much scrapage from Norman's harshly scaled mouth. Myfanwy shuddered at the thought and felt a moment of pity for Thomas, who hadn't been so lucky. *Locked to that mouth, feeling your thoughts slurped out.*

"I think so," said Myfanwy. "I was able to take Norman out before he could tamper with my memories. And I was checked by the medical team in the Apex afterward, bringing my number of hospital visits today to three."

"Are you certain you don't want me to stay in the Rookery with you?" asked Ingrid.

"No, it's fine," insisted Myfanwy. "Once I'm back, the entire place is going into lockdown for the rest of the night. I'm planning to go straight up to the residence, fall into bed, and stay there for many, many hours. Unless there's a whole rash of flesh-cubey things across the nation, I don't want to get any wake-up calls."

Ingrid nodded, smiling.

When the car finally deposited her at the basement entrance, Myfanwy paused.

"I'm really glad you're all right, Ingrid," she said. "Best moment of my life, when they told me you were alive."

"Thank you, Rook Thomas," said Ingrid. The two women clasped hands, and then Myfanwy waved good-bye to her assistant.

One of the security guards approached her diffidently. "Rook Thomas, we're ready to go into lockdown," he said quietly. "The watch office has set up a center in the Apex, so it will just be you and the security staff once you give the word."

"Close it up, please," she said and yawned, covering her mouth with her hand. The guard nodded and signaled to his compatriot in the booth. Heavy metal shutters began to slide down inside the garage door. She reminded herself to activate the security systems for the Rooks' private passages—at least the ones that she knew about. She wondered if she should worry about Grantchester's other secret entrances and decided to sleep in the guest room of the residence. Maybe she would put some cans in front of the door.

The halls of the Rookery were dim as Myfanwy walked toward her office. A few security guards on their rounds nodded to her, but for the most part, she enjoyed the quiet privacy of the building. In the weeks since she'd arrived at the Checquy, the place had come to feel like home.

I think it's all going to work out, thought Myfanwy. *I can keep my secrets. I just need to figure out how to explain everything without admitting that I lost my memory. But I'll do that over a very late breakfast. I don't care if it's three in the afternoon when I wake up. I am going to order the biggest, most glorious English breakfast in the history of mankind, and I am going to eat it in the living room, looking out at my gorgeous view. I'll come up with a tight, rational explanation for all of this. Then I'll call Bronwyn so we can make plans to meet up with my brother. And then I'm going to call a decorator and get the entire residence redone. We'll knock through walls and check for all the secret little passages.*

But first, I am going to bed.

She was humming as she opened her office door and turned on the lights. She was totally unprepared to find a massive, dripping, naked man seated behind her desk.

"Good evening, Rook Myfanwy Thomas. Please allow me to introduce myself. I am Graaf Ernst von Suchtlen."

★   ★   ★

Myfanwy stared at him. *Of course this happened,* she thought wearily. *After the longest day and night in recorded history, of course there's a naked man in my office. And he's a Grafter.*
Well, at least this one's got his skin on, if nothing else.

"So, where did you spring from?" Myfanwy asked casually, spinning out tendrils of her mind to ensnare the nervous system of the naked Belgian. It was an effort. After her nightmarish snogging session with Norman, her brain was tired. Still, she was surprised when her powers slid off his flesh. *He's the boss,* she thought. *He's got the best system they can design. Maybe de Leeuwen would have had the same immunity if he'd had the chance to grow some skin.*

"You may recall receiving a heart in the mail a little while ago?" asked the Belgian. Myfanwy nodded noncommittally. Thomas had received it, but she'd read about it.

"Yes, well, that was mine."

Myfanwy took a moment to process this information. "I'm sorry, I don't understand. Did you stop by to pick it up?" she asked.

"No, I am sorry—I do not think I have explained well enough. I have grown myself from the heart, in your scientists' laboratory freezer."

"I see. And how long did that take?" Myfanwy asked faintly.

"The process began twenty-four hours after your scientists examined it," said the Grafter dismissively.

"Well, that is impressive," said Myfanwy. She took stock of her situation and grimly realized that she had left the ankle gun back at the Apex. Almost as distressing was the fact that she was going to have to sit in one of the deliberately uncomfortable chairs, since the couch was too far away. Making a break for it was obviously out of the question. "You weren't worried that they might notice anything strange about the heart when they were examining it?" she asked.

"We are discreet," said the Belgian. "And no one in your organization is good enough to detect that technology. It is very new, and very experimental." Myfanwy nodded. "I'm sorry that I have taken your chair," he continued. "While I was waiting for you, I found that it was much more comfortable than the ones in front of your desk. But if you would like, I could move." To her horror, he began to stand up.

"No! It's fine," she exclaimed. "Please, don't get up." *Let's keep the nudity behind the desk.* Plus, she was not keen to see the mess he had left on her chair with all that fluid dripping off him. *I'm going to have to get a new chair,* she decided. *Provided I survive.* Myfanwy sat down in the uncomfortable chair that did not have a sheen of slime on it.

"May I ask how you managed to get up from the scientists' lab fridge to my office, stark naked, without attracting the attention of any of the staff?"

"Well, it *is* the night," he pointed out. "And the cleaning staff has gone home. Your security guards do regular patrols, but it's not too difficult to avoid them when one can hang from the ceiling. And this body is invisible to video cameras."

"Cool. And now you are here in my office."

"Yes," he agreed. There was a pause that Myfanwy found uncomfortable but that did not seem to faze him.

"I'm sorry, but *why* are you in my office?" she asked finally.

"Oh, yes. Well, I have come here in secret to speak with you. It may surprise you, Myfanwy Thomas, to learn that for the past few decades the Wetenschappelijk Broederschap van Natuurkundigen have been maneuvering themselves into positions of power within the Checquy," he said. "We have also set up a training and experimentation operation, funded by Britain, forcibly drafting British citizens as soldiers.

"The Broederschap has established a weapon of mass destruction based on new applications of our technology; it's powered by yet more British citizens within a prominent British city. Indeed, we have placed operatives throughout your organization, on all levels, including"—and here he paused impressively—"within the Court of the Checquy!"

"Wow," she said flatly. "So, um, how?" she asked. "How did you infiltrate us?"

"Oh, well, it is easy enough to turn your Retainers," he said, a little thrown by her lack of response. "They get sick of being treated like they're second best. No matter how good they are, they will always be normal, and they can never rise beyond a certain rank. Your Pawns strut around with their special abilities, gliding down the hallways and typing with their tentacles. And those poor Retainers watch them enviously, knowing they will never be respected.

"Of course, we haven't been able to turn all of your Retainers. But for those who feel such envy, we offer an opportunity for growth. Not so they can strike against you, but so that just once they can look in the mirror and see a person who is remarkable."

"And the members of the Court?" Myfanwy asked.

"Well," sighed the naked Belgian. "The more extraordinary the person, the more mundane and predictable the bait." He leaned back in the chair. "Wealth. Power. The traditional bribes. One of them has received a substantially increased life span."

Ah, yes, immortality. That *old chestnut,* thought Myfanwy, mentally rolling her eyes.

"And that is how we gained such power over you," he finished.

"How sad," said Myfanwy. "And what now, Graaf Ernst von Suchtlen? Revenge for the indignities forced upon you after the Isle of Wight? Will you smash the Checquy? Without us in the picture, you would be free to take control of England. And then America! I don't know how strong you all have become, but you might be able to take the Croatoan forces, especially if we were not there to back them up. There are many possibilities for you in a world without the Checquy." Myfanwy was proud of herself for remaining calm, but as she spoke, she became abruptly aware of the implications of the Checquy falling.

"We were never interested in invasion." The Belgian snorted. "Not after that disastrous first effort, which, I would like to point out, was done almost entirely at the instigation of the rulers of my country. No, this was a feint, showing you something with one hand while putting a dagger to your throat with the other. The Checquy controls a secret world. An invasion? Please!" He snorted again in disgust.

"The world has grown smaller since the last time we matched

wits, Myfanwy Thomas. We cannot keep the conquest of a country a secret, and we cannot allow our existence to become public knowledge. But neither can the Checquy. Some secrets can be kept, and this one is just about the right size." He raised an eyebrow, and she swallowed, calculating his meaning.

"So, you will take over the Checquy?" she asked. "By force?"

"That idea has found some favor in the higher echelons of the Broederschap," he said, his voice expressionless. Myfanwy thought of the skinless Belgian floating in his tank. There had been hate and resentment in his voice and a lust for violence in his body.

"I'll bet it has," she said.

For a moment, they stared at each other across the desk. A soul that was centuries old regarded a mind that had been alive only a few weeks.

"Graaf von Suchtlen, may I ask a question?" He nodded slightly. "You are one of the two founders of the Grafters?"

"One of the initial investors, yes," he said, nodding. The fluid had thinned on him somewhat, and his muscles were now more prominent.

"You are centuries old and command all the knowledge and power of Wetenschappelijk Broederschap van Natuurkundigen—a force as great as any in history. In your lifetime, the leadership of the Checquy has passed from hand to hand, while you have only gained in experience. I cannot guess at the powers and abilities that have been built into your body, but I suspect that you are the beneficiary of every advantage your organization can give you. The forces that you have described are powerful enough to overwhelm the Checquy without your ever needing to leave Belgium. So why have you come to me now? Secret, alone, and naked?"

The Grafter nodded faintly and smiled.

"That is the question," he said. "And what do you think is the answer?"

"You know that the Checquy would never surrender to you," said Myfanwy. "Even with traitors in the Court, it would not be an option."

"This is true."

"We would have to fight. We might win that dreadful war, but England would never be the same. It would be difficult to conceal an international battle, and that," she said softly, "is our mandate. To protect, in secrecy.

"And you too have come here in secret. Concealing your presence not only from the Checquy but also from your own partner." The massive man in her chair was suddenly still, and Myfanwy realized how small she was compared to him. His fingers were tight on the wood of her desk, and though she could not control his muscles, she could sense the strength within him.

"You have come here, Mr. von Suchtlen, because you do not want to fight us. You do not want to hide from us any longer. You know that we would not—*could not*—permit you to exist freely. Not with your history. I believe you have come to talk terms, not of surrender, but of alliance. You wish to join our organizations together, do you not?"

He smiled.

Perhaps I retained a bit of Rook Thomas's diplomatic skills after all, she thought.

Graaf von Suchtlen settled back comfortably and told her a story.

I remember it was mid-autumn. It was cold, of course, and the leaves were falling in a torrent on the road leading to my door. I was in a reflective mood, sitting on the front stairs of my country house, wrapped in a fur, drinking something hot and sweet. I was the Count of Suchtlen. I was thirty-eight, wealthy, and, thanks to an easily spooked horse and some inconveniently sharp rocks, I had been missing the bottom half of my left leg for eight months.

It had been a genuinely dreadful year, even apart from the loss of my leg. One of my sisters had died in childbirth, and a fire had destroyed the homes of several of my tenants. Politically, it had been a tricky time, with several people in Brussels—mostly Flemings—disagreeing with some of my ideas. Still, I'd had a few exceptionally successful financial ventures and was contemplating withdrawing from politics and seeing about getting a wife and having some children.

And then, down the lane, through the storm of leaves, my cousin came trotting on his horse. He was ten years my junior, the Count of Leeuwen, and not nearly as wealthy as I. He'd lost some money in a few highly unsuccessful ventures—one of them an elaborate con. Once or twice, he had borrowed money from me and been slow in paying it back. But I was fond of him nonetheless, and he was family. We had gone hunting together several times before I lost my leg and had enjoyed each other's company, although he was extraordinarily excitable.

I welcomed him, and he helped me inside while a servant attended to his horse. We were soon settled comfortably by a fire, drinking wine and engaged in the traditional chitchat. I noticed that he seemed distracted throughout the conversation, and I braced myself for his inevitable request for money.

"Ernst," he said, looking at me suddenly, "I've found a rather remarkable investment opportunity that I think you may be interested in."

"Oh?" I asked, trying to sound surprised and (I suspect) failing. He caught my resignation, and his intensity wavered for a moment. He nodded and leaned forward in his chair, casually drawing a belt knife.

"Yes, I concede that I've had some bad luck in business," he said. "But Cousin, I believe this could redefine our future!" He was excited now, and I sat back in my chair. I hadn't liked his use of the word our. And I particularly didn't like the way he was holding the knife.

"Like that business with the man from Florence?" I asked dryly.

"No, not like the business with the man from Florence!" he snapped, his cheeks flushing. The business with the Italian had almost lost him his house and had led to his fiancée's breaking off their engagement.

"All right, Gerd, I'm sorry," I said, casting an uneasy look at the knife.

"This is different," he said. I began to wonder if he was drunk. Or possibly mad.

"I believe you," I said, cautiously reaching down for my own belt knife. My fingers closed around the handle and I drew the blade.

He smiled. "I'll show you."

And he cut off his own forefinger.

"Holy Christ!" I exclaimed. Gerd's eyes were beatific, with an ecstasy *that I found almost as unnerving as the blood gushing onto my carpet. I drew in breath to shout for someone—whether to restrain him or clean up the blood, I wasn't sure—but he held up his unmutilated hand.*

"Wait," he said calmly and I noticed, with a small thrill of horror, that he was still holding his sliced-off digit. Even more distressing, the severed end of the finger was turning a strange sky blue. I darted a glance at his wound and saw that it was turning the same color.

I'll confess that at this point the possibility of satanic possession began to occur to me, and I tightened my grasp on my knife. I was bracing myself to stab the blade into his eye and call for the servants when he brought the severed finger up to his hand. Before my eyes, the blue patches writhed, and I watched tendrils reach out to one another. I heard a faint sucking sound, and then his hand was whole again. He stared at his fingers with rapt fascination as he wiggled them all.

"Holy Christ," I repeated softly. He smiled seraphically.

Needless to say, I was intrigued, if still slightly concerned that my cousin was trafficking with the devil. It occurred to me, however, that if this was not an abomination in the eyes of God that would lead to our eternal damnation, it represented a marvelous business opportunity.

So it was with an open mind, and a couple of extremely large fellows from my estates as backup, that I accompanied my cousin to his residence, where a handful of grubby men were engaged in some extremely complicated experiments in a barn. They were too socially awkward and uninterested in me to be recruiting agents of the devil. Rather than making any sort of overtures for my soul, they spent several hours explaining to me exactly what their work consisted of. Their earnest descriptions gave me a headache, but their optimism about providing me with a new leg was tremendously exciting.

I watched as they sliced mice and hounds and horses in half and then proceeded to glue them back together. Gerd was entranced, and my mind raced with the possibilities. We worked out a deal: I agreed to fund their research, and they signed several binding contracts. Then they returned to their work, which we later moved to one of my more remote properties.

And so it all began.

★   ★   ★

Well, that's fascinating," said Myfanwy. "And a few centuries later, you're sitting naked in my chair. The chain of events is obvious."

"You know the rest of the history," said the Belgian coldly. "I have no doubt that the Checquy has it documented thoroughly. Our rise to power, our connection to the government, the attempt at conquest, the forcible dismantling."

"Yeah, although after that, things get a little shady. A few hints of your presence in Europe," she said. "But you were careful."

"We were obliged to be," the Belgian replied ruefully. "So many of our primary resources had been lost. We were stripped of our estates, and we came close to being utterly destroyed. Fortunately, I have always endeavored to be prepared. Positions to fall back to, hidden funds and resources. It took us several decades to build ourselves up to where we had been technologically. Several of our master *handwerksmannen* had died during the Checquy's counterstrike. Key experiments were destroyed. Both Gerd and I were forced to watch ourselves be killed. We were wearing new bodies by that time, of course. We sat ten feet from the kings of my country and yours and toasted our own corpses. And then, when the gasps had finished and the blood was cleaned up, we walked past the Court of the Checquy and the elite of two countries and out into the world.

"We rebuilt, retrained, and continued to innovate. Our research was on a smaller scale, of course. Our wealth was far more modest. We had to be even more secretive. But still, we grew in power. And then... Well, then I'm afraid that's when the corruption set in.

"Some of our *handwerksmannen* are fascinated by the concept of corruption. They have dedicated centuries to weeding it out of the human body, to staying its inevitable progression. They always chatter on about it. The molecular level. Enzymes. Organs. Unfortunately, there was so much focus on the small scale that the larger corruptions were missed. Instability crept in. Priorities became... skewed," said the Grafter, and he shifted uncomfortably in his seat. "Some of us became erratic."

"Erratic?" asked Myfanwy. *Because you were so completely sane to begin with,* she thought. *Nothing says normal like invading England on horses with antlers.*

"One of our premier scholars, Jan, developed an alarming penchant for cutting off his own toes. They grew back, of course, but you could hardly have a conversation without having to watch him take off a shoe."

"Charming."

"I think," the Belgian mused, "some people simply may not be meant to live so long."

"You don't think it might have been all the genetic messings-about?" asked Myfanwy through a yawn. Tension and fear were fighting a losing battle against exhaustion.

"Yes, well...no, I don't like that idea," he said.

"No, of course not. How many bodies have you had?"

"You lose count after a while," the Grafter replied. "I have sometimes thought that we may attract the wrong people. My cousin has a troubleshooter, a young man named Van Syoc. He is a monster, with disturbing habits."

Yeah, like tearing the faces off prostitutes, thought Myfanwy. She thought about telling him that Van Syoc was dead but decided against it.

"In any case," said the naked man, "I became concerned—"

"About the toe thing?"

"Well, no, not so much the toe thing."

"You weren't concerned about the toes?" asked Myfanwy, mentally kicking herself for prolonging the conversation.

"No, it wasn't really doing him any harm," he said dismissively. "It was not even interfering with his work. What concerned me about the toes was that it was a new habit—he had gone several hundred years without doing it. Now it was compulsive."

"Uh-huh." *As long as it didn't interfere with his work.*

"Yes, but I am digressing. I had noticed some alarming trends. Communiqués were bypassing me. Gerd had become more secretive and was suddenly much more engaged in the details of our international efforts. Previously, he had been content just to oversee the workshops. He has always been keen to enjoy the luxuries in life," the Belgian said, sighing.

Absolutely, thought Myfanwy sourly. *A stretch limousine, a shiny fish tank.*

"He had always been excitable, but now he became fixated on our projects in Britain. I became suspicious, but I did not wish to confront him directly. Not without more evidence. So I arranged to have his *geheimschrijver* detained one evening, when my cousin was at the theater."

"His *geheimschrijver?*" asked Myfanwy.

"Uh, it is his 'secret writer'—secretary," said the Belgian. "I acquired him and had some of my subordinates infiltrate his memory." Myfanwy tensed, thinking of the youth who had been doing a little memory infiltration of his own that evening.

"Guys with scales?" she asked tightly.

"Hm? Oh, no—I know what you are thinking, but those models are only useful for people with standard, unaugmented brains. No, our support staff is augmented to act as communicators—telephones. They tap directly into the phone network through their minds, hacking into the system. We speak to them as if they were the person on the other end of the line, and the words are transferred. When the person we are calling speaks into their telephone, our secretary repeats their words in their voice. It is practically instantaneous, and completely untraceable."

Which explains why Li'l Pawn Alan's compatriots couldn't track the calls, she thought bitterly. *I suppose they can't do faxes—after all, where would they insert them?*

"I watched as they subdued him, insinuated various implements, and downloaded transcriptions. I found, to my intense disappointment, that Gerd had been in contact with our plants in the Checquy, preparing them for a putsch. I must say that one of the double agents in your Court particularly welcomes the prospect of a violent revolution. It is quite unwholesome," he said.

"Frankly," continued the Grafter, "this was a tremendous blow. I had headed their acquisition and indoctrination. It had been my strategy from the beginning. I had personally overseen the establishment of Camp Caius and the development and placement of our fungal weapon of mass destruction. Oh, yes," he said as Myfanwy raised an eyebrow, "it is quite a terrifying little entity. It subjugates human beings and can engulf vast areas once activated."

"With an eye toward marrying our two organizations?" asked Myfanwy dryly. Up until that moment, she had allowed herself to relax. Part of it was weariness, but the Belgian was so pleasant about everything that she'd... well, she hadn't quite forgotten that he was naked and a centuries-old enemy, but she had ceased to hold those facts in the front of her mind. Now his casual mention of the fungus cult in Bath brought back to her the terror of that day. And the dismissive way that he spoke of hacking someone's memory made her shudder.

"Rook Thomas, you must remember that in the eyes of the Broederschap, the Checquy is not a benevolent force. It is the adversary that smashed our efforts and forced our destruction. I was obliged to watch as my homes were razed and my friends killed. My corpse was burned and the ashes were dumped in the ocean. It was only through exceptionally cunning sleight of body that I managed to survive. I will not blush when I tell you that when we emerged from that ordeal, making overtures of peace to the Checquy was not high on our agenda. Indeed, our initial goal was to conceal our existence from you, and then to set about inflicting as much pain as we could."

"So what happened?" asked Myfanwy.

"It is curious how the passing of lifetimes will change a man," mused the Belgian. "For some, apparently, it brings on a compulsion to cut off one's toes. As for me, I found myself forgiving the Checquy. My spite came to seem petty, and as I watched your organization expand and improve, I realized that it represented as good a governing body as could exist in such circumstances. It had flaws, of course, and was subject to the vagaries of humanity, but its goals were noble. I came to hope that we could meet without resentment. Over the years, I broached the subject to my cousin, and over time he grew amenable. I continued the process of infiltration and establishing collaborators in the Checquy. I did *not* do this because I wished to harm you but because the Checquy are still wary of us, and I wanted them to see that it was in their best interests to join with us."

"By making a threat?" asked Myfanwy.

"By demonstrating a position of mutual advantage," said the Belgian diplomatically. "Or perhaps, showing you the stick and the carrot. If we reveal ourselves, and the Checquy decides it cannot countenance our continued existence...well, we have no intention of dying."

"Ah." Myfanwy nodded.

"Recently it became clear that my cousin had become disillusioned with my ideas. He thought our preparations should be used to cripple, rather than..." He trailed off, and shook his head wryly.

"Yes?"

"Rather than to graft."

Myfanwy gave a wan smile.

"He was basing more and more of his choices on personal enmities. A few months ago I learned that the subjects at Camp Caius were selected because their ancestors had been Checquy soldiers at the Isle of Wight. It was petty, and made the operation far more vulnerable than it needed to be. I had a hunch such small revenge was just the tip of the iceberg. And so," continued the Belgian, "I made arrangements to keep my cousin busy for several weeks and had myself transported to see you in order to broker some sort of treaty."

"And you picked the old 'ship a heart to the other party and then grow yourself a new body' trick, eh?" asked Myfanwy.

"Uh, yes," said the Grafter.

"This was the only way you could figure out to get in contact with me?" said Myfanwy. "It never occurred to you to pull the old 'pick up the phone' trick? Or, and here's just a completely random idea, couldn't you have abducted me from a nightclub?"

"Do you think you would have been inclined to accept any proposals I put to you under those circumstances?" asked von Suchtlen mildly.

No, admitted Myfanwy to herself, remembering the rage she'd felt in the skinless Belgian's car.

"And besides, the heart was the only way for me to leave the facilities undetected. My cousin was becoming paranoid—justifiably, I'll admit, since I *did* arrange for his assistant to be interrogated. Phone lines were tapped, and I couldn't risk having *my* assistant interrogated, so I couldn't place any calls through him. In fact, the entrances and exits to my laboratories were being watched. I found, much to my dismay, that I was almost a prisoner. I could not go anywhere without my cousin's being aware of it." The Belgian sighed, and his face darkened as he contemplated the situation. "I left the heart box in the mail-out tray. It was sent to a mail-forwarding service, which forwarded it to a courier, who delivered it to you."

"I'm sorry, but how did *you* send a box containing your own heart?" asked Myfanwy. She was getting one of those M. C. Escher–style headaches.

"You want to know how it works?" asked the Belgian, brightening visibly. "It is quite fascinating, really. Very new technology. Experimental." He took a breath, and Myfanwy cut him off, desperate to forestall a further lecture.

"I'm sure it's amazing, but I don't need the technical details right now."

"Of course," said the Belgian, and she thought he looked a little embarrassed. "I am sorry, the...is it nerds? The nerds can be a little contagious. In any case, you take a sample to grow the heart, and the body that grows from that heart will have all the memories you had at the time."

"So there could be two of you wandering around?" said Myfanwy, her head spinning.

"No, the sampling is thorough, stripping various vital components. The original body begins to break down an hour after the sample. It sticks around just long enough to pack the sample in the box and then undress and go into the shower. Then the remains liquefy. The sample will have grown into a heart by the time it is delivered, and then will pause for a while before regenerating into an entire person in a couple of weeks. It can even be dissected and will still regrow itself." He looked at her proudly and she nodded. It sounded gross, but she thought she understood.

"The person it grows into can select a couple of abilities to be reborn with," he continued expansively. "Nothing like the capabilities we can provide via surgery, of course. And there are some risks involved."

"Oh?" said Myfanwy.

"Some of the early subjects were known to abruptly melt into a sort of slurry. But we had mostly ironed that kink out, and it was a risk I was willing to take. My cousin had been told I would be sequestering myself in my quarters, and he has always recognized my occasional need for contemplation and strategic planning, so he left me to my solitude. Even if he broke down my door, he would not find a body. Thus," said the Belgian, "we are free to hammer out the details of our merger. I can present it to my cousin as a fait accompli. If Gerd is unable to cope with it, then I am certain the combined forces of Wetenschappelijk Broederschap van Natuurkundigen and His Majesty's Hidden Soldiers of the Checquy will be able to subdue him and whatever forces he can muster." The Belgian sat back with a satisfied smile.

"Yes, well," said Myfanwy, "it all sounds delightful, but I am afraid I have some bad news for you. To begin with, your experimental new heart technology still has a few bugs. It hasn't been weeks in the growing, it's been months. And whatever project you arranged to tie up your cousin's attention, um, it didn't work..." Myfanwy gave him a quick précis of his cousin's recent activities.

"...and so it appears that your cousin is dead—killed in the assault," finished Myfanwy awkwardly.

"Dead," repeated the Belgian dully. He had slumped back in the chair and looked a bit shell-shocked. Myfanwy shifted in her uncomfortable seat and wondered if she should offer her condolences. *Maybe the official condolences of the Checquy?* she thought. But she concluded that any sympathies she expressed would be grossly and obviously insincere. She allowed herself to take a good look at the man sitting in front of her. He seemed to be in his midthirties and had the physique of someone who worked out regularly. He had been completely hairless when she walked in the room, but during the course of their conversation, stubble had appeared on his scalp.

"Dead," he repeated again quietly. Myfanwy nodded silently. "Still perhaps it is better this way," he said, sighing. "Gerd would have had problems adjusting to the new situation. He had problems adjusting to lots of things of late."

Including the idea of a traceable fax line, thought Myfanwy irreverently and then tried to quash the thought as unworthy.

"Graaf von Suchtlen, I'm not empowered to effect a merger between our organizations," said Myfanwy gently. "You understand, it will have to be presented to the entire Court." He nodded. "And of course, the Croatoan will need to be involved. Speaking of which, what were your intentions regarding the Americans? Why did you have agents there?" Von Suchtlen looked confused and shook his head helplessly.

"A Grafter operative was captured in Los Angeles," Myfanwy explained.

"Ah, it looks as if Gerd enacted one of our contingency gambits," he said. "If the Checquy were to become aware of our presence in Britain, we would allow one of our more expendable operatives to be discovered in the United States. This would be a red herring to distract the Croatoan and ensure that they did not provide inconvenient reinforcements to the Checquy."

"Huh," said Myfanwy. "You said the activation of the mold factory in Bath was another of your contingency plans? What about the flesh-cubey guy in Reading?"

"Not one of mine," said the Belgian, puzzled. "It sounds as if Gerd was doing a bit of improvising." Myfanwy looked at him closely, then shrugged.

I don't buy it, she thought, *but this guy had to have known that activating those plans would have prevented the possibility of any compromises. I'll bet his skinless cousin took a project that was supposed to be a last option and tried to use it as a first strike.*

"Well, as I said, negotiations cannot begin until all the relevant parties are gathered. Still, I'm interested in hearing some of your proposed terms. Are you hungry? I'm always terribly grouchy when I've just woken up, and you've been growing in a refrigerator for several months."

"I *would* like a cup of coffee," confessed the Belgian.

"The kitchens are closed for another few hours," said Myfanwy, "and the office machine is broken. In my residence I have a coffee machine that is exceptionally complicated, but I'm sure I can figure it out. How do you take it?" Myfanwy stood up and moved toward the portrait of Grantchester. The eyes of the portrait caught her gaze. *I suppose somebody will say that we should remove that,* she thought.

"Black with sugar, please," said the Grafter, shifting to get out of his seat.

"Please don't get up," said Myfanwy hurriedly. *At least not until I get you a robe,* she thought ruefully, and with perhaps a twinge of regret.

He was, after all, exceptionally attractive.

42

Monica Jarvis-Reed sat, cross-legged, on thin air. She sipped from a juice box and drank in the view of the deserted Italian beach below her. Sapphire waves stretched on for miles, crested into white, and then washed onto the sand. The bay was small, with cliffs arching up at the sides and olive-green shrubs drawing a perfect line around the sand. The sun was bright even through her sunglasses, and she was glad that she'd worn a long-sleeved shirt and trousers. Monica lifted a pair of high-powered binoculars from the strap around her neck and peered down as a tall figure in a swimsuit wove through the shrubs and made its way to the lonely beach chair on the sand. She pulled a satellite phone from its clip on her belt and put the phone to her ear.

"Signal?" she said.

"Standing by with bated breath" came a bored voice.

"It's him. He's wearing that smirk. And far too brief a swimsuit. Plus, I saw a small puff of smoke when he sat down."

"Well, my darling, biometrics from the satellite verify your findings" came the amused answer. "It's our wayward Bishop. Confirmed."

"Okay," said Monica. "Patch me through to Rook Thomas."

That's brilliant," said Myfanwy. "Yes, please go ahead and take care of that. And then enjoy the rest of your week in Italy. Yeah, thanks, Monica." She hung up the phone and turned her attention back to the coffee.

"So if it wasn't an abusive boyfriend, then what happened to your eyes?" asked Bronwyn curiously. Myfanwy kept her gaze down and continued pouring coffee into three mugs. She added sugar to two of the mugs and milk to one.

"Airbag," said Myfanwy, handing one mug to her sister. She picked the other two up and walked into the living room, where Shantay was lounging on the sofa reading a magazine. The American Bishop had arrived in England three days earlier, accompanied by a Rook of Comanche descent and a cohort of lawyers to help negotiate the terms of the merger.

Shantay accepted the coffee gratefully and pulled her legs up to allow Myfanwy to sit on the couch. Bronwyn sat down in a chair and lifted Wolfgang onto her lap.

"Airbag?" she repeated.

"I was in a car accident," said Myfanwy. "Passenger seat. We got rear-ended, the airbag unfurled, and it hit me in the face."

Shantay rolled her eyes behind her magazine.

"Ouch," Bronwyn said, wincing. "When did this happen?"

"The day after we went out partying."

"Didn't your two black eyes cause any problems during your business meetings?"

"There were some embarrassed stares," said Shantay, "but your sister is so important that no one was brave enough to ask any questions."

"Plus makeup," said Myfanwy.

"Plus that," conceded Shantay.

"And the whole merger thing is going to work out okay?" asked Bronwyn languidly, stroking Wolfgang just behind the ears. It was clear she didn't have any real interest but cared that it was a big deal to her sister. Shantay looked at Myfanwy and raised her eyebrows.

"Yeah," sighed Myfanwy. "Of course, the details are going to take months to hammer out. There will be lawyers squabbling, and compromises, and arguments. They'll be too proud to agree to some of our terms, and we'll be too untrusting to agree to some of theirs, but in the end it will all work out." *And it will,* she thought. *We'll bind them with contracts and oaths and promises of full disclosure. You keep your friends close and your enemies closer, and the Grafters are both.*

In the meantime, we'll be raising up a new Rook, a new Chev, and a new Bishop, and I'm determined to put a few non-powered people onto the Court. And a couple more women. Farrier keeps dropping hints that she wants me as the new Bishop, which is insane. Although . . .

Of course, there will be the typical day-to-day weird happenings around the world that we need to tend to. But with the help of the Grafters we'll be able to do a better job.

"Well, that's nice," said Bronwyn distractedly.

"Yeah, it's pretty satisfying," agreed Myfanwy.

"And Jonathan will be back in two days," said her sister. "You'll finally be able to see him after, what? Twenty-two years!"

"That'll be great," said Myfanwy with a smile. "A brother. A family. A job. A rabbit. It's a pretty good life I lucked into, really."

"Yeah, now all you need is a boyfriend," said Shantay dryly.

"Ms. Thomas, did you want this business card?" asked Val, coming in carrying a basketful of laundry. "It says 'Call me if you fancy that drink' on the back."

"Where did it come from?" asked Myfanwy.

"I found it in the pocket of this *heavily* stained men's business shirt," sniffed Val.

43

Dear You,

I thought that I would scribble you one final note before I took my last set of letters to the bank in the morning. It's late now, and I am at home, sitting on my couch, with my rabbit nestled against my feet. It's snowing outside, but there's a fire going, and it's cozy in here. It's safe and warm, and I'm finding it hard to stay awake. But I want to write these things down—for you and for me.

It's been a long day with no startling revelations or bizarre occurrences (which is kind of bizarre in itself). I had no time to do any detective work—just the day-to-day duties of being me. During my lunch hour, I went to the Rookery infirmary and had a quick checkup. I want to leave you a relatively fit body to inherit.

I want to leave you with as much as I possibly can.

It's so easy to despair. I know that I have no choice in what's coming, and for me it's not a matter of faith or fatalism. It's simply knowledge. I guess you could say this means there's no free will, but in writing these letters, I like to think that I'm making my own choices. And besides, free will has never been something I had too much of in this life. I'm grateful for whatever I can get.

In the back of my mind, there's the knowledge that you might choose the other option, use the other key, and go off to build your own life. I couldn't blame you if you did. Of course, it means that all the work I'm doing now, all the preparations and letters, are mostly for nothing. But they're there for you if you want them.

In the end, no matter what choice you make, I hope you can be happy. I don't know what kind of person you are or what you'll do, but I've written dozens of letters to you, and I find myself caring desperately. You don't exist yet, but you're my sister (identical!). You're my daughter. You're my family. Maybe you'll be Myfanwy Thomas, or maybe you'll pick yourself a new name and never think of me. But no matter what life you choose, know that I think of you and pray that everything works out for you and that you have the very best life you can.

Love, always,
Me

ACKNOWLEDGMENTS

Oh boy. There are so many people to thank. And, inevitably, I will forget someone.

Firstly, my early readers, compassionate and insightful, who consented to go through *The Rook* when it had a different name, then gave thoughtful and merciful feedback.

The staff of the Foundry, who have been so helpful and welcoming. Cecilia Campbell-Westlind, Kendra Jenkins, and Hannah Gordon, especially, endured several thousand ludicrous questions from me, and still resisted the urge to have me assassinated.

My copyeditor, the eagle-eyed yet astoundingly tactful Tracy Roe, who gently pointed out that I have been misusing hyphens my entire life.

Stéphanie Abou, foreign-rights agent and international woman of mystery.

Jerry Kalajian, my ambassador to the West Coast.

My editrix, the glorious Asya Muchnick, whose work and belief were invaluable and who made this story so much better. She was willing to engage in long and entertaining debates about the most incidental of points, such as what color of fungus was funnier. And her colleagues at Little, Brown, whose efforts have made all the difference.

ACKNOWLEDGMENTS

The incomparable Mollie Glick, queen of agents, she of the diplomatic tongue and the razor mind. I am so fortunate to have a friend as enthusiastic, encouraging, and wise as she.

My dad, Bill O'Malley, the font of all knowledge, who was willing to answer spontaneous questions about a multitude of topics, ranging from the etiquette of government reports to how best to dispose of a duck that can tell the future.

And finally, my mom, Jeanne O'Malley, who really made it all happen. She comforted me from the other side of the planet when I called, utterly distraught because my aging computer had eaten the first two hundred pages of this novel. She congratulated me twenty-four hours later when I found a backup copy hidden in the bowels of the hard drive. (People, I implore you, back stuff up! The novel you save may just be your own.) My mom was the first to read the book, and she pronounced it good. She believed in it, and in me, and it was she who urged me to get an agent and then helped me find one. (The perfect one!) My mom gave me invaluable advice on how to proceed at every step of the way. She always thought big, and it is because of her that you are holding this book.